RAVE RE

W

"Action packed and poignant...builds tension from the very beginning and will keep you turning pages until the very end. Ms. Tanner's straightforward style never allows for a dull moment."

—Linda Sandifer, author of *Embrace The Wind*

"Susan Tanner captures the fierce independence and adventurous spirit that marked the developing West. A heart-touching read."

—Elizabeth Leigh, author of *Prairie Ecstasy*

EXILED HEART

"Emotionally charged and powerful...a passionate portrayal of the times in the strong and compelling style that typifies Ms. Tanner's writing."

—Libby Sydes, author of *The Lion's Angel*

CAPTIVE TO A DREAM

"A wonderful combination of obsession, madness, lust, violence, and desire that will enthrall readers from page one."

—*Romantic Times*

HIGHLAND CAPTIVE

"Brimming with the aura and atmosphere of Scotland and its tumultuous history. Susan Tanner's obvious understanding of the Scots shimmers within its pages."

Romantic Times

"WITH A LITTLE PRACTICE MAYBE I COULD HAVE BECOME A VERY *GOOD* WHORE!"

"Honey, you'd starve to death in a week."

Hot shame flooded her cheeks with fiery color. Hannah wished she'd never opened her mouth. She was not any more experienced at fencing with words than she was at any of the other things Jeb Welles was good at. No doubt lovemaking was one of his greatest talents.

Jeb didn't miss the look of humiliation of Hannah's face. "Aw, hell, Hannah, I didn't mean you wouldn't find any takers. I just don't think you'd know what to do with them."

Through the tears glittering on her eyelashes, Hannah glared at him. "I'm sure *somebody* would be willing to teach me!"

Jeb could just picture her saying something like that to some other man. In her innocence, she couldn't begin to imagine what would happen. He could. All too easily. His blood was surging at no more than the thought of teaching Hannah the many ways there were to pleasure a man.

Other *Leisure Books* by Susan Tanner:
WINDS ACROSS TEXAS
EXILED HEART
CAPTIVE TO A DREAM
HIGHLAND CAPTIVE

SUSAN TANNER

LEISURE BOOKS  NEW YORK CITY

For Don, Kris, and Jeremy

A LEISURE BOOK®

August 1994

Published by

Dorchester Publishing Co., Inc.
276 Fifth Avenue
New York, NY 10001

Printed in the United States of America.

FIRE ACROSS TEXAS

Chapter One

Texas, June 1859

The Reverend Caleb Barnes often went out into the wilderness to pray, much as he imagined the prophets of old had done and as the Bible assured him Jesus had done. When the Spirit led, he would drop to his knees, heedless of bramble or stone beneath his thinly covered flesh. The pattern of his prayers was always the same. Each time he would deliver up praise for God's many blessings, then follow these with heartrending prayers of contrition for his own shortcomings, while all around him the green woodlands of central Texas faded into the arid deserts of the Old Testament.

This cool June midnight, he was on his knees, thanking God for the child that would soon be born to him and asking forgiveness that he had not yet made his Hannah a humble servant of God. The failure was not for lack of trying. Behind clenched eyelids, he pictured her, slender hands clasped in prayer, head bowed meekly. He'd seen her in that same pose every morning and every evening of their marriage, but he feared that Hannah prayed only by his insistence. She had not truly tamed her thoughts or her ways.

He'd come upon her too often during the long hours of the day smiling and singing when she thought Caleb was not within sound or sight. Only this evening, God help him, there had actually been a flower tucked into her hair. He could still see those tiny yellow petals against the gleaming copper coils that began the day neatly but never stayed so. By each day's end, soft tendrils would have escaped to caress the smooth skin of her temples and high cheeks.

"Forgive her, God," Caleb whispered. He would spare God's retribution for his wife if he could. Evil did not live in Hannah, just youth; the levity would pass as she gained in maturity. Caleb would see to it.

A rustling in the undergrowth disturbed him slightly, but he pushed the sound of the woods creature from his consciousness and pulled the image of Hannah forward again. In his mind, he made her somber and unsmiling, filled with an awareness of the woes and the evils of this world. Even her hair he tamed with that inner portrait, subduing the bright hue of it so that it did not reflect the sun back to the onlooker and conquering the riot of curls so that they lay in an orderly coronet of braids.

Caleb gave an inward nod of satisfaction. Thus should his wife look, and Caleb would see to it that the image eventually became the reality. "She's young, Lord. She'll learn."

The rustling came closer, became louder. Caleb heard the sound of a human voice and grew still, allowing the night to cloak him. He had settled intentionally where there would be no neighbors to distract him from his Lord's work nor Hannah from her duties. Rarely did any travelers wander near enough to disturb them.

Gradually, the words became clearer, clear enough to discern. There were at least two men, maybe more.

"You shouldn't have shot the old man." The voice held an edge of worry.

"He shouldn't have been taking shots at me." The second man sounded more confident, belligerent even. "It don't matter none, anyway." Caleb could almost imagine a shrug. "We're laying a good enough trail, straight to the reservation. They'll blame his death and the slaughter of his porkers on the Comanche for sure."

Caleb stiffened. He had come to this place to convert the heathen red man, to teach the Indians confined to the Brazos Reserves about the forgiving grace of the Savior. He'd had little success thus far. Maybe with good reason. How could they accept God if they did not trust, and how could they trust when they could see the deceit of white men such as these?

Many Texans resented the establishment of the reserves. They wanted the red man out. Even knowing this, Caleb still had not fully realized the lengths they would go to vent their resentment.

Righteous anger filled him, but he held tight to his caution. He would need proof of what these men were about before he confronted them.

Though the men were mounted, they rode unhurriedly. Without hesitation, Caleb followed them on foot, striding tirelessly just out of their hearing. Not that they would have heard him even had he not taken care to be quiet. They made enough noise to cover any sounds around them. Caleb scarcely felt any weariness, though he had been up since dawn. He was doing God's work, and God would sustain him.

Dawn had not yet broken when the three he followed splashed across a shallow bend of the Brazos River. Moonlight glinted upon the surface of the water, and Caleb's eyes widened as he saw the objects of his pursuit for the first time in the open. The reality of their deed was even worse than he had first realized. These men—men who had committed murder and other atrocities in order to focus blame upon the reservation Indians—wore the distinctive coats of United States soldiers.

"Halt," he roared in a thundering voice. "Go no further."

The three ahead of him erupted into immediate commotion. Putting heels to their horses, they cursed. One horse slipped on the rocks of the sandy bank and whinnied, but though the animal was in pain, he was not allowed to stop. Spurs gouged his side, urging him on.

Like the wrath of God, Caleb marched into the cold waters of the river after the soldiers.

Answering the threat of unrest along the Brazos, a small company of soldiers had established a camp of tents on the reservation side of the river, not too far distant from the loosely clustered tepees of their charges.

Garrett, the temporary officer in charge, tried not to show frustration as his gaze followed the black-garbed figure pacing in front of him. The Reverend Barnes had blundered into camp a short time ago. He'd been immediately stopped by the guard and brought to Garrett with his wild tale. Garrett wished fervently that his captain had not chosen this particular time to ride out on patrol with a few of the men.

"Are you *sure* they were soldiers?" Garrett persisted.

The preacher wheeled to face him. "As sure as I am of my salvation."

Garrett wasn't about to question that. Taking a deep breath, he tried to think. Though he was wide awake by this time, his mind still felt weighted by sleep. He glanced at the aide who'd been watching him steadily, waiting for Garrett to need him. "Get Captain Brown over here right away." He looked away from the surprise in the aide's expression.

Maybe it wasn't standard practice for this company of military to look to the Texas Rangers for assistance, but Garrett was at a loss. Indians he could fight, even horse thieves and cattle rustlers. But this . . . well, this was beyond the realm of his experience. The one person he knew he did not want to involve was the Indian agent responsible for the well-being of the Brazos Reserves Indians. Major Robert S. Neighbors would have a field day with this incident. Garrett winced just thinking of his superior's reaction were he to return to that kind of an uproar. As far as Garrett could see, that left the Rangers.

The reverend was still striding about and holding forth on the great evils of mankind when Garrett heard the clip-clop of hooves and knew his man had returned. The young private was accompanied—but not, as Garrett had intended, by the captain of the Rangers.

Relief vied with irritation when Garrett recognized the figure astride the bay mare. Rugged and confident, Jeb Welles had made a reputation for himself among soldiers and rangers alike. Few men could claim to know him really well, but most liked him and all respected him. A few feared him. Personally, Garrett found his methods too irregular to admire. Garrett suspected Welles's own superior officer felt the same. Welles wasn't even a regular with Brown's company. He had been specially assigned by the governor just a few weeks earlier.

To Garrett, Welles remained an unknown element in an uncertain life. Garrett straightened his shoulders and stepped forward.

By the time Jeb dismounted, he had a clear image of the scene displayed by the light of the campfire. Garrett, not youthful but green to life in the West, appeared anxious. An aide stood nearby, looking no more than sleepily curious. The stranger, clothed in homespun dyed a dull black, wore an expression of militant righteousness. Inwardly, Jeb groaned. He didn't mind a little excitement now and then, but this had all the earmarks of a pain in the ass.

There was no trace of this reaction when Jeb turned an inquiring gaze to Garrett. "What's going on?"

For answer, Garrett gestured toward the restless figure. He would prefer that the man told his own story. "This is Reverend Barnes." To Garrett's complete relief, the reverend ceased his striding about and turned a fierce gaze on Welles, who appeared undaunted by that piercing stare.

Caleb matched the ranger look for look, then nodded his satisfaction. The soldier had done nothing, absolutely nothing to find the guilty parties; this man would. Caleb shot Garrett a scathing look of condemnation before he refocused his attention on the newcomer and began to speak. "I was at my prayers when God sent three men near enough for me to overhear their speech. They didn't see me, and they were bragging amongst themselves as they rode. Bragging because they had killed a man and slaughtered his livestock—pigs, I think. Killed him in cold blood so that the Indians would be blamed for their misdeeds. I followed them to the very edge of these reserves."

Damn! For a long while, Jeb said nothing. He'd been expecting something like this, had warned both the Rangers and the U. S. Army, with little result. Jeb addressed Garrett first. "Have you sent out a patrol to confirm the murder?"

Garrett flushed slightly. "Of course."

Jeb couldn't have cared less about Garrett's offended sensibilities. He turned back to the reverend. "Did you get a look at these men up close?"

Caleb shook his head regretfully. "I saw only their backs, but they wore military clothing and their saddles were standard issue. I can only add that one of the three was particularly tall, and one particularly short. However, I'm sure if you check the horses here, you'll find three that have been ridden all night—and one of the three has an injured leg."

Again Jeb glanced at Garrett, but this time the officer shook his head. Inwardly, Jeb sighed. Total competence would have been too much to ask. "You"— he gestured toward the aide— "check the string for any animals that have been ridden recently." He turned his attention back to Garrett. "Muster your men for inspection."

Seething inwardly at the ranger's clipped tone, Garrett did as he was told. His shoulders slumped somewhat in resignation. It was his own fault for asking for assistance. He should have handled this himself. Plummer was going to have his hide as it was. Worse, he had a sinking feeling he'd just shot his own career in the foot. A charge of this nature should have been taken care of internally and covered up externally—something Garrett should have thought of sooner, he realized now. Somehow he didn't think Jeb Welles was going to allow for any secrecy around the event.

Moments later, they were surrounded by hastily dressed men standing at attention in the murky half-light of dawn. Jeb surveyed their faces one at a time, some disgruntled—particularly those who had been on evening watch a few hours ago—some merely curious, almost all of them sleepy. Almost. "Which of you are on watch now?"

Five men stepped forward. Clear eyes, respectful gazes, no sign of either guilt or alarm at being summoned.

Jeb gave a short nod of his head. "Return to your posts."

He then signaled half a dozen men to stand to one side, men who did not look either sleepy or merely curious. He dismissed the remainder. One of those who stayed, smooth-cheeked and blue eyed, looked particularly shaken. Jeb, pacing in front of them all, stopped in front of him and pinned him with a hard gaze.

The minutes stretched between them, with Jeb hard and accusing, the other more guilty by the moment.

"Sir," the youngster blurted out when he could stand no more of that steely stare, "I—I never meant to get the young lady pregnant." His face darkened with his embarrassment. "Her father . . ." He swallowed hard and straightened his shoulders visibly. "I'm willing to marry her, sir."

Jeb snorted and cut a glance toward Garrett. As he watched, Garrett's face slowly darkened with outrage and embarrassment. Muttering a curse, the officer grasped the young man's shoulder and dragged him toward a tent.

The reverend, his attention claimed by this admission of sin, followed. "Neither fornicators nor adulterers shall inherit the kingdom of God," he rumbled in dire warning.

With scarcely a backward glance, Jeb resumed his slow walk in front of the men who were left. He studied the remaining five even more closely.

Three of them returned his stare laconically. The other two shifted their gazes each time they happened to cross Jeb's.

The aide returned, bursting with news. "They were there, sir. Three of them, all still with sweaty saddle marks on their backs. And one has a fetlock swollen like a melon."

Jeb turned back to his quarry and asked softly, "Do any three of you share quarters?" Though he had heard the reverend return to stand at his side, silently listening and watching, Jeb ignored him.

The laconic look faded from one of the men as he nodded darkly. He had grey eyes as hard as the stock of the weapon he wore. "Me and Shaw and Wilkins bunk in the same tent."

"Shaw?" Jeb's gaze swept the group until a reluctant hand went up. The owner was at least six feet three. "And Wilkins?"

"Yeah." The man who spoke stood less than five feet five.

They were the two who had not been able to meet his gaze.

"You other two men can go," Jeb said quietly, without looking at them. They were no longer of any concern to him.

Garrett had remanded the young philanderer to his quarters until appropriate action could be taken in the matter, and he now moved to stand between Jeb and the preacher.

Jeb jerked his head toward the three tentmates. "Those are your men. I suggest you take them into custody." Without waiting for Garrett's reaction, he returned his attention to the men. His gaze traveled over them with disgust. "I'd hang you."

They looked back at him, and not one of them looked as if they doubted his word. Only the one who'd spoken, the one with the hard grey eyes, didn't flinch under his stare.

Lips thin, Garrett nodded to his aide, who in turn motioned toward the guards who stood waiting for their orders.

Watching as the guilty were shackled, Jeb spoke quietly to their commanding officer. "I meant what I'd said. I'd hang them within the hour." He paused. "But if you plan a career with the military, I suggest you not do anything until you make sure they weren't under orders."

"I hand out all orders here!" Garrett countered stiffly, outraged at the suggestion. Welles's charge was ludicrous. The army was here to protect the Indians, not to harrass them.

Jeb smiled without humor. Somehow he didn't think Garrett's ideals were going to last long out here. "Even those from Austin?"

Garrett's outrage flared, then faded at the quiet suggestion that the deed might have been committed by orders of the governor of Texas. At first thought it seemed inconceivable, but was it? The hell of it was, Garrett couldn't be sure. "Captain Plummer will decide their fate. Until he returns, they will be heavily guarded."

As the three under discussion were being led away, Jeb felt their glares of hatred and turned to look at them calmly. Carefully he committed their features to memory in case he ever needed to recall them. If they survived this, he had a feeling that day might come.

Jeb spoke to the preacher. "Reverend, I don't suppose you hold with carrying a gun, but

I'd recommend it as long as these men draw breath."

For answer, Caleb swept his coat aside. The handle of a pistol gleamed in the early sunlight.

When the ranger lifted a brow in surprise, Caleb shrugged. "For as many have sinned without law, shall also perish without law."

Because the preacher had quoted from the book of Romans, Jeb did also. "For it is written, Vengeance is mine; I will repay, saith the Lord." Stifling a grin at the preacher's stunned look, Jeb tipped his hat. "Like I said, Reverend, keep your gun on you and watch your back."

Jeb turned away and any urge to grin left him. Soldiers who murdered the settlers they were sworn to protect and preachers who carried guns. It was getting a mite hard to tell the good guys from the bad.

Chapter Two

From time to time, Hannah slowed the movements of her hoe against the dark soil and gazed off into the distance, but she never ceased work entirely. Caleb didn't hold with idle hands, particularly hers, and he always expected her to accomplish a lot during his absences. For that matter, Caleb didn't hold with much of anything except praying and working and more praying. Neither did he seem to think a woman should work any less hard for being six months pregnant.

As for the last, Hannah couldn't say her husband was overly hard or unfeeling. There had never been any opportunities for her to discuss having babies, or anything else, with other married women. She only hoped she would know what to do when the time came, but that was something she preferred not to dwell on too often.

Hannah tried not to be a disappointment to Caleb, just as she tried not to mind that he left her so often alone with no protection. He never worried about the people he'd managed to rile over the past months. It was an amazement to Hannah how a man of the cloth could be the cause of so much hatred and be so unconcerned over it. "The Lord God shall be our armor," he had told her only that morning when she had voiced her concern. "Put on the armor of the Lord." But Hannah hadn't been "called" as Caleb had been. She wasn't sure God's armor fit her quite as well or offered her quite as much protection, and she wasn't the one carrying the long-nosed pistol.

Lifting her eyes from her work long enough to stretch her aching back, Hannah stilled. Puffs of dust rose in the distance. As she watched, hard-riding horsemen became distinguishable from the clouds of dry Texas dirt their mounts kicked up. Her heart gave a funny little jump, because she couldn't keep herself from remembering the many threats that had come Caleb's way since he'd decided to convert the heathen red men of the Brazos reserve lands.

Folks hereabouts didn't want the red men converted. They wanted them gone, including the Army, which hypocritically made use of them as spies and scouts against those of their own kind still roaming the plains, murdering and scalping. Not that Hannah had heard any of this firsthand. She rarely saw anyone but Caleb, but she was all Caleb had to talk to each evening. She suspected that if it weren't for that fact, she wouldn't know anything at all of what was going on in this world.

As the horsemen drew near, Hannah slowly tightened her grip on the handle of her hoe, holding it less as a gardening tool than as a weapon. Caleb would have frowned. Her stance definitely indicated a lack of trust in God's grace. "I'm sorry, Lord," she whispered, but she didn't loosen her grip on the handle, not even when the riders were close enough for her to see the fastenings on their shirts. She was not all reassured to realize that the men were soldiers.

Their carefully buttoned uniforms made her more aware than ever of the heat of the midday sun. Beads of sweat trickled down between her breasts even though her gown was of light cotton. Of course, Caleb always insisted that her gowns have high, tight necklines and long, tight sleeves. Even so, she felt cooler than these men looked. Their shirts and pants were made of sweltering wool.

There were three of them, all young, all low-ranking by their insignia. As they pulled their horses to a stop just at the edge of her garden plot, one of them touched a finger to the brim of his hat and pushed it away from his face. Hannah acknowledged that it was a nice-looking face, but marriage had cured her of being affected in any way by a handsome man. Or, more accurately, her marriage bed had cured her.

"Ma'am," he said, looking appreciatively at the soft coils of red hair slipping from the pins that caught it in a knot at the back of her neck. He tried to see what color her eyes were beneath the brim of her bonnet. "We'd like to speak with Reverend Barnes."

"My husband isn't home," Hannah said evenly. No use telling a lie. It was as clear as spring water that the horse and buggy were gone. The shed door gaped open, revealing an interior as bare as the paddock.

"When do you expect him back?"

Hannah hesitated. His voice remained quiet and polite, but there was something about his eyes, grey and glittering, that made her uneasy. He wasn't looking at her the way a man should look at another man's wife, particularly if the other was a man of God, and more particularly if the woman was swollen with his child. "Caleb is on God's business," she said at last, hoping the reminder would bolster God's armor. "He's always home by nightfall, but beyond that, I'm never sure. He could be here in minutes or not for hours."

The tallest of them, silent and still until now, nudged his horse forward. He looked at Hannah, but he spoke to the grey-eyed man. "We could leave our calling card."

His eyes held the same look of hunger. As much from that look as from his words,

Hannah knew intuitively that she was in trouble. The perspiration on her skin began to turn clammy as the third man eased forward.

"What business do you have with my husband?" she said in a rush, hoping against hope to stall them, to give herself time to think. She didn't pray. Caleb believed prayers should be reserved for a soul's salvation, not a body's comfort or even safety. He also believed that God helped those who helped themselves.

At her question, the three exchanged a look. And then Hannah knew. These were the same three Caleb had seen just two evenings ago laying a false trail from a burned-out farm to the boundaries of the Brazos Reserves. Caleb had followed them, then taken his accusations to their commanding officer. Even as Caleb had told her the tale, his voice ringing with righteous pride in his actions, Hannah had wondered why God hadn't given his servant some kind of reasoning intelligence. Their closest neighbor, in distance not friendship, had already warned Caleb that there wasn't a soul around who would be the least sympathetic to Caleb's view of the reservation Indians. The people hereabouts wanted the good Brazos bottom land the reserves took in, and they expected the army to help them get it—by whatever means.

"I think you had better leave." Hannah tried to keep the quiver from her voice, but she knew she didn't quite succeed. Caleb would have been disappointed in her lack of control.

The tall man stepped down from his horse, and Hannah took a hasty step backward. She wasn't stupid enough to run. She couldn't get far in her condition, and she knew better than to turn her back. Although what she could accomplish by keeping her eye on them was beyond her. There were three of them. They were going to do whatever they wanted to do.

And what they wanted to do was made abundantly clear when the one with grey eyes stepped down from his horse as well, his pants already bulging. Men were pigs; Hannah already knew that. This was just additional proof she neither needed nor wanted. Here she was, round with child and clumsy past belief, and these men felt lust for her.

The third man, stocky and sweaty, joined the others on the ground and began to circle behind her. Hannah felt salt burn her eyes as terror hit her, but she'd be cursed if she would let the tears fall. She couldn't even threaten them with what Caleb would do if they hurt her. They'd never believe a preacher wouldn't leave any vengeance-taking to the God he served.

She tried to keep all three in sight, but they dodged around her, trampling her garden heedlessly. The sweaty man chuckled at her efforts. "This won't gain you anything," Hannah spoke to grey eyes. He seemed to be as much a leader as there was among them.

"It will if it convinces that holy husband of yours to take himself away from here. We don't need or want his kind. He saw something he shouldn't and didn't have sense enough to keep his mouth shut about it. The stupid son of a bitch needs a lesson!"

The other two gave growls of assent.

"He follows God's direction! He's a preacher," Hannah said, more shocked at his lack of respect for a man of the cloth than for what he was about to do to her. There wasn't a doubt in her mind that she was going to be the "lesson."

"But I'll bet he's not much of a man," the tall one told her, slipping in close while she was distracted. "Not nearly man enough for you, in spite of that big belly he gave you."

Hannah wheeled and tried to take a step backward to give herself room to swing the hoe at him. Instead, she managed to trip on the skirt of her own gown. She felt herself falling and bit back a sound of despair.

The fall sent a paralyzing pain through her back and knocked the breath from her body. Before she could regain either her breath or her feet, a heavy hand was on her shoulder and pale blue eyes were boring into hers. "Don't," she whispered, as close to begging as she had ever come in her life. "Don't do this. It's wrong."

The shortest of them, who was also the heaviest and the one with the biggest bulge in his pants, began to fumble at the fastenings of his breeches while the grey-eyed man Hannah had decided was the leader gazed calmly out across the field. Her glance dropped to the swollen member thrusting through stubby fingers. The owner fell to his knees and dragged her skirts above her waist. The tight swelling of her belly didn't seem to deter him as he gripped himself harder. Hannah felt bile hit her throat, and she struggled against the iron grip holding her down. Useless. Her efforts were useless.

She met a dark, greedy gaze as pain rippled faintly across her back. Anger overtook fear. "May God wither your manhood for all of the rest of your days!" She spat the words at him.

"Shut up, damn you. God ain't going to help you now." For all his bravado, he looked a little anxious as he rubbed himself harder. "Damn you," he said again.

Before Hannah's eyes his shaft withered in his hand, but she was beyond rejoicing as the rippling of pain grew stronger, radiating from her back across her belly. Her eyes glazed, and she drew her knees upward, keening softly with the burning cramps that gripped her.

She was distantly aware when the iron grip left her shoulder and all three of them drew away from her, whispering amongst themselves. The thought came to her that they might simply kill her now and leave her, but she hurt too much to care.

Blood gushed from between her legs just as the hurried sound of their departure reached her. The drum of their horses' hooves on the hard ground pounded against her eardrums. Then she was alone with the soft sound of the breeze against the grass and the warmth of the sun on her face—and the agony of a too early birth.

Her last conscious thought was that Caleb was going to be so disappointed in her.

Chapter Three

Though she stared with wide, soulful eyes at the dust-laden man flapping the wide brim of his hat at her, the cow wouldn't budge. At her feet lay a still-born calf. From time to time, the cow bawled piteously.

"Move, you old rack of bones," Jeb growled, fighting an urge to just let her lie down and die with her calf. God knew, she didn't look as if she would ever survive even the short trip north of the Red River. Angular hips made sharp ridges against a starvation-dulled hide. He sighed and flopped his hat against his leg again. "Move, damn it!" He couldn't leave her. Her bags, heavy with milk, might be all that made the difference between life and death for a Comanche child or elderly person once they were off the reservation.

Jeb chafed at the fact that he was out here at all, fighting the heat and the dust to round up these pitiful excuses for cattle. He was a sonuvabitchin' Texas Ranger, not a cowboy. It didn't help his feelings much that this was his own idea, and against orders at that! Anything had been preferable to guarding Indians too disheartened to be a threat to anyone and watching his captain and the Indian agent bicker between themselves.

As Jeb watched, the old cow lurched away from her calf and started toward the Indian reserves, which lay over the next few shallow rises of land. He tipped his hat back on his head and turned the bay to ride after her. Sweat had begun to trickle in slow rivulets down his neck. Christ, it was hotter than the devil's front porch.

A sound reached some level of his consciousness, and he froze until it reached his ears as well. Hoofbeats of a single horse. Then, as their beat came closer, the gasps of hard-drawn breath from someone who raced ahead of that threateningly steady rhythm.

Abruptly, a Comanche youth burst into view, the determined expression turning to dismay at the sight of Jeb. With a sideways dart, the youth sought to evade this additional obstacle, but an unexpected gully thwarted that effort. Black braids flying, the wiry form tumbled just as the unseen pursuer topped the rise, pistol drawn. Frustrated curses from the hunter turned to delight at finding his quarry sprawled ignominiously on the ground. His pistol waved in the air, then aimed downward toward the hapless Comanche youth.

Jeb sighed. *Son of a bitch.* Reluctantly, he drew his own pistol and trained it on the soldier, who noticed him at last.

The other man lifted his brows at the short barrel staring him in the face. "Welles," he began, cautious despite his unrelenting hatred as he wondered just how much danger he was in.

"Wilkins," Jeb acknowledged with that touch of disdain he knew would make the other man crazy. Jeb was certain he wouldn't have liked Wilkins even if the incident with the Reverend Barnes had never happened. Most of the soldiers guarding the reserves found their duty distasteful. Wilkins always appeared to be enjoying himself.

Wilkins read the dislike in Jeb's face. "I was apprehending this warrior." His tone took a defensive edge. "He was escaping."

Jeb turned to look at the warrior. He was ten, maybe eleven. Unarmed, winded, and scared right down to the calluses on his bare feet. Jeb's gaze traveled upward, and his eyes widened. He'd known Wilkins was a fool; now he knew he was just plain stupid as well. Warrior? There might be no tangible proof in that bare brown chest, but any poor sod could read the femininity in the delicate line of shoulder and collarbone. This was no warrior but, perhaps, the future mother of warriors. Jeb wondered briefly at her state of undress. She was surely past the age of running around bare-breasted.

Jeb looked back at Wilkins. "I'll take over from here." He didn't bother to keep either the animosity or the disgust from his voice as he holstered his pistol. He would have greatly preferred to smash the butt end of it into Wilkins's ugly face.

"You don't outrank me," Wilkins protested furiously.

Jeb merely looked at him, and Wilkins subsided. No, Jeb didn't outrank him, but only because Jeb had turned down each promotion offered to him. Jeb was handed every tough assignment that came to the attention of either the head of the Rangers or the governor of Texas. And he received triple the pay that any other ranger drew for the dangers he was willing to face.

For years, he had found this life uniquely satisfying, but in the past twelve months, that satisfaction had slowly diminished. Protecting the borders of Texas from Mexicans and the homes of its citizens from hostile Indians had kept him from boredom for a lot of years. And he still wasn't bored—but he was sickened. The once proud Comanche, already herded together and confined on reservation lands, were now being hounded from the very boundaries of Texas itself.

And, little as he liked it, Jeb was here to help ensure that the move from the Brazos Reservation to the Indian territory beyond the northern border of Texas was accomplished with as little bloodshed as possible. And he was going to do just that, even if it meant watching a disgrace like Wilkins ride away unpunished for tormenting a helpless Comanche child. Just as he had gone unpunished for the murder of a Texas civilian.

As he watched, a disgruntled Wilkins turned his horse to head back the way he had come. "Wilkins," Jeb called before the other man rode beyond the range of hearing.

Wilkins reined in his horse and glanced over his shoulder.

"I'm going to be watching you 'til we're out of here. Every minute."

Wilkins gave him a murderous look, then glanced at the youth, whose expressionless face assured the furious soldier that the child, at least, did not comprehend Jeb's words. Slightly mollified that there was no witness to this additional humiliation, Wilkins gave a short nod and wheeled his horse away with a heavy hand.

Jeb wasn't fooled. Wilkins wouldn't forget that insult. Shaking his head, Jeb nudged his horse toward the girl, who cautiously gained her feet at his approach. He reached out his hand to her, and, almost to his surprise, she took it, vaulting up behind him as lightly and easily as any warrior. Unlike a warrior, however, she grasped Jeb's waist rather than the back of the saddle. Jeb grinned at the giveaway, then was glad she couldn't see his face and be shamed.

They were within sight of the Indian encampment when Jeb finally asked her, "Where were you headed?"

Because Jeb had spoken in English, that was how she answered, "Hunting. My mother is ill. She needs meat."

"Have you no father or older brothers to take care of her?"

She was silent, and Jeb knew he had insulted her. "Your people will need strong women as well as strong warriors." He knew he'd either make things better or worse by revealing his knowledge. He hoped for the best.

The silence continued until the first tepee came into view, when she observed, disdainfully, "Not all blue coats are stupid, then."

"I do not wear a blue coat," Jeb pointed out, as insulted now as she had been only moments earlier.

"The heart is all that matters, and your heart is that of a blue coat." Her words held a wealth of sad wisdom.

The last Texas home of the Comanche people lay in the shimmering heat before them. Looking at the pitiful encampment, Jeb could not agree. Whatever his heart held, it was not the cold-blooded, hard-nosed bigotry this girl suspected existed in all whites. Unfortunately, in most cases, Jeb knew she was right. Texas had given this land to the Comanche; now Texas was determined to take it back.

For two years, every depredation committed by the last roving bands of Comanche had been attributed to the reservation Indians—even though Neighbors, their agent, argued otherwise. The reservation Comanche had proven themselves willing to act as allies on more than one occasion. But when the bloodshed continued, so did the charges.

The heat of the infuriated Texans had reached beyond the point of reason. They were determined to drive the Indians from Texas, and, rightly or wrongly, their government was more than willing to assist them. With tempers increasingly explosive, John Henry Brown had led his company of rangers to preserve the peace in the area until the reserves could be broken up and the Comanche moved. And Jeb had been sent with them. Jeb wondered how he was supposed to stand as Indian advisor to Brown when the man was too puffed with pride to take the advice of what he considered to be a mere enlisted man. Jeb had years of experience with the Comanche, but Brown saw only his lack of insignia and the fact that Jeb disagreed with many of his decisions.

Like the one that wouldn't allow the Comanche to gather their stock without a white escort. Neighbors, realizing the insult to his charges would be insuperable, refused to allow Brown's men to go trailing the Indians. As a result, the Indians were not allowed to find their stock. So Jeb was out here, on his own, doing just that with as little cooperation as a scattered herd of stringy cattle could give him.

Although Jeb couldn't share Major Neighbors's altruistic view of his charges, he couldn't agree with Brown's hard-nosed treatment of them either. As a matter of fact, Jeb didn't agree with Brown on much of anything, and he hadn't been happy since being assigned to Brown. Even knowing it was as temporary as any other task he'd been given didn't help much at this point.

Jeb was honest enough to admit that he hadn't quite felt the same about Texas since Slade had taken a wife and moved on to the New Mexico Territory. Jeb and Slade had been on-and-off partners for most of the past decade. The thought of the new territories and new challenges facing Slade tempted Jeb more every day, just as Slade's infrequent letters tempted him. Slade was the only lawman in a settlement that was fast growing into a town, a settlement that had been the sanctuary of outlaws for more than a dozen years. Helping Slade clean it up sounded far more appealing that watching the final insult to a once mighty and still proud nation of people.

Jeb barely noticed when the slim, brown girl slid from his horse and moved as gracefully as a young deer toward the scattered tepees.

Still thinking about Slade's last letter, Jeb covered the short distance to the Ranger camp. The youngest of Brown's rangers sauntered up as Jeb reined in his horse and grinned at the poor excuse for a cow Jeb had managed to herd back. "If you're through wranglin' cattle, the captain wants to see you."

Jeb looked toward the tent Brown used as headquarters and sighed. No doubt Wilkins or his superior officer had been there before him.

Might as well get it over with. "Thanks," Jeb told the young ranger sarcastically and nudged his horse forward. New Mexico looked better all the time.

During the course of his career, John Henry Brown had become unused to defiance of any kind. He'd been dealing with Jeb Welles for less than a month, and already he'd met with challenge upon challenge from this one man. Brown tried to quell the admiration he couldn't help but feel as he studied the ranger seated across the narrow table from him. It took a courage most men didn't have to continually place themselves beyond the rules and regulations of an entire military force while upholding the laws and the principles of that entity.

Jeb Welles was one of the best, if not the best, of all of the men Rip Ford laid claim to as head of the entire force of Texas Rangers—best at tracking, scouting, fighting, deductive reasoning, and, from what Brown had gleaned from the occasional comments of other rangers, the best with women. That last surprised Brown somewhat. Welles certainly didn't cut a dashing figure. He shunned any uniform, and his oiled leather vest and felt hat had seen better days.

The only thing about Welles that Brown had never seen less than perfect was the gleam on his Whitney six-shooter.

"The removal of the Comanche begins in two days at dawn. Captain Plummer has requested that you be assigned to his company for the length of the journey." Brown didn't have much hope that Welles would agree to that willingly.

"No." Simple, direct, uncompromising.

Brown smiled faintly that he had read Welles correctly. But, then, he usually did. "I could make it an order," he suggested.

Jeb's answering smile held little humor. "Two days ago you could have. It'd be a waste of your breath now."

A sigh escaped Brown. He'd known Welles's enlistment was up—he'd hoped Welles hadn't realized it. A lot of men found it hard to keep up with the passage of time while on the trail. Idly, he recalled the note from Rip Ford demanding that he gain Welles's re-enlistment at once. He had a feeling that wasn't going to be as easy as Ford thought it would be. Of course, Ford had good reason to be confident; Welles had been with the Rangers for nine of his twenty-seven years, and he'd shown no sign of wanting to change his lifestyle.

Abruptly, Brown pushed a folded paper toward Jeb. Less hastily, Jeb took it and unfolded it. He moved his gaze with equal lack of haste from Brown to the words he'd read every six months for nearly ten years now.

Without speaking, he refolded the page and handed it back to Brown. Until this moment, he hadn't been sure what his answer would be to re-enlistment.

For a long while, Brown simply sat and studied the man, trying to read what was in his mind. "Why not?" he asked finally.

"I can give you three reasons—or a hundred times that number," Jeb said grimly.

"Nelson, Shaw, and Wilkins." Brown had known it sat ill in Welles's gullet that the three men had been released to their duties. "Those men are the Army's business."

"Bullshit."

Brown drummed his fingertips on the rough surface of the table. "There was no proof, Jeb. What the hell did you expect Plummer to do? Hang three men because you've got a gut feeling they were guilty?"

"My gut feelings have saved my neck more than once."

"And several other necks as well," Brown acknowledged without hesitation, "but you can't blame Plummer that your reputation wasn't enough for him to risk hanging the wrong men. All he had to go on was the word of some crazy coot who calls himself a preacher. The man didn't even see their faces, for God's sake."

"I saw their faces."

Brown shifted uncomfortably. Welles's voice was as hard as his eyes, eyes that had lightened to a dangerous, mesmerizing green.

"They're guilty." The answer held quiet finality. "And they'll cross my path again."

Probably intentionally, Brown agreed silently. He'd seen the eyes of the three when they'd been released to return to their duties. Hatred for Welles had burned in every one of them. Welles might not have cost them their lives, but he'd cost them a secure career. They wouldn't be discharged for something that couldn't be proved, but when their time was up, they wouldn't be allowed to re-enlist. Plummer had trusted Welles's instinct enough for that.

Brown backed away from something he hadn't a prayer of altering in Welles's mind. "What about the other three hundred reasons you mention?" Brown knew he'd meant the Reservation Indians. But why would Welles care so strongly about a people he'd spent the last half dozen years fighting with the ferocity of a Comanche brave himself?

"Those poor sons of bitches trusted the word of the United States Government when they were given these lands. The Texas Rangers represent that government," Jeb said flatly. "I'll be damned if I will."

Although Brown sympathized with Welles's feelings, he never let it show. "You can't stop the night from falling on these people, Jeb. It's over for them—at least as far as Texas is concerned."

"You think it will stop at Texas? We'll push them into the California sea and watch them drown before we're done. Every last man, woman, and child."

"You've spent half your life putting bullets in Comanche." Brown knew his frustration was beginning to show. That always happened when he dealt with Welles.

"Yeah. The ones who were occupying themselves trying to put arrows into me. Damn it, I've got no problem with protecting innocent farmers, but I don't want any part of sending these people to their death. Go outside and take a good, hard look around. Tell me how many of those women and their babies are going to make this trip—or survive the winter to come, if they do make it?" Knowing he was railing at someone as helpless to stop the tide of events as he was, Jeb stood up and clamped his hat on his head.

Brown got to his feet as well. He'd failed; it was time to give in gracefully. "Do you want to send a message to Ford?"

Jeb shook his head. "I reckon he'll get message enough when you send him my papers back unsigned."

Feeling better than he had in months, Jeb started toward the door. He was already thinking about New Mexico, but he paused and turned back questioningly when Brown spoke his name.

For a moment, Brown hesitated. "Plummer wanted you to know that Nelson's, Shaw's, and Wilkins's enlistments are all up within the next few weeks." Brown cleared his throat. "Watch your back."

Undaunted, Jeb grinned. "I've been doing that for years." He moved to the door, then glanced back. "But thanks—and thank Plummer for me."

Brown stared at the empty doorway, feeling that the Texas Rangers had just passed a milestone, whether or not anyone but him realized it.

Chapter Four

Texas, July 1859

A light wind rippled the grass along the low rise, brushing golden stalks against Hannah's skirt. The grass ended abruptly at the tiny grave. Hannah wanted those golden stalks to encroach, to cover that bare mound, but there hadn't been enough rain. The naked dirt mocked her; she had failed to keep that helpless life safe within her. Abruptly, she knelt and swept her hand across the surface.

Hannah's mind groped for words that would bring her soul comfort but found none. She suspected none existed. Caleb's words did not comfort. *For whom the Lord loveth He chasteneth, and scourgeth every son whom He receiveth.* Hannah didn't think she could bear much more of God's love.

Straightening, she turned away from the grave and shivered as she realized how far the sun had dropped in the sky. She hadn't meant to be out here so long. She started back toward the cabin, feeling anxious. Caleb would be home soon. She didn't want him to find her here. He had forbidden it.

Halfway back, she saw something move in the distance, and she hurried her stride. In another moment, she caught a glimpse of her husband's dark clothing, recognized his horse, and her heart sank. She gave brief thought to running but discarded it instantly. Caleb would be certain to see her, and she wasn't sure which would be the greater shortcoming in his eyes—mourning for what the Lord had chosen to take or arriving breathlessly before him with heightened complexion and her hair sliding from its knot.

He was waiting for her in front of the lean-to, holding the reins loosely in one hand. Hannah knew there was no need for him to keep a tight grip on the horse. Like Hannah, the gentle animal accepted the servitude life held for him. Unlike Hannah, the horse did not seem to regret his fate.

Caleb's eyes were sorrowful as they moved from his untidy wife to the distant grave.

"I'm sorry, Caleb," she said simply, knowing it wouldn't help.

"So disobedient still," he murmured.

Hannah knew he wasn't talking to her, not really. The message was for her, but he conversed with his God. Hannah held her tongue, knowing there weren't any words that would mitigate her sin in his eyes. She was sorry to be such a disappointment to him, but there never seemed any way to change the simple fact of her nature. She wasn't the righteous woman Caleb wished her to be.

"Can you not give thanks in every thing as the scripture would have us do, wife? Can you not accept the will of God concerning you?"

Hannah bowed her head at the reproach in his voice. She wanted to accept, she earnestly tried, and she managed in most things. But Hannah didn't know if she could ever give thanks for the emptiness that would not leave her.

Caleb sighed, giving up for the moment. "Is my supper ready?"

It shouldn't have been possible for Hannah's heart to sink any lower, but it did just that at his question. "I'll hurry." Speaking the words, she lifted her head at last, waiting for his dismissal.

He shook his head, his expression reflecting his sadness. "I've prayed and prayed for you, Hannah, these years since the Lord led me to take you as my wife. I've had such hopes. Such hopes. But you never did become the woman your pa promised me you would." His voice changed slightly, ringing with his convictions. "But God does not err; my prayers will not go unanswered." With a final sigh, he patted her shoulder clumsily. "Tend to my supper, Hannah. I'll be in soon."

The inside of the cabin was as barren and devoid of color as all of Hannah's life, but it was her home and she felt some measure of peace as she worked. Quickly, she sliced two thick slabs of salted meat and dropped them into the pot of greens that had been simmering all afternoon. Then, with equally efficient movements, she stirred cornmeal and water, adding one of the eggs she'd gathered that morning. When the grease in the skillet was sizzling hot, she dropped spoonfuls of the mixture onto the hot surface.

Lifting the last griddle cake from the skillet, she gave a tiny sigh of relief. Everything had gone well. Nothing was burned.

She wiped her hands on her apron and moved to the door to let Caleb know she was putting his food on the table. To her surprise, she realized that a lantern would need to be lit before they could sit down to eat. For just a moment, she paused in the doorway, enjoying the cool breeze that swept across the grassy hills. The sweet air felt good to her face, flushed as it was from the heat of the cabin.

Across the yard, Caleb was just barring the door on the small shed that served as shelter for both horse and buggy. Hannah had opened her mouth to call to him when the thundering of hooves stopped the words on her tongue. Hannah could make out the shape of several horsemen in the shadowy distance. They were riding hard toward the cabin. Their haste alarmed her, reminding her of her ordeal a few weeks earlier, then sending her mind skittering to the possibility of an Indian uprising. It was what most folks in the region seemed to fear would happen. Hannah wasn't so foolish as to think Caleb's calling or his goodwill toward the Comanche would be any protection.

Caleb turned to look at her in almost the same instant that he heard the horsemen. His haste as he moved toward the cabin told Hannah that he felt an alarm similar to hers.

The horsemen drew near, and Caleb paused mid-stride, halfway between the lean-to and the cabin. He turned his large frame toward the horsemen and waited.

There were three riders, and they were bearing down upon Caleb when Hannah's frozen tongue thawed at the sight of gunmetal gleaming dully in the last rays of the evening sun. She screamed Caleb's name at almost the same instant that a single shot was fired.

It took only that one shot to drop Caleb's massive frame like a felled oak. Blood poured from the gaping hole in his chest, soaking into the dust of the yard. Looking down at him, the man who had fired the shot laughed, a horrible sound that rang through the air.

Hannah took a stumbling step toward Caleb, her gaze lifting to the three horsemen, who never paused but rode hard past her husband as he lay in the dirt only a few feet away from the hooves of their horses. They were too far from Hannah for her to discern their features, but they were close enough for her to see that one was very tall and another short and stocky. She knew them. God help her, she knew these men.

She did not bother to watch them disappear from sight as she raced to Caleb's side. His name was an agonized cry on her lips as she knelt in the dirt beside him. His blood soaked into her skirt hem. Dear God, could a man lose this much blood and live?

Sobbing, Hannah tugged at him. She had to get him inside. "Caleb, please!" She didn't think she could do it alone, but she didn't have any choice but to try.

As she pulled at his arm, Caleb moaned. "You've got to try to help me, Caleb. I have to get you inside."

To her relief, he stirred slightly. Hannah suspected it was the sheer force of his will that gave Caleb strength enough for even the little assistance he was able to give her. Sheer force of will that held him swaying on his feet once she had him up. She knew from experience that Caleb's will was indomitable.

She staggered under the weight of him pressing down on her shoulder, but she managed to direct their steps toward the open door of the cabin. The shallow step up to the porch was almost too much, but they were finally inside.

At last Caleb lay stretched out on their narrow bed, bare to the waist, his breathing filling the small cabin with horrifying rattles. Hannah stared helplessly at the blood welling from the gaping hole in his chest. So much of it. Even more than she had lost with the baby.

"Caleb," she whispered, "I've got to lay a hot iron to it. I'm sorry. You'll bleed to death if I don't."

Caleb moaned hoarsely, but Hannah knew it wasn't really a response. She suspected he was past understanding her, perhaps past hearing as well.

The fire she had stoked to prepare their evening meal served a far different purpose as the flat iron that usually smoothed the wrinkles from Caleb's freshly laundered shirts heated to a malevolent, glowing red. Too soon, Hannah gripped the handle with a thick cloth and turned to look at her husband. Even in agony, his broad face appeared harsh and judgmental, and she fought the urge to apologize for her inept nursing. Her experience in caring for wounds was limited. Though Caleb carried a gun, he'd never used it on anyone that she knew of, nor had anyone ever used a weapon on him. Until today.

Slowly, Hannah approached him, her stare fixed on the ragged edges of the gunshot wound. The sweat that popped out on her brow had nothing to do with the heat of the cookstove in the closed cabin.

"Please, God, you've got to hold him still. I can't do that and put this iron to his chest, too." Despite her fear, she didn't speak the words out loud. She wasn't completely sure Caleb would consider his own survival important enough to bother the Lord about.

Caleb grew quieter as she approached, and she took that as a sign that God was indeed listening. That didn't stop her knees from trembling or her hands from shaking. She fought to keep from gagging on the bile that hit the back of her throat. Biting her lip, she lowered the iron to his chest.

In the instant before she snatched it away again, the sound of Caleb's hoarse screams filled the cabin and Hannah's ears. The silence that followed was so abrupt it was painful, almost as painful as the sounds of his agony had been. The iron clattered loudly against the cookstove as Hannah released her grip on the padding she had used to cover the handle.

With silent tears flowing for the pain she had caused, she surveyed the results of her effort. Although the blood had slowed almost to a trickle, she had no way of knowing if that was enough. If Caleb continued to bleed on the inside, stopping the flow on the outside would accomplish nothing. Desperation washed over her. The nearest medical help was the Army doctor at the Brazos Reserve. She might have as little wits about her as Caleb seemed to think most of the time, but she knew enough not to make that trip. At best, it would be futile; at worst, fatal. Even most Christians found it difficult to aid those who cursed their very existence, and Caleb said he'd not found a

God-fearing man among the soldiers.

Straightening her back, Hannah brought fresh water to his bedside and began to bathe his fevered brow. It seemed alien to touch him like this. Caleb initiated all physical contact between them, and that was confined to the dead of night with the lights out. Even at those times, Hannah's hands never lifted to caress him, but lay quietly at her sides the way she'd been taught.

Now, her fingers passed lightly over the bushy black of his eyebrows and beard. To her shame, she felt nothing a wife should feel. No tenderness, no grief at the thought of losing him. She simply did what needed to be done, hoping he would live because he was her husband and the thought of being alone in this world terrified her.

It took most of her concentration to keep from seeing over and over again the moment when the three men of her own nightmare had returned, from hearing the gunfire and the laughter that followed. That was what Hannah remembered the most. She flinched each time she heard that single blast of gunshot repeated in her mind, but her blood ran cold when she recalled the laugh as Caleb hit the ground.

Caleb's breathing changed abruptly to a harsh rattle, and frightened tears slid slowly down Hannah's cheeks as she realized that he was dying and she could do nothing to help him. "I'm sorry, Caleb," she whispered. "I'm so sorry."

The next instant, he simply quit breathing, and she was alone. For a time, she sat there, the sound of the silence around her deafening.

Slowly, she got to her feet. Caleb had taught her better than to sit when there was work to be done. Reluctantly, she began removing his boots.

Caleb had married her when she was fifteen years old, and for the first time in almost four years of marriage, Hannah saw her husband's body unclothed.

Wearily, Hannah threw out the water she had used to clean Caleb's wound and heated fresh. She felt numb as she bathed him and dressed him in his single black suit. When she had done all she knew to do, she stepped out of the cabin.

Surprisingly, it was a beautiful night, soft and warm and alive with stars. Somehow that didn't seem fair, when Caleb lay in that cabin unseeing. The beauty of God's earth was the one thing he had allowed himself to take pleasure in.

Hannah took the spade that Caleb had used to bury the son she had miscarried just five weeks earlier and walked out to the low rise of land. She began to dig next to the small grave of her child and found the ground there was much harder than the moist dirt nearer the cabin where she had her garden. After a while, her muscles screamed in protest, and a while after that, she couldn't feel them at all. Tired as she was, she couldn't just quit. There was no one else here to do it for her.

Daylight found her staggering toward the cabin, away from a grave that was much too shallow but all she could manage.

She had just reached the threshold when she saw a tiny cloud of dust in the distance. Wondering why she bothered, she stepped inside and took the rifle from the rack beside the door. Lifting it, she stood in the open doorway and waited.

Moments later, she found herself staring into hazel eyes she had never seen before.

Cautiously, Jeb tipped his hat to the girl. It wasn't uncommon to be greeted with a rifle first and a welcome later. Folks had to be careful, after all. It was uncommon, however, to be greeted by a female with blood all over her gown and eyes that looked as if they'd seen hell.

"My horse has a loose shoe. I was hoping to borrow any smithy tools your husband might have." Jeb was careful to keep his voice low and soothing. Something was wrong here, very wrong. But whatever instinct it was that had kept him alive through numerous dangers reassured him there was no immediate threat. And, he knew better than to go pushing his nose into someone else's business without an invitation.

Hannah considered his words for a moment, never lowering the barrel of the weapon she held. Slowly, she nodded and pointed the rifle toward the shed. "What he has are in there.

You're welcome to them."

"I'm grateful, ma'am." Jeb rode his horse toward the barn, but the girl's face stayed with him. He'd seen prettier, but he'd never seen any more vulnerable—or more troubled.

He'd dismounted and reached the door of the shed when his gaze took in the mound of raw dirt on a slight hill just beyond. His hand rested on the drop bar that secured the door, and he glanced back at the cabin. The girl was gone; the door to the cabin stood wide.

Leave it be, he told himself. *Take care of your horse and go on.* Yet, he couldn't bring himself to go about his business as if he'd noticed nothing unusual.

Damn. He left his mount and his packhorse ground-tied and strode back to the cabin. His footsteps rang on the shallow porch. Hesitating at the open door for only a moment, he walked inside.

Hannah looked up and stiffened. "Go away." Her fingers fumbled over the task of sewing their best blanket around Caleb as a shroud. She finished the last few stitches and knotted the thread, very aware of the man watching her. His presence felt threatening after all she'd been through, and she wondered if he would try to rape her on top of Caleb's body. The rifle was across the cabin, but she supposed it wouldn't do her much good if she had it. It wasn't loaded, and Caleb had refused to show her how.

"Your husband?" Jeb kept his voice gentle even as he wondered if she'd killed the man.

That would explain the blood covering her. He sighed as she simply nodded without answering. "Ma'am, I'll be glad to ride out and bring some folks back to help you. Your family, maybe."

"I've got none." Actually, she had five older brothers, but they were scattered to the four winds. Hannah hadn't seen any of them in half a dozen years. She met his gaze squarely, wanting him to understand and go away.

Jeb tried to recall if he'd seen any signs that would indicate neighboring farms as he'd ridden in. He didn't think there had been. *Well, hell.* "Are you through here?"

Hannah realized that he wasn't simply going to go away and leave her in peace. She stood there, feeling lost and trying to think what else she should have done and hadn't. "I think so." She looked back at the stranger. His hazel eyes were disconcertingly clear and sympathetic. She wasn't used to sympathy.

Jeb stepped forward, and the girl moved hastily away. He frowned, but said only, "If you've got a Bible, bring it."

Her husband had been an uncommonly big man. Jeb staggered a little as he hefted the weight of the body, then gained his bearing and started toward the door, the dead man draped over his shoulder.

Hannah followed, trying to convince herself of what was happening. Her husband was dead, and a stranger was carrying him to his grave, and then—her mind would go no further. She could not imagine anything beyond that. Where she would go or what she would do.

Jeb was aware of the blankness to the girl following him. He supposed that was to be expected. They were burying her husband, after all. Last night the man was alive, probably loving her; this morning all that was left was the shell that housed what had been.

He tried to lower the body carefully, not to let it scrape and thump against the sides of a grave he realized suddenly wasn't nearly deep enough. *Damnation!* He should have noticed when he could still lay the body aside and take up the shovel. He didn't want to drag the man back out of his grave. He didn't know how much more this girl could take. Glancing at her, he suspected that it wasn't much.

"Ma'am," he said gently, waiting until she tore her gaze from the distant hills. "You'll want to read from your Bible now." He pulled his hat from his head.

Hannah nodded slowly and opened the well-worn book. The pages fell open to words heavily underscored, which was how Caleb marked all of his favorite verses. It seemed appropriate, somehow, to read over him in death words he preferred to read in life.

"The Lord revengeth, and is furious; the Lord will take vengeance on His adversaries, and He reserveth wrath for His enemies."

The soft voice was so clear and melodious that for a moment Jeb didn't comprehend the words. His eyes narrowed as he glanced at her.

Had *she* taken revenge on her husband for some real or imagined wrong? He didn't fool himself that she was too fragile. He'd seen a gun even out a great many inequalities.

With a start of surprise, he realized that she had stopped reading and was regarding him as steadily as he was watching her.

"I'm through," she said simply.

Jeb nodded and cleared his throat. He couldn't let a man meet his Maker with nothing but those harsh words spoken at his grave. From memory, he began to quote from Ecclesiastes. "To everything there is a season . . ."

Hannah stilled as memories washed over her. Sweet Sunday mornings, her father's voice, clear and resonant, from the pulpit. This stranger had evoked sensations she hadn't felt in years. On the third verse, her voice joined his. "A time to kill, and a time to heal; a time to break down, and a time to build up."

When her voice trailed away, Jeb's did also. He saw that she had once more focused her attention on the hills rising in the distance. He touched her arm. The look she turned on him was heartbreakingly lost. "Go wash yourself," he said quietly, "and change your gown. When I've finished here, maybe you can find some flowers to put on his grave while I put together a marker."

Without a word, Hannah moved away and walked toward the cabin. None of this was real. She'd wake up sooner or later and find that it was all a bad dream. She wanted to wake up *now*, but didn't know how.

Alone in the cabin where Caleb had died, she bathed and dressed herself in a gown as dark and drab as the grave she had dug. All her gowns were drab; Caleb had selected the material for each one of them. She had only protested once, when they were first married, when she was still young and dared to dream.

She belonged to him, Caleb had told her, his voice thundering through the small mercantile—rib of his rib, a part of him; and the Lord commanded, if thy right arm offend thee, cut it off. Meeting Caleb's piercing glare, Hannah had been convinced of his belief in those words. If she offended him, he would deal with her as if she were an offense to God. She had never questioned his commands again.

When she stepped back out into the morning, the stranger was piling rocks on top of Caleb's grave. The sight made her feel better about the fact that she had not been able to dig deep enough that wild animals could not tear open the grave. She shuddered at the mental image her thoughts drew and quickened her steps toward the fields of summer flowers that grew all about the cabin. They would be dying soon. *To everything there is a season.*

Jeb placed the last rock securely on the pile and straightened to watch the girl. She moved gracefully through the tall grass, adding flowers to the bunch she held in her hand. She was slender almost to the point of being too thin, but that didn't detract from the near perfection of her body—narrow waist, high breasts, hips that swayed without conscious thought.

Whoa! Jeb drew his mind away. He had just helped bury her husband. For that matter, he wasn't altogether sure she hadn't sent the man to his grave.

Shaking the tempting picture of her from his mind, Jeb stalked to the shed to find enough lumber to make at least a rough cross. The cool, dark place was meticulous, giving Jeb a tiny insight into the man who had owned the tools neatly lining the wall. He had been orderly, but no craftsman. The saw was barely used; the hammer not much more so.

After he fed the nickering horse some hay, Jeb set to work on the cross. He was just finishing when a shadow fell across the rays of sunlight coming through the open doorway.

Jeb glanced up to find her studying him. She was the quietest damned woman he'd ever encountered. He picked up the chisel.

"What was your husband's name?"

"Caleb. His name was Caleb Barnes."

Something vaguely familiar about the name pricked at Jeb.

Chiseling the letters took longer than covering the grave with rocks. Despite that, however, the girl never moved, never spoke.

"When was he born?"

"I don't know."

Jeb glanced up in mild surprise, then

shrugged. He began to add the date the man had died.

"Put on there that he was a preacher."

With narrowed eyes, Jeb rocked back on his heels to study her. Now he knew where he had heard the name. Recalling the ranting and raving figure in black, Jeb recalled also his instinctive dislike of the man.

Hannah read the displeasure in his face and realized that she had dared to tell him what to do. Caleb had taught her that wasn't a woman's place. "Please," she added softly. "That was his whole life."

Jeb nodded and added the word Reverend before the man's name. When he was done, he put the tools carefully back in their place.

"That looks heavy. Shall I help you carry it?"

The calm way she spoke began to get on Jeb's nerves. Any other widow would be weeping and wailing. He'd damn sure want any wife of his to be!

"No," he said curtly, "I can manage."

Abashed at his rough tone, Hannah followed him silently back to Caleb's grave. She'd been too forward. Caleb wasn't cold in his shroud, and already she was forgetting everything he had taught her.

At the grave, Jeb stood the cross in place, then watched as Caleb's wife placed her bouquet of flowers at its base. They were already wilting in the morning sun; by evening they'd be withered and brown. He stepped away to give her a moment's quiet with her husband, but she turned from that grave to the tiny one and placed a second, smaller bouquet there. For the first time, Jeb read the marker and felt the sting of self-recrimination. This girl had lost a baby, an infant son, and her husband in the space of a few weeks. She needed compassion, not judgment.

But when she faced him again, her features were without expression, and the question taunted him. How had her husband died that she should be so covered in his blood? Not an accident chopping wood. His axe hung alongside his other tools, the blade clean and gleaming. Jeb told himself it didn't matter. The man was dead, and speculation wouldn't bring him back. By sundown, Jeb would be long gone and the girl forgotten.

"I'll make use of those smithy tools now," he told her.

"Of course." Hannah had forgotten how he had come to be there; his help had seemed so natural after the first little while.

She turned to go with that graceful way she had of moving, and Jeb had to force himself not to stare at the sway of her skirts. "And I could use something to eat." She owed him that much.

Hannah looked back and wondered at his obvious irritation. What had she done wrong this time? "It will be ready by the time you're through."

Jeb doubted that, but she proved him wrong.

He stepped into the cabin just as she pulled a pan of biscuits from the oven. Deftly, she slid fried eggs from a griddle to a plate which already held chopped, browned potatoes.

Hannah burned her wrist on the oven as she withdrew the biscuits, but other than a quick intake of breath, she gave no indication of pain. Caleb had never liked outbursts of any kind.

Jeb glared at her stoicism. Didn't she feel anything at all? Maybe she couldn't, not grief or the fierce burning of hot steel. "Put it in cold water," he said roughly.

The look Hannah gave him was blank. "What?"

"Your wrist—put it in cold water." Maybe she was simple-minded, and he just hadn't realized it.

Amazed that he would notice what she had done, Hannah nodded. But before she did what he told her, she put his plate in front of him and poured a glass of cold water.

"Any coffee?" Jeb asked.

Hannah shook her head. "I'm sorry. Caleb didn't hold with drinking coffee." She hurried outside to the well . . . away from the man. He had begun to disturb her in a way she didn't understand or like. But though she could no longer see him, she couldn't rid herself of the way his hair clung to his freshly washed face and neck. His hair was too long; Caleb would never have allowed his to cover his ears. And his jaw was too hard, almost as hard as the cool hazel of his eyes. She had always thought of brown and green as warm colors, but on this man they sure as the Lord weren't warm.

Obediently, she drew water from the well and poured it slowly over her wrist. It did ease the burning, and she wondered why Caleb had never told her that it would. She had burned herself many times when she was learning to cook for him.

Jeb cleaned his plate hastily, feeling a sudden urge to be gone. Whatever else she was, the girl was a damned fine cook. He wondered why he couldn't think of her as a woman. She was old enough to wed, carry a child, and bury a husband, but he held an impression of a girl, a child-woman, in his mind. And he wanted to be away from her, away from here.

He jammed his hat on his head and walked to the door. She had her back to him, the bucket from the well dangling emptily upon its rope, her attention fixed on some distant object.

"I'll be leaving," he said to bring her thoughts back from wherever they had wandered.

She faced him then, her eyes blue and disconcertingly light. Jeb had never particularly cared for blue eyes in a woman, but he could tolerate them if they were the dark of an autumn sky. Hers were the washed-out shade of high summer.

"I appreciate your help. I wish I could pay you for it." She frowned faintly. *Did* Caleb have any money?

"I don't need payment. I did what any man would have done."

Hannah's face cleared. Of course. It was what Caleb would have done in this man's shoes.

She waited where she was while he got his horses from the shed where he'd left them. He tipped his hat to her, then stepped up into the saddle.

Hannah watched him ride away, then stared about her and wondered what in the world she was going to do now.

Chapter Five

Dust rose with each step his horse took, reminding Jeb that it was going to be a long, hot ride to the New Mexico Territory. He tried to keep his thoughts there, ahead of him, but with every puff of dust they turned backward, to the girl he'd left alone with two graves. He recalled her answer when he'd offer to ride for her family. *I've got none.* She appeared not to have any neighbors either. The Brazos Reserves were officially closed, Indians and military alike gone for good. With that closing had come Jeb's freedom. He'd completed his final assignment and refused to re-enlist, despite all pleadings, threats, and blusters.

Not that Jeb would have considered a military outpost much of a comfort to a grieving widow. If she did, indeed, grieve. If she hadn't killed her own husband. And what if she hadn't? The question came unbidden. Was she alone now, with only her husband's murderers knowing how defenseless she was? *No one said the man was murdered.* Once the possibility came to Jeb's mind, however, nothing could chase it away.

She would have been frightened, he argued with himself. She would have asked for help. But would she? An image of her came to mind, shoulders too slender, face too pale against the dark red of her hair. But a delicate appearance didn't always mean fragility. Katherine Slade was proof of that. Jeb tried to think what Katherine would do in this girl's shoes, but he couldn't picture Katherine in her place at all. They were as different as any two women he had ever known. Katherine was strong, everything a woman should be. But wasn't there strength in the stoic way the other had buried her husband beside her son with never a tear falling? Or was it nothing more than a cold lack of feeling that made her seem courageous?

He shook his head. Whatever was or was not in her, she was no concern of his.

So why did he feel like she was?

Damn! Jeb was used to having his mind on women, but not like this. He liked the feel of their soft flesh against his, liked the scent of them lingering with him after he rode away, satisfied and knowing he had satisfied them. But he'd be damned if he liked this feeling that was akin to worry.

"And why should I worry?" he asked the bay as he turned him back the way he'd just ridden. "Why the hell should I care that she's alone and unprotected? She probably killed that poor son of a bitch just so she *could* be alone." A picture of the preacher came to mind. "Can't much say as I'd blame her if she did."

Damn!

Jeb rode back up to the tiny cabin, thinking it looked smaller and meaner than it had before. There weren't two straight boards to the whole structure, and what passed for a front porch looked as if it had sagged from the day it was built. Somehow he wasn't surprised to see a small calico figure sitting on a narrow bench at the door, a rifle across her knee. The thought crossed his mind that she might just use that rifle on him. But as she recognized him, he saw the fear in her eyes fade to relief.

The realization that he had left a frightened woman alone fueled his anger. "Christ! What do you think you're doing with that thing?"

Hannah blinked. Caleb had never taken the Lord's name in vain. "I'm . . . I'm waiting for them to come back."

Jeb's frown deepened. "Who?"

"The men who killed Caleb," she said simply.

Jeb felt like all kinds of a fool, and he didn't like the feeling. Perversely, he blamed her for it. "Why the blazes didn't you tell me he'd been murdered? That you might be in danger?"

"I didn't know I should." Hannah wondered

why he was so furious with her.

That queer light gaze made it difficult for Jeb to think. "Didn't know you should what?" he repeated.

"Tell you." Maybe he wasn't quite as bright as he'd first seemed. Caleb's mind had jumped from subject to subject more quickly than hers, and there wasn't any trail a conversation could take that he couldn't follow.

"Well, of all the fool . . ." Jeb stepped down from his horse. "Do you know how to use that thing?" He glared pointedly at the rifle.

"It doesn't matter."

Straining for patience, Jeb pushed his hat back on his head. "What doesn't matter?"

"Whether or not I can use the rifle," Hannah said patiently. "It doesn't matter."

"It damned sure will if you point that thing at someone!"

"It isn't loaded." Hannah felt a kind of triumph at being right. She hadn't been right too often with Caleb.

"Sonuvabitch! Give me that thing!"

Before she could move to comply, Jeb was on the porch with her, snatching it from her grasp. "Pack your clothes."

"What?" Hannah felt as if her mind had failed her. Now she was the one who couldn't follow the conversation.

"Get your things together," Jeb said between gritted teeth. "You're going with me."

"But . . . where?" This place wasn't much, but it was all she had. It was her home. There simply wasn't anyplace else for her to go.

Jeb didn't have an answer for that one, and the fact that he didn't infuriated him even more. She'd already said she didn't have any family. And if she did have, they probably wouldn't have wanted the little idiot. "Anyplace you say, ma'am. I'll take you anyplace." As long as he got rid of her as soon as possible. "You must have people somewhere who will take you in. Your husband's family. Friends?"

"I . . . Caleb didn't have any family, that I know of. And I don't have any friends."

Jeb leaned forward until his nose nearly touched hers. Sweet Jesus, if the first woman he'd ever bedded had been like this one, he'd have become a monk! "Lady, I'm not surprised. Now pack your damned clothes!"

He was almost shouting by the time he finished speaking. To his satisfaction, the girl got to her feet. He didn't even care that she was looking at him as if he'd lost his sanity—or never had any. Just so long as she didn't ask him another question. Ever.

Hannah stepped into the cool interior of the cabin and wondered what she should do. Sitting alone on the porch after the stranger had ridden away had given her more time than she wanted to consider the future. She'd begun to realize that if she stayed here with only her own company, she would soon go crazy. Caleb had been gone a lot, it was true, but she had always known he would be back. And the times he was home were enough to remind her that being by herself wasn't always bad. But alone forever? She didn't know about that.

She thought about the man on the porch, about riding away from the only place she knew with him. He seemed safe enough. His hazel eyes were hard, but they weren't mean. She had noticed that they tended to become more green than brown when he was irritated. She'd never had that much warning with Caleb. He couldn't be a bad man, she reasoned with herself; he'd helped her to bury Caleb, after all. A lot of folks might have just ridden away. Not that she'd been around a lot of folks lately.

Turning in a circle, Hannah looked about the bare little cabin. There was sure nothing to keep her here. And, somehow, doing something always seemed preferable to doing nothing, a trait Caleb had done his best to change in her. If the stranger wanted her to go with him—well, then she would. And after that . . . Hannah shrugged a little helplessly. After that, she just didn't know.

Jeb had just prepared himself for a long wait, leaning his back against a post that he wasn't quite sure was trustworthy and stretching his legs out in front of him, when the girl stepped back out of the cabin. She carried one small cloth bag. He might have known she wouldn't take long simply because he had thought she would.

"I'm ready."

For just a moment, Jeb didn't move. He just sat there studying her. Her voice suited her, cool and clear. Personally, Jeb had always preferred warm, husky voices, like Katherine's. Voices made for summer nights of loving . . . not singing in a Sunday morning choir.

Jeb shoved to his feet and lifted a skeptical brow at the bag she carried so easily. "That's *it?*"

Hannah nodded. "This and the rifle."

Following her glance to the weapon he still held, Jeb shook his head. "Lady, you ain't touching this thing again until I teach you how to load it and aim it," Jeb returned flatly.

She thought about that. "Fair enough."

To her surprise, he stepped back into the cabin. From the doorway, she watched as he grabbed the remaining blanket from the bed and rolled it up tightly. After a brief search, he found Caleb's little pouch of gunpowder and shot. Then he rifled through her sparsely stocked shelves, grabbing what few staples she had. As he thrust flour and meal toward her, she thought his look was almost condemning.

"We eat—ate mostly from the garden," she said by way of explanation, if not outright apology.

His only answer was a nod as he moved past her through the door. He was already off the porch and walking toward the shed when she spoke again. "What do I call you?"

The question stopped him in his tracks. He glanced back at her and felt a sudden sympathy. She looked kind of lost standing there. And why shouldn't she? She was leaving the only home she had, and her only family was resting side by side on that little rise of ground. "Jeb. My name's Jeb." His answer brought no change of expression, and his sympathy faded to quick irritation as he realized that wasn't sufficient for her. Jesus, but she was particular. "Welles," he added, trying to recall how far it was to the nearest town large enough for him to leave her, large enough to have a church and a pastor who would feel honor bound to look after her for a while at least. Texas was full of men. Some fool would surely be desperate enough to think her the prettiest thing he'd ever seen and marry her before he realized she was probably the most bothersome as well.

When he walked away without another word, Hannah followed him to his packhorse. He took her small bag and the foodstuffs from her and added them to the burdens of the packhorse. Then Hannah followed him quietly to the shed. She stepped into the cool interior in time to see him toss a saddle to the horse's broad back.

"No."

"No *what?*" Jeb asked without turning to look at her.

"I need the buggy."

He did turn around at that. "We won't be able to take a buggy where we're going."

Hannah lifted her chin. She didn't want to admit she couldn't ride. "Caleb brought me here in a buggy," she pointed out reasonably. "Caleb thinks it unseemly for a woman to sit in a saddle."

With great restraint, Jeb kept himself from reminding her that Caleb didn't think anything anymore. "I don't have the time to spare to find paths safe for a buggy. I wouldn't even know where to look for them." He turned back what he was doing. "You'll ride."

"I can't. I don't know how." She made the admission in a very small voice.

An image of himself bent over a broken buggy wheel every few hours stiffened Jeb's resolve. "I reckon it's time you learned."

Trepidation filled Hannah as she watched him tighten the girth around the animal's middle before strapping her rolled blanket behind the saddle. Suddenly that horse, which had always seemed so friendly, had a malevolent cast to his eyes. "M-maybe it isn't such a good idea for me to go with you. Likely, I . . . I'd be a bother."

Jeb never looked away from the bridle he was slipping over the horse's ears. *Likely,* hell! There was no damn doubt about it. "Are you telling me you have enough courage to sit with an unloaded rifle and wait for your husband's murderer to come after you, but you don't have guts enough to learn to ride?"

With that, he turned and held the reins to her, silently daring her not to take them.

Not in a million years, Hannah knew, could she ever make him understand. It wasn't a fear of getting hurt that paralyzed her. Not once in four years had she disobeyed Caleb. Caleb said she wasn't to ride. Somehow, Hannah felt this horse would know she was disobeying his master, would see to it that she failed and looked ridiculous in the attempt. No, Hannah thought, looking Jeb Welles in the eyes, she'd never make this man understand. He had a quality to his chiseled features that said he would dare anything—and never fail.

Slowly she lifted her hand and took the leather reins from him. Somewhat to her surprise, the animal followed her docilely from the shadows of the shed to the bright sunlight beyond.

Jeb watched as she put her foot hesitantly in the stirrup and eased her weight up. To his surprise, she made the movement seem graceful, somehow, as if she'd done the same thing so many times as to make it an unconscious part of herself. Then he felt something other than surprise as he watched her tug at her skirts, trying to cover the length of slender leg revealed when she sat astride. Her flesh there, like that on her face, had a soft, creamy tint to it.

Hannah was too worried about her naked flesh showing in the light of day to worry about the fact that she was now at the complete mercy of an animal who had no reason to be loyal to her. Caleb had always taken care of everything, from feeding to grooming. When she looked up and found Jeb staring at her, she blushed.

The rose color staining her cheeks reminded Jeb what the sun could do to unprotected skin, especially skin as translucent as hers. He noted her bonnet dangling down her back by its strings. "Put that thing on." When she looked at him questioningly, he gestured to her bonnet. "Cover your head."

Hannah blushed darker. She hadn't meant to be immodest. While she did as she was told, Jeb mounted his own horse with the quick efficiency with which he appeared to do everything. He checked the wrap of the packhorse's lead around his saddle horn, then started both animals moving.

To Hannah's surprise, he veered toward the graves on the hill. For the first time since he'd ridden up to her door that morning, his glance held real compassion.

"You'll want to say good-bye. I'll ride a little ways and wait for you."

Hannah wondered why he thought she'd be able to convince the animal she was on to go in the proper direction without Jeb's horse to follow, but all she did was nod. As he rode away, she slid from the saddle, keeping a death grip on the reins. She knelt beside the baby's grave and tried to pray, yet the only words that came to her were, *I'm sorry.* Sorry she hadn't wanted to conceive, sorry she couldn't grieve more at the loss. Though she would have loved any baby, the child would surely have grown to be more Caleb's than hers—would, in time, have become another human to judge her and find her wanting. Even so, she felt the emptiness of the child's loss.

From the tiny grave she turned to the larger one, recalling Caleb's last words to her. "You never did become the woman your pa promised me you would." She didn't exactly know what her pa had promised, but she was sure Caleb spoke the truth. His disappointment in her over the years had been all too apparent. She had always known she did not meet his expectations, no matter how hard she tried.

"And I did try, Caleb, I swear I did," she whispered.

As she stood there, it occurred to Hannah that she was about to fail Caleb one last time, and it would be the greatest failure of all. She was going to ride away and leave her husband's murder unavenged.

She stared down at the grave once more and stiffened her shoulders. After four years of marriage, Caleb deserved more than this from her. She stepped back up into the saddle and hoped the horse would instinctively rejoin the kindred soul that awaited him a few hundred yards away.

Jeb watched her ride toward him and thought that, for all her inexperience, she didn't look at all awkward on a horse. That was good. He wouldn't have to take a lot of time teaching her how not to fall off.

The nearest town lay in the opposite direction of where he wanted to go, and Jeb had decided that an extra day or two with her was as little to his liking as backtracking. He'd take her to Fort Belknap. What she decided to do there was her business—and her problem.

A few moments later, he didn't feel nearly as

distant from her problems as he would have liked. "You're going to do what?"

Hannah flinched at his roar. "I'm going to the reservation. I think the men who killed my husband were soldiers he'd caught at wrongdoing. That has to be told."

Jeb calmed himself. She was just a woman. She had no idea how farfetched her suggestion was. And he had to admire the fact that she wanted to see her husband's murderers punished. He thought of the three weasel-eyed soldiers he'd told Garrett were guilty of murdering the settler and laying a path to the reservation, thought of the sullen hatred in their eyes as they'd been led glaring past the preacher. Likely the girl was right. They'd done the killing here, too. But Jeb had no intention of letting them go free.

"I'll send a wire to Austin from the first town I can. The men will be punished."

For a moment, Hannah hesitated, then shook her head decisively. "I don't know their names and I couldn't describe them well enough. But I'll know them if I see them."

Jeb pushed his hat back on his head and glared. "You're just going to walk up to them, point your finger, and say, 'There. Hang them!' "

Hannah blushed. It sounded ridiculous coming from him, but that was exactly what she had planned to do. She squared her shoulders. "It's something I have to do." He didn't look at all appeased by her declaration. "Look, Mr.

Welles, I truly appreciate all you've done, and I don't expect you to go with me. I can find my way."

"Lady, you couldn't find your way out of a church pew!" Jeb took a deep breath. There was an easy way to end all this foolishness. "Besides, there *is* no more reservation. The Indians are being moved. Everybody bundled up and left. Everybody." He felt a certain satisfaction that he'd thwarted her outrageous plans.

Hannah considered his words for a moment. "Then I'll follow them. They can't be traveling far—all those women and children on foot."

"Mrs. Barnes," he began with gritted patience, "I was there the night your husband accused the men. I can recognize them. I'll make sure they're properly punished."

After only the first few words, Hannah realized that he was speaking to her in the tone one might use with an imbecile. She hadn't minded his irritation, but she minded this. Sometimes Caleb had spoken to her with just that tinge of sarcastic intolerance. She wasn't stupid. She wasn't.

Something Caleb had told her came back to her; something about a man who had stood up to the officer in charge about the men's guilt. "Weren't you the one who pointed out the three you thought were guilty that night?" she asked slowly.

Jeb nodded, sensing a trap. How had she maneuvered him into it?

"They didn't believe you then, did they? They didn't take your word for it, because Caleb hadn't seen their faces. I have. They'll have to believe me."

It took a moment for Jeb to realize that she had spoken in the same coolly sarcastic tone he'd used on her. Why did he keep thinking she was a mousy thing afraid of her own shadow? He recalled the way she'd sat on the front porch with an unloaded rifle, waiting for her husband's murderers to return.

He made one last effort to dissuade her. "Vengeance is a two-edged sword, Mrs. Barnes. It cuts both ways."

Hannah knew he was right, but she had a duty to discharge. If not to Caleb, then to God. "Those men cost me both my son and my husband. I know of at least one other life they've taken. I'll not turn my back and let them kill again."

Jeb felt pinned by that light blue stare. He lifted his gaze to the graves outlined on the slope of ground behind her. They'd murdered her baby? *Son of a bitch!* "All right. I'll take you to Plummer and let you say your piece."

With a feeling of resignation, he realized that he would have been well along on his way to New Mexico by the time they caught up to the cavalcade of Comanche and soldiers. Too far to turn back. What was he going to do with her then?

Jeb watched as she nudged her horse past him and started away from the cabin, then he shook his head. She was riding in the wrong direction. *Damn.* It was going to be a long journey any way he looked at it.

Chapter Six

Leon Wilkins glared at his captain, but Plummer, seated in the open at a small table, appeared not to notice the enlisted man's lack of patience. At the very least, he wasn't disturbed by it. Late afternoon sunlight gilded the inkpot on the table next to Plummer's hand.

They were two days' ride away from the reservation. Two slow days. Women and children on foot couldn't travel nearly as fast as the soldiers, Wilkins included, would have liked. He didn't care much for playing nursemaid to a bunch of redskins, and he wanted to get this duty over with. Maybe he'd get lucky enough to be stationed at a post that wasn't on the forsaken edges of the earth. Someplace that had bars and whores within hollering distance.

In addition to his impatience, Leon felt a

trickle of alarm. Since the night Welles had picked them out as the men guilty of murdering that pig farmer, Wilkins had managed to avoid Plummer. He'd had to face him only one time, when the three of them had been released, and Plummer had made his suspicion of them very clear then. Fortunately, Nelson insisted that none of them had ridden their usual mounts the night of the killing. Wilkins was convinced that it was the only thing that had caused sufficient doubt in Plummer's eyes—the only thing that had saved them.

Plummer was taking so long to answer that Wilkins wondered if the captain had even heard his request. "By my calculations, tomorrow is the first of August, and my time will be up," he repeated. "I want to sign my papers."

All around them, the sounds of men settling into evening camp and the smell of coffee boiling reminded Wilkins that the Army was the best thing that had ever happened to him. Farming was too hard, gambling too risky, and robbery downright dangerous. Since he'd enlisted at Todd Shaw's urging, he'd never missed a meal of some sort, and there was always at least one coin in his pocket. It hardly even mattered that it was rare for that one coin to have any company. The only time he needed money was to pay for a whore.

Soldiering wasn't even all that dangerous. What little bloodshed he'd seen had always been in the company of men fighting on his side, men who were well-armed and well-trained. As far as Wilkins was concerned, there was enough security in that fact to offset the risks of fighting Indians, particularly lately when those Indians were half-starved and far outnumbered.

Plummer finally looked up from the stack of papers he was perusing and stamping one by one. Slowly he shook his head, forestalling Wilkins's protests with a lifted hand as he began to speak quietly, but emphatically. "There isn't going to be any re-enlistment for you, Wilkins. The Army doesn't need your kind of soldiering."

By the time the last word had left Plummer's mouth, Wilkins's eyes were narrow slits of fury, and he'd forgotten all about the need for caution. "What do you mean the Army doesn't need my kind? What the hell are you talking about?"

"The pig farmer," Plummer said succinctly.

Leon felt the sweat bead on the back of his neck despite the cool breeze coming through the trees from the river. "If I'm guilty of something, why am I still walking around a free man?"

"Not something, Wilkins—murder. And if I could prove it, you wouldn't *be* walking around—not free or any other way. You'd be a dead man."

For a long moment, Wilkins considered arguing, but something in the cold depths of the captain's eyes stopped him. Plummer would hang him if he could. No doubt about it. Maybe it would be wisest to put as much distance as possible between himself and the Army. Or at least between himself and Captain Plummer.

It occurred to him that if Plummer had been in camp the night the preacher followed them, he and Shaw and Nelson might not have seen daylight the next morning. They'd just been lucky it was Garrett, instead, and Wilkins had never been one to press his luck.

"You're making a mistake," he mumbled as he took a step backward. "I'm an innocent man." But he didn't protest that innocence too loudly or too long, and he didn't quite meet the steady, disdainful gaze of the captain.

Glaring murderously at any who dared to look his way, Wilkins stalked through the close-growing trees. Just what the hell was he supposed to do now? He tried to think of somewhere he could go, somewhere he hadn't already made himself unwelcome. Unfortunately, there weren't too many such places left.

A movement through the branches to his right caught his eye, and he wheeled about. His gaze honed in on dark skin and gleaming black hair. Damned Indians! There was one skulking about everywhere he looked. He'd be glad to see the last of them, at least!

This was a young one, eleven or twelve, but there was nothing innocent about the youth of a redskin in Wilkins's eyes. They grew up to be murdering savages or the mother of murdering savages. That was what this one was. A female.

As Wilkins peered at her, she met his stare defiantly, standing her ground as if she was as good as anyone. His eyes narrowed. For some reason, she seemed familiar. He shook himself mentally and started walking again. Damn it, they all appeared familiar, because they all looked alike to him.

But just before he passed her by, it struck him where he'd seen this particular female. At the time, she hadn't been dressed as one. He recalled chasing the "warrior" until she had stumbled into Jeb Welles's presence. And he recalled his claim to Welles that the "warrior" was escaping.

Damn it all! No wonder Welles had taken the little bastard under his protection. Welles, like a lot of misguided soldiers and rangers alike, had some kind of chivalrous attitude toward the females, as if they wouldn't put a hunting blade through your gizzard as quick as their men would. Maybe quicker.

The idea that Welles had been laughing at his ignorance bit deep. Thinking with his anger, he took a step toward the girl, but she disappeared into the woods so quietly that she didn't even disturb the leaves in her passing.

No, he wouldn't follow her now—but he'd find her later, by God. Right now he had other things to think about, like where he was going to go. At least, he reasoned, Shaw and Nelson would soon be in the same boat he was. A boat that was cut adrift.

Wilkins hastened back to where he'd left them. "That son of a bitch is going to pay," he growled as he stepped into the small, clear area they'd chosen to stand their tent. He wasn't even sure, at the moment, whether he was talking about Plummer or Welles. But someone for sure was going to be sorry.

Chapter Seven

Along about nightfall, Hannah decided that she was as stupid as Caleb had ever thought her. She was in the middle of nowhere, headed someplace she didn't belong, with a man she didn't know, on a horse she couldn't ride. As she slid painfully from the saddle and looked around at the campsite Jeb had chosen, she fought an urge to give in to tears.

"Wh—What can I do to help?" she managed, surprised to find her voice rusty with disuse after only one day. Though frequently alone, she was used to singing and chattering to herself through the long hours. She hadn't felt much like either today. Even if she had, she wouldn't have indulged in such frivolities in Jeb's or any other man's presence. Caleb's lessons went too deep.

At the sound of her question, Jeb turned and stared, really seeing her for the first time in hours. She looked like hell, covered in dust from head to toe, with her hair slipping from under her bonnet in wispy remnants of color.

His gut tightened right along with his loins. He'd been too long without a woman if he could have this reaction just looking at her. Not in a hundred years would he have selected her from a dozen others to take up the back stairs of the Golden Gal or any other saloon.

"You can gather firewood," he said at last, realizing that she was returning his stare as she waited for an answer. He hesitated. "Can't you?"

Stung, Hannah lift her chin, the urge to cry leaving as quickly as it had swept her. "I can," she returned shortly. Did he imagine Caleb had gone out gathering dried limbs and buffalo chips? The thought of Caleb brought a pang. What kind of wife was she? She'd scarcely given him a thought the entire day. In fact, her mind had been amazingly devoid of anything but the unusual opportunity to study the world around her without any other demands on her time. At least, once she had mastered the skill of riding. Well, she amended, perhaps not exactly mastered.

With a shake of his head, Jeb turned his attention back to unsaddling and unpacking the horses. He hoped Hannah Barnes never took up poker. Every feeling she had showed on her face. He'd been surreptitiously watching those feelings play across her features that whole day. Mostly he'd seen excitement and pleasure, though what pleasure she felt was only revealed by a brightening of blue eyes and a tiny crinkling at their corners, never by a smile. He wondered what Hannah Barnes had against smiling—and against conversation. Maybe preachers' wives didn't indulge in either one.

Then he reminded himself. She'd buried her husband that morning. What the hell did he think she had to smile about?

By the time he had the three animals unsaddled and rubbed down, Hannah had a small, neat fire going. "Where'd you learn that?"

Surprised, Hannah glanced at her handiwork and realized that she had reached far back into her memory for the skill to build a fire that neither smoked nor blazed too high, past her twelfth year to a childhood that had been happy and normal. "My brothers."

Jeb glared. "I thought you didn't have any family. That *is* what you said." The possibility that someone existed whom he might have dumped her on before now irked him. And gave him hope.

"For all I know, I don't anymore." Hannah poked at a fire that didn't need poking. "The last of them rode away from home the year after Mama died. I haven't seen one of them since. I don't even know where they are."

Jeb made a study of finding a pot and a small bag of beans. Lord, he hated beans!

He turned back to Hannah. "How old were you then?"

Hannah stared. Why did he care how old she was when her mother died? "Thirteen," she said at last.

As usual, Hannah's features revealed her thoughts. How long, Jeb wondered, had it been since anyone had shown any interest in the girl? Woman, he amended. He kept forgetting that Hannah was old enough to be a wife and a mother, although he'd kept the fact of her recent pregnancy in mind for most of the day, holding the horses to a walk and stopping every few miles to let Hannah walk and stretch.

"How many brothers do you have?" Jeb asked as he poured a small amount of beans into the pot and added water. It was early, and these beans were going to take a while. About the only thing he could picture himself and Hannah doing for the next little bit was talking. Well, maybe not the only thing, but for sure the only *smart* thing.

After a moment, Hannah shrugged. It couldn't hurt for him to know about her family. At least, not as far as she could see, and if she couldn't understand his interest, it was likely because she didn't understand *anything* about Jeb Welles. "Five. All older," she added, before he could ask.

"Did your father remarry?" He'd seen more than one family torn up over a second wife moving into a home, especially a houseful of sons. Most folks tended to think it was girls who were closest to their mother. From what Jeb knew, it was the opposite. At least, that was the way it had been in his family. He never thought of his own mother without experiencing a pang of homesick longing.

"Papa?" Hannah felt a shock run through her at the very thought. "No, Papa died still grieving for Mama." He'd just never gotten over losing the only woman he'd ever loved. In the long months after he lost her, Hannah had watched him slowly sicken and die. She sometimes thought he might have taken his own life sooner than that if he hadn't truly believed it to be such a sin.

Jeb watched as she sank to the ground by the fire, drawing her skirts around her with as much natural modesty as she did everything else. She was a graceful woman, he'd hand her that.

"When was that?"

"The year he married me to Caleb."

A slight tremor of sympathy went through Jeb at her words. Not so much because of her expression, which was little more than pensive, nor because of her tone, which held only the faintest suggestion of sadness. No, it was more because of the words themselves. Most women would have phrased that statement as the year they married their husbands. Hannah made it sound as if she'd had no say in the matter. Likely she hadn't. There were still a great many arranged marriages, Jeb supposed.

The beans had begun to boil in the battered pot, and Jeb automatically reached to pull them a little farther from the center of the fire. Hannah wondered how many years he had been sleeping in the wilderness. She didn't wonder why a man would choose such an unsettled life. That would have been her choice, but women weren't allowed choices of any kind.

"What are you thinking?" There was no doubt she *was* thinking. He could see a myriad of expressions chasing each other across her face.

Hannah flushed at the mere idea of telling a man, this stranger, that she'd been thinking of something as personal as the way he lived. "You sure like to hear the sound of your own tongue, don't you?" she asked to hide her embarrassment. Then she flushed more at her rudeness.

For one moment, Jeb felt a spark of anger, but Hannah's immediate reaction to her own words assuaged it. He suspected she would have given a great deal not to have said them. "It's all right, Hannah. I expect a grieving woman's got a right to be a bit tart."

Hannah lowered her eyes to the fire, then lifted them almost at once. She couldn't live a lie even if it was only the lie of silence. "I'm not grieving," she said.

Well, she thought some time later, that sure stopped the questions.

High above Hannah, the heavens displayed a glittering brilliance that few earthly phenomena could match, much less rival. She'd heard diamonds were as brightly beautiful as the stars over her head, but she had a difficult time believing that, particularly of something that came from beneath the ground.

As she watched, a flare of light streaked from the upper corner of the sky to the lower. Unexpected tears stung her eyes. Caleb had loved to see a shooting star—as if God had shown some special wonder just for him.

If she had ever allowed herself to think about the possibility of being without him, Hannah suspected she wouldn't have thought she'd miss Caleb. But she did. After all, she had lived with him for four years, and though he'd never been kind, he'd never been deliberately unkind either—just harsh. His harshness had cost her many tears in the early days of their marriage until sometimes Hannah thought the ability to cry had been burned right out of her. But she had cried over the baby, and now she found silent tears slipping down her cheek for Caleb.

And for herself. What, she wondered, was she doing here out in the open with a complete stranger? What had possessed her to just ride away from the only home she had?

What else could you do? The silence mocked her. She didn't have an answer to her own question. What indeed?

Surprisingly enough, she still felt totally safe with Jeb Welles. He was crude and rough, but Hannah hadn't a doubt that he would get her safely . . . where? She couldn't stay with the Army once she had accomplished her goal of identifying Caleb's murderers. Would Jeb just ride away and leave her after he'd made good on his promise?

Somehow she couldn't picture him doing anything that callous. She hoped he wouldn't, anyway. At least she was getting used to Jeb. The thought of being abandoned with an entire company of soldiers who were irrevocably headed toward Indian Country was definitely *not* reassuring.

And, she thought sleepily as her eyes began to close on the sparkle of stars overhead, she was actually getting kind of used to his questions.

Chapter Eight

The small tent stank of sweat and unwashed flesh. Ike Nelson kept his eyes fixed on the narrow tent flap as if that would help him breathe the fresh air that lay beyond.

At the moment, that air was being split by wicked streaks of lightning that had accompanied the wind-driven rain. Normally, Ike didn't mind storms, even liked their violence and the raw energy so powerful he could almost reach out and touch it.

But Ike didn't care for anything that kept him cooped up with the likes of Shaw and Wilkins. The two were useful at times, but most times they were simply disgusting. Like now. Ike's thin upper lip curled at the noises coming from Wilkins's corner of the canvas shelter.

"Havin' fun, Leon?" Todd Shaw's grating

voice cut through the sounds of nature's fury from outside the tent and the hoarse pants from inside.

"Shut up, damn you!" Wilkins howled. "That bitch has ruined me."

Panic welled up in Wilkins as the preacher woman's words reverberated through his mind. *May God wither your manhood. . . .* Over and over. *May God wither your manhood. . . .*

His hand moved harder, up and down, as he tried to prove to himself that his manhood wasn't affected, not by mere words. That just wasn't possible; it wasn't! His hand pumped. Nothing! He moaned and felt a cold sweat pop out on his forehead.

Wilkins hadn't worried much about her words until he'd awakened a few mornings ago from an arousing dream and found himself completely limp. Dreams like that had always been a source of intense pleasure, mostly for the release he could bring himself immediately after waking. But on that morning—nothing. Just like now. Nothing.

Wilkins squeezed his eyes shut more tightly and envisioned a whore poised over him doing the things he liked best. But the fantasy turned to an image of a painted slut pointing a red-tipped finger at his drooping male organ and laughing. Then the whore turned to a calico-drab preacher's wife. Still laughing.

"I'll kill her for this," he whispered, his voice hoarse with a kind of horror for what that pious little bitch had done to him simply because she didn't know what to do with a real man.

Though Wilkins spoke to himself, Shaw heard him and grinned in the dark. "Why don't you just go back and get her to lift the curse?"

Abruptly, Wilkins's hand stilled. The thought had never occurred to him—but why not? If she could do such a thing in the first place, surely she could undo it.

Why not? In another twenty-four hours, he would no longer be a part of the Army. He would no longer have a sure bet for a meal, for boots to put on his feet, or for shot to load his rifle. Yeah, he could go after her and force her to undo this curse she'd put on him. Who'd have thought a preacher's wife would be practicing witchcraft, going about putting curses on people?

His eyes narrowed. And after he had taken care of her, maybe he'd just keep looking until he found Jeb Welles, too. That son of a bitch owed him something, if only a piece of his flesh. If it wasn't for Welles, his enlistment papers would be nicely signed by now, and he wouldn't have to be worrying where his next meal was coming from.

"Hey," he whispered to the other two, "think Plummer's going to let you join up again?" He sure wouldn't mind some good company while he was looking for Welles—but most especially when he caught up with him. Good company, to him, meant someone who held a gun pointed in the same direction as his.

"Naw." Every word Shaw spoke held the faint twang of the northern states where he'd been bred. "Welles fixed us real good there."

Shaw's outrage was so apparent that Wilkins grinned in relief. "I'm going after him," he said happily. He'd bet his last coin he wouldn't have to go alone, either.

"After Welles?" Shaw's voice held interest.

"Hell, yeah." Wilkins grew braver. Nope, he wouldn't have to go gunning for Welles by himself. "The way I figure it, he owes me. Thanks to him, there ain't nothing to keep me from taking what I owe, either." He paused. "But first, I'm going after that little gal that stole my . . . that cursed me. You can have her once she's fixed me," he added generously. "I sure as hell ain't going to want her more than once!"

Ike Nelson broke into the conversation, his comment carrying the cruelty that was always just beneath the surface with him. "What are you going to do if she just looks at you and commands your lungs to quit breathing?"

For a moment, a chill went all the way through Wilkins at the thought that any woman had that kind of power. He could almost feel his chest closing in, as if she'd already spoken the words. Then his fingers curled reflexively around his limp shaft. Hell, he'd rather be dead than go through life like this.

He shook his head, then realized Nelson couldn't see the movement in the dark. "A preacher's wife wouldn't do that. That'd be murder. She might think a little pleasurin' is a sin and that it wouldn't be no harm in keepin' a man from it, but she wouldn't take his life."

"She's mine after she's taken the curse off you." Shaw had been thinking of that soft little body squirming under his since the day they'd ridden off and left her bleeding on the ground. She wouldn't be all swollen with the kid either. He'd seen the slender curve of her shape the night they'd murdered the preacher man.

Wilkins almost rubbed his hands together. Now he had someone to ride with him. And Shaw was a damned good hand with a rifle.

"Fine," Nelson said flatly. "You can have the girl—but Welles is mine."

The other two were almost surprised to hear Nelson's words—especially Todd Shaw, though he'd known Ike the longest. A man never knew what Ike Nelson was going to decide to do from one moment to the next. He was a cold bird.

"Sure," Shaw said easily. "You can take Welles. I just want the pleasure of watching him die."

"You'll get it."

The words held a flat tone that drew a shiver from Wilkins. "What'll we do after that?" he asked, more to change the subject that from a need to know.

"I reckon there'll be plenty places for us once we secede from the union," Nelson suggested.

"You really think that's going to happen?" Shaw queried with a faint tone of disbelief. He still recalled Texas's struggles to gain statehood less than fifteen years earlier. At least he recalled hearing about them. He'd been nothing but a snot-nosed kid at the time.

"Sure it'll happen. Texans want it. That's why Houston ain't governor and Runnels is. Houston wasn't smart enough to see the writing on the wall. Can't no union of states tell a Texan how he ought to live—that he can't own slaves."

Shaw was silent, thinking about that. It was the first time he'd ever heard any kind of passion in Nelson's usually cool voice. Shaw wasn't rightly sure he could agree with him about busting up the union, but he sure as hell wasn't stupid enough to argue the point. Not with Ike Nelson.

Wilkins snorted, feeling brave now that things were going his way. "What do you care, Ike? You ain't ever going to be rich enough to own another man, no matter what color he is." He gave a little chuckle at his own joke.

"I don't give a damn about slavery," Nelson said flatly. "Neither do half the other people who want out of the union. We just don't want any damned Northerners telling us what is and what ain't." He paused. "Do we, boys?"

There was a ripple of tension in the air, and Shaw decided it was time to turn the conversation back to its beginnings. Nelson was getting entirely too heated over the issue. He might just recall that Shaw hadn't been born in the South and that he might have a different outlook on the subjects of slavery and secession. "Well, even if Tex—even if we do secede, how's that going to help the three of *us?*"

"Easy. All these United States soldiers will be gone, and there'll be nothing but Texas Rangers to defend Texas."

It *did* sound easy when it was put that way. Still . . .

Shifting positions, Shaw accidently kicked Wilkins, who cursed. "Sorry," he said absently, his mind still on Nelson's words. "If the Army won't have us, what makes you think the Rangers will?"

Nelson smiled into the dark. "The Army won't have Ike Nelson, Todd Shaw, or Leon Wilkins. But that ain't who we'll be by the time we take care of Welles and get to Austin."

Shaw liked that idea. He liked it just fine. "When do we cut out of here?"

"No need waiting around for them to boot us out. Welles already has more of a head start than I like."

"You want to leave now?" Wilkins peered dubiously at the jagged lightning still piercing the sky at regular intervals.

"First light," Nelson said. "Now shut up and let me get some sleep."

Wilkins closed his mouth.

But Nelson wasn't sleeping. He was thinking about the pouch of gold Shaw kept in his bedroll.

Wilkins wasn't sure what woke him. Maybe it was the gurgle of sound a dying man makes when he's struggling for his last breath. All he knew for sure was that he opened his eyes to the sight of Nelson silhouetted against the murky half-light of dawn creeping in through the open tent flap. The tall man was pulling his long blade from Shaw's chest.

"Wh—what are you doing?" Wilkins stammered, immediately wishing he had pretended to be sleeping still. But then, maybe Nelson would have turned that knife on him next.

Very carefully, Nelson wiped the blood on his pants, then sheathed his knife. "Leaving," he said as calmly as if he'd just gutted a rabbit. "You coming? Or maybe you want to be hanging around when they find him." He nodded carelessly in Shaw's direction.

Wilkins scrambled from his bedroll. He didn't need to be asked a second time. The choice he'd been given was no choice at all. He might not be real happy to ride out with a man who could kill a companion without a flicker of his eye—but he'd be a damned sight less happy being hanged for that man's crimes. He'd escaped justice once; he had a feeling Plummer would seize on any excuse to balance the scales.

With hasty movements, Wilkins gathered his belongings. There wasn't much. Army ways didn't encourage a man to hang on to anything that wasn't necessary for survival.

It was only when he noticed Nelson plundering Shaw's bedroll that he dared to ask, "Why'd you kill him, Ike?"

Slowly Nelson straightened and hefted a

worn leather pouch in one hand. "For this."

Wilkins thought of all the times Shaw had opened the drawstrings on that bag and turned the contents over onto his bedroll, playing with the unevenly sized nuggets that had come tumbling out. Reluctantly, Wilkins nodded agreement. Yeah, he would have killed for those gold pieces, too—if he'd had guts enough.

"Besides," Nelson added, "if it comes to war, me and that Northerner would've ended up on opposite sides. I just saved myself the trouble of doing it later."

Again Wilkins nodded as he ducked to follow Nelson from the tent. He couldn't argue with that either. He felt a little easier about traveling with Nelson. Nelson knew he didn't have a penny to his name, and they were both staunch Texans. Yeah, he reckoned those two facts would make him safe enough. At least, he hoped they would.

Uneasily, Wilkins realized that Nelson was veering toward the captain's tent rather than toward the remuda of horses. "What are you doing?" he asked in a loud, urgent whisper.

Nelson smiled coolly. "I've got pay coming to me. You do, too."

Wilkins licked his lips nervously. His palms itched as surely as if he'd just killed Shaw himself. "Tell you what. I'll get the horses ready. If Plummer will give you my pay, I'll split it with you." He jerked at the gleam in Nelson's eye. "Hell, you can have it all."

The other man thrust his saddle at Wilkins. "Sure. You get the horses ready. I'll be right there."

A chill rippled through Wilkins at Nelson's grin. The man loved danger, Wilkins had always known that. He was a fool for sure.

The whole time Wilkins was pulling their horses from the string and cinching their saddles, he was whispering the same word over and over to himself. "Fool, fool, fool." And he didn't know for sure if he was talking about himself or Nelson.

Nelson didn't say much when he rejoined Wilkins, and Wilkins didn't ask any questions. He was curious though. Had Plummer given him their pay? Was Plummer dead? Somehow, he couldn't picture Nelson getting a jump on the captain. But the possibility existed.

He handed Nelson's reins to him. They mounted and eased their horses to a lazy pace.

Around them the camp stirred to life. Wilkins began to sweat. At any moment, someone might step into the tent where Todd Shaw lay in his own slowly congealing blood.

Instinctively, he urged his horse to a faster walk and saw Nelson grin sideways at him, as if he knew why. Wilkins didn't care. No sane person would think it cowardly not to want his neck stretched by a hangman's noose. He cut Nelson a sidelong glance and shivered. No sane person would have taken the time to go to Plummer's tent for a few meager coins when he might be discovered a murderer at any instant. Especially not when he already carried Shaw's pouch of gold nuggets in his pocket.

In the path ahead, the Red River curled around a bend of trees. A layer of faint mist clung to the flat surface of the water, silent testimony of the cool morning air. The air was washed as clear as the gradually lightening sky after the night-long rains.

Wilkins relaxed a bit as their horses took the first splashing steps into the water. Maybe they'd get clear of this place, after all. The ground leveled away from beneath the horses' hooves, and the animals began to swim with slow, powerful strokes. If the river was any deeper from the torrential rains, Wilkins couldn't tell it.

He gave an audible sigh of relief as his mount's hooves struck solid ground. The sun was almost fully above the horizon, and there was still no outcry from behind.

With his mind on the dead body waiting to be discovered, he almost didn't see her standing there, her back relaxed against the trunk of a gum tree. She was dressed in a soft deerskin sheath, unadorned by the beads most of the women loved to sew onto their clothing. Her innocence and youth lay over her as subtly as the mist lay over the river, but the pride of the Comanche people was boldly evident in the haughty tip of her chin.

To his surprise, and deep relief, Wilkins felt the stirring of lust in his loins. Lust and a deep-burning need to quash that pride as his had been quashed.

Without a word to Nelson, he jerked his reins so that his horse wheeled in her direction. He saw her straighten from the tree and maybe that was a flicker of something like fear in her dark eyes. Wilkins hoped it was fear. The thought was a balm to his manhood.

He rubbed the vee of his pants in satisfaction as he rode toward her. He'd just been tired lately was all. Fed up with the Army. Yeah, that was it. Hell, the thought of a curse seemed ludicrous now. He'd prove it with this girl. And when he'd done with her that way, why hell, he might just flip her over on her belly and pretend she was a boy for a while. See how she liked the pretense when it wasn't her idea.

Less than three feet lay between them when the first shout went up. At almost the same instant that Wilkins's mind registered the noise, he heard Nelson's muttered curse, then the thundering of hooves as Nelson put spurs to his horse's flanks.

For a moment, Wilkins froze. The son of a bitch hadn't so much as shouted a warning. He'd leave Wilkins without a backward glance. Bastard.

Wilkins glared at Nelson's swiftly disappearing back, then at the girl. Almost without thinking about it, he gouged his horse in the side, causing him to leap forward as Wilkins leaned down and grabbed for her.

The girl kicked and clawed as Wilkins

dragged her across his saddle, but she was no match for his compact muscles. He felt her hip bone rubbing against the growing thickness in his jeans and wondered if he was going to come right there in the saddle with the United States Army riding hell for leather after him.

Chapter Nine

Hannah woke to a morning alive with some of the most colorful cursing she had ever heard in her life, which was saying something. Even around Hannah, her brothers had never been bashful about the lurid strength of their invectives. Despite her lack of years, Hannah had been smart enough to suspect that her brothers' profane streaks surfaced because of, rather than in spite of, the fact that their father was a minister.

But Jeb Welles could put even her brothers' worst oaths to shame. And did.

Blinking, Hannah sat up and did her best to rub some of the stiffness from her back. She couldn't help but be uncomfortably aware that her hair now tumbled haphazardly from its knot at the back of her head. A sigh escaped her. She should have braided it before she lay down to sleep, no matter how tired she'd been. Not that it mattered a fig to her how she looked to Jeb Welles. It was her natural fastidiousness, not vanity, that made her wish she could rise looking as neat as if she'd just lain down. She hoped.

Looking around their campsite, she tried to determine the cause of his wrath. It certainly couldn't be the weather. Despite the rumblings of thunder that had come from the north during the greater part of the night, the morning sky was clear and the air pleasingly cool. Cooler, Hannah knew, than it would be an hour from now when the sun began to burn in earnest.

As she watched, Jeb stalked to the thicket of trees and glared at a tangle of offending brush. At least he was looking at it as if it offended him. To Hannah, it appeared an unassuming clump of weeds. She considered asking him the cause of his anger, then decided she was safest not drawing attention to herself. That was the tactic she'd used with Caleb. Of course, Caleb's anger had most often been with her, and there was little use for tactics on those occasions.

She pulled the last of her tangled locks free of the tousled coil and began to comb through them with her fingers. Her comb was in her pack, but she wasn't going to go about finding it until Jeb calmed down. Almost dispassionately, she noted the play of sunlight through the silky strands of her hair, turning them varying shades of red and gold and copper. For the hundredth time, she wished her hair was a nice golden brown, maybe even blond. Blond hair was so delicate-looking.

Favor is deceitful, and beauty is vain. Caleb's voice mocked her with the scripture, and for a moment Hannah closed her eyes. The truth of the words stung as surely as any her husband had ever spoken in the years of their marriage.

When she looked up, Jeb Welles was standing directly in front of her, staring down at her hands working their way through the knots. She blushed and wondered if he guessed at her vanity. Or, at least, her wish for something to be vain about. Somehow Caleb always had. But when her eyes lifted further, meeting Jeb's, the blush was for a different reason. She'd never had a man look at her quite that way. She wasn't sure what it meant, or if she liked it—or even if she was supposed to like it.

Jeb tore his gaze from the sparkle of sunlight on autumn red. *Damn!* For a minute, he'd forgotten his wrath and the reason for it. "Your horse is gone."

Still mesmerized by that look and trying to discern what it meant, Hannah looked at him without really hearing his words. "What?"

Jeb snorted. There she went again! "I said, your sonuvabitchin' horse is gone!"

Instinctively, Hannah recoiled from his anger. Did he think she was to blame? "He was hobbled," she offered. She knew, because she'd watched Jeb tie hobbles on all three of the horses.

"I know that," Jeb snapped, angered even more by the way she shrank from him. He'd never mistreated a woman in his life, yet this one acted as if he would lift a hand to her at any minute. *Maybe her husband had.* The possibility bothered him. A lot.

Hannah watched him warily. *Well, you knew better than to speak up. Even if it did seem like he was waiting for a comment.*

Trouble, Jeb thought—that woman is nothing but trouble. He didn't understand her, didn't much like her. And if it weren't already enough that he was stuck with her, now this! It had to be because the gelding was *her* horse, damn it! The other two were still grazing peacefully, just where he'd left them. *His* horses hadn't caused any problem. "Don't look at me like that!"

Hannah jumped and blinked. "Like what?" she asked cautiously.

"Like you are, damn it!"

As confused as ever, Hannah averted her eyes from his, but the memory of his angry green gaze stayed with her. Odd, Caleb's eyes used to darken when he was infuriated with her. Jeb's lightened and brightened.

At her withdrawal, Jeb felt instant shame. What had happened wasn't her fault. Not the missing horse—or his sudden, unwelcome arousal at the sight of slender fingers embedded in tangled red-gold coils of hair.

"Hannah," he spoke her name softly.

She lifted her eyes back to him and waited.

"I apologize."

Her eyes widened. Try as she could, she couldn't recall one instance in which a man had ever apologized to her for an unfairness. Not her father, because he never *was* unfair. Not her brothers, because they were too stubborn to ever admit they were wrong about anything. And not Caleb, because . . . well, because he was Caleb. "Thank you," she said softly.

Thank you? Suddenly, Jeb chuckled at himself. He'd actually expected her to tell him he had nothing to apologize for. Maybe he'd been around whores for too long. Their way of thinking was that the man was always right. But then, they were paid to think that way. Hannah most definitely didn't think like a whore. Swiftly on the heels of that thought was an image of her posed like one, languorously supine. Waiting.

Damn, again. Jeb quashed the image. The last decent woman he'd tried to treat like a whore was Katherine Bellamy Slade—and he thought he'd learned a lesson from that. Jeb reckoned he was a slow learner.

Hannah was still watching him, and Jeb smiled wryly, glad he'd long since learned to keep most of what he was thinking from his face—at least, long enough to know whether he wanted it to show or not!

Disconcerted by his silence after her acceptance of his apology, Hannah dared to speak again. "He's a good horse, but he isn't used to being hobbled. Maybe he broke the tie."

For an instant, Jeb felt insulted. Did she think he was careless enough to use a weak strip of rawhide to secure something as vital to their safety as the horses? The feeling passed as he remembered her lack of trail experience.

He held the piece of leather toward her so that she could see the smooth edges. "It was cut."

Hannah felt a sudden leap of fear. "Someone was that near while we slept?"

Jeb wasn't too comfortable with that fact himself. Of course, the horses had grazed some distance away while the two of them were sleeping. "They were near enough," he admitted. "What's really got me puzzled is why him, and why *just* him. Someone wanting to put us afoot would have cut all three hobbles. If they needed an animal for themselves, he's the most useless of the three of them. Anyone with half an eye can see he hasn't got near the muscles or conditioning for the trail. He can't take nearly what that bay mare can."

Hannah nodded, enlightened. She understood now why Jeb had been taking it so easy on the trail. She'd realized they were traveling with extreme slowness, but she wasn't as strong yet as she'd been before her pregnancy and miscarriage, so she had remained silently glad for the fact.

"Well," she offered, "he *is* the prettiest." And

he was, too, with his flashy white stockings and blazed face.

Jeb grinned. "There ain't much demand for pretty on the trail, Hannah Barnes."

Hannah stared, thunderstruck, not by the use of her given name, but by the way it made her feel to hear it on his tongue. And by the way his face changed when he grinned. She didn't even mind that he was laughing at her. Much.

"Then why him and not one of the others?" she asked pointedly.

Jeb quit grinning. "I don't know, but I aim to find out. Get yourself ready to move out. We're going tracking."

Tracking. The idea intrigued Hannah. She'd heard of men who could "read" a trail the way a hungry dog could pick up the scent of quail. With hasty movements, she walked to the stream and bathed.

The water was crystal clear and ice cold. Jeb had told her there were dozens of these tiny tributaries, mostly feeding off or into the Brazos River. He sure did talk a lot, but she didn't much mind when he wasn't asking questions. It made her feel uncomfortable to have attention turned on her as he waited for her answers. On the other hand, it was almost pleasant to have him talking to her as they rode. Maybe the things he'd said would be inconsequential to anyone else, but to her they were meat and drink. There was so much she didn't know about so many different things.

And, she realized, she desperately wanted to know, to learn.

Jeb was waiting when she got back from washing up. He had his horse saddled and the packhorse loaded. Her saddle was slung over one shoulder. She reached out her arms to take it, and his eyes widened, then narrowed. He shook his head in disgust, and she felt like a little child who'd had her hand slapped.

Silently, Jeb handed her the reins of his horse. Just as silently, she took them.

Very aware of the woman behind him, Jeb led the way. What kind of a husband had that preacher been? Did Hannah, half his strength and barely recovered from a miscarriage, really expect to have to carry a saddle that weighed almost as much as she did? Jeb wondered about other things, as well. Things that had made Hannah the woman she was.

For one thing, he'd never seen a woman so totally lacking in conversation, yet she did not strike him as a dour, silent sort of person. In fact, there were times when he looked at her and saw the questions fairly bubbling out of her eyes—all unspoken.

And she seemed totally unaware of him as a man. That was disconcerting. Not that Jeb thought that every woman should fall at his feet. But even the most innocent of women normally had some subtle, almost undetectable reaction to a male presence, some awareness of sensuality. Hannah had none or, at most, only an aura of being intimidated. Jeb had no desire to intimidate her, but she'd learned that behavior somewhere. Reason pointed to her marriage, given the fact she'd been married to the man when she was little more than a child.

The thought he'd had earlier nagged at him. "Did he beat you?"

Hannah almost ran into Jeb's back. When he turned to look at her, nothing broke the silence of the morning but the warbling of songbirds and the wind sighing through the few trees that had struggled their way to life along the stream bed. Hannah had thought Jeb totally engrossed in picking up the trail of their horse thief—and she had been totally engrossed in watching him. More than ever, he reminded her of a predator, silent and strong and threatening.

Jeb was still watching her. She noticed the stubble of his unshaven face and wondered inanely how he would look with a beard. "No," she said slowly. "Caleb didn't beat me."

Wondering at himself for even having asked, Jeb nodded once, then turned back to his task. Hannah Barnes had the strangest effect on him, but at least—he grinned faintly—at least she hadn't responded to his question with *"Who?"*

"He prayed over me." Hannah surprised herself. She didn't usually volunteer any information and couldn't think why she did now.

"What?" Jeb stopped dead still and turned around to look at her again. Then his lips twitched. Now she had *him* doing it!

"Whenever I sinned, Caleb prayed over me."

"Lady," Jeb said with dead certainty, "you have never sinned in your life."

To her chagrin, Hannah blushed. She would like for him to continue thinking her without sin, but she was far too honest for that. "Well, Caleb sure found a lot to pray about."

Sensing that he was about to lose her first efforts at conversation, Jeb turned his gaze back to the ground and starting walking again. "For instance?" he asked casually.

"My frivolous nature," Hannah offered reluctantly, wishing she'd never started this.

Jeb snorted. The woman never laughed, tried her best not to smile, wore her hair as severely as it would allow her, and covered herself in the drabbest cloth he'd ever seen on a female. Frivolous? "What else?"

"Shouldn't we be quiet so the thieves won't hear us coming up on them?" She didn't *want* to confess her sins to this man.

"Thief," Jeb corrected. "There's only one, and it's either a woman or a kid."

Hannah wanted badly to ask how he knew. She'd already been more daring than she ever would have thought. Strange how good it felt simply to talk to another human being. But that was the way of sin. It felt good and seemed so easy. Like idle chatter. Caleb had told her over and over that all speech ought to edify, not entertain the speaker or the listener. That was a lesson she had learned early on and learned well, but a body listening to her this morning would never know it.

Instead of watching the sign on the soft ground ahead of him, Jeb found himself glancing back too frequently at Hannah's face, trying to read it the way he read the light footprints intermingled with the hoofprints of the stolen animal. One moment she was almost a normal person; the next a shutter dropped between her and the world. This wasn't the first time Jeb had seen it happen, and each time it did it confounded him. He'd seen people shield themselves from pain, both physical and emotional. He'd seen people close themselves away from what they considered a dangerous or evil world.

Hannah's shield was different from either of those, and Jeb wasn't completely sure it was deliberate. In fact, he wondered if Hannah was even conscious of having erected a wall between herself and everything around her. Her eyes still glowed with lively curiosity, and there was an air of expectancy about her, but her lips remained pressed together and she retreated physically from Jeb, if only by a few inches.

Whatever the reason, Jeb liked the times she forgot herself and laughed and questioned. Maybe he liked them all the more for their rarity.

Behind him, Hannah wanted to duck her head each time Jeb looked back at her. His piercing gaze pried at her, but yielded nothing in return. She hoped he'd forgotten his question about her sins, because she didn't mean to answer it.

Between his sharp looks and the insistent nudging of his bay mare, Hannah began to feel almost exasperated. She tried pushing back at the dark nose, but that only seemed to delight the confounded animal, as if they were playing a game.

Unexpectedly, Jeb stopped in the same instant the mare gave a particularly hard shove.

Hannah found herself shoved firmly against Jeb's back, her cheek pressed to the roughspun linen of his shirt, the masculine but not unpleasant scent of him filling her nostrils.

Jeb barely felt her heart beating against him for the sudden thumping of his own. Instinctively, he turned. Her wildflower-blue eyes were inches away from his. So were her lips.

An instant later, Hannah responded to her need to increase the distance between them and inched carefully backward. "What is it?" she whispered. When Jeb continued to stare, she tried again. "Why did you stop like that?"

Shaking his head as if to throw off the effects of strong whiskey or deep sleep, Jeb stepped aside so that Hannah could see what lay in the next shallow dip of the land.

"Indians," she breathed. But not like any Indians she had ever seen or imagined.

Caleb had never let her go to the reservation with him, so her clearest picture of red men came from one incident. On their way to the Brazos reserves, she and Caleb had stopped at a fort for supplies. As they were leaving, a band of Indians had entered. The braves were laughing and shouting to one another, their brown torsos gleaming in the morning sun, though a frost lay on the ground. Caleb had assured her that the paint streaking their faces was not the garish patterns they applied when making war.

More than the warriors, the women had fascinated Hannah. They held their heads as high as the men, and their black, braided hair caught every ray of sunlight, throwing it back in blue-black glints to those who watched. Several of them wore cradleboards strapped to their backs, the infants within solemn and watchful. Hannah thought them beautiful, and her arms had ached for a child of her own.

The Indians Hannah saw just beyond Jeb's broad shoulders looked nothing like those from her memory. There were no laughing warriors. Only one man, his face withered by his years, sat cross-legged in front of a tepee. Two women tended a fire nearby, while a youth of perhaps ten or twelve sat with his back propped against a tree trunk. In the age-old tradition of young boys, he whittled at a small stick with a sharp knife.

Over them all lay an air of hunger and desolation. Their cheeks were gaunt, though the lands around them surely abounded with small game in these summer months. They wore the cast-off clothing of whites, most of it appearing almost rags to Hannah. Sleeves and hems were frayed; rips were unpatched.

Hannah turned her eyes to Jeb, and he read her silent question and nodded. "I'd say the boy is the culprit. The size of the prints and the weight would be about right."

"For the old man to ride?" That seemed most logical to Hannah.

Jeb sighed. The world must seem a harsh place to a sheltered female. "No. His pride wouldn't allow that." If anyone rode, it would be the almost-old-enough-to-be-a-warrior. Jeb thought it likely that the old man would soon throw himself away. When he determined he was no longer a help but a burden to his family, he would step aside from the trail they followed, sing his death song, and wait for his spirit to leave his body. But Jeb didn't tell Hannah that. She wouldn't understand. Jeb almost didn't.

No, the old man wouldn't ride Hannah's horse—but then, Jeb suspected that Hannah's horse had not been stolen to carry any burdens. In fact, he thought he understood why the youth had taken the gelding instead of the mare or the packhorse. Jeb's animals were trail hard, with wiry, muscled strength and no excess flesh. Caleb had fed his gelding well and the weight of him had been apparent in the creases that lined his back and hips.

What confused Jeb was that any Comanche male would choose to steal the horse rather than wild game to feed his family. When Jeb stepped forward, drawing Hannah with him, the youth rose warily to his feet and Jeb's understanding increased. One arm was withered and shorter than the other by perhaps two inches. Age had robbed the old man of the strength to draw a bow; something else had robbed the boy of that strength.

Though Jeb saw the shuttered look of fear in the young boy's eyes, he could not reassure him without causing him shame by revealing his awareness of that fear. So all he did was lift his hand in a universal gesture of greeting that betokened peace.

Straightening his shoulders, the boy returned the gesture. Jeb glanced at the old man who remained seated, content to let the younger male dominate. From the pride in the ancient gaze, Jeb suspected that the boy was a grandson, beloved in spite of his physical weakness. Likely the affliction had been caused by injury. If the boy had been crippled at birth, he would have not been allowed to live.

"I don't see the horse," Hannah said softly from just behind Jeb's shoulders. She had accepted his words that the horse wouldn't be for the old man to ride, adding the assumption that it was for the women. Perhaps Caleb had been wrong, and the Comanche treated their women with greater respect.

"I expect he's well hidden." That was only partly a lie.

Hannah waited to see what Jeb would do

next. Somehow she wasn't surprised when he lowered her saddle to the ground, then took the mare's reins from her hand and dropped them, leaving the horses ground-tied while he strolled up to the fire and hunkered down on one knee.

When he glanced back at Hannah and lifted one brow questioningly, she followed, wondering if the warriors of this small group would come shrieking from the brush at any moment.

Chapter Ten

Wilkins looked back over his shoulder one more time and felt the sweat trickle down his back. Sweat from the heat of the midday sun mingled with sweat from fear. There was nothing behind him but the empty ridge he'd just crossed, nothing ahead but another ridge dotted by more skimpy-looking trees.

He fixed his eyes on the back of the girl's head. She was arched up and away from him as far as she could get, but her slender buttocks were cradled against his lap. He thought about reaching one hand around and playing with the nipples of her budding little breasts, but even as quiet as she was at the moment, he didn't think she was subdued enough not to fight him. Right now, he needed to concentrate on survival. He could play later.

He wondered if she could smell his fear. He could smell hers. He'd had to put his fist to her jaw earlier to keep her still. When she had regained consciousness, the whole side of her face looked purple. The sight of it made him feel kind of bad, and he suspected it hurt like hell. Still, it was her own fault. If she just hadn't fought him. . . . And it was her fault they were riding alone in dangerous territory. First her struggling, then her dead weight had slowed them down.

Nelson had long since outdistanced him—just rode off and left him, the son of a bitch. Once or twice, the soldiers had almost caught up to him, but each time he had outsmarted and outmaneuvered them. They were too rigid about keeping to safe ground, too cocky that they would eventually catch up to him no matter how many twists he took in his path.

They were wrong, damn their hides! He'd lost them, outridden the sonsabitches, even with the weight of the girl slowing him down. But a tiny part of him kept glancing back, wondering each time if the next backward glance would reveal them catching up again, riding over the ridge behind him. Each time he looked, his spine would tingle in anticipation of the sudden, burning pain of a bullet fired from a military-issue rifle.

Overhead, the sun had almost reached its zenith and would soon begin its long afternoon descent over miles and miles of prairie grass. Wilkins shuddered at the thought of what lay ahead. Come morning he would be riding alone onto the Staked Plains—Indian territory—with a damned Comanche for a captive!

He gave some thought to the idea of veering off and heading south toward the Mexican border, but there were a lot of forts and soldiers between this border and that one. On top of that, he wasn't convinced he preferred facing Mexicans to Indians. Neither one was any too fond of Texans these days.

Shit! He'd meant to be in the company of a faster gun than his about now. He wasn't sure which was worse, what lay ahead of him or what lay behind him. All he knew was that he had to keep riding and that the little gal sitting in front of him had better make the risk worth his while. At least he didn't have to worry about the curse anymore. He'd lost his hard-on during the chase, but he'd had it, and when he could get his pants down and the girl's legs spread, he'd get it again.

Night came slowly with a gentle settling of the bright ball of fire, a gathering darkness, a soft sighing of the wind. With a sense of satisfaction, Wilkins looked about him at the campsite he'd chosen. Water, firewood, a few scattered boulders. Not bad. Then he looked at the girl and frowned as she glared defiantly back at him. His frown deepened to a scowl. Her scornful looks reminded him of Welles. Maybe she was brave because she thought Welles would be coming to her rescue again.

Then again, he thought suspiciously, maybe she looked less fearful for another reason.

He stooped down and tested the ropes binding her. Damn! The little hellion had worked the stiff coils until they were so loose she would have been able to escape in another few minutes.

Cuffing the side of her head roughly, he jerked the ropes tighter until they were secure enough that he could be sure she wasn't going anywhere. "You little bitch! What were you going to do—wait until I fell asleep and then slip off?"

His eyes narrowed. Or maybe she was going to wait until he had his back turned and plant his own knife in it? And he would never have known if he hadn't checked that rope around her! "Hell, I ought to just leave you tied up here and ride off. It'd serve you right, you little witch. You ought to be grateful I ain't killed you yet."

There was no flicker of understanding in her eyes; no glimmer of fear remained. Only hatred. He liked it better when she was afraid.

"Hell, I'm going to kill me something to eat. I'll tend to you later." He started to stalk away, then turned to glare at her. "You better be here when I get back, damn it! I ain't risked my hide for nothing hauling you out here!"

Moving away from the tiny, flickering light of the fire gave him a feeling of insecurity. He patted the rifle in his arms. Of course, he couldn't use it and risk drawing the soldiers straight to him; still, it provided some comfort. As he settled into a small cluster of boulders, he withdrew a slingshot from his pocket. Along with the primitive weapon, he always carried a supply of stones just right for bringing down small game.

He liked using a slingshot, liked hearing the soft thud against flesh and the cracking of small skulls that followed if he got a real good hit. And he usually did.

Very little time had passed before a scarcely noticeable movement nearby caught his attention. He grinned as he lifted the slingshot. Just as the rabbit bounded away, he loosed the rock.

As he walked back to camp, things looked a little brighter. He'd soon have a hot meal in his belly. He felt smug when he saw the girl just as he'd left her. Even better than that, her eyes were closed and she had an air of defeat to her.

She opened them briefly as he gutted and cleaned the rabbit, and all the time he kept one eye on her, checking for shifty movements that would tell him she was still trying to escape.

When the rabbit was on the fire, he wiped his hands on his pants and crossed the distance between them. He reached down to tug at the rough strands holding her captive, smirking as she flinched. She licked her dry lips, and he thought about tormenting her with the canteen of water. She'd spat the last water he'd given her right in his face! He tugged at her bonds again. "Still tight. Reckon you ain't as smart as you thought."

Behind him the fire crackled and hissed as the juice from the rabbit dripped onto the hot embers and tiny flames. Wilkins smiled at the girl and turned away. She could wait until he'd filled his belly. Yeah, sometimes things were all the better for the waiting. Right now, his stomach was rumbling.

The first taste of succulent meat was melting in his mouth when a cool voice spoke from the dark that waited just beyond the circle of firelight.

"Weren't you planning to share, Leon?"

That lack of passion carried more menace than anger to Wilkins's ears. He nearly dropped the small haunch of roasted meat he jerked from his teeth. "Shit, Ike. You scared the hell out of me."

Ike Nelson stepped into the flickering light cast by the fire. "Weren't you expecting me? I thought we were traveling together, my friend."

Wilkins glared at him sullenly. "You high-tailed it away from me. Why the hell should I be expecting you?"

"Why, Leon"— Nelson affected a wounded expression which did nothing to lessen the cold grey of his eyes— "I was riding shotgun for you the whole time."

"Shit," Wilkins returned morosely. Then as Nelson continued to smile that same skin-deep smile, he relented. "May as well sit down and have some rabbit." He glanced behind Nelson. "Where's your horse?"

"Hobbled next to yours. If it had been anyone but me, my friend, you would have been dead by now." Nelson flicked a glance at the girl. "You should never lose sight of the fact that the ultimate goal is survival."

Wilkins bristled. "I ain't touched the girl. Been too busy trying to keep from starving first." He glared at the rabbit dripping grease down Nelson's hands. The other man had taken more than half.

With the neat movements of a cat, Nelson finished stripping the meat from the bone. "You always were the better hunter, Leon. Much better than me."

Appeased, Wilkins settled more comfortably against the tree trunk behind him. His belly was far from full, but at least the pangs of hunger had been eased. He glanced at the girl, who had refused the strip of jerky he'd given her to chew on. Like her bound hands, it lay uselessly in her lap. "Best not waste that, girlie."

She looked back at him with dark, scornful eyes, and he turned away with a shrug. If she didn't want it, he'd eat it later. She could choose to go hungry if she wanted to.

Across the fire, Nelson was watching him with eyes that held as much scorn as the Comanche girl's. "Riding west was useful while the Army was in pursuit. But our path lies south and east."

A small shudder went through Wilkins at his

tone. This was going to be tricky. Now that the curse was no longer on him, he preferred never to see that red-haired witch again. "S-south?" he asked cautiously. "I don't think—"

"Good!" Nelson's voice cracked across his. "That's what I prefer—that you not think. I'll take care of that, and all you have to do is what I say. The preacher's woman is mine. After her . . . Welles."

A mental image of Nelson pulling his knife out of Todd Shaw's body closed Wilkins's mouth on the protest that was already forming. "Sure, Ike. Sure. Whatever you say." He hesitated. "The preacher's woman will be easy, but I don't know that we've got a snowball's chance in hellfire of catching up to Welles."

Nelson's lips stretched over his teeth in something only his mother could have called a smile. "It doesn't matter. If we can't catch up to him, I can guess where he's headed. We can be there ahead of him."

"Yeah?" Wilkins felt a prick of interest.

"New Mexico. With Slade."

"Holy shit!" Wilkins breathed. Then he just stared at Nelson like he was crazy. In his opinion, anybody who willingly took on Welles and Slade together had to be just that. Crazy.

Wilkins gave a sob of frustration, the sound immediately mocked by the sharp call of a nightbird. He brought the back of his broad hand across the girl's cheek again, but this time she barely stirred beneath the blow. "Move, bitch! Act like a woman!"

It was her fault that he couldn't mount her. Her fault. If she would wriggle and squirm, even if only to escape him, he was sure he would feel some stirring of need. But she was like an empty form made of clay, without life and feeling. There, but not there.

He hit her again. "Come on, Ike," he pled again. "You have her first."

That would surely stir his blood, watching another man grunt and thrust between those skinny little legs.

Nelson looked up from the tobacco he was rolling. "Your sex is limp because that's where your brain is. And it's empty."

"Please, Ike." He wouldn't believe in the curse. He wouldn't. The sweat beaded coldly on his upper lip. "Please."

Slowly Nelson got to his feet. He stepped over the dying fire and closed the distance between them. Wilkins rolled away from the girl hopefully, and Nelson stood looking down at her. His lip curled at her battered condition.

He looked at Wilkins. "She's a kid. I want a real woman, like the redhead."

Dispassionately, he pulled his gun with smooth motions. Before Wilkins even knew what he was going to do, he fired.

Wilkins stared at the neat hole in the girl's forehead and puked his guts into the dirt beside her.

Chapter Eleven

Despite her initial nervousness, Hannah decided she wasn't truly afraid of these "heathen redskin." She almost wondered if Caleb's description of them wasn't inaccurate, in spirit if not in fact. Of course, more than likely they had not accepted Christ as their savior and therefore were, indeed, heathen. And any eye could plainly see that their skin was as red as leaves in autumn.

Yet, as the day wore on, Hannah saw not one example of the cruelty and savagery she'd always heard attributed to the Comanche nation. They were kind, even gentle, toward one another and toward her.

The younger of the women, whose name Jeb had told her but she couldn't pronounce, smiled as she handed Hannah a second tattered shirt. The girl had lovely, dark eyes that seemed always filled with laughter. Even, white teeth flashed with her ready smile. Hannah smiled in return and wondered how she had ever come to be sitting in the wilderness mending clothing for a handful of the people Caleb had wanted so fiercely to bring to know the Lord.

She still couldn't believe that Jeb had left her here in order to spend the day hunting. Not that she would have wanted to go with him, nor even that she did not admire his Good Samaritan desire to feed these obviously hungry people. Judging by the protrusion of bones against dark skin, she knew that the tender meat they had managed to serve her at midday was a rarity. Likely it was something that had been easily caught by a boy unable to wield a bow. Or perhaps the old man had roused his failing strength for a lucky shot.

No, Hannah could not disagree with Jeb's urge to provide fresh game for these people, but she had been utterly confounded when he'd told her simply to wait for him there. She had looked around at four solemn faces that, until that morning, she'd never seen in her life, swallowed hard, and nodded. There had been a sense of relief within her when Jeb had unburdened the packhorse for the boy to ride. Somehow, it seemed a little less threatening to her to be alone with an old man and two women.

She quickly learned that her timidity had been for nothing, her silent fears groundless.

As soon as she showed herself willing to help, a needle and thread were thrust at her, along with a shirt that had more holes than substance. Hannah had done the best she could with a needle far too large for the task and stout, coarse thread of a kind she had never seen before.

As she sewed, she wondered by what miracle Caleb had thought to bring the word of God to a people whose language he did not share. How did you convey God's love and ultimate sacrifice in gestures? It was difficult enough to express things of substance, but material objects could be touched and actions could be mimed. Beliefs and ideals were elusive, beyond the realm of what could be touched and seen.

Unfortunately for Hannah, those thoughts did not occupy her mind quite fully enough. It wandered time and again to the events of the past two days and seemed inclined to linger on the embarrassing moment when she had found herself pressed against Jeb's back. Embarrassing, and something more. Hannah tried not to look too closely at the something more, but every inch of her that had touched him, from cheek to breast to thigh, remained in a state of tingling awareness.

She was both glad and sorry when he and the boy returned with the carcass of a deer slung over one horse and a wild turkey on the other. Neither horse looked pleased with its burden. In fact, Jeb's mare looked decidedly ill-tempered with her ears pinned flatly against her head. For all that, Hannah wasn't surprised that the bay carried her burden without flinching, however unwilling she might be. Hannah couldn't imagine even the beasts of the field refusing to do Jeb's bidding. Look at her. She had left the only home she knew, the last resting place of child and husband, because Jeb Welles had said so. Hannah was still amazed at that fact. Even so, she harbored no regrets for her choice and suspected she would continue to follow Jeb until he chose otherwise, if for nothing save the fact that he represented the only solid thing in her world at present.

Jeb's eyes went straight to Hannah as he led his horse near the tepee, his brows seemingly lifted in question, and she smiled to show that all was well with her.

Jeb didn't like what Hannah's smile did to his guts. He didn't like that he had thought of little beyond her well-being all day, worrying about leaving her alone, concerned that she would be frightened or come to harm. Jeb wasn't used to worrying about anyone or anything. He would be glad to leave her safely in someone else's care, let someone else have the worrying.

He watched as she rose to her feet, graceful as always. He looked at the shirt she held clenched in both hands. Mending. "I see you didn't get scalped," he said with a slight quirk at the corner of his mouth. He had not missed the trepidation in her eyes that morning when she'd realized she would be left alone for hours with these people.

Hannah found she didn't much appreciate having her fears mocked, even if they had been foolish ones. "Not yet," she replied tartly. "They were waiting for you to get back to help them."

The quirk broadened to a surprised grin. "Well, at least you're learning to talk, although I have a feeling I'm not going to like a whole lot of what you say."

Disconcerted by her reaction to that grin, Hannah averted her eyes and found herself staring into the boy's steady gaze. He did not look threatening, but he did not appear as friendly as the women. Instinctively, she kept her glance from his withered arm, suspecting that he would resent any expression of sympathy. Men were surely alike, no matter what their color. She felt a pang as she realized that she could count his ribs.

"I'm glad you had good luck," she told Jeb.

Jeb, caught up in staring at the way the sun lit her hair, met her look blankly. He found himself thinking that her voice sounded a little like the cool downfall of a spring shower. "Good luck?"

"With the hunting," Hannah said remindingly, then wondered at the way he muttered some answer she could not hear and turned away from her. Jeb Welles was indeed an aggravating creature.

If asked, Hannah would have said she would be far more comfortable passing the night in the presence of a number of people than she had been the previous night with only Jeb for company. She would have been wrong.

Within the first hour after curling up on her blanket, she realized that she was going to spend a sleepless night. Her mind was jumbled with more thoughts than she could sort through, and the chief among them was guilt. Once again she had given her deceased husband scarcely a thought throughout the day. Caleb had offered everything he possessed to the Lord—every talent, every thought, every ounce of energy—and all he'd earned in return was a feckless wife. And, of course, his immortal home.

Worse than that, Hannah realized, she had not only made no effort toward securing the souls of these Indians for the Lord; she'd given no more thought to fortifying her own with scripture reading. She'd do better tomorrow, she promised herself, then dragged her mind back one more time from its errant but persistent path toward Jeb Welles. She was altogether too conscious of him propped against a boulder where he kept watch on the night. She wondered what he watched against and when he would sleep.

Hannah closed her eyes determinedly and almost groaned when she realized that the man's infernal image was etched into the inside of her lids.

Jeb had not missed the way Hannah knelt diligently by her bedroll before she lay down to sleep. She'd done that the night before, and he'd wondered then what she prayed about. Her husband's soul? Her safety? Somehow, Jeb doubted the last. Hannah seemed to be her own last consideration in the overall scheme of things.

He recalled the multitude of expressions on her face over the evening, ranging from curiosity to ready sympathy. She did not have a typical white woman's reaction to Indians. There had been no revulsion as she watched them eat from a communal pot with their fingers and no manners—at least none that were familiar to her. And, other than a quickly suppressed apprehension that Jeb was sure only he had discerned, she had shown no fear when he left her.

He tried to picture what her expression would have been if she had realized what kind of meat she had shared with her new friends—and couldn't. But he didn't think he would want to be the one to tell her.

From a short distance, a nightbird called, followed by the haunting sound of a coyote. Muscles along Jeb's ribs tensed reflexively, and he made an unnecessary mental check of his gun. He forced himself to relax. After all, if a Comanche raiding party should stumble upon this little group, he and Hannah were likely in the very safest place they could be—among remnants of the people whom they had befriended.

If he were alone, he would simply fade into the darkness, but he suspected that wasn't a skill Hannah had mastered. Of course, he didn't know why he should concern himself overmuch with her safety. Likely she was prickly enough to send any man running—even a Comanche wielding a war lance.

Though it was early, the morning sun was already hot. Hot enough, Hannah saw, to wilt the dew-touched wildflowers that climbed from a tangle of vines. The vines were beautiful but deadly and threatened to choke the young trees that grew along the stream bed.

Hannah completed her morning wash and returned to where Jeb waited. His horse was saddled, and the packhorse was securely burdened. This time her saddle added to those burdens. She guessed that Jeb had jumped to the wrong conclusion in thinking these people had stolen her horse, but she had found jumping to conclusions to be a tendency among men.

Gravely, she bade the Comanche farewell, knowing but not caring that they could not understand her words of best wishes and hopes for their immortal salvation as well as for their physical well-being. She ignored Jeb's incredulous glance.

Despite the knowledge of scripture he'd shown at Caleb's burying, she suspected he was as lost to the Lord as these people were.

At the last minute, she stepped forward to embrace the younger of the women. Not since her marriage had she had anyone she could call friend. To her surprise, the woman held out an intricately beaded pouch to her.

Hannah's eyes filled with tears as she accepted the gift, knowing the hours of labor that had been necessary to craft its beauty. "Thank you," she whispered, dismayed that she had no similar token to give. Even if she had brought every possession she owned from the little cabin she had called home, there would have been nothing of beauty to give in return. Caleb had not allowed her any vanities or adornments.

Touched beyond bearing, Hannah reached out her hand to touch the woman's smooth cheek, and sunlight glinted on her wedding ring. For a moment, she stared, as if she'd never seen it before. Then, slowly, she pulled her hand back and reached to remove the ring with the other.

"Hannah."

She turned to look at Jeb questioningly.

"Are you sure? She won't mind if you have nothing to give her. She expects nothing."

Hannah looked from him to the ring that represented four years of marriage to a man who could never bring himself to love her and whom she could never bring herself to love, try though she had. "I'm sure."

With a smile, she held out the slender circle of gold to her friend. Tentatively, the other woman took it, awed by the smooth shiny metal. She spoke briefly in quiet, solemn tones, and when she was done, she stepped back, the ring clutched in her hand.

"Ready?" Jeb asked.

Not looking at him lest he realize how pitifully glad she was for a friend, Hannah nodded and began walking toward the north.

"What the—Hannah!"

Startled by the sharp sound of her name, Hannah stopped and turned. Not having the faintest idea what had irritated Jeb this time, she merely stood looking up at him.

"What the hell are you doing?"

"Doing?"

"Don't start that," he warned. He held out his hand to help her up behind him. "Come on."

"I can't sit on that horse with you," Hannah protested instinctively. A blush covered her face at the image that came to mind. Her entire upper body would be pressed against his.

"Why the hell not?" Thoroughly exasperated, Jeb pushed his hat further back on his head. He certainly had no intention of walking while she rode, and he damned sure wasn't going to ride while she walked!

Hannah almost smiled. She was coming to know his gestures. Then she realized that she was actually amused by a man's exasperation rather than trembling before it. There was a trust between them that she had never thought to experience. Something like relief went singing through her veins, and before she knew what she was doing, she had lifted her hand up to Jeb.

Not expecting a turnabout without an argument, Jeb stared at her hand for a moment, then extended his, removing his foot from the stirrup at the same time. When Hannah stepped lightly into the stirrup and swung her weight up behind him, he was struck by her lack of substance.

When he glanced behind to make sure she was settled, he saw a gleam of white skin before Hannah jerked her skirt down to cover her leg. That hint of flesh brought home to Jeb the knowledge that her legs were spread wide to straddle the rump of his horse. The fact bothered him. A lot.

"Best relax," he said gruffly. "We've a ways to go."

The young Comanche woman stood beside the tepee and watched them ride away. Her eyes held a hint of sadness.

"You've made a friend for life," Jeb told her.

"I'm glad you were wrong about them."

"Wrong?"

"About the horse. The Book of John says we are not to judge according to appearances." Her words held just the faintest touch of condemnation.

Jeb made a noise that was something like the snort of a horse.

"Her life must be very hard," Hannah worried. "I wish she knew the peace of God—that I could have told her of Him."

Again, Jeb didn't answer.

"What was she saying . . . after I gave her the ring?"

"She was asking her heavenly Father to watch over you." There was a definite smile in Jeb's tone.

"Oh," Hannah said in a quiet voice. She was silent for a long time. "I'm sorry. I guess you weren't the only one to judge by appearances."

"Guess not," Jeb answered evenly. The woman had also asked that Jeb and Hannah be blessed with many children. Jeb didn't tell Hannah that. But he did think of her legs spread over the back of his horse.

By the time Jeb had selected their campsite for the evening, Hannah was more than ready to climb down from her perch. She would have thought riding pillion to be much less tiring than sitting astride her own gelding, but in trying desperately not to brush against Jeb with each move of the horse, she had held every muscle tense for hours.

She wiped the dust and grit from her face and began to gather wood for their cookfire. It seemed almost natural to her now to be with Jeb. There was something comforting about his presence as he settled the horses for the evening. And something unnerving, too.

Jeb suspected that Hannah was nearing exhaustion. Except for her one burst of conversation that morning, she'd been nearly silent the entire day. She certainly never complained.

He watched her, tensing each time she

strayed a little too far in her quest for dry wood. He felt a little like a broody hen with one chick. Hannah was surely as defenseless as a hatchling. How in the world would she manage when they went their separate ways?

With that thought in mind, he withdrew the preacher's rifle from the pack. It was an early Sharps, the kind that had an external hammer to explode the percussion cap. From the well-oiled gleam, Jeb knew that Preacher Barnes had taken as much care of his rifle as he had his horse and buggy. Jeb's mouth thinned. Far better care than he appeared to have taken of his wife. Maybe it wasn't for him to question the judgment of a man called to preach the word of God, but it seemed to Jeb that a woman—especially a wife—was worth more than any possession or beast and ought to be treated accordingly. If he recalled correctly, scripture placed her value far above rubies. He wondered that a preacher could ignore that fact.

"Hannah." He studied her as she walked toward him. Her features, though weary, were as composed as ever, her walk as graceful as always. "Sit down here." A feather could not have settled more lightly. Jeb snatched his mind back to the task of Hannah's protection—or rather to teaching her to protect herself.

Hannah looked at him inquiringly and waited.

Jeb cleared his throat. "Watch me as I load

this." With slow care, he pushed the lever forward, depressing the block and exposing the barrel breech. The lever also served as a trigger guard while the breech was open. Glancing at Hannah to make sure she was paying attention, he looked away just as quickly. She had taken the edge of her lip between her teeth. Jeb could almost feel those teeth pressed as lightly against his flesh. Forcing himself not to take a second look, he inserted the cartridge into the single chamber and pulled the lever back in place.

He thrust the rifle at Hannah. "Here. You do it."

Jeb's rough tone gave Hannah a sinking feeling. She hated being a bother to him, to anyone. Frowning in concentration, determined to get it right the first time, Hannah repeated Jeb's steps.

"Again."

Hannah sighed. She supposed it was a good thing she wasn't used to praise. She repeated the process, and when Jeb didn't speak, she repeated it over several times more.

He might have known she'd get it perfect the first time. Still, loading a rifle needed to be as smooth as silk and a part of habit when the need to act was urgent. After a time or two, though, Jeb stopped watching her hands and started watching the way she set her mouth in determined little lines that did nothing to harden the softness of her lips. And he watched the light of the setting sun against the unruly tendrils of red hair that just would not stay confined. And . . .

"Damn it, Hannah!"

Guiltily, Hannah lowered the rifle from her shoulder. She'd gotten bored with loading the single cartridge and had lifted the weapon to peer along the barrel at a bluejay scolding them from a skinny tree limb. Trust Jeb to finally pay attention when she was doing something wrong!

Jeb sighed and held out his hand for the rifle. "Tomorrow I'll show you how to shoot it." Maybe. If they hadn't caught up with the movement of Comanche and soldiers. If he was still sane. If he hadn't already tried to make love to her.

His gaze was fixed on her skirts somewhere near the point where thigh met hip. He closed his eyes.

Damn. Damn. Damn!

Chapter Twelve

They caught up to the Army sooner than Jeb had expected, considering the delay over Hannah's horse. But then, the trail of several hundred Comanche and a cavalry troop was ridiculously easy to follow, and its progress painstakingly slow.

Scanning the dusty, defeated faces of the Indians, Jeb found himself more anxious than ever to get Hannah safely settled somewhere. He wanted to be on his way to the clean, fresh dangers of the New Mexico Territory. A wild and perilous Texas had fired his blood; a pitiless Texas was sending him running.

Hannah reacted to her first glimpse of the migrating Indians with piercing dismay followed swiftly by an overwhelming sense of empathy. As Jeb rode past the first Comanche brave, who strode on foot along the outer edges of the group, Hannah averted her face. No man, no matter what color, would appreciate pity on the face of a woman, and Hannah knew she had never been very good at hiding her feelings.

Midmorning sunlight etched bitter lines on every face around her, and Hannah found herself pressing her own face against the rough cloth of Jeb's shirt. Even more surprising than her action was his reaction. He made a sound that blended comfort with reassurance. When he reached back and laid a hand on her leg, however, she found the heat of that touch anything but comforting. She held her breath until he moved it again.

For his part, Jeb hoped it would be another few minutes before they caught up with Plummer, whom he suspected was at the front of the straggling band. Because he hadn't been thinking beyond Hannah's sensitive feelings, the touch of his hand on her thigh had not sent the blood rushing to his sex. Her sharply indrawn breath had done that. That rush of sound signified her awareness of him as a man and reminded him of what lay just inches above the spread of his fingers.

He'd moved his hand as if it had been burned. It had been—by the heat of something he longed to curve his fingers around . . . against . . . into.

The damage was done. He was hard, roused, and ready.

To distract his thoughts, Jeb focused his

attention on what he previously hadn't wanted to think about. The Comanche weren't starving, nor did they look in any way mistreated, but their expressions said clearly that they were dying inside. Especially the older warriors who knew how it felt to streak their faces with the colors of battle and roam the plains on tough mustangs, wielding war lance and tomahawk. Now they trudged through the dust, their war ponies traded for cattle, their pride for survival. Not their own survival, but that of their women, children, and old people. Jeb wondered if any one of them, in this moment, thought it worth the price they had paid.

A young private cantered back along the line, drawing Jeb's attention. He pulled his horse to a halt just in front of Jeb's bay mare. "Sir, Captain Plummer is waiting for you ahead."

Jeb nodded, knowing Plummer's scouts would have announced their approach long ago. Then he frowned at the way the boy's gaze strayed toward Hannah. "Lead on," he said curtly.

Wheeling his horse about, the private kicked him up to a canter again, and Jeb spurred his mare to follow, the packhorse trailing as obediently as ever.

Plummer and Garrett had pulled their horses to one side of the slow-moving Indians and dismounted beneath the scant shade of a few scrub trees. Surprise and curiosity played across Garrett's face. Plummer's expression was completely unrevealing; Jeb admired that.

Jeb moved his leg so that Hannah could place her foot in the stirrup to dismount. When her feet were solidly on the ground, he dropped lightly down beside her.

"Welles." Plummer removed his hat, and Garrett followed suit. "Ma'am." After acknowledging the presence of a lady, Plummer waited for Jeb to speak.

"Captain." Jeb's greeting was a sparse as Plummer's. He wasn't here to exchange pleasantries. Hannah had moved slightly behind him, so he shifted positions until she was at his side. "This is Mrs. Barnes."

Jeb watched, but Plummer's expression didn't change. Garrett's did. "The Reverend Barnes's wife," he added.

This time a flicker of recognition showed in the captain's eyes.

When Jeb didn't speak again, Plummer realized that the woman was the reason for the ex-ranger's presence here. "Mrs. Barnes, how may I assist you?" he asked pleasantly.

"By hanging my husband's murderers," Hannah returned just as pleasantly.

Jeb almost grinned at the other man's look.

"Ma'am?" Plummer queried in a strangled voice.

"The three men who murdered my husband are the same soldiers who killed that farmer near the Brazos. The ones who tried to make it appear that the reservation Indians were guilty."

Plummer glared at Garrett, wishing now that

the young officer had hanged the men the same night Jeb Welles had pronounced them guilty. "Now, ma'am," he prevaricated, "there never was any proof of who committed that crime. Your husband was not able to identify them by sight."

"Well," Hannah said flatly, "I can certainly identify my husband's murderers."

"How can you be sure they were the same three?" Plummer suspected he had her there.

"Because they confessed their guilt when they . . . when they attacked me and caused me to miscarry my son." Hannah's voice had dropped to a near whisper by the time she finished speaking.

Jeb eased his arm around her shoulder. It would be hard for any woman to admit to being raped. He knew it had to be particularly hard for Hannah, who was such a private person.

He noted the way Plummer reddened and tugged at his collar. When the captain shifted his weight from one foot to the other, Jeb frowned. "What's the problem, Captain?"

Plummer sighed. May as well admit it. "Wilkins and Nelson are gone. Shaw is dead."

"Gone?" Jeb asked quietly, his tone belying his sudden feeling of impending doom.

"Considering the possibility—the probability of their guilt, I couldn't let them re-enlist. Nelson's and Wilkins's time was up. They left—and left Shaw lying in his own blood in their tent."

"And," Jeb prodded.

"And we couldn't catch up to them," Plummer confessed, thoroughly exasperated, both at the fact and at having to admit to it.

Jeb glanced at Hannah, wondering if she realized her danger with those two roaming free. Apparently not. She was looking at Plummer with a kind of disdain. Jeb suspected that she was biting her tongue hard enough for it to bleed. She had to be thinking that if the United States Army had listened to her husband, both he and her baby boy would still be alive. Shaw, too, but surely not even Hannah could think that any great consideration.

"What now?" Jeb asked.

"I sent a man to Fort Belknap. Their names and descriptions will be sent out on posters to all lawmen. They'll have a price on their heads, and sooner or later some bounty hunter will bring them in."

So Jeb was supposed to trust Hannah's safety to some bounty hunter. *Shit!* "And Mrs. Barnes?" he asked.

Plummer rubbed his neck, realizing the implications of her being a witness to her husband's murder. "You could take her to Fort Belknap and place her in the care of the U.S. Army. I could have her escorted back east at the first opportunity." Boston, maybe, where he'd never have to see her and be reminded of how completely he had mishandled this entire matter.

Without even looking at her, Jeb pictured

Hannah's red hair as it sneaked its way from under her bonnet, wisping against her face and gleaming in the sunlight. And he pictured everything in uniform seeing the same thing and feeling the same kind of bulge against their pants that he felt when he looked at Hannah. *Like hell,* he thought. *Like bloody hell.* The woman might be a pain in the ass, but she'd been through enough because of the U.S. Army's incompetence.

"Captain," he drawled, "if you'll provide Mrs. Barnes with a decent mount, the United States can consider its obligation to Mrs. Barnes at an end. She'll be under the care of the Texas Rangers."

Plummer's relief was so great that he didn't bother to point out that Jeb was no longer a ranger. He knew, because Brown had been forced to admit the fact when Jeb had refused to join Plummer in escorting the Indians north. He nodded and cut a glance toward Garrett. "We'll see to that at once."

Garrett needed no prompting. He was more than happy to escape the presence of the woman whose husband was dead because he hadn't listened to Jeb Welles. He was even happier to escape the presence of Jeb Welles, though the former ranger had scarcely given him more than a passing glance, and that glance had held not the slightest condemnation.

At a quiet word from Jeb, the young private who'd remained nearby unfastened Hannah's saddle from the packhorse and hurried after Garrett.

Though Jeb generally held the opinion that Hannah's disinclination to talk was a nuisance, this was one time he could count it a reason to be grateful. He hadn't the slightest idea how she felt about his high-handed decision, and if she didn't like it, he didn't care to find out, especially not here and now. Not that her feelings would change things. His mind was made up about the matter.

Hannah felt deflated. The one final thing she could do for Caleb had been taken from her. His murderers, except for the one killed by his fellows, would go free. She hadn't the least notion of how to go about tracking down outlaws. And what would she do if she found them? Load her rifle and wave it in their faces? Nor did she have any faith left in the United States Army. If it was up to them, she doubted the two outlaws would ever be brought to justice. Maybe some sheriff in some frontier town would recognize and apprehend the two. Maybe not.

She was so caught up in her own thoughts that she minded only a little when Captain Plummer drew Jeb aside and began to speak to him in tones too low for her to understand what was being said.

Plummer disliked admitting any further depredations by men who had once been under his command, but he felt honor bound to let Jeb know just what he was up against.

"What is it?" Jeb asked tersely, knowing he wasn't going to like whatever Plummer had to say. The other man was too grimly uncomfortable.

"When Wilkins and Nelson rode out of here, they took a redskin with them. A girl." Plummer glanced at Hannah to make sure she wasn't listening to them. "Maybe eleven or twelve years old."

Jeb felt his gut clench. "Go on." He knew what was coming. Knew it all the way down to the pads of his feet.

"We found her the next day. . . . What they did to that kid was a pure shame, even if she was just a Comanche."

Slowly, Jeb unballed his fist. Punching Plummer wouldn't change how he or nearly every other soldier felt about the Comanche people. *But,* Jeb thought, *it sure as hell would feel good.*

"Where is she now?"

"We buried her. When they were through, one of them put a bullet between her eyes." Plummer felt a little queasy, remembering. He'd seen worse things, he reckoned, but never with a child.

Seeing the grey cast to the captain's face, Jeb felt like howling. He knew which girl it had been, and that it had been Wilkins's idea to take her. Without even closing his eyes, Jeb could see the girl's delicate features and graceful movements, her too-knowing eyes as she spoke of the blue coats. He could feel her sun-warmed skin as he boosted her to the horse behind him. He thought of the future she would never have and tried not to see her in Wilkins's hands, beneath his thrusting body. Wilkins was going to pay for this particular mistake. With his life.

Jeb stared into the eyes of the man whose decision had made the tragedy possible. "By my count, Captain, that puts three lives on your conscience. Caleb Barnes, his son, and the girl." Neither of them counted Todd Shaw. His death just made for one less hanging later.

Plummer was too smart to refute the charge, but he wasn't going to suffer over it. A man made decisions every day of his life. Some of them were wrong. Plummer knew he was a good officer and a decent man, and he'd been in command long enough to learn to live with himself no matter what.

All he did was nod and feel grateful that Garrett chose that moment to return with a horse.

Having said his piece, Jeb let the matter drop. What was done was done. But his plans had changed with Plummer's revelation. Now, after he found a safe place for Hannah, he was going looking for Wilkins and Nelson. He'd see Slade, Katherine, and New Mexico when those two bastards were dead. His only problem was in deciding just where Hannah would be safest. Likely Wilkins and Nelson were long gone from Texas, never giving Hannah a second thought. But he couldn't be sure.

For the moment, he turned his mind to the horse Garrett had led up for his inspection, an ugly grulla gelding with steady eyes. Jeb ran his hands approvingly over the sturdy, muscular legs, then picked up each foot and examined the hoof for soundness. Finally he gave a satisfied nod. "He'll do." He wasn't a flashy animal like the preacher's horse had been, but he would carry Hannah safely.

He glanced at Hannah and smiled with a faint curl of one lip. Evidently Hannah agreed with his assessment of the animal's looks. "You'll learn to love him," he told her.

Doubt lifted Hannah's brow, but she allowed Jeb to assist her to the saddle. She didn't kid herself that she had any say in the matter anyway. She'd thought Caleb was autocratic. This man had reinvented the term.

Jeb sent Plummer a warning look as he asked, "Where were they headed?" He didn't want Plummer making any unnecessary comments in front of Hannah.

Plummer didn't need to ask who Jeb meant. "West, toward the Staked Plain."

With a short nod, Jeb made his decision. He'd backtrack with Hannah, take her east, where he knew there were one or two nicely settled towns with lawmen and decent citizens and churches.

Churches. The thought hit him as true as a hammer against the head of a nail. Of course. Where else would a preacher's wife be happy but with another preacher? Not that it mattered so much to him that Hannah was happy; he just didn't want her misery dragging on his thoughts. He quashed the thought of Hannah being suffocated all over again by some grim man of the cloth. And he quashed the thought, too, of some man putting his hands on the body Jeb had imagined over and over again.

He'd get over the feeling. He'd had too many women in too many places to become obsessed with any one of them. Besides, he suspected that he only thought about Hannah as much as he did because he'd been so long without a woman—and because she seemed as untouchable to him as the moon. What woman would welcome sex when all she'd known was the harsh reality of a man who prayed over her and the rape of three outlaws?

Jeb wanted his women hot and willing or not at all. He knew damned well the heat he felt around Hannah was one-sided and all on his part. And it was just that—heat. A fire he could quench with any woman, and would at the first opportunity.

If Jeb had pushed, they could have made the little town of Sherman before midnight that same evening. He didn't ask himself why he didn't. Nor did he ask himself why he selected a campsite long before dusk heralded the approach of night.

To justify the hour or so of full daylight wasted, Jeb fastened a rifle holster to Hannah's saddle and told her to remount.

Having just dismounted a few minutes earlier, Hannah gave him a curious, slightly disgruntled look, but complied without argument. In the past forty-eight hours, she had learned that sooner or later Jeb answered every question, whether she asked it or not. Forty-eight hours. Two days. So much had happened to change her life in that brief span of time.

Two days ago, she had been a wife with no expectations of a future beyond what her husband decreed for her. Two days ago, she had shuddered at the thought of any man touching her, just as she had shivered each time Caleb reached for her in the dark. Two days ago, she had not known Jeb Welles.

Jeb's hand guided hers to the proper position on the rifle stock. Hannah decided that Jeb had as much strength in his broad hands as most men had in their whole arm. Sunlight gleamed golden on the hair along his wrist where he'd rolled his shirtsleeve back out of the way.

"Hannah! Are you listening to me?"

Guilty of doing anything but listening, Hannah jumped and bit her lip.

Taking note of the mannerism that marked when Hannah felt insecure, Jeb sighed. "I'm not going to ask you to do anything you can't handle, Hannah."

Looking into eyes that blended the browns and greens of a forest, Hannah nodded. "I know." She still wasn't entirely sure she *liked* Jeb Welles, but she trusted him implicitly.

The conviction in her voice made Jeb stare

at her a moment longer than was safe. He'd never had any woman to look at him with such complete faith. He didn't want this one to start now.

"I want you to practice pulling the Sharps from the holster," he said a bit roughly.

"Why?"

"Why do you ask so many damned questions?"

Hannah averted her gaze and took a deep breath. Caleb had hated for her to question him. She looked back and her eyes met Jeb's. "I'm sorry."

In that instant, Jeb realized that he much preferred Hannah's look of trust to the expression on her face now. Much. "I'm sorry, too," he said simply.

As Hannah turned her attention to the rifle, Jeb remembered that this was the second time he'd apologized to her in as many days.

He closed his eyes briefly as she awkwardly slid the rifle out of the holster. He had to get rid of this girl. Soon.

When he opened his eyes, his gaze fell on the drab calico-covered thigh at eye-level to him.

Real soon.

Chapter Thirteen

Ike Nelson stared at the ramshackle little cabin and thought about the red-haired woman. He'd thought about little else but her for days, and he'd finally figured out why. It was the look of horror on her face when the preacher fellow had crumpled in the dirt. It was knowing that his, Ike's, bullet had killed the man and caused that look. Ike liked that.

He moved his horse forward. The sun had started its midafternoon descent in a cloudless sky, and sweat dripped from Ike's forehead. At the sound of Wilkins's heavy breathing beside him, Ike felt a familiar twinge of irritation. The man was a pig. Ike could have smelled his unbathed flesh half a mile away.

"What if she's gone?"

A derisive smile touched the corner of Ike's

mouth. Wilkins's question held trepidation and a certain hopefulness. "Jackass," Ike answered calmly. "There's smoke coming from the stove pipe."

Leon hadn't noticed that. "Don't mean it's hers," he said defensively.

Without glancing at Wilkins, Ike pictured the sweating man down on his knees, begging, Ike's pistol pointed full in his face. Ike chuckled softly at the image, then turned his attention fully on the cabin.

He studied the window, shutters hanging haphazardly open. No need to fear a rifle pointing out from the corner now that her man was dead. Another chuckle rumbled deep in his chest. If Ike had known how killing made him feel, he'd have started a long time ago.

Just outside the cabin, he stepped down from his horse and motioned for Wilkins to do the same. Leaving their horses ground-tied, he eased to the front door and silently gestured Wilkins to the back. Ike didn't think there was but one door to the haphazard pile of wood, but a cautious man lived longer. The preacher had proved that point. He hadn't been a cautious man, no, sir.

Ike slipped noiselessly across the porch. He felt proud of the fact that his steps made not the slightest whisper of sound across boards almost too rotten to bear his weight. The reverend hadn't been much of a carpenter, either. Hadn't been much of anything so far as Ike could tell.

The door stood ajar to catch whatever breeze came through the summer heat. The first thing Ike did was scan the opposite wall. He was right. The cabin boasted only that one door. Almost before he completed the thought, Wilkins's weight creaked across the porch behind him.

Ike signaled him to halt where he was, accompanying the gesture with a vicious look.

From inside, a woman's voice sang a soft lullaby. Ike almost thought he recognized the tune as something he'd heard at some point in his life.

He shifted his position so that he could see a different angle of the single room. The woman sat in a rocking chair beside the bed, oblivious to the man studying her. Her back was to him, but Ike had the impression that she held a child in her arms. He frowned and stiffened. Something was definitely wrong. Instead of a riot of red curls, this woman's hair hung board-straight and almost the color of fresh cream.

Though the woman's attention remained with the child, Ike's moved to the bed. A man lay there swaddled in quilts, though Ike nearly choked on the heat with each breath he took.

Ike swung his head to glare at the little shed that served as a barn. There, against one side, stood a crude homemade wagon. Two mules dozed in the paddock. *Son of a bitch!* That kind of carelessness was what got men killed. He thought he heard Wilkins snicker and turned his glare on the other man. But Wilkins's face was devoid of any expression while he waited with apparent patience for Ike to decide what move to make.

Ike stepped to the doorway with a deliberately heavy footfall, and the woman turned, giving a startled gasp as she did so. Ike knew a thrill at the look of sheer terror she gave him when she leapt to her feet, still clutching the child, a little girl with hair as light as her mother's.

"What do you want?" Her voice held a breathless tone of surprise.

"Good afternoon, ma'am." Ike touched his hand to the tip of his hat politely. He took the three steps that brought him fully across the threshold, just as if she'd invited him to do so. "We were looking for the folks that used to live here—friends of ours." He made sure his grey eyes held nothing that would seem threatening to her.

The woman's gaze shifted nervously to Wilkins and back to Ike. By the rounding of her eyes and the way she clutched her child more tightly, Ike suspected that she didn't like what she saw in Wilkins. Ike didn't blame her. He waited patiently for her to answer.

"We . . . the cabin was abandoned when we got here."

"Sonuvabitch."

Ike's tone had turned low and mean, and the woman flinched. Seeing her tense for flight, Ike slipped the mask back into place. "Sorry, ma'am. I do know how to go on in the presence of a lady, but I reckon I've been on the trail too long." He smiled the smile that had brought many a woman to her knees. "My name's Ike, and this here's Leon."

Some of the tension slipped from her shoulder muscles, but not all of it. "I'm sorry I can't help you more—with the folks you're looking for, I mean. We've only been here a day or two. My man took bad sick, and this was the first place I found to stop."

"What's wrong with him?" Ike tried to put some concern into his voice.

"I'm not certain." She cast a worried look toward the bed, where her husband thrashed restlessly beneath the covers. "He's got a terrible fever, and a rattling in his chest. He shakes this whole cabin with his chills." She cast another, even more anxious look toward Wilkins, who had eased closer while she talked.

Ike smiled. Next to Wilkins, he had to look mighty good. And safe. "Well, I reckon we'll find our folks easily enough. And I expect your care will bring your man around real soon."

At his friendly tone, a little more of the tension left the woman, and she seemed to droop. Ike sensed her exhaustion, her weakness. He decided that the startling contrast of wide brown eyes with such light-colored hair was a pretty combination. Her face wasn't half bad either, though slightly marred by lines of worry. He wondered if she'd enjoyed the making of that little girl she held.

"I don't reckon you could rustle us up a bite to eat before we go on our way?" Ike warned Wilkins with a threatening look. He'd have the woman feed them willing-like if he could. That way he wouldn't have to sit with a gun trained on her. Time enough to bring the gun out when they searched the couple's belongings for anything useful. Time enough, then, to use it.

There remained more than a hint of reluctance in the woman's face as she nodded. After watching her glance about the cabin and then at the child she still clutched tightly, he realized that she was afraid to release the kid from the safety of her arms.

"Leon," he said abruptly. "Go take care of the horses." As Wilkins complied with a disgruntled look, Ike eased himself into one of the two chairs at the rickety table. Very carefully, he placed both hands on the table in front of him.

He tried another smile at the woman. "Where are you folks heading?"

After a moment, she responded to Wilkins's absence and Ike's nonthreatening position, and set her daughter on the floor. "San Antonio. We've got kin there."

Ike barely heard her answer to his question, because the little girl turned to look at him, and a flash of memory brought another yellow-haired child to mind. And the memory brought pain. Ike shook his head to clear it.

"Mister?"

Ike looked up.

"I asked if ham and potatoes was okay? It's about all we got left to eat."

The little girl took a step toward Ike, drawing his attention again. He nodded. "That'll be fine. Anything." He felt the pull of the child's curiosity toward him. "What's her name?"

"Elisabeth." The woman's whole face softened when she looked at her daughter. "We call her Beth."

Beth stuck three of her fingers in her mouth and stared at Ike. He tried to look away from her blue gaze. "She don't have your eyes."

"No." Her mother began to slice ham with efficient motions. "She's got her father's coloring there, but his hair's carrot red."

With that reminder, Ike tried to focus his thoughts on the red-haired preacher's wife. Anything but the little towheaded child watching him.

She took a shy step closer. Beth. A pretty name. For a moment, he fought panic as he tried to recall that other child's name and couldn't. Then, as clearly as he heard the rattling of the sick man's breathing in the tiny cabin, he heard his mother's voice calling across the glen for Ike and Sarah to come in for supper.

Sarah's smile and Sarah's laughter tugged at him from across the years that separated him from his brief youth.

So many years ago. Ike and his father hadn't

been home when the Comanches came. But his mother had. And Sarah.

Barely thirteen at the time, he'd become a man the day he helped his father bury his mother and his sister. The next morning he rode away from the little farm that was all he'd ever known. He had fixed his gaze on the dirt path ahead of him and tried to keep from seeing his father's body as it swung gently from the rafters of the bedroom he'd shared with the only woman he could ever love.

Wilkins stood in the barn and rubbed his crotch and tried to imagine he felt a stirring there. Maybe Ike would let him watch. Maybe then he could do it himself. Maybe.

He had to find the preacher's wife and make her take back the curse she'd put on him. Then he was going to kill her for sure.

After that . . . Well, somehow he had to find a way to get away from Ike. Wilkins didn't have a doubt that the man was crazy. Any man had to be who would deliberately track Jeb Welles.

When Wilkins had rubbed the horses down and given them a little of the hay that had been left in the barn, he walked back toward the cabin. Maybe Ike had already had the woman and killed her. Wilkins hoped not. He wanted to try. Wanted to real bad.

Wilkins stepped through the doorway of the cabin, not sure what he expected to find. He stopped and stared. Ike still sat at the ramshackle table—and the kid rested contentedly in his arms.

Far from raped and far from dead, the woman bustled about, putting plates on the table.

Without saying a word, Wilkins took the chair opposite Ike and tried not to stare. He suspected Ike might kill a man for staring at him like he'd lost his mind.

The food tasted as good as it smelled, and they ate in near silence. From time to time, the child would stir restlessly, and Ike would pause in his eating and soothe her with wordless sounds. The woman seemed content to leave her child in his arms while she tended to her husband.

Wilkins saw the color in the man's face and knew he was as good as dead.

He finished eating and shoved his plate away.

"Go saddle the horses," Ike said without looking up from his food.

Wilkins stared at him disbelievingly, and Ike lifted an ugly gaze to his face.

"Do it now."

Wilkins did.

Carefully, Ike stood up and crossed the room to the woman. He placed the child at the foot of the bed where her father lay dying. When he reached toward his vest, he saw a tremor of renewed fear shake the woman, but he didn't say anything. The pouch he withdrew jingled slightly with his movements.

He took out several coins and held them toward the woman who accepted them cautiously. "You'll be needing this, I expect. The food was mighty good." He looked at the man, at the soaked bedcovers, then at the woman. "Take care of the kid."

He felt her eyes on his back as he walked toward the door and thought he heard her whisper her thanks for the money, but he didn't pause. He had a sudden urge to put these people far behind him, like the other ghosts of his past.

Wilkins held both horses at the edge of the porch. His heavy brows were beetled together in confusion. "Why, Ike?"

Ike didn't say anything until he had picked up the tracks of three horses leading away from the cabin. "That little girl hadn't ought to see any ugliness. And a young'un needs her mother."

Wilkins shook his head. "Not if she's dead, too."

Ike snarled deep in his throat. "I don't kill kids."

"Like hell!" Wilkins blustered before he had time to think about the need for caution. "What about the Comanche? You put a bullet in her without blinking. And she was just a kid."

When Ike swung his flat, grey stare around, Wilkins swallowed a moan of fear and waited for Ike to speak or shoot him dead.

"Ain't you learned by now?" Ike growled. "Comanches ain't human."

Chapter Fourteen

The little town of Sherman appeared about as peaceful as a town could get in Texas. Jeb noted with satisfaction the whitewashed structures with their dollhouse fences and flowers wilting in the summer heat. He'd always thought Sherman would make a nice home for a settled kind of person. He could picture Hannah here, tending a garden behind one of those little fences that wouldn't keep a tame puppy out if it wanted in, or strolling along the main street. He closed his mind against the image of some man strolling with her.

"This place has sure grown since John Butterfield routed his San Francisco line through here." Jeb spoke more to himself than to Hannah. He was, as a matter of fact, distinctly aware that he and Hannah had exchanged fewer than two dozen words all morning. He tamped back his feelings of guilt with a sense of irritation. There was no reason, by God, to feel guilty for leaving her in a safe little place like Sherman. She was not his responsibility. He'd done more than most men would have up to this point. More than he had ever intended to do.

Silently, Hannah followed Jeb up the dirt street, riding the stocky little grulla as close behind the bay mare as she could get, trying not to imagine eyes staring at her from doors and windows. She could just imagine what a sight she looked by this time.

Of course, she knew he had to leave her somewhere, and she trusted him to leave her somewhere safe. Whether or not she was ready to be on her own was a different matter altogether. Drawing a deep breath as they stopped in front of a weatherbeaten structure in the middle of town, she wondered how it was going to feel to watch Jeb Welles ride out of town without her. She couldn't let him see how much the thought unnerved her. Somehow, she would just have to get used to the idea of being responsible for herself.

A man as ancient as the clothes he wore sat propped in a chair that rested on spindly back legs and the building behind it. When Jeb stepped down from the bay, the old man rocked forward, dropping the front legs of the chair to the rough planks that made up the boardwalk.

"Sheriff around?"

"Yep. Courthouse." A short jerk of a whiskered chin directed Jeb's gaze across the road.

Surprise lifted Jeb's brow. "That's new." The last time he'd passed this way, the courthouse had been a crude log structure.

"Yep." The old man spat in a bucket, and Hannah hastily averted her gaze so that her revulsion wouldn't show. "Tore the other'n down last year." His voice was a slow drawl. "Had to."

Jeb waited patiently, knowing the other man wasn't through despite the lengthy silence that followed his pronouncement. He had all the air of a man with a story to tell, a story he clearly relished telling.

"Some folks hereabouts said an old grey duck had nested under it. Some said it hadn't. Money was laid down on both sides and no sure fire way to settle it without looking. So—" He paused for effect. "We looked."

Hannah watched in amazement as a grin crossed the old man's face. They had destroyed a courthouse to settle a bet? Though she recalled Caleb's many sermons on gambling, she couldn't recall any scriptures which named it a sin.

Her incredulous expression drew a wink from the old man. "No choice but to do it, ma'am. No choice at all."

Jeb grinned as he agreed. "No other way to settle the matter." He glanced up at Hannah, then back at the old man. "I need to speak to the sheriff."

"Your missus will be safe enough here. Ain't much goes on in Sherman anymore." He sounded almost mournful. "Ain't too much ever did, I reckon."

Jeb moved closer to Hannah. "Stay mounted. I won't be long." Somehow he thought he'd feel a lot better if she wasn't standing in the street. She was so slight of stature, so vulnerable. He refused to consider the fact that he wouldn't know if she was safe or not after he rode out of there.

Jeb found the sheriff to be much as he expected—weathered, astute, and fully competent—qualities that would be essential in keeping a town this close to Indian territory clothed in at least a veneer of civilization. Also, as Jeb had expected, there was a twinkle of good humor in the sheriff's eyes. Any man who would allow the town's courthouse to be torn down over a bet had to have a sense of humor.

As Jeb stepped through the doorway, the man swung his feet down from a table and laid the papers he was studying aside. Jeb gave a cursory glance around the long room. It would take some doing to tear this solidly built structure down.

"Sheriff?" Jeb extended his hand.

The sheriff stood and took Jeb's hand in a healthy grip. Despite his muscled bulk, the lawman moved with a kind of grace. "I'm Sheriff Hastings," he acknowledged the faint question in Jeb's tone. "What can I do for you?"

Jeb gave a sigh and warned, "It's a long story."

"In that case, how about you talk while I stretch my legs? I could use a whiskey."

For a moment, Jeb considered Hannah and the amount of trouble she could get into in the time it would take him to down a drink. Hannah being Hannah, that was considerable. A certain apprehension warred with his memories of the smooth taste of whiskey. The whiskey won out. "As a matter of fact, so could I. I'll buy."

Giving a satisfied nod, Sheriff Hastings clapped his hat on his head and led the way.

Emerging into bright sunlight, Jeb narrowed his eyes against the glare. From the corner of his eye, he could see Hannah, still sitting on her grulla. Patiently, he hoped. Likely Hannah wouldn't think much of his need for hard liquor at this time of the morning. For reasons he didn't name, he very carefully did not look her way.

Once inside the bar, Jeb visibly relaxed and the sheriff gave him a curious look. "You got problems, son?" Without waiting for an answer, he met the barkeep's expectant glance. "Two whiskeys."

Only when the lawman had his drink in his hand did he give Jeb his full attention.

"Yeah," Jeb answered glumly, "I've got problems, and her name is Hannah Barnes."

The sheriff didn't quite grin. Somehow he

wasn't surprised whenever he learned that a man's problems centered on a woman. "I'm listening."

And he did listen, very quietly, until Jeb concluded, "So I need to leave Hannah someplace she'll be safe until those two are accounted for."

"I don't suppose you'd consider letting the U.S. Army take care of—Nelson and Wilkins, is it?"

Jeb shook his head without hesitation. "I can't. If it's left up to the Army, Hannah will be no safer than her husband was, and likely just as dead."

Eyes that had seen a great deal already studied Jeb's face. "Is it revenge you're after or the lady's protection?"

Jeb thought about that for a long moment. "Both, I reckon."

"And will you be coming back for Mrs. Barnes when you've settled with these two men?"

The suggestion startled Jeb. And unnerved him. He spoke more abruptly than he intended. "What the hell would I do with a preacher's wife?" When the sheriff didn't answer, he added, "Besides, I've got a job waiting in New Mexico Territory. That's no place for a woman." He thought of Katherine Slade. "Not one like Hannah anyway."

"Well, then what do you intend for Mrs. Barnes?" Sheriff Hastings waited curiously for his answer.

Jeb rubbed his neck. "I can leave enough money to take care of her for a few months. After that . . . Hell, this is Texas. There ain't nearly enough decent women to go around. By the time the money is gone, some man will be standing there ready to grab her. Likely before then." Jeb ignored the funny feeling in the pit of his stomach. As pretty as Hannah was, there would likely be a man camped at her door by morning. More than one.

The sheriff nodded. "Can't argue with that, especially if she's anything worth looking at."

Jeb could almost see the sunlight sparkling on Hannah's red hair. "She is," he said morosely. "She definitely is." He met the sheriff's amused glance. "I'd like to know you'll keep an eye on her until she's safely married."

"Or until she decides to move on," the lawman agreed.

Dumbstruck, Jeb stared at the other man. "On her own? You can't let her do that!" Hannah wouldn't last two minutes out in the world alone.

"Well, I can hardly keep her against her will, now can I?"

Jeb couldn't argue with that—but he wanted to. He had one last question for the lawman. "Does the Widow Ryon still run a restaurant?"

The sheriff didn't answer right away, and Jeb thought his smile seemed a little forced.

Then he shrugged and answered Jeb's question. "You've eaten at the widow's before, have you?" At Jeb's nod, he added quietly,

"Yeah, she's still in business. Sets a mighty good table."

Jeb wondered briefly at the piercing look the older man gave him, but shrugged it off as he thought to ask about a place Hannah might stay.

By the time he parted ways with the sheriff, Jeb felt fairly comfortable that Hannah would be safe in Sherman. As long as she remained there. Now he had to convince her to do just that. He felt better about his prospects when he made his way back to where he'd left her and found her still sitting obediently atop her grulla. Maybe she'd be as biddable about staying here in Sherman.

He walked up to the grulla's nose and looked up at Hannah. "You ready to get settled in someplace?" Sheriff Hastings had recommended a place where he assured Jeb a woman alone could live in safety.

"I'm going to stay here?" Hannah had had plenty of time to look around while Jeb was gone. She hadn't lived in a real town since Caleb had married her and taken her away from her father's home.

Jeb's eyes narrowed. Was she going to be difficult after all? "Unless you've got some objection?"

Hannah looked up the wide, dusty street that ran through the middle of town. The shops on either side appeared prosperous and well-kept. The houses beyond the business section had little fences and flower beds. "No," she said slowly. "No, I've no objections at all." None she would mention anyway.

The idea of never seeing Jeb again stole some of Hannah's pleasure at the prospect of living in a truly civilized place. But of course she couldn't let him know that. He might not realize it was just the natural result of depending upon him for her very existence the past few days. That and gratitude for seeing Caleb decently buried.

Hannah didn't have much to say as Jeb led the way to a three-storied house just beyond the livery stable. To her eyes it looked truly elegant, with ornate scrollwork above the numerous tall windows. Crisp white paint gleamed in the midday sunlight, and a discreet sign proclaimed rooms for rent in precise black lettering.

Jeb stifled a grin at the wide-eyed expression on Hannah's face as she slid from the grulla. He'd like to show her New Orleans. As hastily as the thought came, he pushed it away from him. It wasn't as if he had time to go wandering around showing the sights to some backward preacher's widow. Not even one with silken strands of hair that caressed creamy cheeks and eyes so brightly blue they were almost iridescent.

With a muffled curse, he wrapped his reins around a hitching post and strode toward the door. When he glanced back, Hannah was standing where he'd left her, wearing the faintest of frowns upon her face. He recognized the frown as uncertainty and said, trying to be gruff, "This is it, Hannah."

Slowly, Hannah tied the grulla and followed Jeb's path to the door. Her heart thudded as Jeb lifted the heavy knocker. She was about to face her future, and it was as uncertain as everything else that had happened since Caleb's death.

A faint feeling of dread filled her. She recalled a boarding house from her childhood that had been run by a crotchety old woman who scowled at any children who dared to linger by her gate. Hannah saw herself now as a stranger must see her—untidy and sun-browned and accompanied by a man who was not her husband. She would surely be a scandal to any decent woman. An urgent need to escape overwhelmed her, but before she could turn and flee, the door opened to Jeb's knock.

To Hannah's relief, there was no sign of a self-righteous matron. Instead, a man who looked scarcely older than herself smiled a welcome, and when his glance moved past Jeb to Hannah, that smile became particularly warm.

Jeb scowled. "I need to speak with Mrs. Kipfer about a room."

"Mrs. Kipfer was my mother. She passed away last year. I'll be glad to help you with a room."

Reluctantly, Jeb held out his hand. "Jeb Welles," he said. "And this is the widow, Mrs. Barnes. Sorry about your mother," he added grudgingly.

"She was a good woman. Her boarders miss her as much as I do, but I try to make them as comfortable as she did. My name is Roger." He glanced at Hannah then back at Jeb. "One room? Will that be for yourself or for Mrs. Barnes?"

Hannah had been flooded with varying emotions from the moment Jeb opened his mouth. The first had been relief that she need not face a glaring old harridan, followed by amazement at Jeb's unprovoked bad manners. Next, she felt a warm confusion at the admiration she read in the young Mr. Kipfer's eyes when he looked at her, and, finally, pleasure that he had not assumed she was a fallen woman who would be sharing a room with a man not her husband.

"Mrs. Barnes—if it meets with my approval." Jeb was not at all sure he liked the way Roger Kipfer was looking at Hannah.

"Of course. If you'll follow me."

Hannah felt distinctly uncomfortable as Jeb took her elbow in a grasp that seemed very proprietary to her. But of course, she should be quite used to his domineering ways.

Jeb wasn't the least concerned with what Hannah was thinking, but he definitely wanted Roger Kipfer to realize that Hannah was not all alone in the world. *Maybe not today, but what about tomorrow?* Hannah's arm felt insubstantial against his hand. Irritation swept over him. How could a woman like her ever stand alone? Why couldn't she be strong—like Katherine? Katherine had crossed the wilds of Texas on her own, tracking the Comanche warrior who had fathered her baby, battling a real son of a bitch like Slade, then leaving everything she'd ever known to follow him to New Mexico. Jeb couldn't picture Hannah doing that.

But he could picture her in his arms. In his bed.

Hannah had the feeling that Jeb hadn't seen anything of the comfortable parlor or the winding staircase that led to a tiny hallway with a half dozen doors all neatly closed. A scowl still sat upon his face, and she hadn't the faintest idea why. They passed the first floor and climbed on to the second. It was a mirror image of the first.

Mr. Kipfer opened one of the doors and stepped inside. "I think you'll find this quite suitable."

Jeb caught him staring at Hannah again, glanced around the neat, little room, and said, "I don't."

Hannah almost laughed at the comic look of dismay on the boarding house owner's face. She wanted to reassure him that such rudeness was just Jeb's way, but she was too preoccupied with her own disappointment. The room was enchanting, with pale green curtains of crisp muslin and wallpaper that combined the same soft shade with golden roses.

"Hannah—Mrs. Barnes will need something larger. On the floor below this."

Mr. Kipfer tugged at the collar of his soft cambric shirt. "I'm afraid I have no vacancies on the first level. I do have a larger room on this floor, but it is more—ah, masculine in appearance."

Hannah felt sorry for the young man as color suffused his face. She touched Jeb's arm lightly. "This will be fine. Truly."

Jeb glared at her. He might have known she'd think so. "It won't do." He looked back at the boarding house owner. "Is there anyplace else in town?"

"Well . . . there's the hotel, of course. And down the road just past the bank is Mr. Armen. He and his wife have a few rooms to let. I really don't believe you'll find his rooms more comfortable than what I can offer."

Jeb's attention was caught by the fact that the owner of the other boarding house was married. "We'll try there."

Hannah wanted to argue, both for the sake of Mr. Kipfer's embarrassment and because she truly liked the little room. But a tiny voice in her head reminded her that she owed a debt of honor to Jeb for taking care of her. If he didn't want her to take a room here, then, of course, she wouldn't. At least not until he left town. After that, she figured, she would be well and truly on her own. She smiled at Mr. Kipfer and followed Jeb from the room.

"Ah, miss—I mean, ma'am, will you be in town long?"

Hannah paused to glance back, still surprised by the display of interest in the nice brown eyes watching her. It was difficult to think of herself as an available—and desirable—woman. "Well . . ." She hesitated, aware of Jeb's scowling lack of patience. "I had hoped to find work here, so I suppose I will be."

Mr. Kipfer beamed. "I'm sure you'll find Sherman to your liking." He looked as if he would have said more, but a hasty glance toward Jeb appeared to make him think better of it.

Jeb set his jaw and clamped his hat upon his head. "Let's go, Hannah."

Hastily, Hannah obeyed.

Back out on the dusty street, Jeb turned to her and asked, "What the hell do you mean, you hope to find work?"

"What?" Hannah stared at him in amazement. He seemed almost angry.

"Just what kind of work do you think you can do?"

"I—I'm not sure. I'd hoped maybe one of the shops in town might need assistance. Maybe the mercantile."

Hannah's voice faded. No doubt about it. Jeb was furious. His eyes had lightened to that beautiful shade of green that portended rage. But why?

"I have no money," Hannah said slowly when Jeb merely stared with that wicked way he had of looking at her, almost as if she were a slow-witted child. "How else can I live?"

With a rough gesture, Jeb rubbed his beard-bristled face. "Did you think I would just cast you on the street and ride away, Hannah?"

She shivered. The way he said her name was almost a caress, but of course he didn't mean it that way. "I can't take your money," she said with quiet dignity. What kind of woman did he think her?

"And if no one needs 'assistance'?" he mocked. "What then? Do you stand on a corner and beg? Sleep in an alley?"

Humiliation washed warm color over Hannah's cheeks. "Mr. Welles," she said stiffly, "I appreciate all you've done for me. I truly do, but you may consider your charitable obligation at an end. Whatever becomes of me from this point is hardly your concern."

As speeches went, Hannah considered she hadn't done too poorly, despite the fact that tears were burning in her eyes and threatening to spill over at any moment. Jeb's reaction, however, demolished any satisfaction she might have been feeling.

"Oh, shit, Hannah." He seized her arm and began striding in the direction Mr. Kipfer had given for his rival's place of business.

Smaller and less ornate, Mr. Armen's boarding house had more of an intimate, homey atmosphere than the other. Hannah felt immediately comfortable with the older gentleman and his courtly ways.

She noticed with relief that Jeb was much friendlier than he had been with Mr. Kipfer. When Mr. Armen opened the door of the only room he had available, however, Hannah sighed quietly. It was much the same as the room at Mr. Kipfer's that Jeb had said wouldn't do.

"This will be fine," Jeb said bluntly.

Hannah turned in amazement, but his look dared her to comment.

Mr. Armen smiled in satisfaction. "Will you be sharing the room, then?"

Mortification burned Hannah's ears, and she couldn't have spoken if her life had depended upon it.

"No. Of course not," Jeb said evenly. "I have escorted Mrs. Barnes here in an official capacity. Since the death of her husband, she has been under the care of the Texas Rangers."

Relief eased some of Hannah's discomfort, but she found she still could not meet Jeb's eyes. Instead, she focused on the room. While it was very nice, it was no more so than the first. The only real difference between the two was that this one was at ground level. She wondered what Jeb had against upper floors. She also wondered when Mr. Armen would expect to be paid, and what she was supposed to do when that moment came. She dared not ask Jeb after his earlier outburst.

"I'll just get your things," Jeb said.

Hannah realized that Mr. Armen had left them alone in the room and that Jeb was watching her with an odd look. "Yes," she replied, feeling awkward. "Thank you."

Was this how their parting would be? Hannah wondered as he left the room. Would he just leave her with a polite good-bye and be on his way? She stepped to the window overlooking the street and watched as he untied her small bundle of belongings from the packhorse.

She sure didn't have much to her name, and with Jeb's going, she wouldn't have a friend in the world. Not that she could exactly think of him as a friend, but at least he was someone she *knew*.

Her gaze fixed on his shoulders, on the way his muscles rippled beneath his shirt. Caleb had been powerfully muscular, but Jeb possessed a sinewy strength that had no need for bulk. Even his thighs flexed with that strength as he strode back toward the porch. *His thighs!* Hannah turned from the window as if scalded. Dear God, what had a few days without Caleb's godly teachings done to her?

Jeb thought Hannah looked mighty peculiar when he placed her belongings on the bed. She didn't look as if she had moved an inch since he left her. Poor girl was probably terrified of being alone.

"Look." He cleared his throat. "I'll come by about sundown and take you to the restaurant for supper."

"You don't have to do that."

Hannah would have said more, would have expressed gratitude for all he had done, but he cut her off.

"Damn it, Hannah, don't argue with everything I say. I'll be back for you later, just like I said."

Open-mouthed, Hannah watched him leave the room. Argue? He'd bossed and bullied her about from the moment they rode into Sherman. And she hadn't opened her mouth in a single protest. Never in her life had she met a more maddening man! Or one who made her feel more alive.

Chapter Fifteen

All of Sherman, Texas, knew the Widow Ryon was a lady. Watching her move among them, offering another glass of milk or a refill on a steaming cup of coffee, not one of her customers doubted that. There was a graciousness about her that embodied a great deal of old-world charm, a charm that was reflected in the furnishings of her home.

Polished wood floors gleamed beneath bright scatter rugs. Unbleached linen squares, neatly hemmed, covered a half dozen small tables. The drapes were also of unbleached linen with tiny ruffles along the hem. Because a large majority of the widow's customers were male, those ruffles were the only frills in the room. When available, fresh flowers in tall vases permeated the air with their fragrance.

Despite the fact that most of her customers were men from the stage route or from the trail or even Sherman's bachelors with no one to cook for them at home, several typically male things were not allowed in Jenny Ryon's restaurant. Things like alcoholic beverages, foul language, tobacco of any nature, muddy boots, and dirty hands. Male guests were forced to remove their hats before she would even notice them.

Any man who did not abide by her house rules found himself facing a five-foot-five-inch ball of fury. As legendary as Jenny's meals undoubtedly were, her temper was even more renowned. She had stood nose to chin with more than one unruly customer and backed them down without wavering or blinking an eye. Part of her success in that was due to the fact that any one of her longtime visitors would tear into tiny pieces any man who dared insult or lay a hand on her.

On the day Jeb Welles rode into town, a stranger decided to put the house rules to the test.

From across the room, Jenny watched with slightly narrowed eyes as the man who'd introduced himself as "Hawk" pulled a cheroot from his vest pocket. Every ounce of her was fully composed as she crossed the short distance to his table. Her gown swished gracefully as she walked, drawing the appreciative gazes of several other diners.

"Hawk," she said in her sweet contralto,

"you'll have to do your smoking on the front lawn. I've provided receptacles there for any gentlemen who feel the need."

There was a wickedly appreciative gleam in the dark brown eyes that glanced up at her. Hawk had always been one to admire the ladies, and he was accustomed to receiving their admiration in return. "Well now, ma'am, I do purely take pleasure from a smoke with my coffee. You wouldn't want to deprive me of that, would you?" His voice was as smooth as a physical caress.

Jenny watched him glance around in smug satisfaction to see how his audience of fellow diners was reacting. "Of course, I wouldn't," she answered agreeably, seeing his satisfaction grow until she added, "You may certainly take your coffee with you."

Stung, Hawk felt his smile flatten somewhat. "I can't say as I recall any laws against smoking in Sherman."

"Perhaps not in Sherman, but I make the laws in this house, and smoking is not allowed." She still retained her composure, but she felt it slipping fast.

"And just who enforces *your* laws?" There was a definite sneer to the tone now.

Butterflies rippled through Jenny's stomach. Despite her ready temper, she was not the kind of woman to enjoy a fray. She was, however, too smart to back down from one. If she ever started, it would be impossible for her, a woman without protection, to stay in business. With apparent calm, she picked up the cup of coffee on the table in front of him and lifted it high. With those disbelieving brown eyes daring her, she poured it over the lighted cheroot in his mouth. "I do," she retorted as the hot liquid soaked into his shirt and pants. "Please enjoy your coffee with your smoke."

Her words were drowned in the curses erupting from Hawk as he leapt to his feet. "You damned little bitch! I'll teach you to—"

All across the room, a dozen chairs skittered back as men responded to the threat to a woman they all admired. Before any of them could reach her, however, Hawk found his arm held in the painfully solid grip of a late arrival.

Jenny met the sheriff's eyes above Hawk's shoulder, but only the barest of smiles touched her lips. Long ago, she had learned to curb her growing response to this man for her own protection—and his. "Sheriff," she said softly.

"Miss Jenny." His grip tightened even more bruisingly on the arm he held. "You got trouble with this man?"

From the moment Hawk realized he was held by the lawman, his struggles had ceased. He stood waiting for the woman's response with a face totally devoid of any expression.

Jenny studied his eyes for a trace of threat or pleading. There was neither. "Just a misunderstanding, Sheriff. I believe Mr. Hawk was just leaving."

With a twist of his wrist, Daniel pulled Hawk around until they stood face-to-face. He released his arm then. "You'll be leaving Sherman, too. There's a stage heading out in a couple of hours. Be on it."

"I've got business here!" Hawk protested.

"You may have had. You don't any more. Unless, of course, you'd like to conduct it from jail?" The sheriff's tone was far more pleasant than the look in his eyes.

With a muffled curse, Hawk snatched his hat from the table and stalked to the door. He paused for one look back at Jenny. This time the threat was there.

Daniel saw it as well. He sighed. "I'd hate like hell to have to kill that man." With an effort, he resisted the urge to put a hand out and touch Jenny—just to reassure himself that she was unharmed.

She murmured a protest at the mention of killing, but her eyes were on Hawk's back as he pushed his way past a man coming through the door. Her anxiety about Hawk was swept away by a wave of pleasure as she recognized the latest arrival. That brief feeling faded, too, as she recalled that Jeb Welles was one of the many reasons she could never afford to fall in love with Sheriff Hastings.

Jeb walked away from Armen's Boarding House with two women on his mind. With any luck at all, he decided, an hour or two with the Widow Ryon would allay his nagging suspicion that thoughts of Hannah weren't going to be as easy to put behind him as he'd like. No doubt his fixation on that troublesome redhead had more to do with his physical deprivation than with the lady's charms.

Jenny Ryon ran a respectable restaurant. Her cooking was reputedly the best in all of northeast Texas, and word of it had drifted as far south as Austin. Only a very few people, however, ever heard of the way in which the Widow Ryon discreetly supplemented the income from that restaurant. Those few were men, a very select group. Any man who had been led to expect more of the young widow than food, but did not measure up to her stringent standards, was treated to the sight of wounded womanhood wrapped in a fragile, trembling package of ivory flesh, satiny brown hair, and eyes the color of fine whiskey.

Jeb had never seen that side of Jenny Ryon, but he had seen her trembling with passion. He'd seen that creamy flesh rippled with goosebumps, that soft-as-silk hair wrapped around one of his fists, those golden eyes staring up into his. His loins throbbed just thinking about her. Without a doubt, the Widow Ryon was just what he needed to remind him that Hannah Barnes was the furthest thing from his type of woman. He needed heat and passion, not a cool voice quoting scripture.

When Jeb reached the far end of town, he stood looking up the walk to where the front gate swung open in welcome. A sign proclaimed that the midday meal was now being served. A half-dozen horses were tied under cool shade trees nearby.

Jeb recalled the first time he'd introduced himself to Jenny. He'd been five years younger and five years brasher, but he hadn't exactly been green where women were concerned, nor had he been lacking in a good opinion of himself. When he'd indicated he wanted something more for dessert than her homemade apple pie, the widow had drawn herself up in righteous indignation. Before she could respond, however, Jeb had drawled, "Cut the bullshit, ma'am. I may need a bath, but the dirt that's on me is clean dirt, and when it's gone you might just like what you see. And what it can do."

Somewhat to his surprise, the widow hadn't slapped the smile from his face. She had burst out laughing instead. Jeb smiled now just thinking about her laughter and the hours he'd passed in her arms afterward. He'd made sure she wasn't sorry, made sure that when she gasped his name, she wasn't just giving him his money's worth. And when he left her before dawn the next morning, he followed the tradition of the men she'd allowed into her bedroom before him and placed a discreet roll of bills on the nightstand. She acknowledged neither the money nor his actions, just smiled and asked him to visit her again if he ever came to town.

He had done just that—several times—letting her meet needs that no painted whore ever could. The need to laugh and to talk when the lovemaking was over and done. The need for honesty and no regrets. The need not to feel as if he had used someone or been used in return. Somehow, for all the money she gathered from those who visited, Jenny Ryon made a man feel as if he'd shared in something rare and honest.

Jeb needed that now more than he'd needed anything in a long time. He sensed a weakness in him where Hannah was concerned. A weakness he couldn't afford.

With a muttered oath, he strode up the path to the front door. Inside, folks appeared too busy eating to do much talking. Jeb's stomach growled at the aroma of roast in gravy and freshly baked bread still warm from the oven.

As he stepped through the door, the Widow Ryon looked up from a conversation she was having with the sheriff. A slight smile touched her lips as she recognized Jeb, but she was a lady and all she did was nod toward an empty table.

Jeb took a seat and waited for her to come to him. He didn't have to wait long.

Her eyes were as beautiful as he remembered. "What can I get for you, cowboy?"

That husky voice reminded him a lot of Katherine Slade, and not at all of Hannah, he told himself. "A full plate, a bath—and the pleasure of your company later," he added quietly so that only she could hear.

Jenny's soft laughter turned the head of

every man in the room, inciting a mixture of lust and admiration for the widow and envy for the cowboy who had drawn her laughter. And an entirely different reaction in Daniel Hastings.

She wrinkled her nose, wondering how she had gotten to be so good an actress that she could pretend all her thoughts were not focused on the lawman sitting behind her—watching her every move. "You do always seem to need a bath when you come in here," she said, reminding them both of the first time he'd visited her place.

"Yeah, but I reckon I clean up well enough to suit you," Jeb drawled with a reminder of his own.

The widow smiled without answering the question of her availability for the afternoon. "I'll get a plate for you."

Jeb's eyes fixed on the sway of her hips beneath some soft, shiny material the color of summer roses. He wondered idly how Hannah would look clothed in something so completely feminine instead of that grimly dark calico she wore. Realizing that he was thinking of Hannah when he should be focusing on the hours to come with Jenny, Jeb felt like cursing aloud. Instead he clamped his lips into a thin line and tried to concentrate his thoughts on how he was going to catch up to Wilkins and Nelson now that he had Hannah in a safe place.

Hannah again. Damn!

* * *

With a careful smile, Jenny served Daniel from a platter brimming with tender meat and smooth brown gravy.

"I'd like to talk with you." Daniel felt the way he always did when he tried to speak his feelings to this woman. Like a green kid in half-britches.

"Of course, Da—Sheriff."

"No." He reached out and placed his hand over her. "Not Sheriff Hastings. Daniel."

Jenny licked her lips. No, it couldn't be. There couldn't be that look of honest caring in the man's eyes. No way in the world could Daniel Hastings not know about the true Widow Ryon and what she had begun doing to pay off her husband's debts. What she had continued to do to keep this roof over her head and, now that her home was secure, to stave off the loneliness that sometimes threatened to overwhelm her.

Of course, the first time a man had ever left money on her night table, she had been insulted. She had slept with him freely, needing a man's arms to hold her until the hours of loneliness passed. When she had seen how *much* he'd left her, all her noble plans to return it had fallen away. It had been enough to pay off one of the mountain of bills hanging over her head. A month or so later, when a friend of his had shown up asking for the same kind of friendly reception, she had swallowed her pride and invited him to her room.

It had seemed easier and easier after that.

Those visits were infrequent and usually weeks between. No crude or crass men had ever approached her—at least not in the early days. Later . . . Well, later she had developed enough strength to know how to handle them. For a long time what she did had not seemed so bad. Then Daniel Hastings had come to town.

From their very first meeting, she had found it necessary to hide her reaction to him. That hadn't changed over the months. It had, in fact, grown until her attraction to him had become a cause for pain.

"Jenny?"

She noticed he had dropped the 'Miss'—noticed, too, that he was looking at her the way any woman would want the man of her dreams to do. But it was all wrong. Her tongue wet her lip in a nervous gesture.

"All right then . . . Daniel." She didn't know what to say about his request to talk to her. Talk about what? Instead she just stood looking at him like some half-minded dimwit.

"Would you go for a buggy ride with me this afternoon?" Daniel wondered how he dared try for the attention of someone as lovely as Jenny. A crook of her little finger would bring any man running to drop at her knees.

She flicked a glance toward Jeb. "This afternoon?"

Daniel saw the look. He wanted desperately to tell her not to do it, not to give her time, her sweetness, and her body to a man who wouldn't want them every night for the rest of his life. A man who wouldn't want to wake up beside her every morning, who would be on his way, and whose boastings would send another man to her side to take his place.

Daniel saw the answer in her eyes and felt his heart break.

More than she'd ever wanted anything in her life, Jenny wanted to tell him she would love to spend the sunny afternoon with him. But she didn't dare. Not because of Jeb Welles. His disappointment would not deter her, though she held him in affection. The truth was, she was afraid, terrified, that Daniel Hastings somehow did not know the truth about her. She could not bear to fall the rest of the way in love with him and then be forced to watch the warmth in his eyes turn to loathing when he did learn what she had made of herself.

With painful regret, she shook her head. "I can't this afternoon . . . perhaps some other time."

But they both knew she didn't mean it.

Daniel smiled sadly and nodded, watching as she walked away from him to be a gracious hostess to her customers. The light from the windows picked out the satin highlights in her hair. Daniel wondered how he was going to learn not to love her.

Chapter Sixteen

Jenny had never been faced with the need to tempt her "guests." They usually came to her hot, hard, and randy as young goats. Even if some were a little slower than others, usually by the time she had washed their hair and massaged their scalp, they were in that condition. She noticed, however, as her hands slid a soap-covered washcloth over Jeb's chest, that he was still something less than ready to bed her. As a woman, she knew instinctively how to remedy that; as a whore, she should have been prepared to do so. As a woman in love with another man, she hesitated.

Jeb noticed his lack of desire, too, with a growing sense of unease. The times when he could enjoy this kind of pleasure at the hands of a woman as lovely as Jenny were few enough.

He should have been more than ready to enjoy what she had to offer. Gritting his teeth, he swore not to think about the possible reasons why he wasn't. One came to mind in spite of that oath, but he pushed the thought quickly away. He slid deeper into the tub of water and concentrated on the silky glide of the washcloth over his water-slick flesh.

His movements caused the water to lap at his nipples, and they hardened slightly. A corresponding tightening in his groin made him relax a little.

Leaning his head back against the wooden rim of the tub, he surveyed the room through half-shut eyes. Jenny damned sure knew how to set the scene. Though the curtains were drawn against the afternoon sun, leaving the room in shadows, the windows were open behind them. Every so often, a breeze billowed the ruffled fabric hanging there and disturbed the scented candle that flickered on the nightstand.

With careful expertise, Jenny had made herself a part of the scene she had created, with her hair piled high on her head, tiny tendrils escaping to caress her face. That gorgeous body of hers was completely covered by a wrapper of such fine material that it left absolutely no doubt in the viewer's mind that there was nothing underneath but the widow herself.

"How long's it been since you had a woman, Jeb?" Jenny kept her voice slow and lazy. She'd learned long ago that she could bring some cowboys to the very edge of release just by talking to them—and she knew exactly how to work them up to that point. In that way, she kept the physical part of it, her part, to a minimum. Doing so had never been as important with a man like Jeb Welles, for she'd never minded him thrusting into her, had even taken her own release in the act. She did so now because the pattern had become a habit with her, and because she could not dispel her memories of the way Daniel had looked at her only a few hours ago.

Jeb closed his eyes, savoring the warmth of the water and Jenny's voice. And her hand. He almost groaned at the sensations she was inducing. He'd been right to come to Jenny. "Too long," he answered at last, "but it's hard to find a woman like you in the desert, sweetheart."

"Oh, I don't know," she whispered, leaning just a bit closer so that the soft lace on her wrapper tickled Jeb's ear. "Maybe with a tub of hot water and a candle, just about any woman would do."

Jeb opened his eyes to a narrow slit and turned his head slightly. With no effort at all, his mouth closed over the fabric-covered tip of Jenny's breast.

She gave a little sigh, wanting to find the pure pleasure her body had found before with this man. God help her if she ever let regret for Daniel Hastings rob her of everything else in life. Beyond a doubt, she knew her feelings for him could destroy her if she wasn't careful.

Determinedly, she let her hand travel over Jeb's body. Warm flesh stretched taut and lean over his ribs and belly; taut, too, over the man part of him. To her own surprise, Jenny felt a sudden, hot moisture between her legs. How long had it been since she had been ready before she was barely touched? She realized that she couldn't even remember the last time. Maybe not since the last time Jeb had ridden into town, full of life and laughter.

"I heard you rode in with a woman." Jenny was sure of herself now, made confident by Jeb's reaction to her. She pulled gently at the hair vee'd along his belly. "Couldn't she do what I'm doing?"

Jeb grew very still. "No." He didn't want to think about Hannah, and he damned sure didn't want to talk about her. To his dismay, he felt his hot desire for Jenny fading.

Jenny heard the closed door in his voice and was intrigued by it. "I heard she's a real beauty. Some of my dinner guests even talked about taking a closer look at her."

"Sonuvabitch!" With one movement, Jeb rose out of the water.

Too late, Jenny realized her mistake. Despite the fact that he was here with her, the woman meant something to Jeb.

"Honey, I'm sorry. I'm sure they won't bother with her if she doesn't want anything to do with them. There's not a bad one in the bunch." Jenny closed her eyes briefly, feeling the tingle throughout her body, knowing there would be no release for her with this man. Not today.

Jeb toweled himself dry with rough strokes, thinking of Hannah approached by strange men. Even if they were as harmless as Jenny implied, Hannah would be terrified. She had a right to be, for God's sake; she'd been raped by men who were little better than animals. And he had left her alone! Feelings of guilt swamped him.

He looked up to see Jenny's eyes fixed on the proof that his ardor had died.

"Why did you come here?" she asked curiously, hiding her own disappointment.

Jeb grabbed for his pants and hesitated over his answer. Jenny had been good to him, and he owed her something—for the frustration he sensed he was leaving her with if for nothing else. He pulled his pants to his waist and sighed, reaching for his shirt. "Because I don't want to keep wanting what I know I can't have."

Jenny gave a throaty laugh and shook her head. "What woman do you imagine wouldn't want you?"

Jeb's fingers made quick work of fastening his shirt and pants. "You don't know Hannah."

"You're trying to convince me you couldn't seduce her?"

Jeb stopped all movement and simply looked at her, but in his mind, he saw Hannah. Prickly, defenseless, innocent termagant. "Yeah," he said finally. "Maybe I could. But if I succeeded, it would destroy her." He shook his head. "You don't know Hannah. She's—different."

He touched Jenny's cheek, seeing her beauty but not seeing it, his mind still focused on the redhead who was surely going to drive him crazy. Discreetly, he placed several bills on the chair where the candle still flickered.

Jenny stared at them for a long moment and started to protest payment for services that had not been rendered. Then her mouth snapped shut as she looked around her. Jeb was already gone.

Different, he had said of the other woman. Different from what? From her? From a woman who whored for money? She squeezed her eyes against a hot flood of tears. She would not feel sorry for herself. She would not.

Across the street from the widow's restaurant, Daniel watched the front door open. As he suspected, it was Jeb Welles who stepped through the door. He watched as the younger man settled his worn hat firmly on his head. Before Daniel had time to feel the jealousy choking his throat, he realized that Welles didn't have the look of a satisfied man. If anything, he looked harassed.

Daniel's eyes narrowed. Harassed?

For a moment, Daniel considered walking on, continuing his rounds. That, he'd told himself, was what he'd been doing for the past few hours. Simply business as usual, keeping an eye on things the way he did every day of every week. Being a single man, he rarely even took Sunday completely off, strolling the boarded walks of the streets after church services ended at midday.

Somehow, though, on this particular afternoon, he'd found himself on the west end of town more often than not. On Jenny's end of town, in front of Jenny's restaurant, propped up against a post, watching Jenny's door. Suspecting she was with a man. Suspecting and needing to know and needing not to know. Well, now he knew. She *had* been with a man. Her choice instead of a buggy ride with Daniel, who had only honorable intentions toward her.

Maybe that was what he was doing wrong. Maybe if he changed his tactics to dishonorable, he'd have a chance. He thought of how she might look now after spending hours alone with a man just off the trail, a man who had been frustrated by days with another woman—a woman he couldn't touch. A preacher's wife.

Daniel felt a little ill at the image that came to mind. Jenny, naked on her bed, sprawled and waiting; then her beautiful body slick with sweat from another man's lovemaking, another man's seed.

The sick feeling grew. What if Welles had been rough? What if she had protested? Daniel's fists clenched; then he forced them to relax as he recalled the clear, honest gaze of the man when they'd shared a whiskey. No, if the preacher's wife had been safe when she wouldn't have Welles, then Jenny had been safe when she would.

Still, Daniel felt almost overwhelmed by his desire to see her, to be sure that she was all right. He started forward, then stopped abruptly. Jenny's choice had made her feelings clear. A man could take only so much rejection.

A curtain billowed gently from a second-story window. Her bedroom? Daniel's mouth set. A man could take only so much of *anything!*

He straightened his vest and stepped down into the loose dirt of the street.

Halfway across, he stopped in his tracks when the front door opened again and Jenny emerged. She didn't see him as she slowly crossed the wide porch to the wooden swing that hung from the ceiling. That end of the porch was almost entirely enclosed by the coolness of leafy vines. In the early mornings, a profusion of morning glories bloomed there. Many was the sunrise when Daniel carried his first coffee of the day to stand across from this house and just look his fill. And wish.

For a long moment, Daniel stood frozen in indecision. The sad droop of her shoulders made him ache to hold her, to murmur love words against her forehead and press his lips to the soft, smooth flesh there. Reality held him rooted to the spot. She hadn't wanted his attentions before—had turned from them to those of a cowboy with the dust of the trail still clinging to his clothes. What made him think she would want them now? Whatever had made her sad had nothing to do with him, no matter how much he wished that wasn't so.

Daniel turned away, telling himself it was the last time he would go mooning after the woman. It was past time he got on with his life, past time he settled down. He wasn't old, but the years were passing with slow inevitability. He wanted a wife and a real home. There were plenty of other women in town who would welcome his interest. Maybe, even, the beautiful redhead who had ridden in with Jeb Welles. After all, she was a widow, alone in the world.

Daniel just wished he thought she was half as beautiful as a certain woman with glossy brown hair.

Jeb's anger grew with every step. Anger and something else, something he didn't want to define. He'd teach those trail-horny cow-punchers to bother a decent woman. *But what if he was too late?* They wouldn't forget in a hurry to keep to the saloons and bar girls. *What good did that do Hannah if they'd already been around bothering her?*

A woman in a bright cotton gown and bonnet stepped out of the mercantile into his path. With no hesitation in stride, Jeb circled her. Three men sauntered out of the saloon. Jeb pushed his way through them.

His steps quickened almost to a run as he turned up the path to Armen's Boarding House.

Without pausing to knock, he shoved the front door wide and paused just inside the spacious hall to allow his pupils time to adjust from brilliant sunshine to near shadow.

When he could see, he ran up the stairs and knocked on the door to the room Mr. Armen had given her. No answer. He pounded. "Hannah!"

Behind him, he heard a door click open just as he twisted the knob. It gave, and he pushed the door wide enough to put his head into the room.

"We do not allow our young female guests to have visitors in their rooms."

Jeb wheeled around to face a woman whose severe style of dress and hair belied the youth of her face. "Who are you?" he asked brusquely, more than a little put off by the heavy dark cloth of her gown.

"Amanda Armen."

"Armen's daughter?" Maybe she knew where Hannah was.

Her expression turned haughty. "I am Jacob Armen's wife."

Jeb abandoned the conversation. His only concern was for Hannah. "Where is she? Where's Hannah?"

"Mrs. Barnes is in the parlor. With gentlemen guests."

For some reason, the young woman appeared to take a perverse pleasure in the pronouncement.

"Shit!"

Jeb didn't hear the censorious comment that followed. He was halfway down the stairs.

The murmur of voices drew him unerringly to a set of wide, double doors that stood open, perhaps in an attempt to channel a breeze from the many windows in the room through the rest of the house.

Jeb froze in the doorway for one instant, willing his heart rate to slow as the fact that Hannah was unharmed registered with him. In the next instant, all the fear he had carried with him burned into rage.

"What in hell is going on?"

The teacup in Hannah's hand clattered to her saucer. Eyes very wide and brilliantly blue, she stared at Jeb in surprise. "Jeb!" She blushed. "Mr. Welles."

By now, Jeb's narrowed glance had taken in the entire scene. Hannah, looking dismayingly beautiful in her drab gown, was perched on a narrow settee. Seated in a far corner of the room was Mr. Armen, with a peculiarly satisfied look on his face. Scattered about the room were four other men, one little more than a boy in his late teens, two others somewhere near Jeb's age, and the last old enough to be Jeb's father. They all had one thing in common. Every last son of a bitch was looking at Hannah as if she were a tempting slice of apple pie waiting for them to sink their teeth into.

Somehow, Jeb felt sure, this was Hannah's fault: His fear for her safety; his haste in leaving a woman who was warm and willing;

his jealousy. His damned jealousy! An urge to punish her stung him. He stepped forward, propping one shoulder against the door frame just inside the room.

"Well, now, Hannah," he heard himself drawl, "I reckon after the past three days on the trail with me, you can go on calling me Jeb."

It took Hannah a moment to realize what he'd done. She watched as the expressions on the men's faces changed subtly. The interest was still there, but there was something else as well—a sort of speculation about just what Jeb's familiarity implied.

Very slowly, all of the color faded from her face, then rushed back. She wasn't sure why Jeb had wanted to insult her, but there was no doubt in her mind he'd done so quite intentionally. And quite effectively. Though she wanted to run from the room, she lifted her chin instead. "Thank you," was all she replied, as if Jeb had just conferred some great honor on her.

Jeb would rather have been slapped. As he looked around the room at the men who were still looking at Hannah and realized the damage he'd done to her reputation, he felt like cursing a blue streak. He'd considered only the effect of his insult on Hannah, not on her audience. Even old Jacob was looking at her with something akin to condemnation—and interest. Fixing him with a glare, Jeb realized with a burst of irritation that Armen wasn't quite as elderly as Jeb had taken him for. His hair was certainly silver, but in the clear light coming through the parlor window, his lack of wrinkles suggested that it was a premature condition.

Amanda Armen chose that moment to sweep past Jeb into the parlor, crossing to stand beside her husband's chair. The interest on the man's face faded with her arrival. Critically, Jeb decided the woman wouldn't be half bad-looking if her hair escaped its tight confines in little wisps the way Hannah's did. Then maybe Armen's attention would remain with her, where it belonged.

While Hannah sat watching Jeb with the quiet dignity of a wounded doe, he searched his mind for a way to salvage a bad situation. *Aw, hell.*

He looked at the boarding house owner. "Sherman does have a church, doesn't it?" He didn't wait for the man's nod. "Hannah lost her husband just a few days ago. I promised her the comfort of a real preacher as soon as possible."

Hannah looked at Jeb as if he was crazy. Jeb ignored her. He didn't have the slightest idea if being a grieving widow would lend some sort of respectability to the fact that Hannah had been alone with a man not her husband for the past few days. Judging by Mrs. Armen's reluctant look of sympathy, he had hopes that it did.

Jacob Armen cleared his throat. "Sherman is quite civilized, Mr. Welles. Actually, we have more than one church. Which religious persuasion do you prefer?"

Jeb looked at Hannah. He was damned if he even knew.

"My father and my husband were Baptist ministers," Hannah said quietly. She was now so thoroughly confused by Jeb's behavior, she wasn't sure what to think. Or to say.

"Warren Salters is our Baptist minister," Armen replied with the faintest of frowns.

Jeb took it the Armens were not Baptist. "Where could we find Reverend Salters?"

"His church is at the east end of town. He has a room in the back." The tone indicated that the proprietor of Armen's Boarding House felt some chagrin that the reverend did not choose to make his residence there.

Good, a bachelor. All Jeb said, however, was, "Thank you," as he crossed the room to stand before Hannah. He glared at the youth who had managed to sit closest to her until that poor unfortunate burned a dark red and jerked his gaze from Jeb's. Satisfied, Jeb turned to Hannah and extended his hand. "Hannah?"

Gracefully, Hannah placed her cup and saucer on the small table before her. She would have much preferred flinging it in Jeb's face.

Her eyes were telling him just that as she placed one hand lightly in his and murmured her thanks.

For his part, now that he'd made what amends he could, Jeb was rather enjoying the flashes of fire coming from her light blue eyes. Her heightened color reminded him of a woman flushed with lovemaking. He wondered what Hannah would be like if she ever really lost her temper—or gave herself to the passion of a man. The thought gave him the immediate reaction Jenny had worked so hard to gain earlier.

He was relieved when they were safely out on the street away from the eyes of those other men. They had watched him steal her away with a great deal of indignation in their expressions. Jeb didn't care one whit about their chagrin, but it wouldn't do to let them catch sight of the evidence of his desire. He suspected he'd done more than enough harm already.

He guided her in the direction of the church. "I guess you're not real happy with me."

Hannah flashed him another look of smouldering anger. "If my faith were as strong as David's, I'd be searching for a slingshot."

Jeb considered that in uncomfortable silence. Maybe he deserved to be likened unto Goliath, but his mental image of the giant had always been of a dark and uncommonly ugly man. Was that how Hannah thought of him?

The next moment, he reminded himself that it didn't matter. With any luck, Warren Salters would be overcome by an immediate affection for a woman so clearly suited to be a minister's wife. In any case, come morning he and Hannah would be well rid of each other, and she could think whatever she wanted of him.

And once he was gone from here, Jeb told himself, he wouldn't give her another thought as long as he lived.

Chapter Seventeen

A low stone fence separated the churchyard from the street. Jeb took Hannah's arm as he guided her through the gateless opening and along the worn dirt path. The path forked just in front of the solidly closed door, and Jeb took the side path that led around to the back. He recalled Jacob Armen's statement that the Baptist minister lived in a room behind the church.

Hannah stared at the neat, white building and tried to imagine what her life would have been like had Caleb pastored a church such as this one. Afternoon teas and box luncheons. Friends who would come to call, sharing needlework and conversation. But Caleb had thought town preachers a tame lot, wasting the calling that God had given them. A man of God, Caleb had often said, should be about God's business of finding the lost and bringing them in, not nurse-maiding a church full of folk already saved. Nor would he ever have tolerated Hannah's hours being so idle that they allowed time for socializing of even the highest nature.

Hannah sighed deeply.

Hearing, Jeb scowled. "It looks like a fine church to me."

"Oh, it is," she said hastily. "It's . . . beautiful." And she truly thought that despite the plain leaded windows and boxlike appearance of the building. Church and grounds both were beautiful because they were so evidently cared for.

Turning a corner, they stumbled onto the Reverend Salters. Almost literally. He was on his knees in a flower bed.

With a good deal of aplomb, the reverend gained his feet and tossed his spade aside. "Welcome," he said warmly.

For a long moment, Jeb studied him critically, from his neat if dirt-stained garments to his round face and kind eyes. He was of medium stature and strong-looking, though not brawny. Jeb thought he looked a little young to be a pastor. He tried to determine if a woman would consider his features handsome and decided with some satisfaction that the reverend was presentable but hardly dashing. Somehow, Jeb didn't quite want Hannah swept off her feet by Reverend Salters. He just wanted her to marry the man.

Refusing to examine the reason behind his feelings, Jeb thrust out his hand. "Reverend Salters? Jeb Welles."

Warren Salters took his hand in a firm grasp. "Mr. Welles." He smiled pleasantly at Hannah. "Mrs. Welles."

Hannah blushed profusely at the mistake.

"No," Jeb said, startled, then realized he'd spoken much too forcefully. "No, Mrs. Barnes is a recent widow. Her husband was a Baptist minister," he added meaningfully. "That's why I brought her here to you. I'm hopeful that in Sherman, she can find a new life for herself. A family."

Reverend Salters blushed more darkly than Hannah had at his own mistake. And at Jeb's meaningful look.

With gritted teeth, Hannah endured the reverend's condolences, then turned her back on the two men as Jeb began to explain her circumstances more fully. Too fully, to her way of thinking. If it had been possible, she would have put miles between herself and the two of them instead of only a few feet. How *could* Jeb discuss things that were so personal to her with a complete stranger!

She wished the ground would open up and swallow her. Considering the fact that she was standing almost in a cemetery, the idea didn't seem all that farfetched. All around her sunlight dappled the grave markers, some of stone, others of time-silvered wood. With the grass neatly clipped and flowers blooming at every turn, the small fenced enclosure appeared a place of serenity.

Hannah, however, felt anything but serene. She turned back to steal a glance at the young man deep in conversation with Jeb. They were discussing her as if she were a lost puppy. In desperation, she sent another totally ignored glare Jeb's way. There might have been a time in her life when she was angrier, but she didn't think she had ever felt quite so humiliated. And still Jeb continued to talk about her as if she didn't have sense enough to speak for herself.

Maybe that was the way he felt. After mortifying her at the boarding house and dragging her half-way across town, Jeb had stood her in front of the Reverend Salters and all but asked the man to marry her! Clearly, he couldn't wait to be rid of the responsibility for her well-being. She hadn't been *that* much trouble to him. Had she?

Overhead, a squirrel barked furiously. In his indignation at the presence of humans so close to his territory, he shook the very branch of the tree he was perched upon. A leaf, curling brown at its edges, drifted to rest by the toe of her shoe. When Jeb continued to ignore her fulminating looks, Hannah fixed her gaze upward, trying to concentrate all of her attention on the squirrel's pluming tail. It wasn't possible. She could hear every word spoken as Jeb explained Caleb's death and Hannah's dire straits.

Warren Salters cleared his throat for perhaps the fifth time. "I am vitally concerned with the well-being of all my church members. And, uh, Mrs. Barnes will, of course, make a welcome addition to our congregation."

Hannah turned to face them. The young minister's face was the same red color it had been since Jeb had introduced her as a widow in need. She considered telling both men she never had any intention of going to church again or that she had come under conviction to join a Presbyterian church.

Before she could open her mouth to make either remark, the Reverend Salters spoke directly to her for the first time since their introduction. "Where was your husband's ministry, Mrs. Barnes?"

Ministry? Hannah supposed Caleb would have called it that. She conceded she had too, at one time. Now his tactics seemed more like bullying. The realization startled her, and she licked her lips nervously. Caleb, a man of God, a bully? How long had she felt that way?

"Mrs. Barnes?" Though he retained enough wits to prompt her to answer his question, Warren Salters was fascinated with the glimpse of tongue as it escaped her lips long enough to dampen them. He stared at her mouth.

If Hannah had not been blushing before, she was now. Why was he staring at her? The possibility that he could discern her less-than-respectful thoughts about a husband who had been buried just days earlier shamed her. "On the Brazos, near the reservation," she said at last. "Caleb . . . Reverend Barnes was teaching salvation to the Indians there."

"A godly calling indeed," the reverend agreed with a nod. A thought struck him. That was more than a day's ride from here. He glanced from the fragile-looking woman to the hardened ex-ranger standing beside her. She had been in this man's company overnight? Maybe for more than one night?

Hannah saw the look in his eyes. He was looking at her the same way the men in the boarding house had when Jeb had spoken so familiarly to her. Somehow he had seen through to her real feelings. She *hadn't* loved Caleb, it was true. Not the way God intended a wife to love a husband. She had respected him; surely that meant something. Still, if she was honest, Hannah knew she had lost even that in the days since Jeb had buried him. Her heart squeezed painfully. Jeb had been the one to show her what should be respected in a man.

No wonder the Reverend Salters was looking at her with such condemnation in his eyes.

Jeb frowned and moved to place a hand under Hannah's elbow. Like Hannah, he hadn't missed the change in the other man's expression. Unlike Hannah, he didn't mistake the cause.

"Mrs. Barnes, I think you should sit down," he said in concerned tones. Ignoring Hannah's amazement at the suggestion, he glanced at the Reverend Salters. "Perhaps you have something cool to drink? Mrs. Barnes has very recently suffered a miscarriage as well as the loss of her husband."

The look on the young minister's face cleared to one of genuine concern. "Of course. Please follow me inside." Certainly no woman who had recently been through the throes of birth, even stillbirth, would be capable of indulging in illicit behavior. His unfounded suspicions shamed him.

Hannah shook with added fury. If Jeb revealed one more intimate detail about her, she was going to scream!

The reverend took Hannah's free arm solicitously in his, feeling her delicate trembling to the very soles of his shoes. To his pleased relief, Jeb Welles immediately loosened his own hold. Thank God, there appeared not the slightest suggestion of intimacy between the two. Warren Salters could not in good faith have taken a fallen woman under his wing. It would be one thing, if he had the presence of a wife to shield him from the inevitable gossip. As it was, a young, unmarried minister was always at risk. Gossip could take his pulpit from him. It had happened to others, and it could happen to him. This had been pointed out to him and to the other students in seminary several times over.

He patted the slender hand resting quietly on his arm and enjoyed the soft warmth of the touch. When he'd first seen her walking up with the rough-looking man, he'd thought the woman entirely too beautiful for a man's good.

Now, after a few minutes in her presence, that beauty did not seem so disturbing as he realized that it was coupled with a modest demeanor and a disinclination to chatter. He'd often felt women should be silent when men conversed. Unfortunately, he'd seen few instances of that in his own congregation.

Only when he had finally directed a question her way had she spoken. He'd found her hesitancy in answering very refreshing and her voice coolly melodious. He could hear it lifted in songs of praise, even now. Mrs. Barnes must have been ideal as a minister's wife. Ideal. With great care, he kept his gaze from falling to the well-defined bodice of her dress.

Jeb saw the admiration in the minister's eyes and cynically defined it as lust in disguise. Lust was what any man must feel when he looked at Hannah. That is, until he came to know how infuriatingly troublesome she could be. Jeb reminded himself he would be well rid of her.

This was best for Hannah, too. In a few years, her children would fill up the front pew, a half dozen pair or more of blue eyes watching their father preach the Sunday sermon to his duly attentive flock. Jeb could almost see them now, blue-eyed and red-haired like their mother, lined up beside her. The image gave him a funny feeling in the pit of his stomach, but with hard determination, he shook it away. Ignoring a faint feeling of unease between his shoulder blades, he followed Hannah and the preacher into the church.

Warren Salters was too aware of the proprieties to take the young widow into the room that held his narrow bed and personal belongings. Instead, he seated her in the vestibule and rushed away to fetch a dipper of cool water from the well.

"What possessed you to—"

Hannah found her furious question silenced by Jeb's finger pressed to her lips. She felt a ridiculous urge to run her tongue along the callused length of it. Instead, she opened her mouth and bit.

"Shit," Jeb yelped, putting the wounded finger to his mouth and sucking. Unexpected heat hit his loins as he tasted the dampness from her tongue and lips.

Hastily, he dropped his hand to his side. "I ought to beat the living daylights out of you," he growled, dismayed that he would react so strongly with such little provocation.

Hannah smiled sweetly.

Jeb stared. When had he realized she was beautiful? How could he not have realized it sooner? And where the hell was the irritation he could always muster when he knew he found her desirable?

The next instant, a feeling of pride struck him as he realized something else. Hannah hadn't shrunk from him when he growled at her. The old Hannah would have. He'd taught her that much anyway. Certain parts of his body wished he could have taught her more.

He heard the reverend returning up the front steps of the church. "Hannah—" He stopped. What the hell could he say? He was leaving, and she was staying. That was the way it had to be and it was best just to leave it at that.

Reverend Salters beamed as he proffered the dipper to Hannah, who took it gratefully. She might not have felt weak-kneed when Jeb was pretending it for the preacher's sake, but she certainly did now. There was something about the look on Jeb's face. . . .

The next moment, she thought she was surely mistaken, for he was chatting genially with the Baptist minister as if there were nothing on his mind but seeing her well and truly taken off his hands.

He thanked Reverend Salters for his time and helped Hannah to her feet. She handed the empty dipper back to the preacher with a polite smile.

"I'll take you back to the boarding house," Jeb told Hannah. "You can rest for another hour or so before I come by to take you to supper."

When the reverend cleared his throat, Hannah decided that she could learn to detest that sound before long.

He looked at Jeb seriously. "Although your protection of Mrs. Barnes is only commendable, I think perhaps it would be best for your association with her to discontinue now."

"What the—" Jeb bit off the curse. He was in church after all. "What do you mean?" he asked ominously.

The reverend held up one hand in a gesture of good will. "Please understand. I mean you no insult. However, as her minister, I must be careful of Mrs. Barnes's reputation. It is imperative that she be accepted by the good women of my congregation."

"You mean the old biddies would tear her to shreds given half a chance," Jeb clarified crudely.

The reverend frowned faintly, but refused to back down. Nor did he deny Jeb's accusation. "I think you have Mrs. Barnes's best interests at heart, do you not?"

Reluctantly, Jeb nodded. All too easily, he could see Hannah in the churchyard, standing apart from a bunch of busybody old women, whispering and pointing in her direction. No, he didn't want that for Hannah; and yes, he could see it happening. He'd grown up in a small town that was much like this one. It had been filled with good people who didn't understand anything or anyone who deviated from the rules of behavior they had laid out for themselves.

When Hannah opened her mouth to protest, Jeb silenced her. "No, Hannah. He's right. You're a fine woman, and I don't want folks around here to think of you any other way." His mouth twisted as he stared into her blue eyes. How could he have ever thought that pale shade unattractive? "Maybe Reverend Salters could walk you back to Armen's."

"Of course," the other man inserted, pleased

at the direction Mr. Welles had taken. "And I'll arrange for you to have supper with some of our congregation. Mrs. Graham will be just the one."

Hannah wondered if she was going to have any more say in the direction of her life now than she had for the past few years with Caleb and the past few days with Jeb. She sighed and set her lips against any protest. If this was what Jeb wanted to see happen, she'd do it. She owed him something. Later, when he was gone for good, she'd decide what she wanted to do with her life. When he was gone for good. The phrase had a distinctly bleak sound.

With quiet dignity, she held out her hand to him. "I don't suppose I'll ever see you again. New Mexico is a long way from here." Her voice faltered a moment, but then she went on. "I want you to know how much I appreciate everything you've done for me."

For the first time, Jeb thought he heard a husky quality to her voice. A knife twisted in his gut. He fought the urge to take her in his arms and took her hand instead. "If you ever need anything . . ." What? In a few days, he would be too far away to do her any good. And he'd be out in the middle of nowhere, tracking two good-for-nothing killers. "Just remember the name Slade in Taos. If you ever need anything, send word to him and use my name."

Reverend Salters decided he did not care for the personal tone of the other man's comments.

"I'm sure Mrs. Barnes will find everything she needs here in Sherman."

"Then she'll never have to call on Slade," Jeb said evenly, releasing Hannah's hand abruptly. No use undoing everything he'd worked on to get her accepted here.

Still, he couldn't resist touching his knuckle gently, briefly to her chin. "'Bye, Hannah."

He barely heard her say good-bye as he walked out of the church. He didn't turn around.

Chapter Eighteen

One man cursed, and another triumphantly dragged a pile of coins to his side of the table. Jeb hesitated for one taut moment with his whiskey halfway to his mouth, then relaxed and drank when the cards were dealt again. A man never knew when a friendly game of poker would erupt into tempers and gunfire. The three winning and losing money by turn had already displayed a volatile mood. One thing Jeb figured he didn't need was to become embroiled in a barroom clash over a winning hand. Or maybe that was just what he needed.

Hell, who knew what he needed.

"Hi, cowboy." A light touch drifted across his collar.

The soft voice belonged to the prettiest girl

working the bar. The prettiest, youngest, and cleanest. His senses had honed in on her when he walked through the door earlier, but he hadn't given her any encouragement. Maybe *she* was what he needed. He sure as hell didn't have nerve enough to go back and start over with Jenny.

Jeb knew what the girl was asking by her greeting. He returned her smile and said, "What the hell." When he held out an arm to her, she obligingly settled on his lap. Any extra wriggling she did was subtle and pleasurable.

As Jeb pulled her warmth close against his ribs, he felt the soft crush of her hips against the front of his pants and the heavy weight of her breasts against his forearm. He hardened at once.

"That feels good." She sighed as she pushed against him.

Jeb chuckled. "I haven't done anything yet."

"Mmmmm. You've done more than you know," she said obliquely, eyeing the three men playing poker. The one whose coarse black beard brushed his collar had already slapped her roughly on the bottom; his friend with the fierce eyebrows had pinched her nipple hard. A protest had merely served to increase their attempts to torment her. Some of the girls here liked the rough stuff. She didn't.

From the minute he'd walked in here an hour ago, she'd had her eye on this one. Maybe the ugly customers paid better sometimes, because they were so grateful for even a pretense of affection from a woman, but she was new enough at this to still prefer the good-looking ones. Especially when they treated her like the lady she wanted to be someday. The lady she was *going* to be.

"My name's Coral," she murmured, fingernails caressing the cloth of his sleeve with a light touch.

Occasionally, one slender finger would slide beneath the cuff, touching the flesh along his wrist. Jeb closed his eyes, concentrating on the delicate touch and the images the girl intended to bring to mind. She was good. Real good.

"What's your real name, honey?"

One sharp fingernail traced a slow path from Jeb's wrist to the inside of his hand, pressing deep into his palm. "You don't like the name Coral?" Her voice held a teasing quality but no pout.

Jeb made a grab for the hand that had begun a wandering exploration of his pants. The light in the barroom might be dim and none of the other customers paying them the least attention, but Jeb had never cared to make a public exhibition of his lovemaking. He didn't plan to start now.

He forgot his question about her name and stood up, steadying the girl on her feet in front of him. "Where's your room, honey?"

Coral glanced up at him over her shoulder, her smile reflecting her satisfaction at the question. "Over there." She gestured to a door near the long bar.

Jeb raised his brows at the unusual arrangement, and she shrugged. "If any of the—men get too rowdy, we can call for help. Hirsch, the bartender, kind of takes care of us. We're all crazy about him."

Looking at the bartender's beefy arms, Jeb decided the girls working here were well looked after. "You won't need him tonight, honey."

Coral almost purred. "I never expected I would."

She took his hand and sauntered toward the door. They were almost there when another girl stepped into their path. She looked Jeb up and down and evidently liked what she saw. She smiled and licked her lips.

Jeb revised his initial opinion of her age after a closer look. Though still attractive, she was well past girlhood. Upswept hair pulled most of the lines from her face, but couldn't disguise the finer ones along her neck. Wide brown eyes, edged with dark color, held age-old knowledge.

Flicking a glance at Coral, she focused her attention on Jeb. "Might want to change your mind, cowboy. I've forgotten more than little Coral's learned yet."

Jeb didn't doubt it, but all he did was smile.

"Go to hell, Jericho," Coral said in good-natured tones, then lifted her voice sightly, "Hirsch!" The bartender looked up from wiping the scarred surface of the bar. "Get her out of here."

He grinned good-naturedly. "Come on, Jericho. Be a good girl. We'll find you a customer."

"One like him?" Jericho queried, her hungry gaze still fixed on Jeb.

Embarrassingly, her glance dropped from his face to below his belt. Jeb sent his own prodding look toward Hirsch.

When Jericho showed no signs of budging, the barkeep sighed and stepped from around the bar. Jeb tensed, but all the big man did was take her arm and lead her, unresisting, to a seat at the bar.

Coral patted Jeb's arm. "It's all right. She does that all the time. She gets plenty of customers, but she always wants mine, too. No one else's—just mine."

Jeb chanced one last look at the woman. Her gaze had transferred itself to Hirsch and held something akin to adoration. Everybody, it seemed, loved Hirsch.

Pulling Coral's warm body a little closer, Jeb smiled down at her. He could see her better here in the light from behind the bar.

Her eyes were blue. *Damn.*

Hannah waited patiently in the dress she had done her best to clean and freshen. Though it had survived its journey tied to Jeb's packhorse, it didn't look in much better condition than the one she'd worn. There wasn't a great deal Hannah could do about the fact, however. The two were all she had.

Her feet dangled from the single chair the room boasted as she considered her options. She did not, she realized, wish to dine with Mrs. Graham, whoever that woman might be. Nor did she care to spend an entire evening in the company of Warren Salters, no matter how good and pleasant a man he was. But that was exactly what Jeb expected of her. In fact, Hannah felt certain, Jeb expected her to spend the rest of her life with the reverend. Or someone like him.

Well, she couldn't deny she owed Jeb Welles a great deal—but not the rest of her life. She squared her shoulders. She might well decide never to marry again. A bit of the starch left her back just as quickly as it had come. If only she could figure out how to take care of herself when she had not a dime to her name.

A knock on the door brought her leaping to her feet, heart pounding, half in guilt for her less-than-eager thoughts about the minister, half in hopes that it would be Jeb standing there when she opened the door.

"You have a guest." Amanda Armen's voice seemed always to hold a touch of censure when she spoke to Hannah.

The guilt faded, leaving nothing but anticipation. "I'll be right down," Hannah called. She made no further move to open the door. Mrs. Armen made her feel less than comfortable and far less than welcome. Maybe tomorrow she would move to Mr. Kipfer's boarding house. Jeb would be furious at the idea, but then Jeb wouldn't be here to know.

"I'll tell Mrs. Graham to expect you shortly then."

The anticipation fell away, leaving Hannah feeling flat and drained. Studying her too-thin face in the mirror, she told herself it was for the best that Jeb would be gone come morning. Then she wouldn't be hoping to see him around every corner.

Hoping? Hannah met her own blue gaze in dismay. Maybe it was a good thing she wouldn't be spending any more time with that man. Clearly she had become much too dependent upon him. She wasn't a homeless waif after all. "Just homeless," she told her image.

Taking a deep breath, she went down to meet Mrs. Graham.

Yolanda Graham was prepared to pass judgment. After all, she had seen for herself the arrogantly good-looking man this young woman had been alone with since the death of her poor husband. Warren Salters had pointed the man out to her, a rough-and-rugged sort swaggering into the saloon. Of course, Reverend Salters had been entirely sympathetic toward the recent widow, but then he was quite gullible. Good, but gullible.

Yolanda had no fears for herself on *that* score. Hers, she flattered herself, had always been a discerning character. One look at this young miss, and Yolanda had no doubt she would know exactly how to put Mrs. Barnes in her place.

As it turned out, one look at Hannah changed her mind. No man as virile as Mr. Welles appeared to be—at least from a distance—would take more than a casual glance at the pale girl poised in the doorway. There wasn't a drop of color to her cheeks. The only thing about her that didn't appear washed out was her hair, but that too-bright color was properly confined in a severe knot. And she looked properly miserable.

"My dear child," Yolanda cooed, rising gracefully to her feet, "our little town is so pleased to welcome you." There was no doubt in her mind that this *was* Hannah Barnes. After all, Yolanda knew everyone in town.

She noticed with satisfaction that Hannah's gaze did not so much as stray to the two gentlemen seated beyond Yolanda, although both jumped eagerly to their feet when Hannah stepped into the room.

"Mrs. Graham," Hannah murmured a greeting, shrinking just slightly as the woman decided her worthy of a welcoming hug.

"Yolanda, dear girl, call me Yolanda. Reverend Salters did not do you justice." Actually, Yolanda thought he had been a little too generous in calling the girl attractive. She was thin rather than slender, and her womanly attributes, what she had of them, were well disguised by the drab sack she wore. True, her features were quite pleasing but altogether unremarkable. Well, except perhaps those eyes. They were quite the oddest shade of silvery blue. On the whole, however, there was nothing distinctive about the girl.

Content with her own claim to beauty, Yolanda was more than happy to take this little sparrow under her wing.

Hannah felt a bit overwhelmed. She had expected a matron with graying hair and pursed lips. This woman had vibrant, dark hair and lips that looked more used to pouting than to pursing. Handsome rather than pretty, she bore an air of command.

"Come along, then. Mr. Graham and Reverend Salters are waiting for us in the restaurant at the hotel."

With a feeling of going to her doom, Hannah followed the woman out into the street.

Dusk was falling, and one by one lights began to appear in the houses along the street. Merchants and businessmen stepped out of their shops, locking doors and hanging signs to indicate they had closed for the evening and were going home to their suppers.

Hannah breathed deeply of the heavy summer air. Somewhere nearby roses grew. "I haven't been in such a pretty town for a long time."

Yolanda glanced about with a far more critical eye. "Well," she conceded grudgingly, "it's a nice enough place, I suppose, but some of these buildings could definitely use sprucing up a bit."

Hannah thought of the places she and Caleb had called home and said nothing.

Better and better, Yolanda thought as Hannah yielded to her opinion. Not an argumentative type of girl. Perhaps Reverend Salters's interest in her wasn't a bad thing, after all. He had to marry sometime, and from time to time a bachelor preacher did present problems for a congregation. If Yolanda were going to be forced to yield her place as leading matron of the congregation, she would rather it be to someone she could bend to her will. Hannah Barnes seemed bendable enough, and Yolanda felt up to that task.

With her chin lifted for whatever battles were to come, she shepherded Hannah into the lobby of the hotel.

Hours, I've been trapped here for hours. Hannah sighed as the first course of soup was removed from the table.

Warren Salters had definitely grown in stature and appeal in Hannah's eyes as he deftly parried Yolanda Graham's determined questions while the woman's dignified husband looked on with an air of detachment. Hannah felt sure Mr. Graham had many opportunities to perfect the art of distancing himself from his wife's inquisitions. Yolanda was too skilled not to have had frequent practice.

The woman peered her disapproval at Hannah's dress from over her wine glass. "You must have left in quite a hurry."

Hannah looked at her blankly. "I beg your pardon?"

"Well," she said vaguely, "you must not have had time to gather your . . . nicer gowns."

Warren cleared his throat softly. "Now, Yolanda, Mrs. Barnes was forced to leave her home the same day her husband died. I'm sure she gave very little thought to what she took with her."

"Actually," Hannah said in a low voice, "I had ample time to gather everything I owned. Its just that Caleb didn't hold with owning more than a body needed."

The reverend smiled approvingly.

Yolanda frowned. She did not at all care for the way Hannah had squared her shoulders before answering. "Whatever did you wear to church while your husband was in the pulpit, my dear?" No minister's wife worthy of the name would have worn such rags!

"There weren't any churches where my husband preached."

"But . . ."

As Yolanda's appalled voice trailed away, Warren Salters explained, "Reverend Barnes carried the word of God to the Indians, Yolanda. Our Hannah has dutifully followed her husband into the very wilds of Texas."

Both women stared at him in dismay. *Our* Hannah?

Setting her back a little straighter, Yolanda reconsidered her strategy. She might be almost ready to place her approval on a match between these two, but not quite yet. It had not occurred to her that the reverend might decide to rush in before the girl had been properly filtered through Yolanda's diligent scrutiny.

She flicked an invisible speck of lint from the sleeve of her own fashionable gown. "Well, we must certainly see about finding some suitable things for you—mourning, of course."

"What I have will be fine," Hannah said firmly. "I am already in debt to Mr. Welles. I won't add to that before I find employment."

"Employment!"

"In debt to Mr. Welles!" Yolanda's shocked voice completely overrode Reverend Salters's tone of dismay.

It also diverted him momentarily. He patted Yolanda's arm reassuringly. "The man is quite honorable, Yolanda. He told me he would leave sufficient funds with the Armen's to take care of Hannah until she can make . . . other arrangements." He reddened.

His blush was nothing on Hannah's. She might have known Jeb would, once again, have told the man everything that was none of his business. Or anyone else's. She longed to see Jeb Welles just to give him a piece of her mind. Of course, that was the only reason the thought of him was so vivid in her mind.

And he *was* vivid. If she closed her eyes, she was sure she would be able to hear his drawling tones—insulting her no doubt! Her eyes flew open.

Yolanda's lips were pressed firmly together,

and Warren Salters was looking at her as if she were manna from heaven.

Hannah blinked back tears. What on earth was she doing here?

What in hell am I even doing here? Jeb thought, as Coral wriggled her soft body against him. Her breasts, full and lush, pressed against his ribs while her hand explored him with light teasing touches. The smell of her perfume irritated his nostrils.

Coral knew she was losing him. Her questing fingers told her that. *Hellfire!* He was the first man she'd actually wanted to bed in a long time. Almost desperately she searched for a way to pull his thoughts from wherever they had wandered back to her.

"You wanted to know what my real name was," she purred close to his ear, making sure her lips just brushed the tender skin there. "It's Emily Ann." No response. "I don't use it because some guy told me it reminded him of an old maiden aunt or a preacher's wife."

"I'll just be a son of a bitch!" Jeb howled.

Coral blinked at the man who had been in her arms only a moment ago and now stood snatching his pants up over his hips. "You don't like any talk?" she asked petulantly.

Jeb looked at her without blinking an eye. "No," he said at last. "No, I don't like any talk."

She smiled softly. "Come on back and I'll keep my mouth closed." She made her smile a little more wicked. "Well, maybe not closed—just real quiet."

He reached for his shirt. "Maybe some other time, honey." Dropping some money at the foot of the bed, he thought, *Hannah's getting damned expensive.*

In frustrated disbelief, Coral watched as he walked out of the little room and pulled the door closed behind him.

Jeb flinched as something hit the door about level with his head. He was glad he'd thought to shut it.

He began to chuckle as he returned Hirsch's friendly wave and headed for the street. Preacher's wife. Damn, nobody had this kind of luck! Nobody.

Chapter Nineteen

Jeb breathed deeply of the evening air and caught the tempting aroma of food drifting from the hotel opposite the saloon. The door of the hotel stood open to the steady night breeze.

A decent meal, he thought, would appease the only appetite his body seemed to have.

Small puffs of dust rose with each step as he crossed the deserted street. The closer he got to the hotel, the more distinct were the sounds from within—light music from a well-tuned piano, muted conversation, and soft laughter. The sounds of civilized living.

Jeb paused in the open doorway, and his eyes were drawn unerringly to the quartet of diners in one corner.

Hannah. Her hair escaped its confines in

tendrils of curls; the pale blue of her eyes caught and reflected the light from the chandelier above her. A touch of rose brushed her cheek as she leaned slightly toward the Baptist minister, listening to words Jeb could not hear from where he stood watching.

For one moment Jeb hesitated, drawn toward her by ties he had not known existed. Slowly, he turned away. This was what he had manipulated for her. Gleaming tableware, sparkling crystal, delicately etched china. Refined conversation and genteel manners. Jeb didn't know what kind of life Hannah had known before she married Caleb Barnes, but he'd seen the poverty she'd endured afterward. For all she irritated the hell out of him, Hannah deserved good things. She looked apt to get them here in Sherman.

Setting his jaw, Jeb clung to the thought that Hannah *had* irritated him, nearly every mile of the way to this little town. No woman could be more hard-headed or perverse.

By the time he reached Armen's Boarding House, he had recalled every annoying thing she had managed to say to him in the past three days. No doubt about it, he'd be well rid of her once he was on his way. He would put her out of his mind and concentrate on finding Ike Nelson and Leon Wilkins.

He rapped sharply on the boarding house door and waited impatiently until Jacob Armen opened it.

Armen greeted him courteously, then said,

"Mrs. Barnes has gone out for the evening."

"I know. I'm not here to see her."

One lifted brow was all the curiosity Jacob Armen allowed himself to display.

"How much do you need for Hannah to stay here a month?"

The boarding house owner named a figure that seemed reasonable enough, and Jeb pulled some bills from a leather pouch that hung around his neck. "If Hannah's still here a month from now, send a message to the commander at Fort Belknap. I'll wire this same amount to you again."

"You are a gentleman, Mr. Welles." Jacob Armen smiled graciously at him. "A true gentleman."

Jeb doubted that, but all he said was, "Tell Hannah she can sell the grulla to buy whatever she might need. I'll leave word at the livery."

"Will you be leaving town soon?" Armen asked.

"I'm riding out tonight." He didn't, after all, have any further reason to hang around.

"Shall I give Mrs. Barnes a message for you, then?"

For a moment, Jeb considered several things he'd like to say to Hannah, but in the end, he simply shrugged. "No, I reckon it's all been said."

Turning away, he settled his hat more firmly on his head. He gave fleeting thought to Jenny Ryon's warm bed, then began to whistle a bawdy tune as he made his way to the livery stable. At least it wasn't raining. He damned sure hated sleeping in the rain.

"We'll be looking forward to seeing you in church tomorrow morning," Warren Salters told Hannah as he stood with her at the Armens' front door.

Hannah looked over his shoulder at the Grahams. As usual, Mr. Graham was gazing off into space. His wife's eagle eye was fixed firmly upon Hannah. "I'll be looking forward to the morning." She glanced at the sky, half expecting a lightning bolt to come ripping out of the blackness to smite her. How did one be polite without ever telling a fib? She hadn't mastered that piece of diplomacy. Perhaps the Reverend Salters's sermon would prove sufficient to overcome Yolanda Graham's daunting presence. Hannah could only hope.

"Well . . ." The reverend hesitated. "Good night, then."

"Good night." Hannah gave him no reason to linger. She liked Warren Salters, but she wasn't going to give him any false hopes. Not to please Jeb Welles or Yolanda Graham or anyone else.

"Good night, dear," Yolanda called with dubious warmth as the reverend joined her and her husband on the walk. As the evening had progressed, she had seen less and less in Hannah Barnes to recommend her as wife to Warren Salters. Her eyes had shone a bit too brightly, her cheeks had taken on too much color, and by the evening's end, her responses to Yolanda had seemed almost pert. Even her hair had proved rebellious as it slipped free of its tidy knot at every opportunity.

No, Yolanda really didn't think she would do at all as a bride for the preacher. With a final shrug, Yolanda decided to turn his attention elsewhere. She had managed it easily enough the last time the reverend had shown interest in an inappropriate direction. She had no doubt she could do so again with as little difficulty.

Hannah watched the trio fade into the night, then stepped inside. A lamp glowed softly in the dim hall. The Armens' Boarding House was more than comfortable, but she really thought she'd be happier at Kipfer's. She wondered uneasily if Mr. Armen would refuse to return the money Jeb had paid for the room. Surely not. He seemed an honorable man.

Despite her best efforts, Hannah did not manage much sleep that night. The smooth sheets of the bed felt alien after a bedroll on a hard ground. When she opened her eyes, she saw nothing but a dark ceiling rather than a liberal sprinkling of brilliant stars, and her ears caught only silence where they were accustomed to Jeb's even breathing.

Hannah didn't rest at all, and morning came too soon. Reluctantly, she dressed once more in her drab calico and thought of the exquisite fabric that graced Yolanda Graham's proud form. "Hannah!" she scolded aloud, shocked to realize that she was envious of another woman's possessions. How wicked she had grown in the past few days!

She refused to look in the mirror as she combed and tidied her hair into a neat knot at the back of her head.

"Warren Salters would be dismayed at such envy," she added for good measure, telling herself that she would learn to care what his opinion of her was. Jeb had all but betrothed her to the man, after all!

Jeb. Hannah sank to the bed, dismayed that she'd let the thought of him sneak in after all her careful efforts.

"He's gone, Hannah," she whispered. "Forget him." But she wondered if she really could.

With her mind carefully blank, Hannah waited in the parlor after breakfast for the morning bells to call her to church. From time to time, another of the guests wandered in and she greeted each one politely, careful to give no opening for conversation. Incredibly enough, she missed her little cabin and her daily routine. Hard as that life had sometimes seemed, it was familiar to her, each moment filled. And she had known what each moment would bring—or at least, she had always thought she did.

The bells rang at last, and she stepped out into the street, unsurprised to see the number of townfolk making their way toward the source of that vibrant ringing. Hannah's stride was unenthusiastic as she walked to the church where Warren Salters waited to greet his congregation.

His smile deepened as he caught sight of her coming up the walk. "Mrs. Barnes." He took her hand for no longer than was proper, but the slight squeeze he gave held a world of warmth.

"Reverend," she murmured. He was truly a nice man. But she didn't want a nice man. She refused to ask herself just what it was she did want.

Hannah hesitated just inside the church, her glance taking in an entire building filled with strangers. It was almost a relief to see Yolanda Graham pat the pew beside her. Almost. With some reluctance, Hannah joined the woman, looking beyond her to nod at Mr. Graham, who nodded politely in turn. Hannah thought he would probably need permission from his wife before he dared to return her smile as well.

Following Yolanda's lead, Hannah turned to face the front of the church and planted a look of pleasant expectation upon her face. All around her, she could feel the stares of others. She hoped they were looking at Yolanda, whose emerald-green gown was eye-catching to say the least. Gathering all of her courage, she squared her shoulders rather than shrinking against the back of the pew.

The congregation rose to sing, and Hannah felt a quick relief when the hymn proved to be one she knew. Just ahead of her, a young girl with dozens of freckles twisted around to steal a peek at the stranger, her eyes wide with curiosity. Hannah smiled at her, and the youngster smiled in return, revealing a missing front tooth. For the first time, Hannah honestly considered a future in that town, a future that included a home and children.

From the front of the church, Warren Salters opened his mouth to speak. "The book of Matthew tells us we should take no thought for our lives, what we shall eat or drink. Our future is in God's hands."

As he continued, Hannah felt a warmth steal through her as she realized that his sermon was aimed at her. He spoke sincerely and eloquently, reminding her a little of her father. With his cherub's face and kindly smile, she really had not expected a hellfire-and-brimstone message, but while his voice did not thunder from the pulpit, he certainly spoke with all the passion and conviction that any staunch believer could wish.

After the service, she felt a bit self-conscious as she walked to the door, where he reminded each of his flock of that evening's special song service. Perhaps her self-consciousness was the result of Yolanda Graham's pinched expression as she followed close behind.

Reverend Salters looked straight into Hannah's eyes. "You will, of course, join us again, Mrs. Barnes?"

"Of course," she murmured. Anything would be preferable to sitting alone in a boarding house room while she wondered how many miles Jeb had put between them in one day.

"I had thought to invite you to dine with

me at the widow's, but Mrs. Graham has reminded me of an obligation I made last week. I can't imagine how I could have forgotten." He appeared a little flustered. "That really isn't like me at all." The flustered look deepened. "I hate to think of you being alone all afternoon. At least until you've had a chance to meet more of our congregation," he added hastily as Yolanda frowned.

"That is very kind of you, but I understand Mr. and Mrs. Armen have quite a nice Sunday luncheon, and with so many other boarders present, I couldn't possibly be alone."

"There, you see, Reverend," Yolanda inserted smoothly. "Mrs. Barnes will be just fine."

"Of course she will. Of course," he agreed, but his eyes followed Hannah as she moved down the steps to make way for those behind her who waited to shake the reverend's hand.

Hannah was careful not to cast any backward glances as she stepped out onto the street. She did not want Reverend Salters—or Yolanda Graham—to misconstrue any move she made. The freckle-faced child scampered by, giving Hannah a tiny wave before she reached her mother's side and took the hand held out to her. In a little while, the family would doubtless be seated at a Sunday table surrounded by good food and friendly smiles.

Despite her brave words, Hannah felt very lonely indeed as she walked back to the boarding house. At the last minute, she turned aside. The thought of sitting at that formal oval table with a roomful of strangers was entirely too daunting. Hannah rather thought she wasn't hungry after all.

She tried to look completely carefree as she strolled down the street that ran between the major businesses of Sherman. At the far end of town, she passed the sheriff, whose stride appeared much more purposeful than hers.

He paused and tipped his hat to her. "Mrs. Barnes."

"Sheriff." She didn't question the fact that he knew her name. Jeb would have told him everything about her. As for that, she supposed every person in town was aware of her presence, how she came to be there, and where she was staying. Hannah noticed that his eyes crinkled at the corners when he smiled. Like Jeb's.

"I hope you're enjoying our town." He didn't think she possibly could be, judging by the forlorn look she had been wearing before she noticed him in front of her. Daniel forced himself to admit that she was more than passingly attractive. Some men might even find her prettier than Jenny Ryon. At least when she smiled. He tried to think of something else to say. "I saw you walking to church this morning."

"Yes. I quite enjoyed Reverend Salters's message. Where do you attend?" Hannah asked more to be polite than out of any real curiosity.

Daniel coughed lightly and wished he hadn't brought up the subject. He'd forgotten she was a preacher's widow! "Actually, I'm one of Warren Salters's flock when duty allows."

Hannah felt an instant sympathy as her glance dropped to the star pinned to his vest. "Oh—I suppose you don't have much time that is truly yours alone. Being sheriff, I mean."

Her sweetness made him feel low-down for the half-truth. It hadn't been duty, but self-pity that had kept him from church that morning. Instead of getting dressed in his best clothes, he'd just sat on his back porch and thought of Jenny.

"Not much," he agreed, "and I'd best be getting on now." He immediately scolded himself. How was he ever going to get over Jenny if he ran away from other women? Nevertheless, he didn't say anything to halt Hannah Barnes as she resumed her even pace along the dusty street.

Hannah didn't stop again until she was just at the edge of town. She stood looking out toward the hills, picturing how Jeb must have looked as he rode away. She blinked very hard, mortified that someone might see a tear fall from her eye.

As Hannah was leaving the church that evening, Reverend Salters called her name as she descended the steps into the warm night air.

Hannah turned and waited politely while he joined her.

"I'd be honored to walk you back to the boarding house."

Despite an instinctive hesitation, the remembered loneliness of that afternoon weighed on Hannah oppressively. Just as she opened her mouth to accept the invitation, Yolanda swooped forward.

"Oh, Reverend Salters, I do need to speak with you about something . . . personal." Her glance bored into Hannah's.

Hannah did not think the reverend looked impressed. Nevertheless, she responded as she was expected to do. "I'll be fine on my own, Reverend. It's no distance at all to the Armens'."

He frowned, ever so slightly, at Yolanda. "Perhaps we can chat when I've returned from seeing Mrs. Barnes safely home."

"Why, how dear of you, Reverend," Yolanda said. "So concerned about all of your congregation. But never worry"—she prodded her husband forward—"Mr. Graham will be delighted to see to Mrs. Barnes's safety for you."

"I'll be fine," Hannah said hastily. "It's scarcely dark yet."

"Nonesense," Yolanda said firmly, before Reverend Salters could say anything more. "Mr. Graham and I wouldn't dream of letting you go alone."

Looking resigned but faithful to his calling, the reverend allowed himself to be led back into the church while Hannah accepted Mr. Graham's dutifully extended arm.

"You really don't have to do this, you know," she said quietly.

"Oh, but I assure you, my dear, I do. If I

would have any peace at all for the remainder of the evening, I do."

With that, they walked side by side to the boarding house in complete silence. Hannah was very aware that Yolanda's husband waited until his charge was safely inside before he turned to go.

In the dim hallway, she nearly trod on Amanda Armen's foot.

"Did you enjoy the song service, my dear?"

Hannah wondered how the woman managed to sound unpleasant with so innocent a question. "Very much," she said and started up the stairs. The newly polished handrail felt smooth and cool beneath her fingers.

Jacob Armen waited at the top. "Mrs. Barnes."

Although it could have been no more than a genteel greeting, Hannah stopped halfway up the stairs. "Mr. Armen," she returned. The scent of perfumed oil from the well-rubbed wood of the handrail filled her nostrils unpleasantly.

Armen appeared hesitant, then squared his shoulders. "Did you plan to make . . . ah, financial arrangements this evening?"

A faint roaring started in Hannah's ears. "I—I thought Mr. Welles had done so."

"Actually, my dear, he did not." Mr. Armen sounded apologetic. He touched his mustache in seeming embarrassment. "Well, I'm sure we can take care of this later. You must need a good night's rest now."

A prickly feeling along the nape of her neck

caused Hannah to glance down the stairs behind her. Amanda Armen stood with a smirk upon her face. Hannah's face burned. Filled with distrust, she looked back at Mr. Armen. "I can't accept your charity. I'll leave now." Somehow she knew she would regret accepting any offer of assistance from these people.

"Don't be hasty, Mrs. Barnes. After all, wasn't charity what you expected to receive from Mr. Welles?" There was a subtle change in Jacob Armen's tone. "Or was it payment for services rendered?"

The meaning behind his words sank in, and Hannah blinked back tears. No one had ever spoken to her so crudely. At least not since the morning the three soldiers had come looking for Caleb. "I don't know what you mean," she said faintly. But she feared she did know. Too well.

Jacob Armen assumed the same smirking look that sat upon his wife's face. "Perhaps you would be as willing to"—he appeared to be hunting for the right word—"to provide the same kind of services for one or two of our male guests." Jacob had made a similar arrangement with a previous female resident. It had been profitable for all concerned until the silly girl had decided to marry one of the men.

Hannah stared at him, scarcely able to believe he'd made such a proposition to her. "No." To her dismay, the word came out barely a whisper, and she repeated it in a stronger voice. "No." She started up the stairs, hoping he would move out of her way before she reached him. She did not think she could bear for the man to touch her. "I'll get my things and leave. As soon as I can, I'll send money for last night's board."

"And just where will you go, my dear? You'll come to the same choice when you leave here. Accept charity or live on the only means you have at hand." Jacob felt frustration building in his breast. This should have been easy. After all, the woman had traveled several days and nights with a man not her husband. And Jeb Welles had not appeared a man of abstinence. Why was she balking at so convenient an arrangement?

It occurred to him that the Barnes woman was hoping to force some kind of concessions from him. He'd put an end to that. "This is the only offer I will make, Mrs. Barnes. I suggest you take it, if you would not find yourself starving on the street at my front door."

Hannah met his gaze, feeling stronger. "Like the fowls of the air, my Lord will feed me," she said quietly. She tried not to think of the trust she had placed in Jeb. She wasn't his responsibility, after all.

"Ah." Armen looked smug. "You think the preacher will take you in, don't you? Well, that pious little air of yours won't last one minute after I've spoken with him!" He folded his arms on a note of triumph.

"Move out of my way." Hannah had not

known she could feel such loathing for another human. The worst of her feelings toward Caleb's murderers had been watered down by fear and horror. She did not fear the man standing in front of her, and he did not horrify her. He disgusted her.

Somewhat to her surprise, he actually recoiled from the contempt blazing in her eyes and moved slightly to one side of the staircase. Hannah climbed the stairs past him and reached the door of her room.

It took her only a moment to gather what little she possessed and stuff it into her cloth bag. When she emerged from the room, the hallway and the stairs were empty.

She reached the front door without encountering either of the Armens and walked out into the night.

As she gazed up at the starlit heavens, it occurred to her that for the first time in her existence, she was completely on her own. And she hadn't the faintest idea what to do.

Near daylight, Daniel Hastings found himself once again outside Jenny's house. He brought his tin mug to his mouth and tested the metal rim. Still too hot to drink. He sipped anyway.

A light came on in an upstairs window. Was Jenny alone in that room? Daniel wished he hadn't come this way. No use torturing himself.

Just as he started to turn away, a movement in the shadows near her front porch caught his gaze. His eyes narrowed as he discerned the broad shoulders of a man. Whoever it was couldn't be up to any good skulking about in the pre-dawn grey.

As the man stepped quietly up onto her porch, Daniel started across the road. He reached the steps just as one long leg eased through a window that had been left open to release the heat of the day from the house.

His fingers closed on a stiff collar, and he dragged the man back through the window to snarled curses. He spun the man named Hawk around to face him.

Hawk's lips curled to a sneer. "Going to arrest me, sheriff? It ain't a crime to visit a lady, is it?"

Daniel felt the heat of his rage build to the boiling point. "No," he gritted between clenched teeth. "I'm not going to arrest you. I'm going to beat the living hell out of you."

He drew back one large fist and let it fly.

Jenny dreamed someone started a brawl in her restaurant, something that had never happened. Men cursed and grunted as fist pounded flesh. Her eyes opened slowly, and she stared into the darkness above her. The sound of cursing continued.

For one startled moment, Jenny froze, then realized that the noise was coming through her open window. Hastily, she swung her legs over the edge of the bed and reached for her wrapper. It sounded as if the fight were at her very front door!

With light, quick steps she descended the stairway and reached the tiny vestibule where her customers hung their hats and coats. The door scraped lightly along the wood of the porch as she pushed it open.

Two men battled by the faint light of dawn.

"Daniel," she breathed.

The other man stumbled away from him and put his hands up in a gesture of surrender.

Daniel dropped his fists and dragged heavily for breath. This kind of thing was damned hard on a man.

"Hawk," he said when he could breathe again, "you've got one hour to get out of town, and before I'm through today, every sheriff in Texas will have your name and description."

With excruciating effort, Hawk retrieved his hat from the porch where it had fallen at the first blow from the sheriff's fist. "Don't waste your time, Sheriff. I'm headed for friendly hills—maybe Indian territory," he snorted in disgust. Hawk didn't so much as look at the woman standing in the open doorway.

At his words, Daniel's lips twitched in a smile that he found immediately painful. He watched until Hawk had limped down the walk and into the street.

Jenny took a step toward Daniel, one hand outstretched. "You're hurt."

In the tradition of men, Daniel shook his head. "It's nothing."

"Come inside and let me bathe your face." Her loving gaze picked out every bruise and knuckle scrape.

Daniel stared at Jenny. Her hair was tumbled around a face that was perfection itself in the pale light of breaking day. Her eyes were luminescent. His gaze dropped to the wrapper she had donned over her nightgown. He thought of what people would say about her if they were seen together like this. If Jenny would marry him, it wouldn't matter. He'd tell the whole world to go to hell. Besides, he didn't know if he could trust himself with her. Not when she looked like this, soft and warm and vulnerable.

"No," he said at last. "I'd best not."

Jenny understood. She had seen the look in his eyes and guessed what he was thinking. No doubt she looked like she'd just been with a man. Maybe he even thought Hawk had been there at her invitation.

She bent down and picked up his hat. Holding it toward him, she waited until he took it from her. "Good-bye, Sheriff."

He hesitated, then put his hat on his head, wincing as the action stretched the skin over sore ribs. "Keep your windows closed, Mrs. Ryon."

Jenny waited as he walked away. With a shiver caused by more than the cool morning air, she pulled her wrapper closer and went inside. He'd called her Mrs. Ryon. Not Jenny.

Chapter Twenty

Jeb opened one eye and glared at the edge of sun peeping over the horizon. For the second night in a row, he'd managed to get only a few hours sleep, and he wasn't ready for morning to break. With a groan, he eased out of his bedroll. A man ought not to ache down to the center of his bones just from sleeping on the ground. The fire he'd built for his supper was nothing more than embers, but the coffeepot was still hot to the touch.

Instinctively, he glanced around, as if expecting to see Hannah smiling brightly back at him. She liked mornings better than he did. Once again, her absence brought an empty feeling to the pit of his stomach, which he tried unsuccessfully to fill with stale bread and coffee that wasn't worth swallowing. He would have given a month's pay for a decent meal.

Deciding to ignore his lowering mood, he whistled for his mare. When she did nothing more than lift her head and look in his direction, he scowled. Females. Nothing but worry and trouble even when they weren't around. It made no sense to be worrying about Hannah. He'd left her in the safest place he knew, but there was no denying she was on his mind.

He dumped the last of the coffee on the ground and cleaned up his campsite. When he began rolling his bedroll, the mare curiously followed his packhorse over to see what Jeb was up to. She had preferred the grulla, but she tolerated the pack animal.

"Temperamental," Jeb muttered. "You all are. Hannah wasn't happy with that preacher husband of hers. No reason in hell for her to be so starry-eyed over another one just like him." He conveniently overlooked the fact that Warren Salters had been his idea. "Reckon she wants someone else to pray over her."

The idea was depressing. A woman like Hannah deserved to be spoiled wicked. Instead, he pictured cherub-faced Reverend Salters standing at Hannah's back while she kneeled for hours at a time. She had just begun to show a little gumption. He reckoned the preacher would snuff that out soon enough.

With a savage jerk, Jeb tightened the packhorse's load, then had to relax the leather straps as the animal grunted. He snapped his fingers, and the mare stepped docilely forward.

"Forget Hannah," he told himself as he swung the saddle onto the mare's back. "Thinking about a woman while you track the likes of Nelson and Wilkins will get you killed."

He couldn't let that happen. If he got himself killed, there would be no one to keep those two from finding Hannah. He could hardly envision that smooth-cheeked minister standing between her and danger, even if he did look as if he spent more time chopping wood than planning sermons. No, if he didn't take care of them, she would spend the rest of her life looking over her shoulder and feeling guilty that her husband's death was unavenged. Of course, even once they were jailed or dead, she wouldn't know unless he sent word back to her.

He wondered how she would feel about getting a telegraph from him weeks or even months from now. Would she even remember his name? The idea that she might not was more than a little daunting.

Jeb mounted and looped the lead from the packhorse around the horn of his saddle. No use hanging around here all day fretting over a skinny little red-haired woman. He had a job to do, and he'd just as well get to it. He'd wasted enough time the day before, leaving camp late and dawdling along the way at little more than a jog. Hell, he probably wasn't but a few hours hard ride from Sherman now.

He let the mare amble along at a walk for the first mile or so, conscious that he was putting Hannah farther and farther behind him. He hoped Sheriff Hastings was as capable as he appeared to be. There was no telling what direction Wilkins and Nelson would decide to take. They could be miles on the other side of the Mexican border, or they might be wandering aimlessly around Texas. The thought that they might unwittingly ride into that quiet little town where he'd left Hannah sent a shiver up his spine.

The second mile, he put the mare to a trot and argued with himself. He'd done the right thing in leaving Hannah. She would be safest in one place. Besides, he told himself, he couldn't possibly drag her with him while he hunted outlaws, especially outlaws who had every reason to want to see her dead. His mind presented an image of Hannah, lying in the dirt, torn apart by bullets.

"Damn it!" he bellowed, startling both horses. Exasperated both by the mental picture and by his inability to control his thoughts, he snatched his hat from his head and threw it on the ground. The mare danced sideways at the action, jostling the gelding, who promptly stepped on Jeb's hat.

Muttering curses, Jeb pulled the mare to a stop, climbed down, and retrieved his battered hat. In one fluid motion, he remounted and reined the mare in a circle—back the way they had come.

Hannah very carefully removed a bug from the berry in her fingers. She couldn't say the plump berries were very filling, but they were ripe and sweet and had staved off the worst of her hunger pangs and eased her thirst. The squawk of a bird drew her gaze upward. Rays from the midday sun created a rainbow of blue and black on the feathers of a blue jay as he swooped toward her. Hannah was eating his lunch. She wondered what Jeb was eating.

By daybreak, she had begun to suspect she might have made a big mistake in not throwing herself on the mercy of the Reverend Warren Salters, but so far a delicious feeling of freedom outweighed that niggling suspicion.

Hannah, girl . . . She tried to remember the exact tones in which her father used to speak to her. *You can't go through life doing first and thinking last.* Frowning, she tried to determine a point in the past week at which careful thought on her part might have prevented her from becoming a widow or ending up in the care of a man as hard as nails or receiving a proposition to sell her body for food and board.

If one existed, she couldn't see it now any more than she had recognized it then.

Scrambling to her feet, she picked up her bag and dusted her skirt. All she could do was the same as she'd always done. Trust God.

She sure wasn't trusting any more men. Her judgment wasn't good enough for that. She'd actually thought Jacob Armen an honorable man. And Jeb—well, Jeb could have been honest with her. After all, she'd never expected him to take care of her for the rest of her life, but she would have appreciated a warning that she was being left completely destitute in a strange town!

The blue jay flew at her again, and she scowled. "I'm leaving! And besides, I didn't eat *all* your berries."

She hoped that bird was the worst animal that came at her. Jeb might at least have returned her rifle! After all, it belonged to her now that Caleb was dead, and Jeb had shown her how to load and draw it. She could have learned to aim at something on her own. Maybe.

With every step, Hannah became increasingly aware of two things. Blisters were developing on the heels of both feet, and the sun was getting hotter. At least she wasn't lost. Not really. All she had to do was keep following these wagon ruts. Even if the path wasn't well enough traveled that she would encounter someone willing to help her, she should surely come to another town before long.

Feeling defiant, she loosened the strings of her bonnet and let it hang freely down her back. After a few more steps, she reached up and slowly began to pull the pins from her hair as well. All her life she'd been proper, trying to do just what her father and then Caleb had exhorted her to do. Look what it had gained her. She was alone in a land likely to prove more hostile than friendly, with no food, no shelter, and no money to buy either.

Hannah supposed she ought to feel more anxious than she did, and perhaps she would. Later.

Jeb figured he was better than halfway back to Sherman when he thought he saw a woman strolling toward him. Which was ridiculous. Hannah must really be on his mind. He not only had he imagined a woman, but one with red hair.

He used his neckerchief to wipe the sweat from his eyes and looked again. "Well, I'll just be a son of a bitch." The bay twitched her ears at the sound of his voice.

Jeb rode right up to Hannah, pulled both horses to a stop, and just sat there staring at her. She looked like a ragamuffin with her hair hanging loose and wilted in the heat. He wouldn't have been surprised to see her shoes dangling from her hands and bare feet peeping out from under the hem of her skirt. The sun had burned her cheeks just slightly. She was the most beautiful sight he'd ever seen in his life.

Hannah stared back, too hungry for the sight of him to think about hiding the fact.

Jeb was so glad to see her that it took a moment before a feeling of fury swamped him. How dared she put herself in this kind of danger? "What are you doing?"

"Me?" Hannah tried to gather her thoughts. They had scattered like leaves in the wind at the sight of Jeb riding toward her.

"Oh, no!" Jeb swung down from his horse.

"Oh, no, you don't! You're not answering every question I ask with another question, damn it. Don't even start!"

Because Hannah had forgotten the question and didn't dare ask what it had been, she stood there silent. Tall as she was, Jeb was taller and he glared down at her. The fact that his eyes were very light and very green would have warned her he was angry, even if she hadn't already known. But she did know.

"Hannah?" he growled.

"I don't know what you want me to say," Hannah offered. That was true enough. "And I don't know why you're so angry." That wasn't. The enormity of her actions had hit her. What if it hadn't been Jeb who found her?

"You don't know why I'm so angry? I left you in a safe place, and what do you do? You wander off like you're on a Sunday picnic!" He pushed his hat back on his head in order to glare at her a little more effectively.

"I didn't wander," Hannah pointed out, not the least disconcerted by Jeb's anger. That was one area where she *did* trust him implicitly.

"Well, just what the hell did you do? Take a walk and lose yourself?"

Thinking hard, Hannah looked at the toe of her shoe. It was obvious to her that Jeb wasn't going to like any answer she gave at this point. "I couldn't stay there," she said at last, still not meeting his eye.

Jeb wanted to shake her. Hard. "You could live with that—with your husband in a half-rotten cabin in the middle of God knows where, but you couldn't stay in a boarding house that is as comfortable as any home I've been in. Would you tell me just why the hell not?"

Hannah looked up at that. "I couldn't do what he wanted me to do."

Something about her quiet dignity triggered a sense of foreboding in Jeb, and he grew very still. "Couldn't do what *who* wanted, Hannah?"

"Mr. Armen."

"And just what was that? What did Jacob Armen ask you to do?"

His suddenly gentle tone disconcerted her. "He wanted me to whore for other men," Hannah said bluntly. "I'm not a whore."

A deadly feeling started deep down in Jeb's chest. "What about the money I left him?"

"What money?" Even as she spoke, sweet relief swept Hannah. Jeb hadn't abandoned her.

The deadly feeling grew. Jeb didn't even point out to Hannah that she was answering him with questions again. "And the grulla?"

"I thought you had him."

Jeb touched Hannah's sunburned cheek. "Put your bonnet on, Hannah." The killer instinct every Texas Ranger learned to cultivate was in full force.

Without another word, Jeb remounted and

held out his hand to Hannah. Obediently, she clambered up behind him. This new mood of his was far more worrisome to her than his anger had been.

"Where are we going now?"

"I'm going back to kill that son of a bitch," Jeb answered matter-of-factly.

Hannah rested her head against his back. It felt sturdy and oh so secure. "Thou shalt not kill," she murmured.

"Shut up, Hannah."

Sherman was bustling with afternoon activity by the time they rode back into town. Jeb went to the livery first. The grulla was still where he'd left him, but the owner raised bushy eyebrows in surprise at seeing Jeb leaning against the door of his stall.

"Armen came by to look at him this morning. Said he'd bought him off you."

"He lied." Jeb straightened away from the stall. "I'm leaving my horses here. I'll be back—for all three."

Jeb turned and walked away, and the other man felt no inclination to question the reason for the vicious look in his eye.

When they reached the bright sunlight of the street, Jeb looked at Hannah. "Go to the hotel lobby and stay there. I'll be back for you in a minute." He started away, but wheeled back after a single step. His eyes narrowed. "Hannah, I swear I'll skin you alive if you don't do exactly like I say."

Hannah nodded gravely. "I'll be fine," she said, careful not to lie.

She watched him stride purposefully toward Armen's Boarding House, then hitched up her skirts and ran toward the building where Jeb had first talked to the sheriff.

Sheriff Hastings looked startled as she nearly fell into the doorway. Startled, but capable.

Her expression jerked him to his feet. "What the hell—"

"If you don't hurry, there's going to be a killing." The words fairly tumbled from her mouth in a breathless rush.

In two strides, Daniel was at the door, buckling his gunbelt low on his hip. "Where?"

Hannah followed him into the street. "Armen's."

"Tell me," Daniel demanded, still walking fast.

Forced to run to keep up, Hannah explained as clearly and quickly as she could between gasps for breath.

Jeb shoved open the front door of the boarding house with all the force of the anger bottled up inside of him. He didn't speak a word as he walked past the open door of the parlor to a closed door with a plaque that read "Office."

Without knocking, he turned the knob on the door and swung it open with a hard push. Jacob Armen looked up from his papers. His look of irritation faded swiftly, replaced by one of dawning dismay.

"Get a gun," Jeb said in an ugly voice.

Jacob stood and straightened his vest. "What are you doing here?" he asked nervously.

"Get your gun and get out to the damned street, or I'll put a bullet between your eyes right here." Jeb felt no sympathy for the sweat that broke out on the other man's forehead. He intended to make Armen do more than sweat for what he'd tried to do to Hannah.

"Jacob?" Amanda Armen's worried voice came from the open doorway. "What is all the noise?" She stepped into the room. "What's going on?"

When Jeb turned to look at her, she blanched. "Oh."

"Best get your husband a weapon, ma'am, if you don't want him to die defenseless."

Sheriff Hastings moved Amanda out of his way with little ceremony. "No one's going to die, Welles."

Jeb looked past the sheriff at the pale face peeping around his broad shoulder. "Damn it, Hannah," he said helplessly. Now why in hell had he thought she'd do what she was told?

"Come on, Armen," Daniel said heavily. "You're going with me." He wished he'd found the widow's story a little harder to credit, but it was all too easy to believe, especially with the look of guilt these two wore.

Now that he felt in less danger of dying,

Jacob swelled his chest. "And just where is that, Sheriff?"

"Likely to jail," Daniel retorted. "I would imagine either Mr. Welles or this little lady has some charges they'd like to see brought against you."

"I'd rather kill him," Jeb said with a feeling of resignation.

"You can't do this, Sheriff," Amanda Armen protested.

Daniel pinned her with a look. "Would you like to come too? I can handle more than one prisoner at a time."

Her mouth dropped open. "We're respected people in this town. We won't be treated like this!"

"I'd say any respect you've been given in the past is going to be scarce after today." He glanced back at her husband. "I'm waiting, Jacob. You want to be dragged or"—he gestured toward Jeb—"you want me to leave you with him?"

Jacob moved hastily around the desk. "You're going to regret this, Sheriff Hastings," he warned in dark tones. He was careful to put the sheriff between him and Welles.

Daniel smiled grimly. "Not likely." He tipped his hat toward Amanda Armen. "You have a real good day, ma'am."

Jeb took Hannah by the arm and followed the sheriff and Armen from the room. "What did I tell you?" he whispered furiously.

"You would have regretted killing that man

the minute it was done," Hannah said unruffled. "I couldn't let you do it."

"I'm going to beat the living daylights out of you, Hannah. I swear I am."

Hannah sighed. "Could you feed me first?"

Chapter Twenty-one

Jeb sat across from Hannah and watched her eat. For the first time in a long time, he was at a dead loss as to what to do. He'd finally accepted the indisputable truth that he wasn't going to be able to ride away and leave her here. Judging by the last two days, it seemed unlikely he could convince himself to leave her anywhere. How he'd gotten to this point didn't bear examining. Now that he had, the question was—what was he going to do with her?

Hannah lowered her spoon. "You're staring at me." She looked around the hotel restaurant. "And so is everyone else in here."

Jeb followed her gaze. Everyone else consisted of two other diners and three of the hotel staff. The trio of workers had gathered in one corner of the room, waiting for one of the guests to need something and clearly hoping it would be Jeb and Hannah who called for their attention. Jeb wasn't surprised by the stares. He suspected that the story of their return to town had spread like wildfire through a dry forest. Sherman wasn't big enough to have much scandal occur with any regularity.

"Don't worry about them," Jeb told Hannah. "We'll be gone by this time tomorrow, and you'll never lay eyes on any of them again."

"Where are we going?"

Jeb wished she hadn't asked that or, at least, wished to hell he knew. All the same arguments he'd had with himself as he rode away from Sherman the first time presented themselves to him again. He couldn't haul Hannah around the countryside chasing outlaws. She wasn't someone like Katherine, who could stand up to that kind of rigor.

With the thought of Slade's wife came the answer, clear as the crystal tumbler of water at his fingertips. He'd take Hannah to Katherine. Katherine would know what to do.

"We're going to New Mexico," he heard himself say. "Katherine will take good care of you."

His supposition that she needed another woman to take care of her stung. The only person she needed to look after her, Hannah decided, was Jeb Welles. "Who takes care of Katherine?" she asked quietly.

Startled, Jeb met her clear, blue gaze. "Well . . . Slade does."

He wondered why Hannah looked so satisfied by his answer.

An hour later, Jeb, with the sheriff's assistance, had retrieved the money he'd given Jacob Armen and was ushering Hannah into the mercantile.

To Hannah's dismay, Yolanda Graham was just leaving.

The matron straightened her perfectly straight bonnet and fixed Hannah with a disapproving eye. "You have behaved most unwisely, my dear. Most unwisely. The story is all over town. I am sure it will take some time for me to overcome the ill effects of your behavior enough so that you will be acceptable to decent folk. Imagine! Wandering about the countryside quite alone! I shudder to think how poor Reverend Salters is taking this."

Somewhat to her own surprise, Hannah found she was far from crushed by the condemnation. All she could think was how glad she was never to have to pretend a polite interest in this woman's unceasing criticisms again. She felt sorry for Warren Salters, who had no choice.

Jeb bristled, wishing Hannah would speak up for herself. No doubt this was one of the old harpies who would have made Hannah's life miserable if she'd stayed here. When Hannah didn't speak, he did, with deliberate crudity. "You're saying you think Hannah should have accepted Jacob Armen's offer to prostitute her?"

"I beg your pardon?" Yolanda gasped. She was affronted that someone like the ex-ranger would even dare to speak to her, much less so provocatively.

"You criticized Hannah's choice of leaving town rather than becoming a whore. I take that to mean you think she should have earned her living on her back," Jeb drawled. Giving the woman no time to argue, he added, "I guess it looks glamorous to someone like you, but, lady, you wouldn't earn a dime if you tried it. You'd starve inside a month."

With that, he tightened his grip on Hannah's elbow and pushed her past the sputtering woman.

"You shouldn't have said that to her," Hannah said, looking around the store with a great deal of interest.

Jeb stopped, dumbfounded. "What about what she said to you?"

"You said yourself we'll be leaving here soon," Hannah answered reasonably. "Why should I care what she says or what she thinks about me? I'll never see her again."

Jeb began to think he should have felt a little more compassion for Caleb Barnes. Maybe praying over Hannah was the only way the man could keep from strangling her!

The storekeeper took one look at Jeb's glowering expression and hurried over to assist him. Jeb listed a half-dozen items he needed, then nodded shortly in Hannah's direction. "And whatever she wants."

Startled, Hannah turned to look at him. "I don't need anything."

Jeb glared at her dark gown, ready to take issue with just about anything Hannah said at this point. "What about some decent-looking dresses?"

Hannah colored. "My gowns *are* decent!"

"They're ugly as sin!"

"Caleb chose the cloth!"

Seeing the shine of an embarrassed tear in the corner of her eye, Jeb caught himself before he said anything worse.

As he searched for something to say that might make Hannah feel better, the storekeeper inserted an apology. "We don't have anything here that is already made up. I only carry yard goods."

Jeb gave up, knowing Hannah couldn't do much sewing of any kind on the trail. He made a mental note to have Katherine take care of Hannah's clothing.

"What about soap or . . . something?" Jeb ended lamely, having no idea what ladies needed.

Obviously still furious, Hannah simply looked at him without saying a word.

Frustrated, Jeb thrust ample money at the storekeeper. "Add whatever she needs to the bill and give her the difference. I'll be outside."

He stalked out onto the boardwalk and nearly ran into Sheriff Hastings.

Daniel wondered what had the younger man's color up, then shrugged it off as none of his business. "Still planning to ride out today?" He glanced at the lowering sun. "It'll be dark soon."

"We have rooms for tonight." Jeb had intended leaving immediately and would still have preferred that, but he didn't think Hannah was up to it.

"No need to rush. You could stick around a day or two. The Armens aren't all this town has to offer."

Jeb shrugged. "It's a long, rough ride to Taos. No need to get used to the comfort of town."

"What about Mrs. Barnes? I'd think she might be more used to comfort than to hardship." Daniel wasn't too sure Jeb Welles had made the right decision in planning to take the woman with him. Jacob Armen might have left a bad taste in his mouth, but most of the townfolk were nice, friendly people.

Jeb thought of the cabin where he'd found her, the grave she'd dug for her husband, the baby she'd buried. "You'd be wrong," he said without insult. "She's one tough little lady." He realized with a faint feeling of surprise that it was true. Hannah looked fragile, but she had a grit to her that he hadn't seen at first. He just wished she wasn't so always in control. To his way of thinking, it would be good for her to kick and scream and fight about something just once. Then he could speak without worrying about crushing her feelings—a worry that would never have occurred to him a few days ago. Lord, what was happening to him?

"Well," Daniel said, "it's her choice, I reckon."

Stepping from the mercantile, Hannah still felt warm inside from hearing Jeb describe her as tough. Maybe some women might not feel it was a compliment, but they didn't know Jeb Welles. "That's right, Sheriff. It *is* my choice." She smiled to take any sting from her words. Smoothly, as if it was something she'd done many times, she handed Jeb the package the storekeeper had wrapped up for her.

Half-amused, half-dismayed, Jeb looked at the wrapped goods, then at the sheriff, daring him to comment. "Well, if we don't see you come morning, I appreciate the help."

Daniel Hastings grinned. Now that looked like a tamed man. "I hope you'll pass our way again someday—and maybe decide to stay. Sherman can always use more decent citizens."

He almost said families, but decided that would be salt on an open wound. Jeb Welles might be fairly and surely caught, but he damned certain didn't know it yet.

Watching them walk away, Daniel wondered what Jenny was serving for lunch. And which of the men sitting at her table would share her bed tonight.

Knowing Jeb was in a room just down the hall and not on a trail taking him far away from her, Hannah enjoyed every minute of the luxury afforded by a hotel room. The hot bath, rich soap, and scented water were a wonderful indulgence. No doubt she'd take equal pleasure, however wicked, in the smooth feel of clean sheets. Later.

Now, she waited for Jeb to knock upon her door and take her down to dine. When the knock came, however, it wasn't Jeb on the other side of the door.

The desk clerk scuffed his feet apologetically. "Begging your pardon, ma'am, but the Reverend Salters is asking after you. He's waiting in the lobby."

A tiny dart of trepidation mingled with Hannah's curiosity. She couldn't picture Warren Salters mouthing any insults at her, but the possibility existed. Above all, he was a man of the cloth, and he might feel betrayed that a woman he had taken under his wing had found herself involved, however innocently, in a situation that gave rise to gossip.

"I'll be right down," she said slowly, but when she stepped out into the corridor she turned, not toward the stairs, but toward Jeb's room.

She knocked lightly at his door, unsurprised when he opened it immediately. A light blush colored her face. He was dressed, but his shirt hung open, and the damp hair on his chest and head was evidence that he'd stepped from his bath not long ago.

"R-Reverend Salters has asked to speak to me. I wanted you to know I was going downstairs now." The grim look that crossed Jeb's face startled her. "Is . . . is something wrong?"

"No," Jeb said shortly. "Go on. I'll be down

in a minute or two." He ignored the brief look of hurt in her eyes at his curtness.

Jeb didn't close the door when Hannah turned away. He watched as she walked toward the stairs, her skirts swaying gently with each step. Even in sack cloth, Hannah would be a real lady. Suitable for a preacher's wife. Jeb slammed the door with a growl just as Hannah's bright hair disappeared from sight.

Hannah flinched at the harsh sound of the slamming door behind her. She supposed Jeb was worried that she'd manage to get into more trouble before he was able to dress and get downstairs. He hadn't seemed to trust her out of his sight all day. That suited her just fine, but it hurt to think the effort might be no more than an irritating necessity to him.

She saw Warren Salters before he saw her. He was standing with his back to the room, his hands clasped behind him while he stared out the window at the darkening street.

Squaring her shoulders, Hannah moved up behind him. She could feel the desk clerk's curious gaze fixed on the two of them. If the Reverend Salters was going to denounce her, she might as well get it over with. "Reverend."

When he turned, the look upon his face reassured and startled her. While his expression held a great deal of warmth, it wasn't the heat of righteous anger. In fact, there wasn't a trace of anger or condemnation on his good-natured features.

"Hannah—" He caught himself. "Mrs.

Barnes! I've been so worried about you! I called upon you this morning, and I was told you had left without a word to the . . . Armens." His hesitation over the name was barely perceptible, as was the tightening of his lips.

He'd called upon her? "It was very kind of you to worry, but as you can see, I'm perfectly fine." Now that Jeb was somewhere close by. Jeb made her feel safe. "I'm very sorry for the embarrassment I've caused you," she felt compelled to add.

"Embarrassment! To me? What makes you think so?" There was honest confusion in his tone.

"I saw Mrs. Graham earlier today." Hannah took a deep breath. "She wasn't very happy."

The Reverend relaxed and smiled a bit ruefully. "Mrs. Graham has been of great help to me in the past, seeing to my welfare on a variety of matters. Lately, however, I've been of the opinion that a wife would be of greater help to me in *all* matters." He glanced over her shoulder. "Mrs. Barnes, would you join me in the dining room, where we could talk more privately?"

Hannah followed his gaze with her own to the lobby desk. The clerk studiously copied entries from one log to another, but the young man's stance held a definite list in their direction.

"Certainly. Je—Mr. Welles will be down soon. Perhaps you would care to join us for dinner?"

"Perhaps."

He held out his arm to Hannah, and she took it.

As they stepped into the dining hall, a waiter nearly stumbled over his own feet in his haste to greet them. "A table for two?"

"Three," Hannah said firmly.

When the reverend closed his mouth over his own reply, she realized that she'd again overstepped what she'd been taught was a woman's bounds. The realization didn't trouble her nearly as much as it would have a few days ago. Jeb didn't consider her bound by the same code of conduct that Caleb had. The thought warmed her.

Warren Salters drew out Hannah's chair, then seated himself across from her. He stared at her in bemusement for a moment before picking up their conversation where he'd interrupted it. "May I presume to ask your plans, Mrs. Barnes?"

"Mr. Welles is taking me to New Mexico—to friends of his." Spoken aloud, the idea sounded a bit haphazard.

"These are"—the reverend hesitated—"mutual friends?"

"No," Hannah admitted. "I've never met them." Even more haphazard.

He sighed. "I know you've not had a very good introduction to our town, Mrs. Barnes, but I assure you, most of the folk who live here are decent, honorable people. People who make good neighbors and good friends."

Hannah responded to the dismay she heard in his voice. Clearly, it pained him that she'd had such a distasteful experience while, at least nominally, under his care. "I realize that," she said carefully, "and I don't hold what happened against anyone else here."

Relief eased the lines around his mouth. "Perhaps you would care to give us another chance, then?"

Hannah thought of Yolanda Graham. "I don't think my circumstances will allow that."

"Circumstances?" His face cleared. "You mean your lack of funds."

Hannah nodded. That was part of it. Somehow it didn't seem so much charity that Jeb was willing to take her along with him to visit his friends. She had a feeling there wouldn't be many hotel bills between Sherman and Taos. As for when they arrived, well, maybe this Katherine Slade needed a housekeeper or nursemaid or something. It would be a different story altogether should she decide to stay here.

"Mrs. Barnes, it has long been the obligation of the church to care for widows and orphans."

"I don't want to be an obligation to anyone," she said quietly.

"And I do admire that. But I am sure you would not remain an obligation long. Mrs. Barnes, you would be a definite asset to our town, to our church." He cleared his throat. "And to my ministry."

Hannah stared, amazed. The look in his eyes had nothing to do with his calling to God's work.

"Mrs. Barnes—Hannah—I am not a man given to haste, and I had certainly thought to give *you* more time to know your thoughts in this regard . . . but I think you would make a fine helpmate."

Hannah was still staring.

"Hannah Barnes, will you marry me?"

Despite the faint roaring in her ears, Hannah heard the tiniest scuffle of sound behind her.

"Better give him your answer, pretty quick, Hannah." Jeb spoke evenly, with no trace of emotion. "We ride out at first light."

After a moment of complete silence, Reverend Salters recovered with remarkable aplomb. "Please join us, Mr. Welles."

Jeb did, careful to swallow any derogatory comment on the notion of Hannah remaining in Sherman. After all, that had been his plan before, and Hannah sure hadn't argued the point. Just because he'd changed his mind didn't mean Hannah had changed hers. She'd been a preacher's wife once; maybe the possibility of being one again appealed to her. No matter what Jeb thought of the idea, Hannah would have to make up her own mind. And, Jeb realized, he didn't like the idea one damned bit.

Hannah did her best not to compare the two men. She really did. It was, after all, an unfair comparison. Jeb Welles was trail-lean and trail-tough. Warren Salters, though no weakling, would have very little use for such broad shoulders and whipcord muscles. They would certainly be of no benefit from the pulpit.

Abruptly, Hannah noticed how quiet it had grown, then realized that the two men were both watching her. Watching and waiting. Surely neither of them expected her to answer a proposal of marriage with an audience?

Jeb leaned back in his chair, an expectant look upon his face. Hannah scowled at him briefly before taking a deep breath and turning her attention fully upon the reverend. "You do me a great honor."

He took pity upon her obvious distress. "But you must decline," he answered for her gently.

Hannah bit her lip for a moment, then decided to be honest. "My first marriage was not a happy one, sir. I will not wed again unless I can be assured of something more than duty and honor between myself and my husband. I'm sorry."

The reverend rose gracefully to his feet. "Do not apologize, Mrs. Barnes. That is no unworthy sentiment, although"—he looked rueful—"I cannot rejoice that you would choose the rigors of the trail over my proposal."

Despite his words, he glanced at Jeb with a mixture of curiosity and chagrin. Perhaps it was not the journey ahead that Hannah Barnes was choosing so much as her traveling companion. Immediately, he chastised himself for his thoughts. They would be more than worthy of Yolanda Graham.

Reverend Salters took his leave, and Jeb and Hannah were left alone. Jeb studied her face, looking for a hint of regret. "I've seen a lot of good marriages based on less than the reverend had to offer." His words surprised himself no less than Hannah.

"Not mine," Hannah said firmly, hiding her unhappy response to his words. Had Jeb wanted her to accept the offer? The possiblity was daunting. Hannah decided she would be glad to leave Sherman, Texas, and all it held far behind.

"I don't think we're following the right tracks."

Ike felt the skin crawl at the back of his neck. If he heard that whining tone in Wilkins's voice one more time, he'd put a bullet in him. "I told you before, don't try to think. It's beyond you."

"Well, it don't make sense they'd turn this way. There ain't nothing ahead of us but a no-account little town." Wilkins puffed up a little at his own courage. It took a real man to argue with Ike Nelson, and lately he needed to prove himself a man any way he could.

Ike rubbed the bristles at his neck, felt the dust and grit mixed with sweat. He sure could use a bath and a shave. Even if Wilkins was right and the tracks he'd been following didn't belong to Welles and the girl, he'd be glad to stretch out in a real bed with some whore. He'd been in Sherman a while back, and the memory of moist lips and perfumed bedsheets eased some of the anger that had been building against the fool he had for a traveling partner.

"Leon, if you don't shut up, I'm going to cut off that piddling little thing you keep worrying about and your worries will be over."

Hot fear sent sweat trickling down Wilkins's spine.

Ike caught the stench of the other man's terror and smiled.

Chapter Twenty-two

Things had definitely changed, Jeb decided. Hannah had changed. She looked the same. Once more that wealth of red hair sat circumspectly coiled at the back of her head, covered with a bonnet. That same expression of curiosity looked out on a world that Jeb had taken for granted so many years ago that he couldn't remember when he'd felt any wonder at the things around him.

Yet, Jeb knew a subtle change existed. Shoulders that had been stiff with trepidation and pride were now straight with self-confidence. Blue eyes no longer held unspoken apologies but danced with a mischief that Jeb both feared and hoped to see unleashed. He wondered if that would ever happen. He'd never in his life seen a woman so determined to keep her feelings to herself. Her expressions continued to give her away, but her speech rarely did.

Glancing sideways at her from the corner of his eye, Jeb decided there were other ways in which Hannah was too much the same, as well—physical ways, like the slender curve of her waist, the fullness of her breasts, the delicate arch of her throat. And Jeb knew his reaction was too much the same. The bay mare laid her ears back as he shifted his weight one more time.

Jeb looked around for a distraction and found one in the lowering fireball ahead of them. In another hour it would be dark. They needed to be making camp. Jeb turned his mare toward a likely-looking stand of trees, and Hannah followed.

At least the grulla followed. The sturdy gelding, Hannah realized ruefully, still did more of the decision-making than she did, but he seemed to be taking good care of her. He'd even begun to look a little less homely to her.

She slid to the ground and automatically reached out a hand to take Jeb's reins.

Jeb grinned at her with an odd sense of pride. "You'll make a trail hand yet, Hannah-girl. I'll see if I can rustle up some supper. Will you be all right while I'm gone?"

"I'll be fine," Hannah said confidently, trying not to look anxious. In spite of all the lonely hours of her marriage, she'd never quite gotten used to being left alone.

Jeb slid his rifle from the saddle and strode

toward the river, where the game would soon be coming in for an evening drink of water. Hannah watched him go, then forced her attention back to the tasks at hand.

Becoming a trail hand wasn't exactly her ambition, and Jeb's words weren't quite the compliment she might have hoped for, but Hannah decided that it was in line with being considered "one tough lady" and not to be disdained. Not quite expertly, she removed the saddles and unburdened the packhorse.

She was careful to stay close to the ground-tied horses while she gathered firewood. They had been traveling along the Red River since midafternoon, and Jeb had warned Hannah that the river itself marked the very boundary of Indian territory. The threat of danger from Indians was far less here than it would be as they moved farther west, but it still existed to some extent. When she walked down to the river to refill their canteens and to bathe herself, she remained alert and watchful. Jeb wouldn't appreciate it, if she got herself captured by Indians. But what, the tiny thought intruded, would she do if *he* were captured?

Pushing the thought aside, Hannah worked quickly and diligently, finding, as always, that work kept her mind from fretting. Still, she couldn't quite help the apprehension that crept in, the little niggling fear that something might happen to Jeb while he was gone. Wild animals or Indians could both be dangerous to a lone man. Hannah tried not to worry about what she would do if he didn't come back, tried not to think about how she would feel.

She flinched when she heard a rifle shot upriver from their camp. That was the sound of supper, she told herself.

Even so, she couldn't deny the relief that swept over her when Jeb emerged unscathed from the trees that lined the bank of the river.

Jeb's quick glance took in the semi-smokeless fire, hobbled horses grazing contentedly, and Hannah waiting expectantly for words of praise for her accomplishments.

He shifted the weight of the turkey he'd killed from one aching arm to the other and stifled a smile. "Did you fill the canteens?"

"Yes." Hannah felt a minute sting of disappointment. Why didn't he notice what she had accomplished and take for granted that she'd done the things he couldn't see?

"And the coffeepot."

Hannah gestured towards the tin pot sitting beside the fire, then turned to walk away.

Seeing the slightest droop to her shoulders, Jeb regretted his game. "Hannah," he called softly, waiting until she turned back before adding, "you did good. I shouldn't have teased you like that."

A tiny frown wrinkled Hannah's brow as she looked at him; then she said something he didn't fully understand and wasn't sure he'd like if he did.

"I used to know how to be picked at. I expect that's just one more thing I'll have to learn again if I'm going to get on in this world."

Jeb thought he caught the implication that Hannah intended to learn a lot of things—on her own. Did she think he would abandon her again before she could take care of herself? Or before she had someone to take care of her?

"You're going to get on fine in this world, Hannah." Jeb's voice sounded strained and a little husky, even to his own ears. He cleared his throat. "I reckon I'll get this bird ready for the fire."

While the smell of roasting game filled the air, Jeb kept a careful watch on Hannah's small explorations along the river bank. He'd cautioned her not to get out of his sight, and he made sure she didn't. He wondered if she'd never lived close to a river when she was young and free to enjoy it. He had, he realized, begun to wonder a lot about the life Hannah had lived before he met her.

Somehow, Jeb managed not to burn their supper despite half of his attention being caught up in keeping an eye on Hannah, both for her protection and for his pleasure. When he called her back to eat, her cheeks were rosy with the same joy that shone from her blue eyes.

Jeb handed her a tin plate already filled and watched a look of suspicion cross her face.

"What's this?" She poked at a heap of wilted greens suspiciously.

"Think I'd poison you?" Jeb asked blandly.

Hannah schooled her features to hide a smile

at the question. "No. You wouldn't enjoy that nearly as much as skinning me alive or beating the living daylights out of me."

Jeb gave a snort of laughter at hearing his own threats quoted back to him. "If you don't eat those greens, I won't have to do either one. You'll die of scurvy."

Settling on the blanket he'd spread, Hannah gave a sigh. "They don't look like any greens I've ever cooked."

"Eat them anyway."

A silence fell as they ate, until Jeb tired of watching Hannah pick at her food. Normally, she downed more than such a slender frame looked able to hold.

"What's wrong?" So, the greens weren't the most appetizing in the world. Jeb had eaten worse. And the fowl had roasted to near perfection over the open fire.

"I guess I'm not as hungry as I thought." Bravely, Hannah swallowed another piece of turkey, the gamy taste hitting the back of her throat. She didn't mind rabbit or deer or squirrel, but she'd never had much liking for wild turkey.

"If you wanted fine cuisine," Jeb said, insulted by the look on her face, "you should have stayed in Sherman."

Hannah flushed. She hadn't meant to offend him. Holding herself rigid, she took another mouthful of bitter greens. Swallowed. And bolted for the river, gagging.

"I guess you like horsemeat better!" Jeb

shouted to her back. Immediately, he felt ashamed and even more so when Hannah returned a few minutes later looking pale.

She sank back to the blanket. "What did you mean about the horsemeat?"

"I shouldn't have said that, Hannah." He shifted uncomfortably. "Forget I did, all right?"

"No."

Jeb rubbed his jaw. Hannah could turn stubborn at the damnedest times. She watched him steadily, and he knew she wasn't about to forget what he'd said. "The stew the Indians gave us when we went looking for your horse . . . well, that was him."

If there had been anything left in Hannah's stomach, she would have lost it then.

"I'm sorry," Jeb said awkwardly.

Hannah closed her eyes. "Once I had a pet bird that died. The next time Mama fried chicken, Simon, my oldest brother, told me it was my bird." She looked at Jeb again. "Papa strapped him."

Jeb felt like a youth in need of a good strapping. "I said I was sorry, damn it!"

When Hannah made no further move toward her plate, Jeb poured two full cups of coffee and handed one to Hannah.

"Tell me about your brothers," Jeb said when she finally began looking a little less green. A change of subject seemed like a good idea to him, and Hannah had opened a door he'd been curious about for a while.

"My brothers? What about them?" Images

from childhood raced through her mind, and as always, she pushed them away. Thinking of her brothers had become a grief to her in the past few years. She missed them achingly sometimes.

"Do you know where any of them are?"

She shrugged. "Papa got letters from the oldest ones every now and then, but they were never sent from the same place twice in a row. California, Louisiana . . . one even came from New York. Papa liked reading them, but then he'd be sad for days afterward."

"And you? Would you be sad?"

Hannah shied from his probing. "More restless than sad."

Jeb knew she lied. Hannah's face still revealed more of her feelings than she ever let herself admit to having. He wondered if she was that controlled in bed, then choked on a sip of coffee as he realized where his mind had gone. Again. "What about your mother?"

Hannah searched his eyes. "What are you doing, Jeb?"

"Trying to find the real Hannah," he admitted.

For a long time she simply sat and looked at him. "I'm not sure there is one," she answered at last. "I was Papa's little girl, then Caleb's wife."

Watching her nearly expressionless face, Jeb felt a flare of exasperation. "And doesn't that bother you?" He recalled her lack of emotion at her husband's death, her lack of anger at the insult Jacob Armen had dealt her. "Doesn't anything bother you? Make you lose control? Cry? Scream? Something to show you're alive inside?"

"Caleb didn't hold with outbursts," Hannah said doggedly, fighting the portrait of a cold woman Jeb was painting for her.

"Caleb's dead, damn it!" Watching the play of emotions across Hannah's face, Jeb forced himself to keep his hands from her, from shaking her until she broke, from touching her, caressing her . . .

Hannah looked at the cup clasped in both hands. "Yes. He is."

"What does that make you feel, Hannah?" Jeb pressed for her response. Something had to break Hannah free of the terrible control the man had clamped on her, a control, Jeb realized now, that extended far beyond the grave.

Fighting not to remember, Hannah clenched her hands into fists. She turned her face from Jeb. "Caleb was my husband. What do you think I feel?"

"No, Hannah, that's not good enough," Jeb said quietly. "It doesn't matter what I think. It only matters what you feel."

"Why?" Cornered, Hannah leapt to her feet. "Why does it matter? It's over."

Jeb rose cautiously, sensing Hannah was close to flight. He had to make sure she stayed to fight instead. He sensed it was important to her, to the woman she could be. "It won't be over for you until you face up to what you feel, to what that man did to you."

"Caleb didn't do anything to me." Hannah felt a lump of panic rising in her throat. She forced her voice past the painful constriction. "Caleb was my husband. A man of God. A good man," she insisted, taking a step backward.

"Who didn't love you," Jeb pushed. "Who put a roof over you head, fed your body, and scarred your soul. He may have been a righteous man, Hannah, but he wasn't a good man."

"Don't," she whispered. "Please don't." She whirled to run, not wanting to acknowledge the truth. The wedding vows she had spoken before God had pledged her to love and obey the man her father had chosen for her. All she had ever been able to give Caleb was her obedience, and even there, she had too often failed him. She had never been able to love him.

Jeb grabbed for her before she could move. His hands held her by the forearm, not letting her turn away, forcing her to face him. "He didn't love you, Hannah. He probably never even knew how. It isn't wrong that you couldn't love him, that you can't grieve for him."

The tears Hannah had fought so hard spilled from her eyes, unleashing the words she had fought not to say. "I'm glad he's dead!" She made no move to wipe away the tears streaming down her face. "God help me, I'm glad."

Jeb caught her close to him, pressing her to his chest, feeling the hot tears soak the front of his shirt. The fragile feel of her drew a wildly protective response, and he cradled her in his arms, sinking slowly back to the blanket with her.

"It's all right, Hannah," he whispered against her temple, breathing in the fresh scent of her. "I swear to God, it's all right."

Chapter Twenty-three

Sunlight burnished the polished oak floor to a soft golden color. Bleached linen graced every table. Flatware sparkled. Even Jenny's critical eye could find not one fault with her restaurant. The diners appeared well fed and content with the service. Used to doing everything herself, Jenny had recently hired a young girl to help serve the increasing number of customers.

A man in the dusty, rugged garb of a trail hand caught Jenny's attention with a discreet gesture. She paused beside his table. "Hello, Rufus." She greeted him with real affection. "I haven't seen you in a while."

"You're as beautiful as ever, sweetheart."

Jenny smiled down into the admiring eyes of the cowboy, who seemed as enthralled with her fried chicken as he was with her. Even while he complimented her, his hand reached for a crisp drumstick from the brightly flowered china platter and brought it to his teeth.

"And you're as hungry as ever. It's good to see you again." In one way, Jenny was being honest; it *was* good to see him. In another, she regretted his arrival. Rufus might be an old friend, but she didn't feel much like renewing old friendships these days.

"Sit down with me." He gestured to the opposite chair. "You'll give me a catch in my neck making me look up at you like this." He grinned a bit wickedly. "Of course, you can always rub the pain away later."

Giving a little laugh, Jenny did as he requested, pulling a chair out from the opposite side of the table and seating herself. It was no use waiting for a rounder like Rufus to remember what few manners he might have been taught in his youth. She was surprised he'd remembered to removed his hat when seated at her table. He'd had to be reminded more than once in the past.

"Where have you been the last few months?" It was a meaningless question, one she asked every "old friend" who wandered back into her life.

Not one of them ever seemed to realize how little their answer meant to her, and Rufus was no exception. He began to speak enthusiastically of his place, a spread of his own he'd finally started. "Someday I'm going to be somebody in this state, Jenny. Just you wait and see."

"I don't doubt it, Rufus," she said gently, hoping things worked out better for him than they seemed to be for her lately. At least her restaurant was prospering.

"When I get rich, I'll buy you fancier gowns than you've ever worn." He liked the yellow one she had on just fine, though. It was plainly cut for his taste, but it made her soft brown eyes look larger and darker than ever.

Jenny shook her head. "You know I don't take gifts, Rufus. Besides, you'll be wanting to buy things for a sweet little wife just any day now." Despite her rejection of his offer, she kept her voice warm and kind.

"Well . . . maybe not just any day," he countered, "but it sure does get mighty lonesome around the ranch come evening. I *have* been thinking a wife wouldn't be a bad idea." He looked at Jenny speculatively. "As long as she looked as good as you." And as long as she knew the things Jenny knew how to do. Of course, he wouldn't want a wife of his learning those things the way Jenny had learned them.

Come to think of it, maybe he'd rather she didn't know anything. Then he could be sure he was the only one to ever teach her.

"And as long as she could cook like me?" Jenny teased softly as he reached for another piece of chicken. Despite her smile, she felt a hint of sadness. His expression had revealed a glimpse of the path his thoughts had taken. No, men didn't look to women like her for wives. They preferred real ladies who would starve to death in genteel poverty before taking the path she'd chosen, even if it offered survival. She'd always known it, but it hadn't much mattered until she'd met Daniel Hastings. Her first marriage hadn't given her any particular desire for a second. Daniel had changed her mind.

Now, though . . . She shrugged the regret aside. What was done was done. Maybe Daniel *didn't* know what she was; maybe he suspected. It didn't matter either way. Even if he wanted her for a wife, she couldn't go to him without telling him the truth. And she couldn't do that without the risk of being crushed by what she dreaded to read in his face when that moment came—the same thing she'd discerned in Rufus's face a moment earlier. With Rufus, it was of no consequence; with Daniel, it would be enough to kill her.

Rufus concentrated on filling his empty belly with chicken, fluffy potatoes, and tiny sweet peas creamed with butter and flour. "Damn, Jenny, you're a fine cook."

"But I'm not being a good hostess sitting here with you." She softened her words with a smile. "I'd better check on my other guests."

Rufus caught her hand before she could rise and caressed the knuckles with a gentler touch than she'd known in a long time. He had, she recalled, always been a tender lover, and a fulfilling one. "I'm going for a bath and a shave. How about I come back later?"

For a moment, Jenny hesitated. Her bruised heart could use a soft touch. But Daniel's craggy face, framed by silver-tipped hair, came between her and the man waiting for her answer. For a moment she considered lying, telling Rufus it wasn't a good time of the month. Somehow she knew, though, that things had changed for her, and they weren't ever going to be the same.

"I'm afraid not, Rufus. The only business I run now is the restaurant."

Rufus's eyes widened in surprise, but he managed to hide his disappointment with a smile. "I hadn't heard that." He hesitated. He sure did need a woman. "What if it wasn't business?"

Reluctantly, Jenny shook her head. "I'm sorry."

"No sorrier than I am." And no sorrier than a dozen other men would be. Jenny limited herself to a select few, and those few had always considered themselves lucky indeed. Rufus sure had. "I don't reckon I could say anything that would change your mind?"

She smiled at his earnest look. It sat as oddly on his boyishly handsome face as did the mustache he hadn't sported the last time he'd been around. "I don't think so. But you'll always be welcome at my table, Rufus."

He grinned ruefully. "I'd rather be welcome in your bed, honey." He leaned across the small table and gave her a swift kiss on the cheek before he released her hand. "If you ever need anything—anything at all—all you have to do is send word to me. I swear it."

"I know." Jenny rose to her feet, feeling like she'd severed a lifeline. She guessed that in a way, she had. Word would spread that the Widow Ryon was no longer available. Sure, there would be some disappointed men, but they'd go on to find other women to fill the empty times. Maybe some, like Rufus, would even realize it was past time for them to take a wife. And Jenny would be left alone, with nothing to fill the vacancy in her life—or in her bed.

Rufus settled his hat on his head, paid his bill, and told Jenny good-bye. As he stepped out into the street, he realized that he had a real problem. He'd been thinking pleasurable thoughts about Jenny the whole ride into town. Now he had a need he wasn't quite sure how to get satisfied. He'd never been one to take a saloon girl who could be had by any man. Still, he didn't know if he could wait, and he didn't know anywhere else to go in Sherman besides Jenny's. He knew one or two other women like Jenny. Widows, who'd had a man in their bed once and needed one again. Wives, who were not satisfied with the men they had. Unfortunately, none of them was here in Sherman. None but Jenny.

Shrugging, he walked into the barber where he could get a good, close shave and a turn at a tub of hot, soapy water. When he confided to the man that he needed a woman, he was told the girls at Hirsch's saloon were skillful and as clean as those anywhere. "Tell Hirsch you want Jericho or maybe Coral." Rufus thanked him with an extra tip as he left.

When Rufus reached the saloon, he headed straight for the massive bartender. "I'll need a bottle of whiskey, a room, and a girl—I was told to ask for Jericho or Coral."

Hirsch shook his head. "Both taken." He pointed across the room, then swung his huge head toward the far end of the bar and gestured to a long-legged beauty perched there. "Hey, Chloe. Come here."

As she approached, Rufus didn't spare a second glance at the shadows where the other two girls were occupied. He beamed at Chloe and seized the bottle the bartender held out for him. "Where's the room?" He never took his eyes from the fancy brunette.

Hirsch took his measure, saw no threat, and directed Chloe to lead him upstairs. He wanted to keep the room behind him open for whichever girl the tall, grey-eyed man decided to take. Hirsch had a bad feeling about that one. A real bad feeling. He propped his hip against the bar and stared broodingly toward the corner.

Feeling Hirsch's gaze, Coral winked at him, then pressed a little closer to the short, chunky fellow who seemed absolutely fascinated with her. She didn't consider him her type, but the last fellow she'd tried to bed had left her feeling rejected. Hell, she *had* been rejected.

Besides, she needed the money, and she damned sure didn't want anything to do with the man who had his hand down the front of Jericho's dress. He might be handsome, but he sent a chill right down her spine that had nothing to do with sensual pleasure.

Ike smiled down at Jericho, but his eyes drifted toward Coral. He sensed her fear and dislike, and the knowledge excited him more than the feel of the other girl's nipple between his fingers. For a moment, he considered making Wilkins switch with him, but something about the knowing look of the dark-haired Jericho changed his mind. He craved a good, long bout of sex, and he suspected this one had more of what he wanted in that direction.

He needed some release for the frustration of losing the trail he'd been following. The tracks of Welles and the woman had mixed in with those of a lot of other travelers a few miles outside of town. The couple could be right here in town, somewhere real close by, or they could be a hundred miles away. Welles might never have intended riding into town. Coming this close could have been a deliberate ploy to lose them—one Ike had used himself a time or two. If so, it meant Welles knew he was being followed. The possibility didn't make Ike particularly happy.

Ike figured he was due a distraction from his troubles. He turned Jericho so that she sat crossways on his lap, her breasts close to his face, then slowly tugged the ruffled top of her dress down past her nipples. Wilkins and Coral were the only others who could see what he was doing, and he watched them while he opened his mouth wide and took one dark tip against his tongue. He grinned when Wilkins groaned and breathed heavily through his mouth.

Coral gaped and wondered if she had the better of the two men after all. Before she had time to wonder further, Wilkins shoved her off his lap.

"Let's get out of here," he said thickly. He was so big he hurt.

Coral stood, straightening her dress while she looked toward Hirsch. Hirsch's gaze moved past her to all that he could see of Jericho, which was her back. He frowned, then jerked his head towards the stairs.

Relief swept through Coral that grey eyes hadn't chosen her. If Hirsch wanted Jericho in the room behind him, he was worried. And Hirsch had real good judgment about which men made bad customers. She turned and looked back at Jericho, thinking to warn her with a look, but Jericho was still facing away from her. Her back was arched, her dark head tilted back, and she rocked against the lap beneath her in rhythmic motions.

"Damn," Wilkins breathed. That whore was going to come right here in front of everybody. The bulge against his pants became more painful, and he tightened his grip on the hand clenched in his. If he didn't bury that bulge in something real soon, he was going to do the same. "Come on."

When Wilkins and the girl had disappeared up the stairs, Ike clamped a steely grip on Jericho's hips, stopping her motion. She whimpered and opened her eyes.

"No." He smiled at the painful need registered on her face. "When you get finished with what I want done, then you get yours."

Jericho licked lips dry from her panting and rose unsteadily to her feet, then watched as the man stood and stretched lithely. He started toward the stairs, pulling Jericho with him, but she instinctively glanced toward Hirsch. The bartender looked almost angry as he jerked his thumb toward the door behind him.

"This way, honey," she said, still husky-voiced with passion. "The upstairs rooms are full."

Ike glanced at the stairs, the barkeep, and the door just beyond the bar. He smiled slowly. Maybe the barkeep took his pleasure from listening. Well, Ike could give him plenty to listen to. He was going to have this whore begging for her pleasure in just a little while.

He leaned down and whispered in her ear, "Come on, sugar. You're going to show me every trick you've got. Then I'll teach you a few more."

"Do something else," Wilkins insisted. He closed his eyes against the flickering light of the candle the girl had lit. It didn't do any good to look at her lush body anyway.

"Honey, I've done all I know how." Coral heard the exasperation in her own voice. She still couldn't believe her bad luck. As soon as she'd stripped and stood before him, his rock-hard condition had melted to nothing.

Wilkins couldn't believe it, either. He'd wanted her a little while ago; he'd been ready, damn it. Hell, he should have pushed her down on a table and spread her legs in the bar while he could still do something. He squeezed his eyelids tighter and tried to picture the other whore with her breast half down Ike's throat. Nothing.

Sweat beaded on his forehead. Jesus, that redheaded preacher's wife had ruined him for sure. He had to find her. He couldn't keep on like this. Even whores would be laughing at him soon. He opened his eyes in sharp suspicion, but the girl watching him wasn't laughing. Worse than laughter, he saw pity in her eyes.

Pity and irritation. "I can't figure this," she said petulantly. "I know I ain't ugly or anything, but you're the second man in as many days who couldn't keep it stiff long enough to get it in."

"Maybe he was cursed, too." Wilkins pulled her hand back down to his flaccid sex, saw the revulsion in her eyes, and flung it away again.

"Cursed. Hell, he wasn't cursed." Coral was still angry over the incident. She didn't want this man so much as she wanted his money, but she'd felt a hunger for that other one. "He was love-bit by that little redheaded gal he had holed up at Armen's."

Wilkins felt a tremor of excitement that had nothing to do with sex. "Redheaded gal?"

"Yeah. Course, I didn't know it until I heard all the gossip about old Armen trying to make her whore for his guests. Humph! If they want that, they can come here. There's hardly enough business in town as it is, without that greedy bastard taking any away from us."

Unable to believe his luck, Wilkins cut in. "What was his name? Who was with the redhead?"

Coral frowned. "His name? What the hell difference does it make?" She'd had really strange customers before, but this one took the prize.

Wilkins took her pointed little chin in his hand and squeezed. Hard. "His name, damn you. What was it?" The heavy scent of her perfume focused his anger. She smelled like a stupid whore.

"Ouch!" Coral tried to jerk away but couldn't. "I—I don't know. Webb or Wells or something like that."

"Welles," he breathed in satisfaction. "He's brought her here." He quelled an urge to hasten back down to tell Ike. Ike would cut off his balls if he disturbed him now. Besides, Leon felt sure anything he learned could wait a few hours—till morning anyway.

He let go of Coral's face, and she drew back with a sob. He'd bruised her, damn him. Hirsch would make him pay for this! She tried to ease from the bed. All she wanted to do now was get away. He could keep his damned money!

Wilkins clamped a hand back on her wrist. "You ain't going anywhere. Not until you've given me what I need."

"There ain't much chance I can do that, if you can't get it up," she taunted, furious because he'd hurt her. He had no call to do that.

Anger welled up in Wilkins, and he grabbed the whore around the throat. "You'll give me what I need all right." The blood pounded in his temples. Her neck felt fragile. Slowly, he began to squeeze.

Jericho watched through half-closed eyes as the grey-eyed stranger pulled up his pants and fastened them. Every muscle in every part of her body was tired and sore and sated. She considered asking him to stay just a little while longer, but doubted her body's ability to withstand another bout of his creativity.

Ike turned to look at her as he buttoned his shirt. By candlelight she was pretty; by daylight, he suspected she would look every bit her age and profession. Not that it mattered, he'd be long gone by daylight. She'd given him his money's worth, and that was all that counted with him right now. He grinned, pleased with the world. "Reckon your watchdog heard what he bargained for?"

Jericho thought of Hirsch, his neck craned, listening. She thought of the things this man had tormented her into saying, into begging for, into pleading for. Jericho had been whoring for a dozen years, and she blushed. The next time she thought she'd seen, heard, and done it all, she would remember this night and the man with grey eyes.

Ike saw the color creep up her neck and laughed. "Honey, if I didn't have places I needed to be, I'd show you the things we didn't get around to."

If another man had said that to her, Jericho would have scoffed. She believed this one. Her eyes widened as he peeled several bills from the roll he pulled from one pocket. Normally, she considered herself good at what she did and worth the fairly considerable amount she demanded in return for her talents. This time, she would almost have been willing to pay her customer. She couldn't wait to show Coral what she'd been given for her time. She'd bet that sweaty little bastard upstairs hadn't been nearly as generous—and not half as much of a pleasure to service.

"Sugar," she nearly purred, stretching tired muscles against the soft mattress, "you come back any time, and I'll be glad to learn anything you have to teach."

With a laugh, Ike bent over the bed. "If I ever come through this way again, I'll be back." He cupped one full breast in his hand and rubbed his thumb lightly over the nipple, while he kissed her. Hard.

Jericho couldn't believe it when her body

responded yet again. She wouldn't have thought she had anything left to respond with.

Ike laughed again and drew away. "Spread your legs, honey."

She did, but to her disappointment, all he did was take her hand in his and place it where she wanted *him* to touch her.

"Don't move," he said, pausing in the doorway to look back. She obeyed, and even he felt his sex harden slightly at the sight of the whore with her legs sprawled and her hand nestled against the curls between them.

Leaving the door open, he sauntered out into the bar. The giant of a bartender stared at him as he emerged, and Ike jerked a thumb back over his shoulder. "She wants you," he told the man, then looked around the bar for Wilkins. He should have been waiting for Ike by now, but he wasn't.

Ike chuckled. Maybe the little bastard had actually managed to keep it up this time. Still, he wondered if he should check to see if Leon was waiting with the horses before he went pounding on doors upstairs.

"Holy shit."

He turned as the choked curse came from behind him, then grinned as the barkeep stepped into the little room Ike had just left and closed the door. Ike bet that was the first time the man had ever walked off and left the bar unattended.

[illegible]

[illegible] ... upon their [illegible]

[illegible]

He turned, as the revolver [illegible] came [illegible] [illegible] ... [illegible] unconcerned.

Chapter Twenty-four

Even with his eyes closed, Jeb could see the stars scattered across the sky above him. He'd stared at them so long that they were imprinted on his mind. Stared at them, counted them, cursed them—anything to keep from rolling the sleeping woman in his arms over onto her back and tossing her skirt over her head. He could just picture Hannah's reaction to that.

He would have laughed if his rigid arousal hadn't been so painful. How a bitterly weeping woman could bring him to this state when a wriggling saloon girl couldn't was beyond him. As far as that went, almost everything seemed beyond his ability to understand where Hannah was concerned. Everything, that is, except one indisputable fact—Hannah Barnes had a firm hold on his emotions. He'd seen this coming, tried to avoid it any way he could, and had no idea how to deal with it now that it was a reality.

As if sensing the turbulence of his thoughts, she stirred against him, murmuring in her sleep, and his hunger bit deeper. If the air hadn't turned cool with the settling of night, he'd be covered in sweat from that hunger. And if Hannah had any inkling of the thoughts and images teasing his mind, she'd be off that bedroll and out of his arms in a flash.

His arms tightened. He wasn't about to let her get away. Without even thinking about what he was doing, he shifted slightly so that they lay nearly face-to-face. Each light breath she exhaled, soft and sweet, tickled his face. Stifling a groan, he pressed a kiss to her temple where soft tendrils curled against her warm skin. He could feel her steady pulse against his lips.

Instinctively, Hannah sought the cradling warmth that held her. A heartbeat sounded rhythmically against her ear. A heartbeat sounded rhythmically against her ear. Slowly, her eyes opened. Her upper lids felt dry and gritty from the crying she'd done. Bit by bit, she became aware of muscled thighs pressing the length of hers, of hard arms holding her to a solid chest. Heat flooded through her as she realized that she lay snuggled against Jeb Welles like the harlot Jacob Armen had tried to make her!

Jeb's hold tightened as he felt Hannah draw

back from him. "Shhh, Hannah. Be still," he whispered, nearly desperate to keep her next to him. He couldn't think of a damned thing to say beyond that.

"I can't," she whispered back, just as desperate. For the life of her, though, she couldn't come up with one reason to give him why she couldn't, or even shouldn't. Despite her words of protest, she didn't move. Everywhere his body touched hers felt exquisitely sensitive, even through the layers of clothing between them.

"I'm not going to hurt you." Even as he said the words, Jeb forced himself not to crush her to him. That might not hurt her, but it'd sure as hell scare her to death.

"I'm not afraid of you," she said softly. No, not of him. Of herself. Of her reaction to him.

Jeb could see the gleam of her pale blue eyes in the moonlight. Maybe that wasn't fear he saw looking back at him, but it came damned close to it.

Jeb wanted to whisper lovemaking words to her, words that would tell her what he wanted to do to her body, what he wanted her to feel and what he wanted to feel in return. The thought of her reaction to *that* made him grit his teeth against uttering them. He'd be damned if he could take hearing her spout scripture against the sins of the flesh to him. Not now when he was on fire with wanting her. And he didn't trust her not to do just that!

Neither, however, could he bring himself to

loose his hold and let her go. Almost without conscious thought, he slid his hand from her elbow to her shoulder and back again in a slow, caressing movement. He felt her breathing become shallow, but still she didn't pull away. Her breasts brushed his chest with every breath either of them took. The beating of his heart sounded loud within his own chest.

"Hannah?" The word emerged in little more than a croak.

Hannah knew what he was asking. She thought of every reaction open to her at this point. Anger. Indignation. Flight. Closing her eyes, she focused on the sensation evoked by the palm of his hand as it slowly caressed her arm. Surely, her heart would pound its way out of her chest. She fought to keep from slipping her hands into his hair where it curled at the nape of his neck. Memories of long nights of lying stiff, knowing Caleb would condemn any sign of affection from her, held her very still.

Jeb felt the instant she tensed and bit back a curse. What had he expected? If she hadn't loved her husband, chances were, she hadn't welcomed his attentions. Sex would hold none of the appeal for her it did for Jeb. Worse than the long nights of a loveless marriage, she had endured the rape of three murdering bastards. What the hell *had* he expected?

Hannah yearned to press her aching breasts against Jeb. The thought of disgusting him kept her from it. Chills rippled along her ribs, raising goosebumps on her flesh and turning her sensitive nipples into stabbing points of need.

The rigidity of Hannah's body slowly cooled Jeb's ardor. He'd persuaded reluctant women in his life, holding them down and teasing them with their own needs until they'd begged him to do what they refused to begin with. He knew he couldn't do that with Hannah. She'd been raped once. Jeb wasn't about to do anything that would place him on a level with those sons of bitches in her eyes. The thought that she might never welcome his touch finished the job of defusing his explosive need.

Jeb's hand fell away, and Hannah almost cried with the loss of his touch. Her reaction shamed her, but not to the point that she could keep herself from asking, "Where are you going?"

"For a swim." He grunted the words, rolling to his feet.

A swim! Was that where his thoughts had been as he touched her?

Hannah had believed herself beyond tears, but salty liquid filled her eyes as she watched his shadowy form fade toward the river. She had never burned for Caleb, but he had wanted her and cursed his need every time he took her. Even when Hannah had learned not to rile him with any signs of affection, Caleb had denounced the weakness of his own flesh. She had thought nothing could hurt worse than her husband's scathing rejection of her. She had been wrong.

Taking a deep breath, she wiped the dampness from her cheeks. She'd survived every other pain life had dealt her. With God's help, she'd survive this one too. Likely it was for the best, anyway. She wasn't sure she could live with herself if Jeb had taken advantage of feelings she hadn't even known she possessed until this moment. Not if it lowered her in his sight.

For a long time, she lay still, listening. Above the muted calls of insects, she could hear soft but distinct splashes as Jeb walked into the river and began to swim. Hannah could almost feel the coolness of the water against her own heated flesh and wished she knew how to swim.

Jeb stayed in the river a long time. When he returned, she feigned a deep sleep. Maybe it would be less embarrassing for both of them if she pretended the incident had never happened. Likely, in Jeb's mind, it never had anyway. The thought filled her with a sadness she hadn't felt since the morning she'd stood at her mother's grave.

Ike didn't like it. Wilkins should have been waiting in the bar for him. He glanced around the deserted room, then at the door the bartender had closed behind him. A cruel grin touched his face as he remembered the condition of that whore when he'd left her. Yeah, old Hirsch was going to have himself a good time.

But where the hell was Wilkins? He didn't

really think the little twit could have managed to do anything with that whore he'd hauled up the stairs. And the dumb clod should have had plenty of time to discover that for himself. Again. Ike almost smiled, thinking how furious the girl must have been. Or maybe not. Maybe she had felt only relief at getting paid for nothing more than a few hours' sleep.

The smile faded. Ike felt the hair bristle along the nape of his neck as he stared up the darkened stairs. Wilkins wasn't up there. Ike would bet a bankroll on it. Something was wrong.

Cursing under his breath the whole time, he left the bar and headed for the livery stable. He stopped near the entrance of the wide, open hallway to watch and listen. He was aware of the sleeping town at his back. Despite the peaceful quiet along the street, a warning still lingered down his spine.

The sound of Wilkins's heavy breathing reached him, and Ike walked into the enveloping darkness. His eyes had adjusted to the dark, and he made his way easily enough.

"Leon." He reached the snoring figure, slumped in a semi-sitting position in front of one stall. Maybe that warning had been a false alarm. Ike nudged him with the toe of his boot. "Wake up."

"What the—" Wilkins rubbed his eyes. He felt like hell. "Ike?"

"Who the hell do you think it is? And what are you doing sleeping out here? That gal run you out when you couldn't keep it up?"

Leon felt a fresh jab of anger toward the girl, and toward Ike, too. Then the anger gave way to apprehension. Ike was going to be mad at him for killing her. They wouldn't be able to stay in town and hunt for the preacher woman. And Welles.

Wilkins's hesitation brought a fresh roil of alarm to Ike's gut. He hadn't stayed alive this long without a sixth sense that warned him of danger.

"What's wrong?" He didn't try to lessen the cold ugliness of his voice. When Wilkins didn't answer, the alarm heightened. *Shit.* "What the hell have you done?"

"She laughed at me, Ike." This wasn't exactly how he'd planned to tell Ike they needed to get out of town. Fast.

"You messed her up?" Still no answer. "How bad?"

"She shouldn't have laughed at me," he whined. "I was just going to shut her up, but my hands were around her neck, and . . ." His voice trailed away.

"You killed her?" Ike's voice rose with his fury. You stupid little bastard!"

Leon cringed a little. He'd known Ike wasn't going to like it. "I d-didn't mean to do it, Ike. It j-just happened," he stammered.

"You don't just *happen* to put your hands around a whore's throat and choke her to death, jackass." Ike felt like strangling Wilkins. "Aw, hell, let's get out of here."

"We can't leave," Wilkins said anxiously. "Welles and that preacher's wife are in town."

"Here?" Ike couldn't believe his damned luck. Welles was here and Wilkins had fixed it so they couldn't do a damned thing about it. He'd have no compunction about throwing Wilkins to the wolves—in this case, the sheriff—but somehow he didn't think he'd be allowed to walk out of here without someone taking a look into his own past. The law wouldn't have to look far to find blood on his hands. He damned sure couldn't survive that a free man.

He glared at Wilkins. "Just how the hell do you think we're going to be able to hang around here long enough to do anything about the fact that Welles and that redheaded bitch are within reach?" Ike didn't expect an answer. As far as he was concerned, Wilkins didn't have sense enough to give him one. He glared toward the dark street. Welles and that preacher lady could be anywhere.

"We can find her, Ike. I know we can."

"Yeah, if Welles or the sheriff in this sod farmer's town don't find us first. Do you think they won't be looking, after what you done?"

"She was j-just a whore."

"And you're just a worthless piece of cow dung. Come on. Let's get out of here." Ike led his horse out of the stall.

"But what about the girl?" Wilkins whined, following suit. He had to find that bitch soon. She was going to take this curse off him. Then he was going to kill her. He would put his hands around her neck, just like he had that stupid whore who'd taunted him, and he'd squeeze and squeeze until she turned purple, too.

Ike didn't understand what it was like. He just didn't understand. Wilkins shivered under the glare the other man gave him.

"Sooner or later they'll ride out of here. Or Welles will ride out alone. Either way, we'll have the girl." And Welles, too. Ike finished saddling his horse and stepped into the stirrup. "Get mounted."

Wilkins wrinkled his forehead in bewilderment. "But what are we going to do 'til then?"

Ike gave him a humorless grin. "We're going to hole up outside of town and wait. And you'd best pray nobody cares enough about that whore to look too hard, 'cause I don't plan on dying on account of you."

Wilkins knew what that meant. Ike would sacrifice him in a minute. Not that he'd ever had any doubt of that. He wiped surreptitiously at the sweat beaded on his brow and grabbed the reins of his horse.

As he followed Ike through the dark street, his anger began to grow. None of this was his fault. It was that preacher woman's fault. All of it.

Chapter Twenty-five

Jericho started up the stairs, feeling every aching inch of her body. The unwelcome light of morning streamed through the windows and hurt her eyes. Maybe she was getting too old for this business. Or maybe she was just getting too old, period. Then she thought of the way Hirsch had been looking at her when he finally pulled his trousers back on and buckled his belt, and she grinned.

She'd bet he wouldn't even have left her then if he hadn't realized he'd left the bar completely unattended for over an hour. Not that there were likely to be any more customers coming in at that hour.

Her grin faded as she thought of the grey-eyed stranger. Hirsch hadn't shown her the things that one had, hadn't made her crave more and more of feelings that were almost too much for a body to stand. What Hirsch had given her instead was infinitely more precious. He'd looked at her like she was a motherlode of gold and touched her like she was fragile crystal. Hirsch wouldn't have taken her to the brink only to call another man to cool the raging fire he'd built.

When Hirsch had walked into that room, her heart had stopped. He had never even seen her naked, much less with her legs sprawled and her hand pressed between them. The shame of that moment might have overwhelmed her had it not been for the barkeep's reaction.

Instead of turning away from her in disgust, he'd reached for the buttons of his shirt. "Let me do that for you, sweetheart," he'd whispered, his hungry eyes glowing darkly as he'd looked into hers.

Just thinking about it made Jericho's lips curve in a smile. She'd never thought about Hirsch that way before. Now she wondered why she hadn't. She liked big men with arms like the forelegs of a bull. That wasn't all that had been bull-like about Hirsch, either.

Lordy, Coral wasn't going to believe her ears. Jericho yawned as she rapped on the first door up the stairs. She hoped she'd guessed right about which one. Chloe would scratch her eyes out if she banged on the wrong door and woke that hellcat. Not that she and Chloe weren't friends. They were, but Chloe was a real bitch if she didn't get what she considered a full morning's sleep.

There was no answer to her knock, but the door swung slowly open on its hinges. Jericho stepped into the room, hesitated, then took one step more before she stopped altogether. The oil lamp was still burning low on its wick. It wasn't like Coral to be so careless as to leave a lamp burning. "Coral?"

A chill ran up her spine when the other girl didn't stir. Coral lay on her back, one leg twisted beneath her. Surely no one could sleep in that position.

Jericho forced herself to take another step forward. The sheet draped over Coral's chest was still, not rising and falling with the movement of her breathing. Blue eyes stared sightlessly at the ceiling. Jericho stopped again, her teeth starting to chatter. "Coral? H-honey?"

Oh, God! The words reverberated through her mind several times before she forced them through her teeth. "Oh, God! Oh, God! Somebody help me!"

"Doc?"

The bespectacled man glanced at the waiting sheriff. He stepped away from the girl's body and removed his glasses, rubbing his handkerchief over the lenses.

"Strangled," he said on a sigh. The dark bruises on the pale neck left little doubt of that. Her neck was broken, too, but Doc rather thought she'd been dead by the time it snapped beneath the force of the hands that had been crushing her windpipe.

He'd been called here before, more than once. A while back, a girl had been treated roughly. Sheriff Hastings had made an example of the man. Before that, another girl had been caught by an unwelcome pregnancy she'd tried to abort on her own. Her death, despite all the doctor could do, had made an example for the other girls.

This was the first time one of Hirsch's girls had been murdered. Doc turned his gaze on the bartender. The man was taking it hard. His eyes were red-rimmed; his face more grey than anything else.

"It was quick," Doc told him.

Hirsch just stared back at him. It couldn't have happened quickly enough. The end wouldn't have come before Coral felt the terror of knowing she faced her death. His fault. The knowledge nagged at him. He'd worried about the wrong man. These girls trusted him. It should have been Coral he put in the room behind the bar, not Jericho. And if he hadn't gone in to Jericho like that . . .

Daniel Hastings placed a hand on Hirsch's broad shoulder. "You know who did this?"

Hirsch nodded grimly. "I know."

"Come down to my office. I'll need a description." Daniel could have gotten the information right where they were, but he wanted Hirsch out of there when the girl's body was removed. He turned a look on Doc and nodded. Doc would know what to do while they were gone.

Daniel nudged Hirsch out of the room ahead of him. Three girls were huddled in the hall, all weeping softly.

Hirsch hesitated and started to speak. Jericho fixed dark eyes on him, accusingly, it seemed to him. He closed his mouth and kept walking.

"Hey." When Hirsch didn't look back, Jericho lifted her voice slightly. "Hirsch."

He stopped and turned, half afraid of what he would read in her face.

Jericho tried to smile, but her lips trembled with the effort. "Hurry back, all right?" Tears sparkled in her eyes as she admitted. "I'm scared."

"I won't be gone long," he promised, feeling a bone-deep relief. Jericho didn't blame him. And she still trusted him.

By the time Daniel Hastings had a description firmly on paper, he knew he was dealing with the men who'd made Hannah Barnes a widow. The men Jeb Welles had sworn to find. Evidently Welles had been right to think the men would be after Mrs. Barnes. It was too much of a coincidence to suppose they'd arrived in Sherman this close behind Welles and the woman by mere chance. They had to have tracked the couple here.

For the first time, the sheriff knew without a doubt that the Widow Barnes had made the right decision when she turned down a decent offer of marriage. Reverend Salters could never have kept her safe from the likes of Ike Nelson and Leon Wilkins. Daniel didn't like to think of that pretty little woman lying all twisted and broken. Didn't like to think of her suffering the horror that poor Coral must have felt. He hoped to hell Jeb Welles managed to keep his mind on what he was doing and his eye on his backtrail.

Daniel walked out into the street with Hirsch. No less than two dozen men lined the wide dirt expanse in front of the jail. Silent men with grim faces, hard eyes, and loaded guns. His posse, ready and waiting without being called. Daniel wasn't surpised. The few times he'd needed a posse, they'd shown up before the call went out. This was their town. Their families were here; their lives were here. They were farmers and storekeepers, but they knew how to ride and how to shoot, and they knew how to protect what belonged to them.

His deputy came from across the street, where he'd been talking with a man too old to go hunting killers, but not so old he didn't wish he was young again. Daniel nodded at the oldster, letting him know he understood and sympathized.

Daniel waited until the deputy stopped beside him before speaking loudly enough for every man there to hear. "Before we head out looking for tracks, we search this town—every building, every alley." He paused. "By two's." He didn't have to tell them to cover each other's backs.

Some of the men looked surprised that they

weren't heading out of town immediately; one or two nodded in satisfaction. No one protested.

Daniel glanced at his deputy and lowered his voice. "You take half these men and start at that end."

The deputy nodded and stepped into the middle of the gathering, dividing them into two groups. Daniel strode purposefully to the end of town that housed Jenny's business, knowing that half the men would follow.

Within moments, he stood in front of the restaurant. He pictured the dead whore's body in his mind, tormenting himself with the knowledge that any woman who made her living with her body put herself at the same kind of risk that had taken Coral's life. Just because Jenny Ryon carefully selected her customers didn't mean she couldn't make the same kind of fatal mistake. Just because he loved Jenny didn't mean the day wouldn't come when some man would put his hands around that lovely throat and squeeze until all life was gone from her body.

A cold sweat trickled down his back. He looked at the man standing next to him. "Come on, Matt." All around him, men fanned out by pairs and entered the businesses and homes lining the street.

Jenny was just descending the stairs when her front door opened. She gave a start of surprise when Daniel entered without knocking. He knew she wasn't open this early. Her glance went from him to the man half a stride behind him, and she felt a tingle of alarm at their grim expressions.

"What's wrong, Sheriff?" She pulled her shawl more tightly around her.

Daniel saw her through a murderer's eyes. Smooth, golden skin. Soft eyes. Silky blue fabric over full breasts and a narrow waist. His gut clenched, and his voice came out harsher than he intended. "One of Hirsch's . . . ladies was killed last night. We're going to search your house."

Jenny colored faintly. "You think I'm hiding a murderer?"

Daniel could hear the hurt. *Damn.* He made an effort to soften his voice. "Not intentionally. I've got to make sure this town is safe before I ride out of here with every able-bodied man."

Jenny's flush deepened. How *could* she have made such a stupid mistake? Of course, Daniel wouldn't think she was sheltering a killer. She carefully stepped aside to allow them to climb the stairs.

Feeling a little weak-kneed, Jenny sank onto a chair next to one of the small tables. Her trembling wasn't due to any fear. She felt perfectly safe in Sherman. What she didn't feel safe from was the emotions that caught at her each time she saw Daniel Hastings. Emotions she began to fear she would never overcome, not entirely. All she could hope to do was keep them in check so that she didn't allow her feelings to destroy her life. But she wondered if that was possible.

She could hear Daniel's footsteps in the hall above. What, she wondered, would it be like to hear those footsteps every day? To know they belonged there? To know Daniel Hastings belonged to her? Oh, God. She took a ragged breath as she heard him pause at the very end of the hall. Her room. The room she'd shared with far too many men.

Daniel glanced around, seeing Jenny in every nuance of the room. Braided rugs and polished wood. Soft colors and fabrics. No ruffles or lace. Her nightshift lay in a crumpled heap, tossed carelessly aside as she had dressed. Daniel had to force himself not to gather it up. His fingers itched to feel the silky texture that had slid against her flesh.

Son of a bitch! Daniel turned on his heel and left the room, stalking along the hallway and down the stairs. Matt waited at the bottom. And Jenny.

Jenny winced at the harsh sound of his footfall on each step. She looked up as he paused on the last one, looked up and tried to smile. "Nothing?"

Her tremulous smile tore at his gut. "Nothing." Matt was watching him curiously. "Let's go. It's going to be a long day."

Jenny followed them to the door. "Sheriff?"

He looked back from the ridiculous little gate that wouldn't keep a good-sized dog out.

"Be careful."

Daniel didn't answer.

"I'll be careful, too, Mrs. Ryon." Matt grinned at her, not the least offended by her partiality toward the sheriff. Everybody in town knew Mrs. Ryon was as sweet on Sheriff Hastings as he was on her. Everybody, it seemed, but the two of them.

She smiled. "Please do."

Jenny's words followed Daniel from town.

Hours later, he had to push them from his mind as he scanned the horizon for the hundredth time.

"They're wily bastards."

Pushing his hat back on his head, Daniel wiped the sweat from his forehead before he answered the deputy who'd ridden up beside him. "Like coyotes," he agreed. "And just as worthless."

Daniel and his posse were stopped on a rise just west of town. They'd lost the tracks they'd been following some time ago. Daniel wasn't even sure they were the *right* tracks, but they were all he had to go on.

"Ain't likely we'll find them now," the deputy persisted.

Daniel knew what he was getting at. The sun had lowered almost to the horizon. The men with him were hungry and ready to get back to their families. They were convinced the two killers they hunted were long gone, and he knew most of them would be thinking the girl had been only a whore, after all. Maybe because of Jenny, Daniel couldn't quite feel that way. But he understood.

"No, not likely," he agreed at last. There wasn't a chance in hell they would pick up the trail again before dark, and the clouds moving in swiftly said there wasn't much chance there would be any tracks left to pick up come morning.

With one last frustrated glance around, he called to the men, "All right. Let's head on back to town. We're wasting our time here."

There was no grumbling at the decision. There wouldn't have been too much if Daniel had decided to press on. Every man of them respected Daniel and depended on him to keep their families safe.

During the ride back to Sherman, Daniel felt an increasing anxiety. What if they'd missed something in town? It was possible. What if those murdering bastards had just hung around, waiting and watching, biding their time to kill again? And Daniel had led every able-bodied man out of town, leaving the place wide open for them. He rubbed his neck, wondering how much harder he could push his weary horse.

Even now, the two could be sitting in Jenny's restaurant, sampling her cooking and thinking about killing her like poor Coral. They could be talking to her, smiling at her, making her think they were to be trusted.

And if not these men and not this time, who knew when it might happen? Jenny lived all alone in that great big house. She could scream for help, and no one would hear her.

The thought of Jenny terrorized and screaming turned his blood to ice. He knew he was going to make himself crazy if he didn't stop. Hell, maybe he already was.

By the time they passed the first weathered building in town, near panic had Daniel's gut in a tight clench. He didn't even stop at the jailhouse, but kept right on riding to the other end of town.

For a moment he just sat there, looking at the light glowing a welcome from every downstairs window. Yeah, Daniel thought as he swung down from his horse, a welcome for every lowdown, whoring, murdering bastard who rode into town. He knew he wasn't being fair, but fair didn't come into it. Fear fed his anger. How dare she put herself in danger like this?

The door swung open at Daniel's touch, and for a moment he stood just outside her doorway as he checked for any threat within. When he was sure there was none, he stepped inside, his eyes seeking her.

She was just coming from the kitchen, a basket of fresh muffins in her hand. Daniel could smell their warm, fragrant aroma from where he stood.

When she saw him, she stopped. Her mouth formed his name.

He removed his hat, glanced around at the customers who'd paused in their eating to check him out. All male. All strangers. Daniel scowled, and the four men carefully turned their attention back to their food.

Jenny's heart went out to Daniel. He'd been out there for hours, and he didn't look as if he'd had any luck. Exhaustion showed in every line of his face. Exhaustion, and something else. Something more.

She crossed the room to stand before him, the hungry diners waiting for the muffins she carried completely forgotten in her concern for this man. "Sit down," she said softly, instinctively knowing he didn't need questions at this point. "I'll bring you a plate."

Before she could turn away, Daniel grasped her upper arm. She looked at him in confusion.

"Get these men out of here."

"My customers?" She stared at him blankly. "I can't do that, Daniel. They're not finished eating."

"I can do it." He meant it, too.

Jenny's back stiffened. She didn't know what was going on with Daniel, but she knew she didn't like it. "Don't."

That was all she said, that one word, but Daniel didn't mistake her meaning. All hell would break loose if he did what he wanted to do. He looked around. To a man, Jenny's customers were focused on the food in front of them. The tension drained from his shoulders, and he dropped his hand from her arm. God, he couldn't go on like this. The woman was driving him insane. "All right," he said finally. "But I'm staying."

Jenny didn't even try to hide her bewilderment at the comment. She hadn't suggested he leave to begin with. "Fine," she said as if they were having a normal conversation. "I'll get your plate now."

Daniel eased his tired body into a chair near one wall.

When Jenny returned with a clean plate and tableware, the slump to his shoulders devastated her. "Daniel." She touched his shoulder gently.

The pressure of her hand through the material of his shirt seared the flesh beneath. "Don't touch me," he said hoarsely, lifting his head to look at her.

Jenny snatched her hand away as quickly as if he'd slashed it with a knife. He'd drawn just as much blood. "Of course," she said stiffly. "I'll bring you something to eat."

"No." Daniel wanted to erase the look on her face, the look he'd caused, but the thought of four pairs of eyes watching as he did so held him to his place. "Just coffee."

Despite her wounded feelings, Jenny decided to ignore Daniel. He needed food in his stomach. She filled one heated serving plate with pork chops smothered in gravy and another with crisply cooked carrots and cabbage.

She walked back into the dining room and placed both platters on the table with solid thumps. She stared at Daniel until he met her look. "Eat." She meant it as an order she didn't intend to have disobeyed. "I'll get your coffee."

All the while she took care of her other

customer, refilling serving plates and coffee cups, she was conscious of Daniel. Of Daniel eating. Of Daniel drinking coffee. Of Daniel watching her. Mostly the last. For some reason, his fixed gaze seemed less reassuring than almost threatening. Which was surely ridiculous.

At least, she consoled herself, her good cooking had managed to take the drawn look from his face. He still looked determined, though, and she still felt apprehensive at just what he was determined *about*.

When the last diner thanked her, paid her, and walked out the door, Jenny turned to look at Daniel. He had long since finished eating and he'd finally pushed his coffee cup away, but he'd never quit watching her.

Drawing a deep breath, she squared her shoulders and walked over to stand in front of him. "What is it, Daniel?"

He didn't pretend ignorance. Mostly because he hadn't thought of any way to do this except head on. "Are you Baptist or Methodist?"

Jenny stared at him as if he'd lost his mind. She suspected he had. "Am I *what?*"

"Baptist or Methodist?" He'd never seen her set foot inside either church. Likely, she thought she'd be run out if she tried. Of course, he wasn't much for church-going, himself. He did it as part of his job and spread his attendance and his tithes between the two.

"Why? What difference does it make?" Jenny

had never known Daniel to pry into other people's business.

"I figured you'd rather be married by a minister of your own faith."

"Married?" she squeaked. What was he talking about? "I'm not getting married."

"Yes," Daniel said firmly, rising and putting his hat back on his head, "you are. You're getting married tonight. To me."

"To you?" Her voice rose, trembling perilously. "You can't even bear for me to touch you." She turned her head. Damn, it'd be just her luck to start crying now.

Daniel reached out one hand and placed it gently under her chin, holding her head so that she either had to close her eyes or look at him. "If I'd let you keep touching me, Jenny, I'd have put you up on the table and pulled your skirt over your head." He smiled ruefully. "I didn't think you'd take kindly to that."

Tears filled her eyes as the truth hit her. Daniel really did want to marry her. Then reality sank its blade into her heart. "I can't marry you, Daniel."

"Hell, yes, you can. And you will," he said grimly. At some point during the day, he'd decided he didn't give a good damn *what* Jenny wanted. She didn't have sense enough to keep herself safe, so he was going to have to do it for her.

"You don't understand." Nor did she want to explain it to him. She just wanted him to go away and leave her with this misery so she could learn to live with it.

"Don't I?" Daniel asked gently. He would have given anything if he could have left her past out of this, but he suspected she would be too honest to leave it where it belonged.

Jenny lifted a tearstained face to his. *Did he? Could* he, and still want her?

"This is *my* town, Jenny. I know who comes and who goes, and I know who stays where and for how long." He wiped a tear from her cheek. "I'm going to marry you, honey, and you don't have one damned thing to say about it."

The touch of his callused finger against her skin was more than Jenny could take. She burst into sobs and felt him pull her against his chest. She buried her face against him. "How c-can you w-want me?"

Daniel locked his arms around her. "I don't just want you, sweetheart, I need you. I love you."

Feeling her body shake with sobs she couldn't stop, Daniel decided he wasn't going to be able to convince her with mere words. With all the tenderness he had in him, he tipped her face up and covered her mouth with his. Her skin was cold, but slowly it warmed beneath his touch.

When her lips parted on a sigh, Daniel knew he had won.

Chapter Twenty-six

"What do you mean, you won't marry us?"

Daniel stood on the back steps of the Baptist church. He considered his calm response remarkable, given the fact that he was on the brink of howling his frustration to the dark skies above. He indulged himself by glaring at the hastily dressed minister who held a lantern high to peer at Daniel.

Warren Salters flinched only slightly at the sheriff's growled question and ferocious glare. "I didn't say I wouldn't marry you and the Widow Ryon," he responded with complete calm. "What I said was I would not perform a hasty ceremony in the dead of night." He paused deliberately. "How long have you known the woman, Sheriff?"

What kind of a damn-fool question was that?

"You know how long I've been in town, Reverend." And he'd wanted Jenny since the first day he'd laid eyes on her.

"And how long have you been courting her?"

Daniel scowled. Jenny never let him court her at all. "Long enough."

"Well, then, since you've waited this long to ask the lady, you can wait until tomorrow to complete the deed."

The reverend thought that reasonable enough and felt he had good basis to force a delay. Marriage was a serious and sacred agreement between two of God's creatures. He would not be party to a union brought about by the heat of passion or, heaven forbid, manipulated by a calculating woman. He knew Daniel Hastings to be a honest and honorable man; he really didn't know Jenny Ryon at all. She had never graced the entrance of his church.

Daniel tortured the brim of his hat as he tried to stare the younger man down. He was the law in this town, by God!

Reverend Salters didn't stare down.

Shit. "In the morning then. Early."

"As early as you like." Right after he'd had pointed out those aspects that made for a successful marriage to the bride and groom. It might be true that he had never shared in that happy state, but it was also true that he'd witnessed a fair number of marriages, both good and bad. He knew what characterized each.

Daniel jammed his hat back on his head,

ignoring the fact that he'd rearranged the shape rather dramatically. "I'll be here to fetch you at first light, Reverend."

The reverend smiled serenely. "I'll be waiting, Sheriff."

Fighting an urge to snatch his hat from his head and stomp it into the dirt beneath his feet, Daniel strode out of the churchyard.

He scarcely noticed and didn't care that it was a beautiful, starlit night. His attention was far from the moonlight that silvered the weathered boards of the storefronts lining the street and created dark shadows that fell from the alleyways. Instead he was plotting how he could keep Jenny from changing her mind about marrying him between now and sunrise.

From the cover of one of those dark alleys, Ike studied the sheriff. Only an hour or so earlier, he'd watched from the vantage of the livery stable roof as the weary posse rode back into town. He had grinned to think how he'd outsmarted half the men of that nothing little town. Even with the likes of Leon Wilkins hanging around his neck, he'd outwitted them! He would outwit Jeb Welles, too, damned if he wouldn't.

But first, he needed to get rid of the sheriff. If there was one man who stood a chance of gunning him down before he reached Welles, it was this one. And Ike didn't intend to let that happen.

He was just about to fall into step behind the

lawman when he happened to glance back over his shoulder. *Damn!* That preacher man still watched the sheriff from the open doorway of the church, the lantern held in front of him like a beacon. Ike wondered if he was getting old. He could remember the time when he wouldn't have even come close to making a mistake like that! With the patience that had kept him alive all these years, he waited for the preacher to go back inside and close the door behind him.

When that finally happened, Ike began to move carefully after the sheriff, skirting the edges of the buildings, keeping to the dark overhangs of the porches.

The sheriff had reached the far end of town before Ike felt confident enough to step into the street behind him and slide his gun from the worn holster strapped to his leg.

Tired of pacing the confines of the room, Jenny moved from the dining area of her restaurant to the porch. Her wedding night. She still couldn't believe it. Had Daniel really asked her? Had she really said yes? The pounding of her heart told her the answer to both of those questions.

In the long minutes since Daniel had left to get the preacher, all the reasons Jenny shouldn't marry him had presented themselves one by one. And one by one, Jenny had chased them away.

No secrets stood between her and Daniel; nothing dark and insidious could rear its ugly head in the years to come and soil what was between them. Daniel knew, accepted, and forgave. Jenny had only to forgive herself.

Wrapping her arms about herself, Jenny gazed up at the thick sprinkling of stars. Their brilliance vied with the moon's silver glow to light the evening. Maybe she wouldn't have blue skies and an armful of fragrant flowers, but she would have stars like diamonds and a man who was proud to have her stand at his side. Still looking up, she whirled, her skirts floating around her.

Every time he sees a man, he'll wonder. Jenny froze, her breath catching in her throat. Where had the thought come from?

"No." She said the word aloud, as if to say it would push the thought away. *Every cowboy who sits at your table will make him ask himself—is that one of them?* "No." This time the word was little more than a sob.

Jenny stepped down from the porch, her steps carrying her toward the street before she even stopped to think where she was headed. The balmy warmth of the evening had turned to a chill that touched her flesh with fingers of ice. A tightness restricted her breathing. Her steps quickened.

When he lies down with you, he'll wonder—how many others?

Daniel was the only one who could make the voice go away. The need to see him, to hold him was an urgent drive deep within her. Jenny was almost running by the time she stepped through the narrow gate.

Every sense seemed heightened in the moment she saw him, his long stride bringing him closer and closer to her. She stopped abruptly so that the hem of her skirt swirled with the sudden cessation of movement, then caressed her ankles as it settled. Fragrances surrounded her, rich earth and summer flowers. Somewhere nearby a small animal scurried through the trees, the sound little more than a rustle of dried grass. She thought she would remember that heartbreaking moment forever.

Daniel was alone. Jenny waited, poised on the edge of her next step, unable to run to him, equally unable to flee. *He didn't bring the reverend. He's changed his mind. He doesn't want you, after all.*

Daniel saw her there and smiled. And his smile drove the voice away. Everything about him beckoned to her. His powerful shoulders, broad hands, sinewed thighs all called to her of the security he offered. Security and love.

Jenny took a step forward, then stopped again, confused by a vague sense of movement somewhere behind Daniel. Her gaze traveled over the shadows and found nothing, and still an uneasiness teased the nerve endings along her spine. She opened her mouth to call a warning to him, then felt foolish. Warn him of what?

His gaze pulled hers back to him. What she found there drew her another step closer. Somewhere behind Daniel metal flashed in the moonlight, jerking her glance from his once more.

Daniel's eyes narrowed as Jenny's lips parted slightly. Her anxious, bewildered expression stirred the hair at the nape of his neck. With a smoothness born of years of experience, he turned and dropped low, sliding his gun free in the same instant.

Though deep shadows veiled the figure on the street behind him, Daniel didn't need more than the telltale gleam of gunmetal to warn him. Friends didn't slink along the fringes of dark with guns drawn. In the same heartbeat in which Daniel whirled around, he judged the position of the gun turned his way, and from that, the body position of the man holding it. Daniel aimed for the heart.

With Daniel's quick turn, the advantage of surprise was lost, and the grin on Ike's face faded. Only the advantage of the moonlight outlining the sheriff's figure remained, and there was no time to wonder what had given him away. Lifting his gun, Ike twisted sideways, his back coming up unexpectedly against a post of the building behind him. The movement jarred him in the instant he fired, and he knew the shot had gone wild.

The lawman's bullets peppered the wooden front of the building at his back, and Ike grunted as he crouched and ran. The whine of bullets didn't bother him too much; he'd been in worse situations. But when the bullets ceased to fly, the almost inhuman howl of the man behind him sent a long chill from the base of his skull to the small of his back.

Disbelieving his eyes, Daniel dropped to his knees in the dust of the street beside Jenny's crumpled form. Blood slowly soaked the front of her blouse. Daniel eased his arms under her and cradled her to his chest as he rose, a sob clawing at his throat.

Lights came on in the mercantile where the proprietor lived in the rooms behind his business. The door opened just enough to permit the man to peer through the crack.

The crack widened. "Sheriff?"

"Get Doc." Daniel didn't lift his eyes from Jenny's pale face. "I'm taking her home."

Chapter Twenty-seven

Though Hannah finally slept, morning didn't come a moment too soon. Her dreams had overflowed with memories of Jeb's touch, memories that filled her with as much restlessness as the reality had done. She awoke with the first rays of sunlight, feeling exhausted from tossing and turning all night. Surreptitiously, she scanned the campsite with her gaze, jerking her glance away when it crossed Jeb's.

He sat across from her, his back propped against the trunk of a tree, one leg bent at the knee, the other stretched out in front of him. The green of his eyes equaled the brightest summer-leafed branch. So sharp and piercing was his gaze that she wondered if he could see into her soul.

With color flooding her cheeks, she murmured a good morning and rose from her blanket. She felt his stare on her back as she walked down to the river to wash her face—a stare that made her so nervous she stumbled twice, once on a tangle of vine and once on a small bush.

Hannah's puffy eyes weren't lost on Jeb. She had needed to cry, just as she needed to laugh. Her tears had been a catharsis as she finally faced the truth of her feelings for Caleb Barnes. But not all of those tears were from facing her past. Some had fallen because Jeb hadn't been able to keep his randy hands away from her. Self-disgust filled him. Hannah was a lady, for Christ's sake, not some two-bit whore to be tumbled on the ground beside a campfire.

In the future, he'd have to be damned careful not to tempt himself beyond bearing. Hannah clearly wasn't for him. His first plan of action was still his best. He'd get her to Katherine and then let her seek her own kind in a man. How the hell he would manage all those days and nights alone with her was his own damned problem, not hers.

Though he tried not to look at her when she returned, his gaze was drawn to her again and again while he gathered their belongings. When she stretched the ache of sleeping on the ground from her back, the movement thrust her breasts forward until he could almost feel them brushing his chest once again. He felt a tensing in his groin and nearly cursed.

"Tie up those bedrolls," he told her curtly. He wished to hell he'd tried that other whore before leaving Sherman, the dark-haired one called Jericho. Maybe she could have brought him the release he needed.

Hannah winced at the tone he used. Those few moments of tenderness the night before when he'd held and comforted her might never have been. Silently, she obeyed, ignoring her hunger and refusing to ask when he planned for them to eat breakfast.

She helped him finish burdening the packhorse and mounted the grulla when Jeb climbed up into his saddle, all without speaking. Not even being handed a piece of tough jerky for her breakfast drew a comment from her.

Jeb's churlishness began to bother him, but he didn't know how to handle the situation otherwise. He'd never before wanted to keep a woman from being nice to him. If he was friendly and natural with her, no doubt she would react the same way. His wanting her would be bound to increase a hundredfold. He could hardly bear it as it was.

But when he glanced back after they'd traveled a few yards and saw the dark, haunted look in her eyes, all he could do was sigh. He reined in the bay until the grulla drew even.

"Don't look like that, Hannah."

She stiffened. "Like what?"

Lord, she made him spell everything out. Sometimes it was best to leave as much unsaid as possible. "The way you're looking now. Like a . . . like a whipped puppy."

Hannah felt the insult all the way to her toes. "Maybe I should have stayed in Sherman." She kicked the grulla, trying to make him walk faster.

Now that was ingratitude! An urge to punish her overrode his guilt. "So you could become a whore for old Armen?"

"With a little practice," Hannah said between gritted teeth, "maybe I could have become a very *good* whore."

She had surprised even herself and was quite prepared for the incredulous look that crossed Jeb's face at her words. She was not, however, prepared for the hoot of laughter that followed her comment.

"Honey, you'd starve to death in a week."

Hot shame flood her cheeks with fiery color. He'd said almost the same thing to Yolanda Graham. At least he'd given the other woman a month! Well, his words definitely made one thing clear, even if it hadn't been abundantly so already from his actions. Jeb didn't find her the least bit appealing, and he didn't think any other man would either. Hannah wished she'd never opened her mouth. She was not any more experienced at fencing with words than she was at any of the other things Jeb Welles was good at. No doubt lovemaking was one of his greatest talents.

Jeb didn't miss the look of humiliation on Hannah's face. "Aw, hell, Hannah, I didn't mean you wouldn't find any takers. I just don't think you'd know what to do with them."

Through the tears glittering on her eyelashes, Hannah glared at him. "I'm sure *somebody* would be willing to teach me!"

Jeb could just picture her saying something like that to some other man. In her innocence, she couldn't begin to imagine what would happen. He could. All too easily. His blood was surging at no more than the thought of teaching Hannah the many ways there were to pleasure a man.

He grabbed the reins of the grulla and glared at Hannah. "I don't think you have any idea what you're saying, but, honey, if you want somebody to teach you the finer points of being a whore, I can do it." Jeb got hard just considering the possibilities. He hoped Hannah didn't push him much further. He didn't know how far his self-control could be stretched.

Hannah had only thought she blushed before. But it wasn't his words that drew the dark color to her skin now. It was her own thoughts. She ducked her head to escape his hard green stare. If she spoke the words that waited on the tip of her tongue, he'd have her stretched out on the ground in a heartbeat. Hannah began to suspect that was what she really wanted, but she didn't quite have nerve enough—yet.

After a moment, Jeb took pity on her and released the grulla's reins. "Come on," he said gruffly.

Those were the last words spoken between

them for the rest of the morning.

For two bits, Ike would have blown Wilkins's head right off his shoulders. Hell, he'd have done it for less than that. He moved carefully around a building, making sure to keep his hat pulled low enough to shade his eyes. He knew from hard experience that their peculiar shade of silver was distinctive enough to identify him to anyone looking for him. And the whole damned town was looking. Maybe not for him in particular, but for any unfamiliar face—anybody they could hang for the death of the whore and for the shooting of the sheriff's woman.

Anger still nipped at Ike. Anger that he'd missed the sheriff and hit the woman instead. Not that he cared about the woman or cared if she died. He just didn't like failing in what he set out to do. And it didn't look like he was going to have another chance. For two days now, the sheriff hadn't stepped foot farther than the front porch of the place where they'd taken the woman.

Two days. Because of Wilkins, he'd wasted forty-eight hours crawling around this no-account town trying to catch a glimpse of Welles or the woman. If Wilkins hadn't killed that whore, Ike wouldn't have been shooting at any tin star-sporting lawman. He could have enjoyed the comfort of a rented room and a willing woman while he strolled the town and simply waited for the couple to show their faces.

As of a few minutes ago, he'd have bet his soul they weren't here. If he had a soul to bet. Some woman, a long time ago, had told him he didn't. Ike was inclined to believe that.

If that redheaded preacher's woman was still in town, she would have been in a church this morning. There were two for her to choose from. He'd watched at the door of one while the churchgoers gathered together and went in for worship, and he'd watched at the door of the other an hour and a half later as those inside came out.

With cautious movements, Ike timed his ride out of town to coincide with the folk heading home to their Sunday dinners. No, Ike was sure the woman wasn't here, and he had a gut feeling Welles wasn't either.

An afternoon thunderstorm built along the horizon as he rode toward the camp where Wilkins waited for him. Wilkins had whined at having to sit and do nothing while Ike rode back into town. Ike could just see that idiot stumbling around, drawing attention with his every move. He was about sick of Wilkins's whining. In fact, he was sick of Wilkins.

When he eased into camp, he found the other man sitting with his back propped against a tree. His rifle lay useless across his lap while he snored and snorted in sleep. For a moment, Ike just stared at him. The man was a pig. He could put a bullet through Wilkins's skull right now and likely spare himself more trouble later.

He dismounted, took the rifle from Wilkins's

lax grip, and kicked him. "Get up."

Wilkins came awake with a jerk and a grunt. He peered at the man standing above him through bleary eyes. "Damn, Ike! I could have shot you sneaking up on me like that!"

"Get your ass up. They're not in town." Ike didn't bother to tell Wilkins that a deaf man could have heard him ride in.

Wilkins scrambled to his feet as quickly as his considerable girth allowed. Wilkins was sure it wasn't as considerable as it had been a few days earlier. Riding with Ike was hard work. He didn't spare much time for eating and resting.

"How're we goin' to find them, Ike?" Wilkins stayed worried that the other man would change his mind about hunting Welles down and killing him. Without Ike along to track Welles, Wilkins didn't think he had a chance in hell of finding the girl on his own.

He wilted under the grey-eyed glare Ike turned his way and focused his attention on saddling his horse.

"I'll find Welles," Ike said at last. "Don't you worry about that."

"We'll make camp here," Jeb said over his shoulder.

Hannah looked at the sky. Early afternoon at the latest. "Now?"

"Now."

Hannah sighed and slid down from her horse. They'd resumed speaking, but conversation remained minimal at best. Silence was, in fact, an easy habit for her to fall back into after all the years Caleb had discouraged her from chatter. That was what he'd labeled her efforts to share in his life. Now, however, she felt a resentment she wouldn't have expected. The last few days had reminded her there was another way to live. She didn't want to lose the freedom of speaking her mind without fear of reprisal.

Jeb turned to look at her and found her watching him with what he could only call a stoic expression. It was a look he remembered from the first time he'd met her, a look that said she could take the worst hand life had to deal her without crumbling. Jeb didn't like feeling he fell somewhere into that category.

"Tomorrow we start onto the Staked Plain," he told her. "It's the quickest way to get where we're going, but it isn't the safest," he said honestly.

Hannah said nothing. For most of her life, she'd heard of the Staked Plain in the same breath with the words murdering savages, raids, and hostages. The prospect of crossing it didn't fill her with joy, but she knew by now that she would follow Jeb into hell itself. Even so, she was just as glad to be postponing this particular adventure, if only by a day.

"Damn it, Hannah, say something!" Jeb wanted her cautious of what lay ahead, but not terrified. If she spoke her fear, he could reassure her that he'd take care of her, for as long as she'd let him. The thought shook him.

He didn't want to feel this way about a woman who didn't want him.

Hannah jumped. "I'm hungry," she said cautiously. No doubt he could turn that into a fault, too.

Despite his irritation at the guilt she made him feel, Jeb couldn't help the smile that lifted his lips before he pressed them into a firm line once more. "I don't want to fire any unnecessary shots, Hannah. Maybe I can catch some fish."

Hannah didn't have to ask why Jeb didn't want to draw attention to their location. "Can I build a fire?" she questioned cautiously.

"A small one. Make sure it doesn't smoke." Jeb fought the urge to touch Hannah's cheek. God help him if he put her in danger. "Take care of the horses first."

He started to walk away, then turned back. "After we eat, I'll teach you how to aim that rifle instead of just using it to prop your knee against when you ride."

Hannah nodded, trying not to show the apprehension his words raised in her. If Jeb had any thought of ever trusting her with a loaded rifle, the dangers that lay ahead were grave indeed.

Jeb walked along the river until he found a place where the water eddied in clear currents around several large rocks. Stepping onto them cautiously, he waited until he knew they were steady before rolling up his shirtsleeve and stretching out on the sun-warmed surface.

Slowly, he lowered one hand into the cool water. Hannah would like this spot. A river breeze caressed the surface of the water and rustled through the shade trees overhead. Jeb thought of bringing her here later, of enjoying the smile that came from the heart of her and sparkled through her blue eyes. Feeling himself grow stiff against the hard boulder beneath him, Jeb groaned. He couldn't even think casually of Hannah without suffering for it.

He focused his concentration on the task at hand. If he didn't catch anything, they would be eating beans and hard tack again.

A trout flirted from the shadowed edge of the boulder beneath him. Jeb kept his arm very still and let his fingers ripple with the current. The trout would be intrigued by the movement, without feeling threatened by the presence of the man he could not see on the rock above him. When the fish drew close enough, Jeb knew from experience, he would actually be able to caress the cool scales of the creature without sending him scurrying back to his dark lair.

Within moments, the trout bumped his fingers. Jeb forced himself to keep them limp until the fish gained reassurance from the lack of threat. Jeb grinned. Catching a fish with your hands was a little like seducing a skittish woman. A man had to take it slow and easy, making sure nothing he did appeared threatening and that no sudden moves caused her to put up her guard. Slowly, the comparison dawned. Jeb had never met a woman more skittish than Hannah.

Jeb almost lost the fish in his sudden excitement at the realization. His hand closed on the scaly creature too near the tail, and he was forced to thrust his other arm, sleeve and all, into the water to gain a better grip. What was it about Hannah Barnes that had made him forget everything he knew about women? Forget all those hard lessons learned painstakingly over a good many years?

He was bursting with elation when he pulled the fish from the water. Yes, sir, just like a skittish woman.

By the time Jeb was through, Hannah would know she belonged with him. Jeb froze at the thought, then slowly relaxed at the warmth that seeped through him as his mind accepted what his heart and body already seemed to know. Hannah *did* belong with him. She belonged *to* him. And Jeb was going to make damned sure she knew it. He just had to figure out how to do it without terrifying her along the way.

Hannah looked up from a tiny, smokeless fire when Jeb returned carrying three large trout. Surprise widened her eyes. "How did you do that with nothing but your hands?"

Jeb grinned. "You just have to know how, Hannah. That's all. Is the fire ready?"

"It's small." Hannah looked dubious. "Did you see any smoke from the river?"

"None," Jeb reassured her. "You did just fine with it."

Her pleased smile made him feel good. Hell, just looking at Hannah made him feel good. Jeb busied himself getting the fish ready to cook before he did something to make Hannah skitter away from him again.

When the smell of crisp brown trout filled the air, Jeb laid a whole fish across a tin plate and handed it to Hannah. "Try that."

Hannah thought it the most wonderful thing she'd ever tasted. She told Jeb so.

"Then you haven't had catfish cooked right out of the river." Jeb wasn't about to try catching one of those sharp-finned creatures by hand. He had a hunch, however, that getting his hands on Hannah would be just as risky.

With Hannah well fed, he began his plan to gentle her. He refused to think of it as seduction, but he hoped the outcome was the same.

At Jeb's command, Hannah slid the rifle from its holster and walked over to where he stood. He'd cut a shallow X into a tree that didn't look to Hannah wide enough to aim at, much less hit.

"I could never hit that," she said emphatically.

"I'm going to teach you."

There was a disconcerting huskiness to his voice that seemed unlikely to have anything to do with shooting a rifle. Hannah peered at him from under heavy lashes. "There aren't any bullets in the rifle."

"After you learn to aim at what you intend

to hit, I'll teach you to really shoot—when it's a little safer to fire the rifle. Come here." Jeb drew her in front of him and pulled her arms into position. Her skirt brushed his thigh. The scent of her hair filled his nostrils. He closed his eyes and gritted his teeth.

"Like this?" Hannah asked innocently.

Jeb opened his eyes determinedly. This had been his idea after all. "Just like that." Hannah's arm wavered with the weight of the gun, and Jeb reached up to steady her aim. His hand quivered at the touch of her thinly clad arm. The swell of her breast was mere inches from his thumb.

By the time Hannah managed to swing the rifle into a position where Jeb thought she *might* have hit the tree, her arms were trembling from the weight of the gun and Jeb had broken out into a sweat. Each swing of her shoulders pressed her body more firmly against his.

Jeb eased the rifle from her grip. "That's enough for today, Hannah. We'll take a break and then see how much you remember about loading a cartridge." He caught the expectancy of her expression as she twisted around to look at him, and he smiled into her blue eyes. "You did just fine, honey. Just fine."

Hannah realized that she liked Jeb's praise. The fact that it was sparing made it all the more meaningful.

Minutes later, she walked quietly beside him toward the river. He was talking about Slade and Katherine, assuring her that she would like them. Hannah wouldn't argue with that. She generally liked most people, but she wondered how the couple would feel about having her foisted off on them. She suspected that was what Jeb intended to do—get her safely to New Mexico and dump the responsibility for her on his friends. The thought hurt.

"This Slade may not appreciate having another woman to take care of."

"Well, first off, Slade isn't going to be taking care of you—I am." Jeb faltered, then decided to test the waters. "At least, until you have a husband to take care of you." He'd be damned if he ever let another man have her. Hannah said nothing. "And second, Slade would be as willing to do it as I am. Hannah, all men aren't like Caleb."

No, Hannah thought. Jeb was harder than Caleb but not as cold and not cruel.

"And they aren't all like the three men who raped you."

Hannah stopped in her tracks. Raped? "But I—those men didn't—"

Jeb stopped, too, and stood looking at the top of Hannah's head, which was all she would show him. "Didn't what, honey?" he asked gently. Just like her life with Caleb, Hannah needed to talk about this or it might haunt her forever.

She lifted her face. "They didn't rape me," she said clearly.

Now it was Jeb's turn to be confused. "But

the day they attacked you—" He stopped and tried again. "The baby—"

"They would have," Hannah said slowly, "but the baby started to come too early. All that blood." She shuddered. "I guess they thought I was dying. They just rode away and left me there."

Jeb felt his rage toward the three start all over again. Hannah damned well *might* have been dying. Another thought ate into the rage. If Hannah hadn't been raped, her resistance to his touch likely had nothing to do with fear of men. Either her husband had given her an aversion to all men, or she simply had none of the feelings for Jeb that he had for her. He didn't like that thought at all.

He tried to think if she had responded even a little to his touch when he helped her to hold the rifle. He wasn't used to this uncertainty where women were concerned, and he damned sure wasn't enjoying it. He'd felt confident when he'd trapped that fish so neatly in his hand, but Hannah wasn't a fish.

Deliberately, Jeb led Hannah out on the rocks where he'd caught the trout. When the rocks shifted slightly beneath their weight, Jeb was ready. He caught Hannah to him, holding her securely.

For just a moment, Hannah rested against him. Jeb could feel the too-fast beat of her heart, and he smiled to himself in relief. Fear of falling hadn't made her pulse speed up like that.

When Hannah would have pulled away, she

felt Jeb's arms tighten. She leaned back so that she could see into his face. His eyes had turned the same brilliant green as when fury gripped him, but Hannah knew he wasn't angry.

"Jeb?" She tested his name on her lips.

Somehow she knew he was going to kiss her. She had all the time in the world to pull away as he slowly lowered his mouth to hers. She had time to avoid any heartache that might come of wanting a man who didn't want her—at least not for more than a passing moment.

Hannah lifted her face to Jeb's.

"Can't we stop for a while?" Wilkins asked for the hundredth time. He could taste the grit of the trail between his teeth, and his bandanna was soaked with sweat.

Ike glanced up at the sun. Barely past midday. "Shut up, Leon."

"Damn it, Ike. I'm hungry, and my canteen's been empty for an hour." They rode within smell of the river, and still Ike wouldn't let them stop.

Silently, Ike unstrapped his canteen and handed it to the other man. "Now shut your damned mouth."

Wilkins was miserable enough to feel almost brave. "We may as well give up, Ike. We ain't never going to find their tracks."

Ike turned to look at him and smiled in a way that made Wilkins shiver.

"You stupid son of a bitch," Ike said softly. "We've been on their trail for half the morning."

Chapter Twenty-eight

Doc placed his hand against the Widow Ryon's cheek one more time, just to be sure. Then he straightened his aching back with a brief stretching movement. He looked down at the pale, beautiful face and wondered how his peaceful little town had become a place where women had to fear being shot down in the street. Being shot down or having their necks broken, he added, thinking of Hirsch's girl. But whores, even one as sweet as Coral had been, knew they lived on the edge. A woman like Jenny Ryon . . . He shook his head. Well, it just ought not to be.

The doctor's unconscious movement frightened Daniel. "What is it, Doc?" he asked hoarsely. If anything happened to Jenny now. . . .

Startled, the old man turned. For a moment, he'd forgotten he wasn't alone. But no, there was Daniel, steadfast and waiting, just as he'd been since Doc was called to dig a bullet out of the woman's torn flesh.

Still fearful, Daniel cleared his throat as Doc beckoned him out of the room and closed the door behind them. For two days, he'd wanted to ask the question, but couldn't force himself to utter the words, fearing what the answer might be. He was still afraid.

Doc saw it in Daniel's anguished eyes—the same question that had been there every time he turned from examining his patient. Doc smiled. This time he could answer. "She'll live."

He was damned glad to be able to say it. Daniel had told him the two of them planned to be married. Even if he hadn't said anything, Doc would have known the sheriff's feelings just from the agonies the man had suffered while the widow's life trembled on a thread. She'd lost so much blood that, for a while, Doc had tasted the bitter despair of defeat. Even then, he hadn't given up on her. And neither had Daniel.

Daniel closed his eyes briefly and whispered a prayer of thanks, to the old practitioner and to God. Weakened knees carried him past Doc to the door of Jenny's room. He paused with his hand on the doorknob. "Do me a favor?"

"Sure." Doc finished cleaning his spectacles and returned them to their perch on his nose.

"Tell the girl downstairs to fetch Warren Salters."

Doc frowned. Not that he wouldn't like to stand as witness to a wedding between these two this very day. He would for a fact. Still, he shook his head. "Now, Daniel, I said she'd live, and she will. But she's not ready to speak words in front of a preacher with you. Give her a few more days to rest and recuperate." He smiled. "At least wait until she can stand on her own two feet."

The steel in the sheriff's eyes faded the old physician's smile and stopped him from saying more.

"The son of a bitch who shot her has two days on me, Doc. I can't wait any longer or the trail will be so cold I'll never pick it up—and when I leave here, Jenny's going to be my wife." If it did nothing else, marriage to Daniel would ensure that Jenny never had to return to the life she had led before. He might be far from rich, but he had enough saved to make sure of that much anyway.

"You could let him go, Daniel," Doc suggested. "Likely he's halfway to Mexico by now, anyway."

"I'm a lawman, Doc. Pledged to protect this town." Daniel shook his head with an air of finality. "The man killed Coral and damned near killed Jenny trying to get me. I can't let it go." Daniel was convinced that one man had committed both deeds. He was equally convinced that it was the same man who'd widowed Hannah Barnes.

Doc didn't back down from the sheriff's hard-eyed stare. "Are you sure protecting your town is what's on your mind—or is it maybe vengeance?"

Daniel could recall asking Jeb Welles that same question when he'd first ridden into town with Hannah Barnes. Now Daniel knew exactly how Welles had felt. "Both. And I can't say for a fact which is foremost," he admitted, "but I reckon I'll accomplish everything that needs doing when the bastard is dead." He pinned Doc with a questioning gaze. "Will you get the preacher?"

Swallowing his last, useless protest, Doc sighed. "I'll get him."

He turned to go, and Daniel stepped into Jenny's room.

Daniel's profile was the first thing Jenny saw when she opened her eyes. A deep rumble of thunder the first thing she heard, a fiery pain along her shoulder the first thing she felt.

With his gaze turned outward, Daniel stood at the window, the curtains drawn back to expose threateningly dark clouds tumbling along the horizon. His face looked as grim as the clouds that held his attention.

"Daniel."

The soft voice tugged at Daniel. For a moment, he thought it came from deep within himself, as it had so often while he waited for her to waken. Or die. The terror of the past forty-eight hours washed over him in renewed waves so great that for a moment he had to grit his teeth against panic.

He turned slowly to look into whiskey-colored eyes that watched him in quiet confusion. "Jenny." Hoarsness disguised his voice to the point that he scarcely recognized it for his own.

Relief swept Jenny. For a moment Daniel had looked so grim she feared he'd changed his mind—or that it had all been a dream. She moved toward him just slightly, then winced. The pain that shot through her shoulder was a sufficient reminder that she had dreamed nothing of what happened.

Daniel crossed to the bed, desperate to touch her, to hold her. He made himself stop abruptly, terrified that he would cause her further pain. With a smile, Jenny lifted her arms in welcome, and Daniel gathered her close.

Nothing had ever felt so good to Jenny as his arms around her, nor ever looked so beautiful as his weather-lined face.

Daniel felt the fragility of her against his chest—the feather-like beating of her heart, a reassuring sound that an outlaw's bullet had almost stopped forever. He brushed his lips across her hair, overwhelmed by feelings. Because of him, she had almost died. "I'm sorry, Jenny, love. God, I'm sorry."

The deep huskiness of his voice was a rumble in her ear, and it took Jenny a moment to comprehend the suffering his words conveyed. "Oh, Daniel," she whispered, tears burning her eyes, "don't. Please don't."

She couldn't bear for him to feel any guilt for what had happened. Any harm that ever came to her because of his work was well worth the risk. *But what about his risk? What if someday a bullet aimed his way didn't miss the intended target?* She shouldn't let him see how much the thought terrified her. Her arms tightened fractionally around his neck, and she caressed his rough cheek with her own soft one.

"I'll find the bast—I'll find him."

Daniel's grim voice frightened her. Jenny tried to swallow her response, knowing she would be wrong to protest what Daniel felt called to do. Daniel's work, his love for her, everything he did and felt was wrapped in a code of honor that would allow him nothing else. Jenny knew she couldn't interfere with that, but in the end she was unable to help herself.

"I don't want you to go after him. I don't want you to leave me." To worry and wonder and wait.

Easing back so that he could look at her, Daniel smiled faintly at the irony of the moment. All this time of wanting her and believing his case hopeless—and now when she was his, he had to leave her. He touched a callused finger to the full, lower lip that trembled with the depth of her terror.

"I'll be back before you even know it." His

eyes darkened hungrily. "I love you, Jenny Ryon, and I'm not going to let anything take me from you." He touched his lips to hers, wishing he could crush her against him, needing to feel her softness against the entire length of his body.

Before he could forget himself enough to injure her wounded shoulder, he eased her back against the pillows. "I'll send your girl up to you. You'll probably want to pretty up before the wedding." Personally, Daniel didn't think anything could look as lovely as the tumbled waves framing her face.

"Wedding?" He wanted to marry her, here and now? Jenny glanced down at her nightshirt, at the ugly bandage padding her shoulder, then lifted her eyes to his.

Daniel grinned faintly at her look of horrified disbelief. "Reverend Salters is waiting downstairs. You'll have to talk to him before he'll begin the ceremony. He's hell-bent on that. He's already had his say to me."

It wasn't hard for Jenny to imagine the kind of discouragement the minister had offered to Daniel. The sheriff was a pillar of the community, after all, someone whom people looked up to and depended on. No doubt Reverend Salters knew just what Jenny was, or rather what she had been. How was he to know—and why should he care?—the reasons for the things she had done, or the fact that the past was behind her?

The bedclothes twisted beneath her nervous

fingers. "Can we talk to him together?" The question came from between suddenly stiff lips.

Daniel shook his head. "He says not." He frowned faintly at the distressed look on her face. "It'll be all right, Jenny. He just wants to be sure this is what we both want." *Wasn't it what Jenny wanted, after all? Maybe she was having doubts now that she knew firsthand how dangerous being a sheriff's wife could be.*

She forced a smile. "Then it *will* be all right." But she didn't believe it for a minute.

When Daniel left her, the smile faded, and she found it difficult to muster another when the reverend knocked on her door a short while later. She thanked the girl who had dressed her hair with as much grace as she waited tables and a great deal more chatter. Jenny had thought she would be glad to see the girl and her exuberance leave, but realized she was mistaken in thinking that the moment the door closed, leaving her alone with the Baptist minister.

Jenny gestured toward a chair and murmured something inanely polite as he seated himself. He asked about her health and listened to her quiet answer before shifting forward slightly in his chair. The movement brought a sudden tension to Jenny's spine.

Warren Salters smiled faintly. He was used to this reaction, but usually from the groom, not the bride. The groom usually feared a frank discussion on marital responsibilities, including the marriage bed and fidelity, while the bride rarely had any misgivings about discussing her upcoming nuptials.

However, he decided, the same technique for easing the moment should work for one as well as the other. At least he hoped it would. "Why do you think I'm here, Mrs. Ryon?"

Jenny considered evasion, then decided that an honest question deserved an honest answer. "To talk me out of marrying Daniel."

He frowned at her unexpected response. "You've been married before; you assuredly know what it entails. I'm inclined to believe you would know better than I if marriage is something that you are suited for."

Hands quietly clasped in her lap, Jenny said nothing.

This wasn't going the way of his usual pre-marriage talks. Not at all. "Do you love Daniel?" he asked curiously.

"More than life." Jenny thought she had never spoken truer words. Now that she had truly allowed herself to believe in a future with him, the thought of ever being without Daniel was devastating. Losing him would probably destroy her.

"Do you plan to be a good wife?"

A chill caused a ripple of gooseflesh across her arms. Now it would come. Her past flung at her with harsh words and accusations. She lifted her chin. "I'll spend every day of my life trying."

"Then I'd have to call Daniel Hastings a lucky man." He smiled gently as Jenny's mouth dropped open. "Now, let's talk about whether or not Daniel can be the husband you need."

A warmth spread very slowly through Jenny as she realized that her fears were groundless, and she told the minister exactly how perfect a husband Daniel would be for her.

By the time Daniel stood at Jenny's bedside, her hand clasped in his, Warren Salters was convinced that at least two people in this world had found the mate God intended for them. With the doctor and a servant girl as witnesses, he spoke the words that would bind them for the rest of their lives as man and wife and through eternity as loving companions.

"Jenny, don't look at me like that," Daniel begged. "I've got to go."

Although Jenny couldn't quite help the dread in her expression at the thought of his riding away from her into danger, she could help the words she spoke. She wouldn't send him off worrying about her feelings.

She managed a low chuckle. "Do you really want me to be delighted that you're leaving me on our wedding day?" Despite her best efforts, her breath caught on a funny little sob.

His gaze caressed her lovingly, from the delicate line of too-pale cheeks to the tender bottom lip caught between her teeth as she waited for his response. He knew what she was doing, knew she wanted to ease his mind. Just as much as he wanted to ease hers.

He leaned forward and touched his mouth to

hers, sucking gently at her lower lip until her teeth parted slightly, releasing it, opening her to his insistent pressure. And then he kissed her long and thoroughly, his eagerness telling her just how little he liked leaving her. "I'll be back, Jenny. I swear it." It was a promise to both of them.

And then he was leaving, and she was left to struggle against the dry sobs that she couldn't quite stop though she kept the salt tears from falling. She heard him descending the stairs with the sure steps of a man who had business to take care of and a need to take care of it swiftly.

When Daniel reached the bottom of the stairs, he saw the reverend seated on a comfortable divan. Waiting, as Daniel had asked him to do.

Warren Salters rose to his feet and looked at Daniel expectantly.

"She'll need some company for a little while," Daniel said gruffly.

"I'll be here until she feels she can be alone. And I'll return every day to see to her welfare."

Daniel felt better at hearing that. The doctor would be checking in twice a day, but he didn't know how good Doc would be at reassuring Jenny. Surely a minister knew best how to do that.

With a nod, he walked out onto the porch, settling his hat firmly on his head. The storm had passed, leaving a steamy heat in its place.

And erasing every sign of trail he could have hoped to follow.

He would have to set out on instinct alone, and instinct told him that the man who had hurt Jenny would never have set foot in this little town if he hadn't been following Jeb Welles and Hannah Barnes. And Daniel knew where Welles and the woman were headed. Taos, in the New Mexico Territory.

He didn't glance at the window above as he stepped out into the street. If he had, he would have seen Jenny, out of bed against doctor's orders, her face pressed to the window.

Watching him walk away, knowing he walked into danger, Jenny wondered if she had survived a bullet only to die of a broken heart.

Chapter Twenty-nine

Hannah stared into the fire, her thoughts on that brief moment two days earlier when Jeb had held her close while the river rippled lazily past. The rifle she'd been loading and unloading at his command lay forgotten in her lap. Nothing had ever felt as good as his lips on hers. She'd been shameless, and the knowledge brought a rise of heat to the surface of her skin. At least Jeb wouldn't be able to see her blush in the light from the fire.

He'd released her after only a moment, but she suspected that it hadn't been soon enough for him not to feel her response. Surely he would have had to be blind not to see the wonder in her heart reflected in her eyes. Likely, Jeb was used to that kind of response from the women he kissed. Hannah had a feeling there were many. She didn't want to be one of a number of others. But what, she wondered, was there about Hannah Barnes that would cause her to stand out in his mind? Not much, as far as she could tell.

Certainly not as far as Jeb's attitude toward her since then could reveal. She might have been someone's maiden aunt for all the attention he'd given her. Maybe for the past few years she had *felt* like some poor spinster despite the fact that she'd been a married woman. But not anymore, not since the touch of Jeb's lips on hers.

One kiss. Just one and then . . . nothing. He'd gently moved her away from him, given her a lopsided smile—and pointed out a turtle swimming against the current. All too aware of the pounding of her heart against her breast, Hannah had known an exquisite disappointment.

Since then, the only change between them seemed to be in the way Hannah felt. If there was any change in Jeb's feelings, she couldn't see it.

Jeb hunkered down across the fire from Hannah and watched the worry chase across her face. There wasn't a doubt in his mind that she fretted over that moment by the river when he'd dared to hold her. She had been troubled ever since. He'd tried to keep the atmosphere between them light since then, tried to give her time to get used to the notion of being touched by him. He sure wouldn't have thought that one kiss would distress her as much as it appeared to have done.

He sighed. So much for skilled fishing. "Hannah, I'd never do anything to hurt you. Not intentionally."

She looked at him wide-eyed. Just how much of her thoughts had Jeb Welles managed to read? As for that, what exactly had she been thinking?

Jeb tried again. "I'm not going to do anything you don't want me to."

Hannah ducked her head and fixed her gaze on the crackling flickers of the campfire. "That leaves the door wide open," she muttered.

"What?" Jeb stared at her, realized that his mouth was hanging open, and shut it abruptly. He was sure he hadn't heard what his ears were trying to convince him she'd said.

Hannah forced herself to lift her chin and meet his gaze. She wasn't going to make a complete fool of herself now! "I know you're not going to hurt me," she said clearly. "I never thought you would."

Jeb could have howled in frustration.

Ike frowned at the circle of ground where ashes had been swept clean, leaving just a trace of grey against the soil. He just couldn't figure the slow pace that Welles was setting, unless it was from a reluctance to cross the river into Indian territory. Maybe something else. Whatever the reason, Ike had slowed to match that pace.

Something else was bothering Ike, too. A handful of Indians, no more than four by their tracks, had crisscrossed Welles's trail a time or two, their wanderings appearing almost aimless though they were headed in the same general direction as Welles and the woman. Ike didn't think they were actually following the couple, but he didn't need any complications—not where Welles was concerned. He intended to keep his distance until the Indians were no longer following the same path as Welles.

He glared at the soft moccasin print near the edge of Welles's cold campfire.

"What is it, Ike?"

Leon's words held an edge of worry, but then Leon worried about everything.

"Something wrong, Ike?"

The sound of that voice was like the irritating whine of a mosquito in Ike's ear. Ike grinned to himself, while keeping his outward expression unrevealing. "Indians," he said flatly. "Get back on your horse." He suited his own action to his words and remounted with grimly efficient movements.

An hour later, he began to regret his moment of fun. Leon's fretting had turned his voice into a dozen droning mosquitos. "How many, Ike? How many, do you think?"

"I saw one print. Could be a single one-legged Indian or a war party too smart to leave more than one print. If you ask me one more time what I think, I think I'll stick you like a pig and leave you bleeding for them to finish off—

however many there are."

Wilkins watched his horse's ears twitch back and forth. Back and forth. Ike would do it. He really would, the bastard. Sweat trickled down between Leon's shoulder blades. From time to time, he glanced nervously over his shoulder toward the vast plains stretching out to the north of them and ahead of them to the west. Every inch of that emptiness belonged to the Indians. They were the intruders. Welles and the woman. Him and Ike.

It was on the tip of Leon's tongue to suggest they turn back for the comforts and safety of town, when he remembered that there might be comforts to be had, but no place in Texas would be safe for the two of them. Not now. And not just because Ike had killed, no, sir, not anymore. Leon straightened his achingly tired shoulders. He'd done his share of killing now, too. He was as much a man as Ike.

Except for one thing, a tiny voice niggled at his pride. Yeah, he thought sourly, except for that one thing the preacher woman had stolen from him. Turn back? He stiffened his spine. Hell, no. He was going to find that bitch. Another glance toward the lonely, sun-steamed plains took some of the stiffening from his backbone. If he lived long enough, he was going to find her.

When Leon finally fell silent, Ike savored the rare and peaceful absence of human sound. Beyond the rustling of their horses through the golden prairie grass, he could actually hear insects clicking around them. Insects and the occasional call of some harsh-throated bird. Moments later, a third sound was added to those. A low keening that seemed to blend with the stirring of the wind through tall, dried grass.

Before Leon could open his mouth, Ike reined in his horse at the same time he held up one hand in a gesture that commanded the other man's continued silence. He didn't look at Leon. He didn't even want to *see* the questions he knew he would find in Leon's eyes.

The grasses around them settled into waiting stillness with their cessation of movement, and in that quiet the keening took on a different sound and meaning. Ike studied the shallow rises of land all around them, then turned his horse toward a lone tree surrounded by a few hardy scrub brush.

Leon felt his skin prickle. Those were Indian chants. Damned if they weren't! Why the hell was Ike headed straight toward their source? Leon shook his head and fell a little farther behind the other man. At the first whirring sound of an arrow loosed from a taut bow-string, he had every intention of turning tail to run. Ike could be brave if he wanted to be. Leon would rather live.

Ike rode right up to the old Comanche and sat astride his horse, looking down at the ancient Indian, whose back was propped against the tree. The remaining strands of the old warrior's hair were completely white, and his skin reminded Ike of leather that had been left exposed to countless seasons. He was dressed in his ceremonial best, a war lance thrust upright into the ground at his side. Brightly painted feathers affixed to the top of the lance floated on what little breeze was available.

The Indian did not deign to notice their presence but kept his eyes lifted to the midday sky and continued his soft chants.

"Ike. Ike!" The hoarse whisper carried on the air like a carrion bird with wings outspread.

Ike winced at the sound. Damn that Leon! Ike turned to glare at him.

"Don't get too close, Ike." As much as the other man angered him, as much as he scared him sometimes, Leon sure didn't want anything happening to Ike. Not just yet. He shuddered to think of himself left all alone on the vast Staked Plain. Alone with the fiercest remnants of every tribe, those who had refused to yield to the white man's insistence that they be herded onto reservations.

"Shut up, Leon." Hellfire and damnation! Couldn't Leon see how harmless the poor old son of a bitch was? He'd thrown himself away because he couldn't keep up with his companions. Or they had thrown him away.

Ike spent another few minutes puzzling over the nature of that group, then shrugged. He hadn't really thought they were a war party, mostly because they were too few, but also because he suspected that at least one set of tracks belonged to a woman. He knew for sure they weren't now. Then he'd thought they might be a small band of raiders, but no raider would have had this old man along.

He shrugged to himself and told Leon, "Come on." The old man was no threat to them. They might as well leave him to his death chant and the buzzards that would be circling in a day or two.

"You ain't going to kill him, Ike?" Leon couldn't quite see walking away from an Indian they could finish off just as easily as not. He couldn't see Ike doing that, anyway.

Ike turned his horse toward the west once more and shook his head, more in disgust than answer.

As they rode away, in the same direction as the remaining moccasin prints, the quavering chants slowed and finally ceased. The old man watched their backs and thought of his grandson and his two daughters-in-law. He tried to thrust those thoughts aside. When he'd awakened this morning, this tree, this place had called to him. It called to him still. He'd chosen his day to die, and it was a good one. The living would have to care for themselves.

Turning his face back to the sky, he took up his chants with renewed vigor, but his former peace eluded him. He'd lived many years and he'd seen many white men in those years. Some who were good, like the green-eyed Texan whose woman had hair the color of autumn leaves, and some who were bad. These two men were bad. He smelled the evil of them even after the wind blew over the earth where they had stood and looked at him.

He fell abruptly silent and glared at the horizon where the two riders were just disappearing into the wavering prairie grass. Grasping his lance with one hand, he pulled himself up. The bones in his old body protested every movement. Soon, he told himself, soon would be the time of his rest. But first he must make sure these bad men did not do any evil to his grandson and the women.

Chapter Thirty

Daniel squinted against the rays of the sun; brilliant rays reflected back from every rock, every scrub tree, every blade of grass. After a time, he gave up studying the empty horizon and lifted his gaze to skies just as vast and just as empty. Not so much as one fleecy cloud marred the blue perfection overhead or gave hope of relief from the blazing heat.

For a moment he let himself think of Jenny, then realized what a mistake it was to do so. In that moment, he wished desperately that he'd never managed to pick up any sign of a trail. He almost hadn't. The thick grass that covered this land was too vibrant, too resiliant. It sprang back into place with every passing, leaving only a few bent stalks that might just as easily have been broken by wild animals as by men on horseback. In fact, if it hadn't been for a single campsite carelessly cleared, he wouldn't have picked up their trail at all. But that scattering of cold ashes had been enough sign for the greenest tracker to find. If not for that, he would be on his way back to his wife.

Daniel spoke the word out loud, savoring the sweet sound of it in his mind. His wife, his bride of three days. Left alone and waiting, probably wondering if she ever should have married him at all.

Damn, Hastings, that kind of thinking will make you careless and get you killed.

With an effort, he refocused his attention on the trail that lay ahead of him. Every now and again during the past few days, he'd caught some faint indication that the outlaws weren't the only ones riding ahead of him. He couldn't think of too many people brave enough or stupid enough to strike out into Indian territory. He wasn't certain which category any of them fit at that point, including himself, but he sure wouldn't mind having Jeb Welles somewhere nearby if it came to a shoot-out.

Taking another wipe at the sweat beading his forehead, Daniel retied his neckerchief and urged his horse back into a ground-eating trot. He hadn't a clue as to why the pace of the outlaws and Welles and the woman—if that was really who he followed—was so slow. All he knew was that he was ready to get this over with so he could get back to Jenny.

* * *

"Now ain't that a pretty sight," Ike whispered.

Leon, busy trying to find the insect that had been feeding on his flesh and causing him acute misery over the past few hours, didn't realize at first that Ike had reined his horse to a complete stop. He nearly let his own horse plow into Ike's before he steered the animal aside. It took another minute after that for Ike's words to sink in.

Ike blocked his view, and Leon craned his neck, trying to see around the other man's broad shoulders. "What is it, Ike? What are you looking at?"

Because Ike had whispered, Leon did too, despite his quiver of anticipation. He was ready for a diversion, for something to look at besides grass and a few trees. Ike wouldn't talk to him, much, and Leon didn't care for the silence that enveloped them for long stretches of time. He'd almost begun to wish Ike would hurry the pace so that they could catch up to Welles and the woman.

Ike shifted slightly, moving his body barely enough so that Leon could catch a glimpse of the Indian woman who crouched at the edge of the water. She gripped a small pouch made from leather which she filled by holding it beneath the surface of the stream. Her attention was divided between her task and a bird that flew noisily along the narrow stream. The bird dipped down from time to time seeking the insects that hovered at the water's surface.

With a minimum of movement, Ike searched the surrounding area with his gaze. Beyond the woman, beneath the sparse shade of a lone cottonwood, a second woman waited. At her side stood a young brave. The youth, Ike realized in surprise, watched Ike and Leon with steady eyes. When he realized that Ike had seen him, he spoke quietly to the woman at the water.

She reacted violently, twisting about to look at the two men on horseback, dropping her water pouch at the same time. Another word from the youth sent her splashing after it. Water meant the difference between life and death on the plains. With shaking hands, she retrieved it before scrambling to her feet and backing anxiously toward the woman and the boy.

The boy waited, silent and stoic. Despite his outward calm, he had no idea what action he should take. He knew better than to show the fear that gripped his bowels. Without knowing how he knew, he felt certain that to reveal any hint of weakness to these men would mean death, not just for him, but for his mother and his aunt as well. The last white man he had encountered had proven to be a friend. He did not believe that would be the case with these two.

Though he longed for the courage of his father to sustain him, he had only the vaguest memory of a warrior in brilliant paint riding away one clear morning. He had not known at the time that that was his father's day to die.

His father's father had been no poor substitute in the years that followed, but now the old one was gone as well, and the boy stood alone between two women and whatever fate awaited them this day. He felt totally inadequate to the task of protecting them. Never had he minded his withered arm as much as he did in this moment. Nevertheless, he manfully grasped his lance with his other hand and prayed for strength.

Ike chuckled. *These* were the Indians he'd been worrying about? For these puny three he'd held off moving in on Welles?

Leon felt a tingle of excitement at the chuckle. Ike was going to do something; he could tell.

With a grunt of disgust for his earlier worries, Ike started his horse walking toward the Indians. Leon followed slowly.

Neither man heard the old Indian who had come up behind them. His lance, readied for his own death, was now held in a grip that was still strong. In this moment, that lance was ready for the death of these white men. It thirsted for their blood.

"You wanted something to watch, Leon?" Welles was traveling so slowly a little delay wouldn't hurt anything. "Well, I'm ready for a woman now, and these are women." He rubbed his crotch. "And I'll let you watch," he offered, feeling generous.

Leon grew hard, but he wasn't fooled this

time. If he even tried to straddle one of these squaws, he'd wilt like a wildflower in a child's grubby hands. Nor did he think watching Ike would keep him hard enough to take a woman, but he didn't say anything to discourage Ike. Not that he thought he could, but he didn't want the other man getting mad at him for saying anything. Seemed like lately everything he said made Ike mad as blazes.

Though the boy did not move a single muscle as they approached, despair no longer overwhelmed him. By whatever miracle, his grandfather was there, watching him. His age-old eyes warned his grandson to make no move, to give no clue of another presence behind the white men. The youth could feel the strength of his grandfather's will. He could feel his grandfather's strength.

Ike flicked a glance over the spear the boy held in one hand. Then he let his gaze travel to the other arm. It hung limp at the boy's side, and Ike grinned openly. A cripple. Damn, how lucky could a man get! Two women and a cripple.

Stopping mere feet from the three, he stepped insolently from his horse and let the reins drop to the ground. He kind of had to admire the boy's courage. The young brave didn't so much as flinch from Ike's stare.

"Hell, boy, you want to watch, too? I don't mind." Ike laughed again and reached out with one hand, grabbing the younger of the two women and pulling her to him.

She struggled against the hateful grasp until her nephew spoke quietly to her; then she subsided, though tears of dread filled her eyes.

Ike despised the gutteral tones of the Comanche, but when the woman ceased her struggles, he nodded at the boy. "Now, that's right smart of you, young'un. Just everybody be real easy-like, and I'll think about letting all three of you live when I'm done here."

He kept his eyes on the woman while he told Leon, "You keep your gun on that boy, now. I don't care how excited you get; you don't let him have a chance to toss that stick of his."

Not that Ike was really worried. The boy didn't look stupid enough to try to take on two armed men with a lance. If he'd thought he might be, Ike would have taken the lance from him and simply broken it in half. Instead, he ignored the boy and lifted his hand to the woman's breast.

She flinched and choked on a sob she couldn't hold back. Ike smelled her fear and smiled as he forced her hand against the bulge in his pants. He took his other hand from her heavy breast long enough to unbuckle his gunbelt and unfasten his pants. He let both slide down around his ankles. His erection jutted out in front of him, drawing the woman's horrified stare.

The harsh voice that came from behind Ike had the same effect as a glass of cold water on his privates. He barely noticed that the woman jerked free of his grasp when he half-turned to look over his shoulder. A long string of curses started from his mouth at the sight of the old man with his weapon raised high. Worse than that was the sight of Leon, his mouth gaped open and his pistol drawn but hanging slackly in his grasp. The stupid son of a bitch was going to get them both killed. And him bare-assed while it happened!

"Leon! For Christ's sake, shoot the old bastard!"

Before Leon could move or Ike could say anything more, the boy spoke sharply, reminding them of his presence. And his lance.

Ike could have howled with his frustration. They were at a standoff. If he told Leon to shoot either the old man or the boy, that left one still standing. Ike wouldn't have minded if Leon took a lance in the chest, but what if it was Ike instead? He gave a brief thought to trying to get to his own gun, but the ugly look in the boy's eye changed his mind.

Very carefully, he lifted one foot at a time and stepped out of his pants. He held his hands carefully away from his body and backed toward his horse.

Leon could hardly believe his eyes. "You just going to let them go, Ike?"

"You stupid son of a bitch! Shut your damned mouth and keep that gun on the old man." He swung up into the saddle, wincing as his bare flesh met leather with a stinging slap. He'd be lucky if he wasn't ruined for life by this. *Shit.*

Without a word to Leon, he put his heels to

his horse's sides, hard. As his horse leapt forward, Ike slid low on his neck, leaning down to pick up his pants and gunbelt from their heap on the ground. He wasn't surprised when he heard another set of hooves thundering along behind him by the time he reached the next rise of land.

Daniel pushed his hat back on his head and watched them go. That was the damnedest sight he'd ever seen, and he wouldn't have missed it for the world. He was still chuckling when he started his horse after them at a slower pace. No need to hurry. He'd already made up his mind to come up on them after they'd made camp for the night. If he was lucky, he'd be able to take one of them before they even realized who he was.

Hannah tried not to watch Jeb as he spooned food onto a plate. She'd been trying for days now, but it was hard when that was all she really *wanted* to do. All she wanted to do was look at him, and all she wanted to think about was how it had been to have his arms around her.

Jeb reached across their campfire to hand her the plate and sank to his heels on the other side.

"Eat," he urged in a gruff voice. He worried that Hannah hadn't consumed enough lately to keep herself strong. He suspected he knew what was bothering her, but he didn't know how to fix it. Despite her disavowal, he knew now that he'd frightened her. She hadn't been easy with him since that kiss. But hell, fear hadn't been what he was trying to stir in her!

Hannah picked at the stewed rabbit. Jeb was better at hunting with his hands than anyone she'd ever known. The thought drew her eyes to those broad fingers with their strength and their calluses. She blushed and looked away.

Jeb rocked forward to his knees, setting his plate aside with a low curse. This had to stop, and soon. "Damn it all, Hannah, I told you before, I'm not going to do anything to hurt you. I swear it."

For one brief moment, Hannah pictured her future, when Jeb had her safely married to another like Caleb. Trading her love and her freedom for security. That day would come, she had no doubt. Hannah's jaw jutted at the thought. Maybe being one of Jeb's multitude of women wouldn't be such a bad memory to carry with her through that lonely future.

"I'm not afraid of that," she blurted out before she could give herself any more time to think about what she was saying.

Holding his tongue, Jeb waited for her to tell him what it was she *did* fear. In the long silence that followed, a peculiar feeling grew in the pit of his stomach. He tried to ignore it, telling himself it was wishful thinking on his part. Hannah couldn't possibly want any part of him.

Before her dread of being humiliated could

stop her, Hannah forced the words past her lips. "I'm more afraid you won't do what I want you to do."

Jeb grew still, knowing what he wanted but terrified that he might be terribly wrong about the meaning of her words. "Spell it out for me, Hannah," he said softly.

"If I've got to spend the rest of my life with a man like—like Caleb, or even if you're going to give me to somebody kind and gentle like Warren Salters, I want to know what I'm missing." Hannah wouldn't look at him. She decided she must have lost her mind completely. She wasn't sure how or when, but it surely had happened.

Jeb's heart sank. He wished to hell she hadn't worded it quite like that. He wanted desperately to take advantage of the moment, of what Hannah was offering. But he couldn't.

"Hannah, I'm not going to *give* you to anybody." Jeb felt like crying as he gave away the only chance he was ever likely to have with Hannah Barnes. "You're going to choose a man. When you're ready to choose. Not before."

"What if I choose a man you don't approve?" Hannah asked softly.

Jeb opened his mouth, then closed it abruptly. He gave considerable thought to her question before asking, "What kind of man?"

He had, he realized, never once thought to ask Hannah what she wanted in a husband. Jeb couldn't think of any man, or any kind of man, he'd want to let have Hannah right now. The thought of another man doing to Hannah the things Jeb wanted to do to her made him crazy.

Hannah met his glance across the softly crackling fire. "A man who knows how to laugh, and to curse. Who knows God has a forgiving side and who knows how to forgive himself and others. A man who can get angry without getting mean." In short, she acknowledged silently, a man like Jeb Welles.

Honest terror formed a lump in Hannah's throat. She could take a chance and risk everything. Or never know. She smiled despite the threat of tears. Maybe she was more of a gambler than she'd ever known.

"The kind of man who isn't afraid to teach a woman to shoot a rifle. One who can catch a fish with his bare hands." She glanced down at the plate in her hand. "Or a rabbit."

Her voice trailed away as she realized that Jeb was staring at her in disbelief.

"Hannah?" He said her name hoarsely, questioningly, unable to believe but wanting to desperately.

Hannah couldn't read his mind, had no idea what his reaction was to her admission. She just sat in silence, looking at him.

Even now, Jeb thought he might be mistaken. He had to be sure. If he was wrong and made a move toward her, she might run in terror. But if she came to him . . .

He took a deep breath. "Come here, Hannah."

With agonizing slowness, her gaze locked

with his, Hannah laid her plate aside and rose to her feet. She circled the fire, then sank ever so slowly to her knees at his side.

Jeb reached out and cradled her cheek in the palm of his hand, brushing his thumb across her lips. "Do you know what you're saying?" he asked huskily. A part of him didn't believe she could know. Not really. "Everything I own is with us here on this trail. Since leaving home, I've never stayed any one place more than six months at a time." And he'd never taken a woman with him when he left, nor ever wanted to. Until Hannah.

He'd never expected to find any woman with the courage of Katherine Slade, brave enough to give her life to a man who had nothing but his gun and his skill at surviving. Jeb knew Hannah wasn't a woman who could give her body without giving her heart, and where her heart went, the rest followed. Nor, Jeb realized, did he want less than that.

"I don't need much," Hannah said, still not quite accepting that she had risked all—and gained all. She opened her mouth and caught his thumb between her teeth.

Jeb drew in his breath at the sensation and reached for Hannah, pulling her off balance so that she fell against him.

He put his lips to hers, using the ridge of his thumb to tempt her mouth open beneath his. Hannah's moan almost covered the soft crackling of underbrush. The sound reached Jeb's consciousness a second too late.

"Now, ain't that tender." Ike stepped out of the shadows, gun in hand.

Hannah froze. That cold voice belonged to her nightmares.

Every foul word Jeb had ever known coursed through his mind as he slowly put Hannah away from him, easing her behind him. His carelessness was going to cost them a future together. "I'm sorry, Hannah," he said quietly. He wondered where the second man was and prepared himself to feel the burning of a bullet through his back.

Ike just stood there smiling.

Wilkins crashed through the brush behind his partner. "Can I have her now, Ike?"

Jeb relaxed the tiniest bit. Both of them were in his sight now. That didn't put a gun in his hand, but it made him feel a little better. A very little.

He'd kept Hannah's hand in his for a moment, but he released it with a gentle squeeze. He needed both his hands free. His gun was within reach, but he didn't dare make a move for it. Yet.

Ike barely glanced at Wilkins. "Stay back, Leon." He'd waited too long to have Welles in this position. No bumbling fool was going to foul things up for him.

Wilkins froze in his tracks, stopped by the ugly threat in Ike's voice. "B-but you promised, Ike. That redheaded witch has got to fix me. She's got to!"

Despite the danger of their situation, Jeb

allowed his curiosity to be drawn. He refrained from glancing back at Hannah, but he could sense her perplexity, could picture the tiny frown that creased her forehead. He wasn't surprised when her cool voice broke the silence. His Hannah had learned a lot about boldness in the past few days.

"What's wrong with you that needs fixing?"

Wilkins jerked, half in surprise, half in a vaguely recognized fear. Despite Ike's earlier warning and his own lingering dread of Hannah's powers, he took a step or two closer, glaring down at her. "I want my manhood back!"

"You want what?" Hannah stared at him blankly. She hadn't the faintest notion what he meant.

His dark eyes were narrowed and mean. "You cursed me—withered my manhood. I'll do worse to you if you don't lift the curse."

Jeb gave a snort of laughter. He couldn't help himself. "Two of us, Hannah?" he asked softly, thinking of his inability with Jenny and after that with Coral.

Giving him an odd look, Hannah decided she'd ask Jeb what he meant later. If there was a later. Right now, her memory replayed this ugly, sweaty man jerking at her skirts, fumbling to part her legs. She heard her own voice. *May God wither your manhood.* It would appear that God had heard her plea. This man considered it a curse. God had made it a promise.

She met the man's glare firmly. "No." Hannah

felt a faint surprise at the strength of her own response.

Jeb nearly groaned. That cool, choir voice of Hannah's was going to get them both killed without a doubt.

"Bitch!" Wilkins howled. "I'll kill you." He lunged forward.

Jeb prepared to launch himself at the enraged man.

"Leon!" Ike felt fury grip him. "Damn it."

Hannah watched in horror as the taller man swung his gun in a graceful arc. The one he called Leon seemed to freeze just inches from her face; then his chest exploded outward, splattering her skirt with blood. Hannah fought to keep the darkness at bay. If she fainted, Jeb would be alone to face this madman with a gun.

Ike grinned at the sick look on her face, and the fury on Jeb's. "Didn't like that, huh?" The grin faded as he focused on Jeb. "Your turn, Ranger."

"You're insane." Hannah scrambled to her feet and backed away from him. Deliberately, she made her voice high and trembling. It wasn't hard.

"Be still." Ike wanted her within the same line of vision as the ranger.

For just a moment, Jeb tensed. What the hell was Hannah up to? She wasn't worth a damn as an actress.

"I'm not going to stay here with you. You're a crazy man." Hannah backed a little closer to the Sharps rifle she'd been practicing with earlier. She prayed Ike wouldn't notice, that her skirts would hide the gleaming barrel for just a moment more.

Jeb's eyes widened as he saw where she was headed. He bit back a curse and an exclamation. "Run, Hannah," he said in an even voice. *Stay away from the gun.*

Ike jerked his attention away from the girl. He'd almost made the mistake of focusing more on her than on the man in front of him.

He'd take care of the woman later. "Stand up, Welles. I like to look a man in the face when I kill him."

"Well, now," Jeb drawled, despite his fear for Hannah and fury at what she was about to try, "I hadn't heard you to be that particular."

Ike growled deep in his throat, but the growl died as he heard the metallic click of a breechlock sliding back. His eyes widened as he glanced toward the sound.

Legs spread for balance, the woman stood with a damned rifle aimed at his face. Her jaw was firmly set; her eyes never wavered.

After the first moment, Ike relaxed a little. Hell, he'd almost let a female call his bluff. "Lay it down, preacher woman. I'll get to you later."

Hannah ignored his command. She couldn't have spoken a word if her salvation depended upon it. Gritting her teeth was the only way she kept from screaming. Jeb's life hinged solely on what she did next. And, God help her, she didn't know what to do now. She'd never even pulled the trigger on the rifle before, on any kind of gun for that matter. Jeb hadn't gotten to that lesson yet. All she could do was hope the outlaw would be more intimidated by the weapon in her hands than he seemed to be.

Desperately, she tried to recall if there was a cartridge in the chamber. Had she been loading or unloading when Jeb had called her to eat? She didn't dare chance a look.

Ike drew the trigger on his handgun back very slowly, grinning at Jeb as he did. "Almost over, Ranger."

In that instant, Jeb heard another faint click from the inky darkness behind Nelson. He chanced a glance toward the source of that sound. Firelight glinted on a metal star.

Jeb couldn't risk betraying the lawman's presence to Hannah.

Hannah sobbed. Now or never. Closing her eyes, she squeezed slowly on the trigger—just as Jeb had told her. The explosion sent her staggering backward a step, and she struggled to keep her balance.

Before Hannah could open her eyes, Jeb's arms were locked around her, holding her in a tight embrace. His broad chest blocked any view of what lay behind him. Tiredly, Hannah laid her cheek against that broad strength, feeling his heart beat with the life another had almost taken from him.

Jeb watched as Daniel Hastings stepped from the shadow and lowered his pistol.

He rocked Hannah gently in his arms and whispered, "I love you, Hannah."

Hannah felt tears squeeze from beneath her lashes as she breathed a prayer of thanksgiving. "I love you, too."

Chapter Thirty-one

Hannah nestled in the security of Jeb's arms, gazing into the flickering heat of the campfire. She savored these new sensations. The warmth of a hard, lean body cradling hers, an awareness of being protected and cherished. The feelings were so sweet that she was not even self-conscious when she caught the sheriff watching her and smiling from time to time. Somehow she was sure he understood.

He and Jeb talked softly, and their voices circled around her head, low and steady, filled with the strength that men had to have in this land. Strength that allowed them to be gentle as well as hard. Each time Jeb spoke, his chest rumbled, tickling her ear and making her smile.

Daniel was envious as he watched the two

of them together. Seeing the almost instinctive tightening of the ranger's arms around his woman when she so much as sighed stirred a need in him to be home. To be with Jenny. He rose and tossed the last of his coffee into the fire.

Jeb looked up at him in surprise. "You're heading out now?"

Daniel nodded. He could probably travel twice as fast by day as he could by night, but he figured moonlight would get him a good distance before a catnap saw him through the day. "Wilkins and Nelson are dead. I need to be getting home. What about you two? What are you going to do now?" he asked.

"Get married." Jeb's arms pulled Hannah a little closer as if somehow he expected her to protest.

She didn't. She smiled and snuggled a little closer to the muscled expanse of his chest.

Daniel didn't even pretend to be surprised. "Well, now, that's good news. Where you headed after that?" He still would have liked to have seen the couple settle in Sherman.

To Hannah's surprise, Jeb shrugged. "I don't know. Hannah and I—we haven't talked about it yet."

Hannah heard the words, but she was slow to grasp their meaning. Gradually it dawned on her that she was actually going to have a say in her future. It wouldn't just be presented to her as an established fact. *Hannah, gather your things. We'll be leaving at first light.* With her left to wonder about their destination until he decided to honor her with the information.

The irony was that she suspected, with Jeb, she wouldn't have minded so much. She'd have followed him anywhere without qualm or question.

No, where they went from here really didn't matter to her, but she knew without a doubt what Jeb wanted. "I've never seen New Mexico," she said softly.

She felt the subtle relaxing of his shoulders behind hers. "Reckon we'll keep on toward Taos," he told the sheriff. "There's bound to be a preacher somewhere along the way."

"Bound to be," Daniel agreed, leaving his disappointment unspoken. He cleared his throat. "I got married before I rode out." It sounded blunt and awkward the way he said it, but he didn't know any other way to bring up the subject. And somehow, before he rode off, he wanted Jeb to know.

Jeb whistled lightly. "I reckon you'll be glad to get back. Congratulations." And, though he only knew a handful of people in Sherman, it seemed only right to ask, "Who's the lady?"

"The Widow Ryon. Jenny." Daniel said her name softly, enjoying the feel of it on his tongue. Jenny Hastings now, he reminded himself. The Widow Ryon was no more.

A faint uneasiness traveled through Jeb and was gone. Like the past. "You won't go hungry for a fact. Hannah here's a tolerable cook, but I'd travel the length of Texas for the Widow

Ryon's cooking." He squeezed Hannah gently before getting to his feet.

Hannah felt bereft without his warmth beside her and pulled the blanket a little closer around her.

"Good," Daniel said easily, "then maybe we'll see you in Sherman again some day."

"Could be," Jeb agreed without hesitation, "but whether you do or not, I won't be forgetting what you did for us tonight. God knows what might have happened to Hannah if you hadn't shown up when you did."

The two men shook hands and Jeb walked with Daniel to where his horse was staked.

Hannah let her eyes close sleepily. No matter how hard these two tried to convince her, she knew she would never really be sure if it had been her bullet or the sheriff's that took Ike Nelson's life. Oh, both men had been careful to tell her that hers had gone far wide of the mark—but she'd seen the look they'd exchanged, and she knew they were capable of a bald-faced lie to protect her from any guilt over having caused a man's death.

Whatever the truth was, she was willing and able to live with it, just as she was willing to accept whatever tale these two men chose to give to her and the world.

Nothing mattered to her except the fact that Jeb was safe. And she knew she would never regret aiming a rifle at Ike Nelson and pulling the trigger.

For a long moment, Jeb stood looking down at Hannah where she lay nestled in the bedroll. He knew she must be exhausted, knew he should let her sleep. Then she murmured anxiously in her sleep, and he remembered the demons that could plague a person in the long hours of the night. She'd been through so much in so little time.

Hannah needed to be held, and Jeb needed to hold her, but he knew he couldn't do that and not touch her the way he'd longed to do for so long now.

Very slowly, he sank to his knees and laid his palm against her cheek. She opened her eyes at the light caress and a drowsy smile curved her lips.

"Hannah?" Her name was a hoarse question.

Without hesitation, Hannah freed her arms from the blanket that enfolded her and lifted them to Jeb. A fleeting worry for the ghosts of Hannah's past flitted through Jeb's mind and was gone with the first touch of her as he gathered her in his arms. He would make her forget every pain that her marriage to Caleb Barnes had inflicted on her. She was his now. His to protect, his to cherish, his to savor.

The gentle movement of Jeb's lips against hers erased the last vestiges of the dream that had troubled Hannah's sleep. She had envisioned herself back in the little shack by the Brazos, waiting through one of the lonely days for Caleb to return home, knowing the evening would be no less lonely for his presence. The sadness that had gripped her had been like nothing she had ever experienced—a sense of loss, of inexplicable sorrow.

When Jeb's touch awakened her, she knew that the sense of loss had been for Jeb, for the thought of living her life and never having known him. Never having felt his touch.

She gave herself up to that touch now, closing her eyes to savor the sweetness of his hands cupping her breasts through the thin cloth of her gown. She felt his fingers at the fastenings along her bodice and held her breath in anticipation.

Jeb spoke her name, compelling her to open her eyes and look at him. He needed to know that she welcomed him with more than her body, that her heart and mind were his as well. Slowly, he slipped her gown from her shoulders, allowing the pale light of the moon to reveal her to his hungry gaze.

With her gown hanging open, he reached to withdraw the pins she used to secure her hair. He pulled the silky strands free to caress her shoulders and bared breasts. Hurting with need, Jeb lay beside her and pressed his lips to her collarbone where one curl nestled against her warmth.

Hannah shivered with longing at the caress, wanting to feel his flesh against hers in so many places that had never known the touch of a man.

Jeb's lips trailed lower, across the first swelling of her breast to the peak that had hardened more with each inch his mouth traveled. When his lips closed on that peak, Hannah arched against him, and Jeb growled his pleasure deep in his throat.

With gentle movements, Jeb removed her gown, then pulled the blanket over her to protect her from the chill of the night. He removed his clothing with far hastier movements before he slid in beside her, gathering her close to his chest.

Hannah's arms encircled the muscular strength of the only man she would ever want, and Jeb took the woman who belonged to him.

Chapter Thirty-two

The broad sky of the New Mexico Territory was blindingly blue. And beautiful. More beautiful than anything Hannah had ever seen or imagined.

When she turned to share her excitement with Jeb, she found him watching her, smiling. He did that a lot. Just watched her and smiled. When he did, his green eyes would glow with a light she knew was only for her.

"What do you think?" Jeb didn't really need to ask. He'd taught Hannah to play poker, but she hadn't mastered keeping a poker face. In a way, he hoped she never did. He liked reading her expressions, seeing her pleasure and excitement—her love for him. "Does this look like any place you'd care to spend the rest of your life?"

"Are we almost there?" Hannah knew Jeb hoped to settle near this Slade he thought so much of.

"Judging from the map Slade sent, I'd say his place starts somewhere along that creek just ahead. He was thinking that creek could be the boundary between our spreads."

Despite her eagerness to embrace a future with Jeb, Hannah felt her stomach drop slightly. "What if they don't like me?" She tried to keep her voice teasing, but it fell short of her effort. It was apparent to her that Jeb put a lot of stock in what these people thought and what they felt.

"They will. You're my wife."

Far from reassured, she just looked at him.

Jeb sighed. "They'll like you, Hannah. They'll love you. Just like I do. Slade's mentioned that Katherine gets a little lonesome for another woman." He moved the bay mare a little closer to the grulla, close enough that he could reach out and touch Hannah's cheek.

He could still see the uncertainty in her eyes. "You and Katherine are a lot alike. You're both strong, determined women."

If he'd had any remaining doubt of Hannah's strength and determination, the days that followed the night she'd shot Ike Nelson would have banished that doubt. He'd tried to convince her that the sheriff had been responsible for the death of the outlaw. He still never admitted to any possibility that it was Hannah instead, but he didn't really know for sure if she believed him. He suspected he might never know.

Hannah had wept at the thought that she might have taken a life, then resolutely put the past behind her. Now they had all of their future ahead of them.

Hannah smiled at his words. *A strong, determined woman.* She suspected she'd never get flowery compliments from Jeb Welles. Somehow she didn't think she'd ever miss them.

"Let's go," she said softly, knowing what he wanted to hear from her. "I want to see what's over the next rise."

Author's Note

In the summer of 1859, John Henry Brown, with a company of Rangers, was sent to preserve the peace in the vicinty of the Brazos Indian Reserves, where local settlers had been at odds with the Indians for some time. Brown soon fell into conflict with the Indian Agent, Major Robert S. Neighbors. Some weeks later, Neighbors, under orders and with an escort of United States soldiers, regretfully moved the Indians under his care north of the Red River into Indian territory.

These two men, as well as Captain Plummer of the United States Rifles, Governor Runnels, and Rip Ford, played a real part in the history of the Brazos Reserves. All other characters and incidents in my story, except one, are entirely fictitious. The other recorded incident is the tearing down of the Sherman, Texas, courthouse on a bet.

WINDS ACROSS TEXAS

Susan Tanner

Bestselling Author of Exiled Heart